The Grande Dame
and Hitler's Twin

The Grande Dame
and Hitler's Twin

A Comedy of Errors

SALLY PATTERSON TUBACH

RESOURCE *Publications* · Eugene, Oregon

THE GRANDE DAME AND HITLER'S TWIN
A Comedy of Errors

Resource Publications
An Imprint of Wipf and Stock Publishers
199 W. 8th Ave., Suite 3
Eugene, OR 97401

www.wipfandstock.com

PAPERBACK ISBN: 978-1-7252-8187-5
HARDCOVER ISBN: 978-1-7252-8188-2
EBOOK ISBN: 978-1-7252-8189-9

Manufactured in the U.S.A.   10/12/20

To Fritz

Acknowledgments

I WISH TO EXPRESS my deep gratitude to all those who have, in a wide variety of ways, aided, inspired, and sustained me during the writing of this novel: Sue Austin, Julie Christensen, Natalie Zemon Davis, Bruce De Benedictis, Antoine Faivre, Trudi Gardner, Patrick Hatcher, Richard Hertzberg, Carolyne Hudson, Nancy Kors, Joanna Kraus, Susanne Lowenthal, Shelley McEwan, Marlene Miller, Susan Nunes, Kaye Sharon, Bernadette Rigal-Cellard, Leslie Rupley, Sheryl Ruzek, Sunny Solomon, Ruth Somers, Harvey Stromberg, Fritz Tubach, Nick Amar Tubach, Michael Tubach, and the members of the University of California, Berkeley Section Club Writers Workshop.

PART 1

The Mentor

Prologue

March 21, 2008, Good Friday, 12:01 A.M.

ALONE IN HIS PENTHOUSE office at De Carlo & Wittgenstein, Bruno De Carlo sat with a thick folder marked "Top Secret" in his lap and pondered the fantastical story in which he now had a role to play. It was just past midnight and the only other people in his spectacular postmodern Treasure Island art-and-auction-house campus were the janitors and security guards. Hitler's twin would be arriving at San Francisco International on 20 April—and he would be in charge of him. But Bruno De Carlo was having serious doubts.

The CIA had vetted De Carlo thoroughly; they had even used him in some minor international capers, and he had performed well. But this was a mission of a different magnitude. At first, he hadn't believed Olaf Knudtson of the agency's Biotechnology and Genetics division, but in the past months he learned it was all true. Klara Hitler had born two identical sons on April 20, 1889. DNA testing proved it beyond a doubt, and the surviving twin would land in California in four weeks.

Sixty-two years old, the handsome and elegant Italian-American entrepreneur had been both persuaded and coerced into accepting this job—to turn Hitler's identical twin brother into a successful artist, thereby keeping him out of politics and preventing him from perpetrating another catastrophe of the type his brother had unleashed on Europe over half a century ago. With his wealth, influence, and prominence in the San Francisco art world, Bruno De Carlo was a logical choice for the CIA, who had studied him for a long time. Bruno sometimes had the uncanny feeling that Knudtson knew him better than he knew himself. The CIA concluded this wealthy entrepreneur had outgrown his own DNA, so to speak, and his modest Italian village background; he spoke three languages, traveled seamlessly from continent

3

to continent, and he knew how to market all kinds of art and artists for extravagant profits. Bruno himself knew he was probably an ideal choice for the mission. He had even embraced it with enthusiasm at first, but his initial confidence waned as the time grew closer, and now he suffered from growing apprehensions and insomnia.

For a moment Bruno realized it was Good Friday, and he thought of his modest Catholic upbringing in the Tuscan village of Monteriggioni, which seemed so far away. Then he opened the dossier to the pages in the middle that were worn from repeated readings. He glanced at them perfunctorily but there was no need to read them again. They contained nothing he didn't already know about the astonishing circumstances of the twin's existence—of that night in 1889, when Frau Alois Hitler, wife of a customs official, bore two identical boy babies in a room above an Austrian brewery, and of the midwife who kidnapped one of the babies but accidentally dropped it in a freezing river, drowning it. Bruno was well apprised of the fateful night's details but felt no desire to review all of them at this moment. It was enough to recollect that the baby's frozen body, along with letters of confession by the midwife and her blacksmith husband, came to travel slowly down an Austrian glacier until they were discovered by an eccentric American scientist almost a century later. And that this scientist, a cryogenic specialist, found the baby encrusted in ice, and—by mistake, not design—reanimated it in 1987, on the same day his wife bore their only child, and how the odd scientist convinced his wife that she had born twins, and how they gladly gave up custody of the glacier baby to American and French authorities at the end of its first year. As he had done countless times before, Bruno could only shake his head at this deeply unsettling story, which seemed so preposterous, but had been proven beyond a doubt.

De Carlo sighed and closed the dossier in its plain grey folder. He stood up and walked over to the wall safe, which was hidden behind a French rococo mirror in an ornate gold frame, which in turn was partially hidden behind a potted ficus tree. In his immaculate charcoal Brunello Cucinelli suit, he paced in his spacious office and ran his fingers repeatedly through his wavy dark hair that was graying beautifully at the temples. Abruptly he stopped and turned on his heel to stare out the huge window that faced north, where he saw the lights of a few boats on the bay, and the dim lights of towns hugging the shoreline. He recalled an evening twenty years ago when the music of Johannes Brahms played in the background as he watched some of the same lights with the person who had literally changed his life.

That person had been his crucial mentor, and he sorely wished she were present now to guide him. She had molded the deceitful and ambitious personality he had been in his forties into something finer, into someone with an elevated sense of purpose and a set of respectable values. Despite her charisma, deep knowledge, and high standards, she had accepted him unconditionally when he was indecisive and spineless. She hadn't judged him but had slowly opened his mind and heart to new insights, new worlds, really. Her manner may have been a bit authoritarian, but her persuasion was patient. Her convictions were sure. She became his anchor when he was drifting at sea.

Bruno began to mentally retrace those two short but important years of their friendship. Someday, to memorialize her, he might write a story about her. He could already draft much of it in his mind. It begins twenty years earlier, in 1988.

1

MYRTLE SPENCER HALSTEAD PULLED out of The Pines's underground garage in her perfectly preserved, light blue 1968 Buick Skylark with its 35,000 original miles. The eighty-five-year-old widow headed up Sutro Street on her way to the appointment at her old house on Russian Hill. It was a week after she presented a brilliant program on "Age and Love in Shakespeare" for the Reading Roundtable, a group she had founded shortly after she liquidated most of her real estate holdings and moved into the finest of life-care retirement residences. She would rather have spent her day savoring the afterglow of her moving literary program, during which she had mesmerized her audience with her formidable voice. But there was much to do, and so much to think about. Several Pines residents had warned her not to show her house on her own without a real estate agent.

"What nonsense," she said out loud for her own benefit and made a right turn into the traffic.

She ran a red light at the corner of Webster and Washington, causing the car entering the intersection to swerve to the side. It screeched to a stop, honking and burning rubber, precariously close to her impeccable Buick's chassis.

"How uncivil! And all-too-common these days," she noted to herself.

She kept going, determined not to waste her energies on such unpleasant trivialities. She had, rather, to preserve her strength for the important matter of her house. It was the last piece of property she owned. Not the most expensive or elegant, but she had held onto the house too long because she especially loved the place. She had lived in it herself for twenty years, ten with Robert before his death, and ten liberated years afterward, finally turning it into a wonderful home. It had been her favorite domicile in the city, and even after she scaled down and moved into The Pines, she continued to rent it because she couldn't bear to part with it. But all of that was superfluous sentimentality now. She had sold everything else and converted the proceeds into investments that provided an ample income for her present and future needs. By character, and by virtue of having survived the Great Depression, she was frugal and prudent. With justification, she prided herself on the wise decisions she had made even though it meant having sacrificed what surely would have been a brilliant acting career.

At the corner of Franklin and Vallejo, she failed to see a pedestrian about to enter the crosswalk and turned the corner, chasing the startled teenager back onto the curb. His profanities and the middle finger he aimed at her Buick were lost on her. Completely absorbed in the task ahead, she continued down Franklin Street. She thought that at eighty-five she wasn't getting any younger, and the repair work and troubles with renters were too burdensome. She had entered a phase in her life where she wanted to devote more time to the important things. She had never allowed sentiment to overrule reason, so why start now?

Although she evicted the renters and put it on the market some weeks ago, the house hadn't moved. And she didn't hold out much hope for the Italian who called her several days ago and wanted to look at it. But here she was at 999 Greenwich Street, an hour early, to show it to him. Her cousin Clara had also warned her against selling the property by owner. But what Clara didn't understand was that no agent would be capable of recognizing the right buyer.

Myrtle found a convenient parking place across the street from the entrance. Backing into it, she rammed bumpers harmlessly with the cars parked behind and in front of her Buick, breaking nothing. Thoughtless drivers, who could have left a little more room for others to park. Well, at least she had a spot. She got out of the car and slowly made her way up the wide brick stairs to unlock the heavy, oak front door. She entered the house and proceeded to walk through the spacious rooms in which she drew back curtains, opened windows, and turned on lights. Upstairs, she leaned out of a bedroom window that faced the East Bay, recalling the electrician who had literally swept her off her feet, when Robert was away on the east coast, when she was still of *un certain âge*—she preferred the French term for a number you didn't divulge. During their summer romance, he insisted on leaving that window open to hear the fog horns while they made love, and she finally put an end to the liaison when she realized she was beginning to confuse pleasure with freezing.

In one of the bathrooms she examined her wrinkled yet distinguished face, pale green eyes, and fine nose in the mirror. She rarely wore her green cashmere scarf with the two gold stripes because it didn't go with any of her clothes, but now it was wrapped snuggly around her neck, because the furnace had been off while the house was empty. It would take a while for the rooms to heat up before the potential buyer arrived. She smiled into the mirror and noticed how the scarf's color almost exactly matched that of her eyes. It also concealed the loose skin on her neck, so she decided to leave it on. She thought of the many friends, now passed on, she had entertained in this house. Bravely, she assured herself she was lucky to still be alive. And yes, others would also have to admit, seeing her wavy gray hair, her perfect eyebrows, and intelligent features, that not only was she a woman still to be reckoned with, but one who had been a beauty in her youth.

She stepped out onto the wide balcony that faced north. The fog was beginning to dissipate toward the Golden Gate, and sunlight filled the street below. Suddenly, a flaming red Thunderbird convertible squealed into sight around the corner and up the street, its radio blaring. An old model, probably from the sixties, like her Buick she guessed, and also in mint condition by the looks of it. The driver, a young man of forty-something with wavy black hair glanced through dark glasses from one side of the street to the other, as if looking for a particular address.

Obnoxious boor.

But she watched as he found a parking spot for the red-hot vehicle. When he turned off the motor, she recognized the music that boomed from his radio as one of her favorite arias—*E lucevan le stelle* ("And the stars were shining") from Puccini's *Tosca*, no less—and she could just make out the seven letters on his rear, personalized license plate: *ABDANZA*.

Contrary to her expectations, the dark, young barbarian did not jump out over the door and spit on the asphalt. Rather, he looked at his watch, slowly lit a cigarette with a glinting silver object, tilted his seat back so that his dark glasses aimed at the heavens, and listened, motionless, as the condemned tenor, Cavaradossi, wailed out his tale of treachery and tragic love for the benefit of the neighborhood. Which is to say, Myrtle, attentive and unobserved on her balcony, also listened to the end of the aria. Now she thought, "What surprisingly good taste!"

Then she turned back inside and shut the door to the terrace—it was still too cool to leave it wide open. She descended to the main floor and continued to wait for her appointment to arrive, thinking that San Francisco was a fine city to live in, after all.

Within the minute, the bell rang, and someone knocked forcefully on the door.

My goodness, he's twenty minutes early. That's a good sign!

"Coming," she called, before adding, "Who is it?" when she stood behind the door, with the chain attached.

"Bruno De Carlo," a deep voice answered. "I have an appointment to see the house."

Satisfied that this was the voice with which she had spoken on the phone, she cracked open the door as far as the chain would allow and peered out. But when she recognized the man from the red convertible, she began to close it again in disbelief. With just a two-inch crack left open, she raised her eyebrow and aimed her good right eye at him critically and said, "But . . . I thought you said . . . are you Mr. De Carlo?"

"None other."

"But . . ." she began to protest.

"Am I too early? I can come back later," he offered. He hoped, however, that she would decline his offer, because he wanted to see the house and get his Thunderbird to the garage to fix the radio, which was stuck on that classical station. He slowly removed his sunglasses and stuck them into his shirt pocket that bore the letters, *CD*.

Christian Dior, Ms. Halstead reassured herself. She expanded the crack back to the width of the door chain. Now, as she refocused on his bare face, it slowly produced and bestowed on her a smile and an exquisite sparkling of dark eyes crowned with abundant black eyebrows, not to mention a convincing sense of dignity, aristocracy, and masculine playfulness that touched a chord in her.

Déjà vu, she thought to herself as she undid the chain and opened the door so he could enter the property.

2

JACK PETERSON, ESQ. WOKE with a start in the middle of the night.

What was that noise? Thunder?

He slipped out of his bed on the fourth floor of The Pines and looked out the bedroom window to check the weather. The sky was clear, but an ambulance was turning in under the neon emergency entrance sign of St. Theresa's Hospital across the street, its siren winding down. Since he moved into The Pines, he had been awakened more than once by these emergency room disturbances. Just about everyone on the lower floors facing west had been, and everyone except Jack Peterson found this constant reminder of their mortality nearly intolerable. All save Jack had signed the long waiting list for apartments on the upper floors—people claimed you couldn't hear sirens from the fifteenth floor on up. Of course, you had to wait for one of the higher-up residents to move out or, in most cases, to die.

During the day, many of the *lower* residents kept their curtains drawn in order to cover up their proximity to St. Theresa's emergency entrance— the final *doctor's visit* for many of them, and the only gall in the honey, the bitter core in the sweet life of The Pines. From the viewpoint of The Pines's administration, it was a matter of practical economics. Acute cases, after all, could be transferred directly from the residence by wheelchair or gurney across the street straight into the best-equipped emergency room in the city. There was no need for an ambulance or medical shuttle bus, which retirement homes located farther away from hospitals had to subsidize. It was a selling point for new residents. And while many were, indeed, favorably impressed by this convenience and efficiency at the outset, once they were established at The Pines, the closeness of the medical security they had sought often became a source of disquietude.

Jack pulled a robe out of his closet, stepped into his slippers, and walked to the next room. He took one of the two vinyl-padded bar stools from the counter that bordered the kitchen and carried it across the turquoise-green wall-to-wall carpeting to his living room window. Perched on the stool, he had a good view down to the emergency room and didn't need to stand. He thought of it as a ringside seat. He peered out now and watched with interest as the ambulance drivers pulled the latest arrival out onto a gurney. Jack couldn't make out whether the victim was male or female, but an IV was already attached to the body, and two nurses came out of the hospital to meet the new arrivals. It must be serious. The small group swiftly vanished into the hospital.

The sight didn't bother Jack in the slightest, and it brought back memories of his long career in Los Angeles as a personal injury trial lawyer. He thought of the two large cardboard boxes in his closet that contained hundreds of messages from satisfied clients. Over the years they wrote grateful notes and postcards from all over the globe—Hong Kong, Bora Bora, Paris, even Tibet and the Gobi Desert—where they enjoyed the fruits of his labors on their behalves, minus, of course, his reasonable, hard-earned share. Jack knew there were many Americans out there who liked lawyers. If physicians and insurance corporations disliked him—he had won sixteen judgments in excess of a million dollars—then they should have been as competent as he was, in the case of the doctors, or less greedy, in the case of the insurance companies.

Jack watched as the paramedics came back out to the ambulance and drove off. He was no enemy of emergency rooms. Miracles took place there. People were brought back from the brink of death, and relationships with tremendous potential for good were born at the very moments when victims were overwhelmed by despair. He had been a master at instigating and developing such relationships in ways that eventually enriched and rewarded both partners beyond their wildest dreams. His motto had been, "Turning misery into money." He was proud of a life's work that had transformed so many seeming disasters into positive stepping stones and replete bank accounts.

It was 3:30 A.M. He tightened his bathrobe tie, ran a hand through his ample head of silver hair, walked in his usual upright posture to his kitchen, and heated some chocolate milk. Warm mug in hand, he returned to the living room. He set the mug down on the glass-top coffee table; then he straightened the framed oil painting of crashing Pacific waves on a white sandy beach that hung above the sofa on the wall opposite the west-facing windows. Now he sank down into his dark brown leather easy chair and tuned the TV to a black-and-white Western. But not wanting to fall asleep in this chair, he got up again, sat down on the couch, placed his slippered feet on the coffee table, and stretched his legs. This two-bedroom apartment was the perfect size, and it was private. He liked it. He had not signed that waiting list. He wouldn't think of moving to a higher level. As far as he was concerned, this was the perfect location.

3

Two weeks after meeting with Myrtle Halstead on Russian Hill, Bruno De Carlo picked up his new mobile telephone with the intention of calling her. The Greenwich Street address was stylish, perfect. He put the phone back down and lit a Gauloises. Puffing on the cigarette, he paced in his Bush Street apartment, annoyed by its mediocrity. He needed to move out of this cramped space with its outdated doorknobs, plumbing, and light fixtures, and establish a permanent West Coast base of operations appropriate to his ambitions. At forty-two, his reputation as an international art and antiques dealer was growing. His aristocratic, old-world family name facilitated the ultimate San Francisco social contact—with the Beattys. He privileged them with the misinformation that he refrained from using his hereditary title— *Count*—out of deference to new-world sensibilities. As a result, everyone in the upper echelons of San Francisco society thought they knew a delightful secret about his lineage. He had been a success at the Beattys' dinner parties, and the billionaires had graciously purchased the minor Watteau from him and a large seventeenth-century Kirman he had found at an estate sale in Paris. His last three society appearances had been duly noted in Marsha Kaiser's column in *The Chronicle*.

But there was a downside that he pondered at this moment, a big problem. He was forty-two, after all, *Nel mezzo del cammin di nostra vita*—midway in the journey of our life, as Dante put it in his *Inferno*. He knew the first few lines by heart, and although he often quoted them in the original

13

to great effect at cocktail parties, he wasn't where he wanted to be in his life. He was alone. His sex life consisted of one catastrophe after another. He still hadn't made his fortune, and his mother back in Tuscany was refusing to give him the capital that would leverage him into the big time and establish him in the life he deserved. Things had not gelled. He flicked some ash angrily into an already overflowing ivory-and-teak ashtray—something he had found in Bali—and grabbed his phone with the other hand.

Now he walked through the living room back to his bedroom window, glanced down into the dreary alley below, and returned to the living room where, with the windows half-open, the traffic noise was always present. He put one foot up on the fifteen-thousand-dollar antique Heriz rolled up underneath the windows as he jammed one of them shut, and when he tried to close the other it got stuck close to the bottom where it always did, leaving a three-inch crack for the outside to enter. He took his foot off the carpet. This was no place for a fine Persian like this one, but there was no point rolling it out here. If he was having a mid-life crisis, he was determined to solve it. He had even formed a plan, something like a New Year's resolution: no more dissipation; no more big spending; no more getting side-tracked by sexy women, or men, for that matter. From now on, he would devote all his efforts to the two essentials, and if he could get them, all the rest would follow. First was this house on Russian Hill owned by that uppity old lady, Myrtle Halstead—the perfect home base for his San Francisco art and antiques business. And second, and much more difficult was the $500,000 from his mother to buy the house in southern France, actually a particular decaying villa near Nîmes, which would award him a sustainable membership in the ethereal circles of the rich and famous.

The money for the San Francisco house was in his local bank account, but all he had on the French villa was an exclusive eighteen-month option to buy, which he had just landed through a French real estate agency. And buy it he must, because this otherwise-ordinary villa contained, buried underneath its cellar and unknown to everyone else in the world, priceless mosaic baths from Roman antiquity. He had been vacationing in a nearby peasant farmhouse the previous summer when the proprietor of both the villa and farmhouse, old Maurice Villebrand, had begun excavating to repair a pipe underneath the villa's cellar. There he ran into the tiles and bath mosaics that were unmistakably from the early Christian, Roman era of Ausonius. Maurice didn't understand the find's value, and when he showed it to Bruno, the latter didn't enlighten him as to its archaeological importance and priceless art value. A value so enormous, Bruno knew, it could enrich the owner's personal pocketbook by a quantum leap and catapult him into international fame in the art world—his world. He, Bruno De Carlo, had to become the owner of this villa. It was the opportunity of a lifetime, his own personal, cosmic Super Lotto, and he held the ticket with the winning number.

Cautiously, diplomatically, Count De Carlo gave Maurice a friendly hand fixing the pipe and helped him rebury some of the cumbersome old tiles. Then, having endeared himself to Maurice's family, he obtained a promise the survivors would sell the property to him someday, when, God forbid, Maurice no longer was. This option, in the form of signed legal documents, was a form of life insurance, as Bruno saw it. Life insurance for the type of life he wanted to lead. One month earlier, Maurice had departed from this world, and Bruno needed to close the deal and cash in this insurance within the next year and a half.

But he was caught with his financial pants down. Who would have thought Maurice would go so soon? Had he known he definitely wouldn't have spent his money as though it came from an inexhaustible source. It did, of course, for all practical purposes, in the form of the monthly checks that arrived from a trust fund at the Banco d'Italia that his mother administered for the benefit of Bruno and his sisters. What was the point of saving? The checks from Italy arrived with unerring regularity, and his mother had always been good for an extra emolument at odd times. Besides, in his enterprise, you had to cultivate the image of the rich and famous if you wanted to join them. He was better at this than at long-term financial planning.

He'd worry about his mother on his next trip to Europe. Now was the time to zero in on the San Francisco project, to secure his local base and a chic residence. But how could he persuade this old woman, Myrtle Halstead, to sell it to him? She hadn't responded to his offer. He sensed with her it was not just a matter of the money. There was something else he had to address to make her move on the deal. But what?

He deliberated another moment, set his phone down on the coffee table and went over to his music collection. He selected a cassette titled "Favorite Classical Hits," inserted it into his stereo tape deck and turned it up loud enough that it could be heard as background music. Then he sat down again, crushed the half-finished cigarette in the ashtray, and dialed her number.

Late afternoon. Ms. Halstead's reading glasses rested on the tip of her nose and her chin on her chest. Joseph Campbell's *Hero with a Thousand Faces* slipped off her lap onto the floor the moment the phone rang, so she didn't know which disturbance had awakened her.

What?, she thought. *Who would call at this hour? No one calls at this time of day. Well, maybe it's that anonymous caller, the one who never says anything, but just likes to listen.*

For the last several weeks someone had called at odd times and had kept the line open, listening, apparently. There had been no heavy breathing, no threats or obscenities, just an open line. At first, she had said, "Hello? Hello? Who is it? Anyone there?" and hung up. But the last time, on a whim, and since she was reading Joseph Campbell, and since the anonymous caller seemed harmless, she had said to him or her, "Well, since you don't seem to want to talk to me, perhaps you would like to hear a few lines of what I'm reading."

Then she read a paragraph about native North American creation myths to the caller, in a well-modulated tone. The caller seemed to listen with interest, but as he or she made no comments on the text, Myrtle said she hoped the caller had benefited from the reading, wished him or her a good day and hung up. But this time there was a voice on the other end: Mr. Bruno De Carlo's.

What was this? He would like to see her. His voice struck her as suave and silky. Well, no, she didn't think so. But, oh, he wanted to discuss the house, perhaps over lunch. It was important. Well, maybe she could have him talk to her cousin, Clara, who was rather knowledgeable about real estate. No, he wanted to see her. Well, perhaps, if it were just for lunch, in a public place, in a restaurant? She'd have to consult her calendar. Just a minute. Monday—impossible. Tuesday, not so good. Wednesday, rather inconvenient. Thursday, well, yes, she just might be able to fit it in—at the Four Seasons Clift Hotel. He assured her it was a splendid choice.

Good, she thought. *He's at least not so gauche as to insist on Fisherman's Wharf or Ghiradelli Square or some other vulgar tourist area. Perhaps this beast can be tamed. What was that music in the background? Vivaldi. Very good.*

And, no, no. He needn't pick her up. She would meet him in the hotel lobby. For a moment after she hung up, she wondered whether this Italian-American could be the mystery caller, but then she realized those calls had commenced at least a week before her ad for the house had appeared in *The Chronicle.*

Myrtle spent Monday sorting and sifting through her closet. By late afternoon she had chosen the right dress for the Thursday lunch. Tuesday, she ironed both it and the appropriate silk scarf and polished the silver jewelry she would wear. Wednesday, she went to the hairdresser. Thursday morning she dressed with great care and read Shakespeare sonnets to calm her nerves before calling for a taxi at 11:15. By 11:40 she was seated in the lobby of the Four Seasons Clift next to an ornate Chinese vase full of extravagant fresh flowers, looking as if she owned the place.

Outside, a red convertible pulled up to the hotel entrance on Geary Street. The car was quickly whisked away by valets, and the elegant Signore De Carlo was ushered into the lobby. In his ivory-colored silk suit—the jacket hanging à la Via Veneto from his shoulders, the latest portable Motorola global telephone swinging from his left hand in a black case—his entrance would have been grand, had anyone noticed it. He waited until he was several steps inside to remove his sunglasses and reveal his deep brown eyes surrounded by long lashes and crowned by ample brows. But this flourish was also lost on Ms. Halstead, who at the moment was surrounded by tuxedoed waiters who offered her cocktails, tea, newspapers, telephones, or whatever her station in life desired. When she managed to disperse this superfluous attention, she looked up to receive Mr. De Carlo's elegant gesture. Holding a yellow rose he had pulled discreetly from the Chinese vase, he bowed toward her from the waist, set down his telephone case, lifted her right hand, and pulled it toward his lips so that her silver charm bracelet tinkled brightly. Simultaneously, he extended the rose toward her face and uttered, "*Buon giorno, Madame.*"

A waiter escorted Myrtle and Bruno to the tapestried courtyard restaurant and seated them in a corner. By 2:20 P.M. they had finished a delicious lunch and were engaged in a wide-ranging conversation about the house, in which Ms. Halstead emphasized not just the financial, but the personal aspects of buying and selling a house—not just a house, but a home, a refuge, an *ermitage* from the world. She elaborated on transitions, both spatial and temporal, and quoted Shakespeare, admonishing, *ripeness is all.*

The Italian count sensed the deal was far from secured when a beep on his mobile phone inserted itself in the form of a curator's call from Los Angeles. For Myrtle, the call was a rude interruption of her dissertation on the philosophy of housing, and it irritated her. She had a difficult time understanding the staccato-voiced conversation with this electronic interloper, punctuated as it was by Italian and French phrases. But at least it ended as quickly as it had begun, and Ms. Halstead immediately led them back to the subject as if the call had never happened.

"So, young man, I believe I understand your professional needs for a dwelling in San Francisco. That's all well and good. On the personal level, however, you are a bachelor, and I'm not sure why you need such a large house."

"Ah, but *chère Madame*," he said and fixed his dark eyes intently on hers, "you yourself have admitted that you lived very happily alone, not lonely, mark you, in this home for years."

"Indeed, *Monsieur*. But to move alone and happily into new surroundings is a much more complex proposition than that of base market considerations, than that of simply buying a piece of property that is viewed as such. The walls, the floors, the ceilings, the very arteries of water and electricity in this particular house have reverberated with the sounds and the thoughts of the great masters of Western literature and music. The very building materials have aged, much as fine wine, with a patina of intellectual discourse and elevated sentiments. This house has attained sensibilities with which no ordinary house in your common multiple listings can resonate. Young man, this house will only be owned by the right person. . . and at the right time."

Somehow, she managed to give her final sentence an inflection that implied the questions, *Are you that person?* and *Is this the right time?*

Bruno De Carlo's face emitted signs he was taking every word into the depths of his soul. He realized this was the crucial moment. He had to come up with the right response. Otherwise he would lose this house forever. An expectant tension hung in the air for an instant before he replied in Italian beautiful to the ear, *Nel mezzo del cammin di nostra vita mi ritrovai per una selva oscura. . . .*

Suddenly Ms. Halstead's voice joined Mr. De Carlo's in a short Dantean duet about straying into a dark forest in the middle of life until Mr. De Carlo reached the end of the lines he knew by heart. When he gallantly dropped out in impressed deference to her, Ms. Halstead soared on in a volume that caused heads in the courtyard restaurant to turn. Those heads then witnessed an elegant old woman—perhaps a retired actress?—come to the end of some Italian recitation. She bestowed a gracious smile and an assenting nod to her table companion and extended her right hand over the table to shake his right hand with a tinkling of silver.

4

MID-MORNING, 15 MARCH. JACK Peterson, Esq. sat in the front row in the Sierra Lounge doodling in his notebook. Halfway into the "Ides of March" Reading Roundtable meeting, he was bored, but couldn't leave. He had arrived early to get a front row seat as close as possible to Myrtle Halstead. He had attended the January meeting of the Reading Roundtable, his first after moving into The Pines, and had been captivated by her formidable voice, which, he learned from other residents, had inspired and intimidated decades of students and budding actors. He had seen how she had enchanted her audience into silent obedience and that, when she had finished her presentation, no one moved until she released them. These were skills any lawyer could appreciate.

He was determined to speak to her on this occasion, but it turned out she wasn't leading the meeting. Someone announced she might not return to the group for some time, until her cataract surgery was well behind her. Whenever it was scheduled, her next performance would be announced well in advance. Now a mealy mouthed old bag from the ninth floor was driving along about this ridiculous story, *Death in Venice*, by some writer with a very banal name. What was it—Tom Mann?

Jack Peterson had been attracted to the title, thinking the work might be a murder mystery about that westside beach community where one of his most memorable clients lived when he was practicing in LA. But this *Death in Venice* story turned out to be about this unsavory old German lecher who

19

took a vacation in Venice, Italy, and got the hots for a good-looking teenage boy, of all things. Then the German dyed his hair an unnatural jet black and died sitting on the beach during a plague. *Good riddance*, thought Jack. He was not particularly fond of Germans, to begin with. Now, this uninspiring old bitty tried to explain the *deeper meaning*, and the *symbolism* of this story, and Lord knew what else. If this was what it took to become literate, maybe he'd switch over to the checkers club.

He ran his hand through his white hair several times and tugged on the tails of his Colonel Sanders moustache. He wished he were in the last row where he could have slipped unobtrusively out the sliding glass door, crossed the roof to the other side of the penthouse, and descended one flight of stairs to the elevator landing on the twenty-fifth floor. There he could have caught a ride back down to his apartment and at least have watched some game shows on TV till lunchtime.

But he was trapped here for another hour, and his mind began to wander and form new associations with the German author's name—Tom, Thomas Mann. It was remarkably similar to that of his ex-client from Venice, CA—Tommy Manchester. Thomas Mann, Tommy Manchester. Strange coincidence! Many years ago, this Thomas Manchester—he called himself Tommy in those days—broke his back during a wild teenage party in someone's house at Venice beach. Now that would make a good story—about how a drunken Tommy tripped down some flagstone steps in a pair of unlaced hiking boots. And how Jack successfully sued the boot manufacturer for its failure to provide warnings about the dangers of wearing unlaced or improperly laced boots. And how the out-of-court settlement made Tommy weep for joy!

Coming out of this reverie, Jack noticed he was doodling pictures of boots and laces on his note pad along with the words, *Venice, Death, Tommy, Thomas Mann, Tom's my man, homophilic? Tadzio, Liebestod,* and *symbolism.* He looked at his watch and back at Ms. Tedious personified, who droned on. Discretely, he glanced back at the audience. Countess Olofsky was snoring softly two rows behind him, and several people around her had also been infected by her narcolepsy. This was definitely a drag, Jack concluded. Somebody should write a new version of *Death in Venice,* an American version—about Venice, California. Something more upbeat than this. He shifted for the umpteenth time in his chair. He smoothed down his hair. He itched for high noon and the moment of liberation. He wondered what Myrtle Halstead would have thought of his idea.

5

THE DEAL CLOSED. BRUNO De Carlo moved into the house on Russian Hill in mid-April 1988. Now he wanted to invite Ms. Halstead to his new home, or, at least, he felt obliged to do so. After all, in a flash of intuition, he had promised her a private housewarming party as he cinched the deal over lunch at the Four Seasons Clift, and she had readily agreed. But there seemed to be a problem he hadn't noticed when he viewed the house. Something was wrong with the electricity. When he turned the microwave on while the dishwasher was running, the refrigerator would go out, and he could only start it again by going outside, down the front steps, and around the side of the house to the basement entrance. He had to unlock it with two different keys and run back upstairs to get the flashlight he'd forgotten (the fluorescent light fixture in the basement didn't work) and descend again to reset the circuit breaker. Good God! He would have to go to the hardware store on Monday—no, Monday he couldn't, because of the trip to Chicago—on Thursday then, to pick up some spare fuses.

There were other flawed electrical combinations in his new home. Running the garbage disposal while the lower oven was on turned off the stereo. And the stereo in combination with the light in the upstairs bathroom turned off the kitchen clock. He was a busy professional and couldn't be bothered with continual trips to the basement—he shuddered to think of these trips during the rainy season—not to mention trips to the store for bulbs, batteries, flashlights, and who knew what else? As an interim solution he tried plugging various appliances into different outlets and running extension cords to lesser-used outlets. But this only provoked new, unprecedented outages. This was his first American house—well, the first house he had owned anywhere—but surely this was not normal.

He called Ms. Halstead, who was much distressed to think Mr. De Carlo would cast negative aspersions on her Russian Hill gem.

"Why, I owned the house for thirty years, as you know, Mr. De Carlo, and lived in it myself for twenty. I was never aware of any electrical problems, and never did any renter of that property, I assure you, so much as hint at an electrical deficiency."

Bruno De Carlo began to wonder whether or not it had been wise to call her. She seemed about to launch into one of her lengthy dissertations, whereas he needed some practical help. Well, now he was caught, and he'd have to listen to another lecture.

"I assure you I'm a thoroughly honest person, all my business dealings have been impeccable. In real estate, I've always made the full disclosures required by law. Why, if you want to call the title company or my banks . . . kachoooo!"

Suddenly Ms. Halstead sneezed, and Bruno seized the opportunity to cut her short and asked whether she might be able to give him the number of her electrician.

"Well, I don't have an electrician. But I can give you a reference. Mind you, I don't know him, and I never used him. But the last renters gave me a name about a year ago. Let me look it up."

A long pause ensued during which Myrtle set down the receiver and thumbed through her address book. Finally, she got back to Bruno with a phone number and a name—Hermann Wittgenstein.

Two days later, at 5:45 P.M., Hermann Wittgenstein arrived at 999 Greenwich Street in a Strom Electric Company pickup truck—a full twenty-four hours and forty-five minutes before appointment time. In his light blue Strom Electric Company shirt and baseball cap with the jagged yellow lightning bolt logo over the company name, Wittgenstein pulled all 235 pounds of his heavy-boned frame out of the truck and shut the door. He stood at six feet two inches, even with slightly stooped shoulders, and walked slowly up the wide brick steps to the front door. He was glad when no one answered his ring. He proceeded now, unimpeded, to inspect the house's exterior, clipboard in hand, making note of this and that—the nearest telephone pole, wires and cables entering the house, gas meter, the master exterior electric box. He peered through all the accessible windows and checked out the mailbox. He took the newspaper out of the slot underneath Mr. De Carlo's mailbox, removed the rubber band, opened it up, noted on his clipboard, *The Chronicle*, refolded it, returned the rubber band, and stuck it back into its place. As he was making a second round of the premises to note any significant details he might have overlooked—color of house, number of stories, estimated height, etc.—Bruno De Carlo drove into his driveway, and, after the garage door opened automatically, into the garage. Clipboard in hand, Hermann Wittgenstein followed a red Thunderbird into the garage. When the motor was off, Hermann approached the window before De Carlo had a chance to roll it up and said, "Good day. I am happy to meet you," in his German accent. He lifted his cap to uncover a bald spot on the top of his head, that was balanced by a four-inch ponytail. He extended a muscular arm worthy of a wrestler toward a startled Mr. De Carlo, who remained glued to the seat of his Thunderbird. "I am Hermann."

On a Sunday morning two weeks later, Bruno woke up and thought of Myrtle. The electrical work was going to take longer than expected, but he felt he shouldn't postpone the dinner he had promised her. After all, he was a man of his word, a nobleman, as she had called him after lunch at the Clift Hotel. Besides which, he had learned about her reputation in the city as a *shrewd real estate lady*, but he didn't know how far her influence extended. In his business you could never know too many prominent people. And you never knew when some odd contact might lead you to a basement full of treasures. In the broad palette of female friends and acquaintances he had taken out for lunches, dinners, and more, she was by far the oldest—at least seventy-eight, he guessed—but that was immaterial. In California all types of relationships were tolerated. And furthermore, she had given him a very good deal, despite the electrical problems, the repair costs of which were unknown at this point, while Hermann investigated. Moreover, if she had as much money and taste as she seemed to possess, he might also be able to sell her or one of her rich old friends a Persian carpet or some Venetian candlesticks.

Mr. De Carlo got out of bed and, in his dark blue silk robe, went downstairs and stepped out his front door onto his entrance. Cigarette in in hand, he took his newspaper out of its box.

"Good morning, pal, Mr. De Carlo, sir," a German accent greeted him from the sidewalk below. Hermann Wittgenstein was leaning against the Strom Electric truck writing on his clipboard. Bruno took the opportunity to tell him he needed to give a dinner party, and he asked the electrician if there was any way to rig things so that at least his kitchen, dining, and living rooms would function for an evening.

"Ja, you know I cannot so soon be done with the main work, but if I can another look inside the house take, I can tell you maybe if this is possible."

Bruno nodded his assent. Delighted to be of service, Hermann lumbered up the stairs, the yellow lightning bolt pointed toward his generous nose, ponytail riding behind the baseball cap.

"I will look around a little bit here again, if that is OK with you, Mr. De Carlo, sir. And then I will say you what I can do for your party. If it is agreed, pal?"

Hermann had been there most of the previous day, so Bruno was used to his linguistic peculiarities and reconciled to a certain amount of disturbance in order to solve the wiring problems in his house. They were, in Hermann's opinion, ultimately solvable, but would take time. While Bruno had his breakfast and took his morning coffee on the balcony facing Alcatraz—it was another glorious California drought day—Hermann rooted throughout the house. He delved into closets, attic accesses, and crawl spaces that barely existed. And he wrote copiously everywhere he went.

After three hours, Hermann emerged, smudged and dusty from his expeditions, baseball cap reversed so the lightning bolt seemed the beginning of his ponytail. He had a veritable patient's chart on his clipboard, which Bruno sensed boded ill for the diagnosis and eventual repair costs. He glanced at Hermann's notes, but everything was in German. Yet Hermann announced cheerfully, "Ja, I think that for your evening meal I can do some things, but these things can be different from the other things I can do for the whole house. The costs for these things I do not yet know, but do not make yourself worries Mr. De Carlo, pal, sir, because I will make a plan for all. A first plan for your evening meal, for that I will ask no charge, and then a plan for the whole house. Both jobs are good for me to learn better the American electrical house system. Ja. You may not make worries, because I will do all OK and if you are agreed you call me two days before you want your evening meal."

Bruno De Carlo was surprised to hear so many consecutive English words from Hermann's lips, but he immediately wanted to believe that this meant there were solutions, and that he'd had the good fortune to find a German to work on them. Only in America. He couldn't be bothered with these things and was anxious to entrust them to Hermann.

Bruno would call Hermann to return next weekend to do the work. Ms. Halstead would arrive in a taxi on Sunday at 7 P.M. Mr. De Carlo would cook. He loved to cook and eat well, so the evening was assured at least one redeeming feature.

6

SATURDAY MORNING, HERMANN ARRIVED at 9 A.M. at Mr. De Carlo's house and waited to announce his presence until the Italian emerged on his front entrance to retrieve his newspaper. Then he set to work and labored all day in the basement, the attic, and throughout the house, stringing cables and wires and setting up a generator that would serve Mr. De Carlo's culinary arts in case of emergency. Toward evening Hermann announced everything was prepared for the next day. But just in case anything should go wrong, he, Hermann himself, would volunteer to return and man the electrical command post he'd rigged in the basement. And furthermore, for good measure, he'd bring along his sleeping bag and spend Sunday night there, if need be, if, and only if, this would not disturb Mr. De Carlo. The basement housed an old sink and toilet, and it was really best to err on the side of caution, he warned Mr. De Carlo.

"I am happy to do this for you, Mr. De Carlo, pal, sir. For free, for love, naturally. This is all—how do you say?—volunteer work I will do. Ja."

After he'd found the right English expression, he repeated it.

"Yes, all is volunteered, so you do not have to make any thoughts about running up too high costs. I will man the post. This is really a . . ." Again, he looked for the word and came up with, "challenge! Ja, a challenge and an honor for me. I must learn more about antique American home current systems for my profession and for my career. This is so."

Myrtle had not consumed so much alcohol since that night on board ship between Piraeus and Trieste in 1925 when she lost her virginity to the British student she met in the Athens youth hostel. Making love to him had been extremely pleasant in her intoxicated state, and she had immediately afterward fallen into a deep sleep despite the swaying of the ship. She did not get pregnant. Nor was she struck by lightning, God's wrath, or disease. But she did wake up the following morning with such a miserable hangover that further association with the Englishman was out of the question. When they debarked at Trieste, she vowed never to see him again, and she didn't. Cutting people out of her life, paring her list of friends and acquaintances down to the essentials, had always been one of her important guiding principles. Lately, it had become a virtual obsession, since she had no more time in this life to waste.

Now, as is typical for intoxicated people, Ms. Halstead was not thinking about the morning after. Rather, she was blissfully content to gaze into the candle across from her handsome and charming Italian acquaintance, having finished off the dinner he had prepared for them in his new home— tender beef carpaccio with extra virgin olive oil, capers, and freshly grated Parmesan; a green salad with nutty arugula leaves; and penne with the best homemade tomato, garlic, and basil sauce she had ever eaten. This third glass of Chianti Classico was by far the smoothest wine she had ever imbibed. And all of this served by this attentive, young aristocrat, *Signore*, no Count—as he had confided to her this evening—De Carlo, to candlelight and the Brandenburg Concerti. She forgave him Pachelbel's *Canon* earlier in the evening.

During a pause in the conversation, they both raised their glasses to sip the wine at the same time. When she noticed he was aware of their simultaneous gestures, he bestowed on her an open, unabashed smile she was happy to give back. She knew it was up to her to do something in return for all this generosity of spirit and effort. What could she offer him that he didn't have? She reflected on this question for two seconds. Well, the finer things of life, of course. That which uplifted and made you see things whole. Shakespeare, for example! The great books! Knowledge of Western civilization and literature! Things that elevated your sights, your intellect, and your spirit. After all, she had learned during this remarkable evening that he had suffered an oddly deprived upbringing in his Tuscan villa south of Florence, with its servants, the mandatory polo, sailing, and riding lessons, and the obligatory appearances at opening nights. It was deprived precisely because of all these frivolous pastimes, she concluded, based on the misinformation he had given her. When he attended those glittering opening nights at La Scala or Rome, hounded by the paparazzi of Europe, did he know or care whether it was von Karajan or Van Cliburn, and who was the director or the pianist in such a case? At the theater, could he distinguish Olivier from a second-rate imitation? Did he understand what was behind Hamlet's hesitant ruminations, or Goneril and Reagan's machinations, or the merchant's insistence on the pound of flesh? She studied his face now and saw before her an inquisitive, brown-eyed boy who had done his duty and now awaited his reward. But he spoke first.

"Now for the *pièce de résistance*, my dear. That is, if you are ready for it?" Bruno queried Myrtle.

"*Mais, bien sûr*," she replied, and he rose to prepare the dessert in his kitchen.

The boy has everything else, she thought as she set her glass down and waited for the last course. But she could offer him the something more that was lacking, something not of transient worth but rather of lasting, even eternal value. Something independent of the economy that could never be taken away. A form of riches that would be there when the stock market crashed, when your Persian carpets were eaten by moths, when your precious Velasquez was stolen. She could offer him *Geist*, as the Germans called it, and *Kultur*—high culture. She could take him on an intellectual voyage that would cause his spirit to soar high above the frenetic titillations of Wall Street, above crass commercialism, above base—necessary, she granted, but nevertheless—base monetary considerations. Thus, she resolved to launch her private campaign after they had consumed the last bites of ripe, half-papayas filled with fresh raspberries, marsala, and lemon juice.

In due time the candles were low, the lights of downtown twinkled brightly, and the first wisps of fog curled magically in and out of the sky-scrapers. The Brandenburg Concerti had long ended. Now she pulled herself cautiously into a standing position—no, no, she didn't need his help and brushed away the proffered arm—went to his music collection, and with the help of her reading glasses and the miniature pocket flashlight she always kept on a chain around her neck, spied a new cassette of Brahms's *Third Symphony*. As she expected, the plastic wrapper was still intact—it was she who had given him a year's subscription to the Tape-of-the-Month Club as a housewarming gift, and she had made the initial six selections for him. Now she asked him to insert the tape into the cassette player and spool ahead to the third movement. When he accomplished this with her help, she took his hand and led him to his own window, saying, "Hush, not a word for the next ten minutes. And do only what I say!" He looked puzzled but nodded in agreement.

She released his hand but gestured that he should continue to look out his window at the city lights. She sat down in an easy chair and said nothing while the sad, yearning strains of the third movement filled the room.

Bruno was, admittedly, also a bit intoxicated by the smooth Chianti and his own good cooking. He had forgotten about Hermann's presence in the basement, and of course, Myrtle was oblivious to the fact that a German immigrant was manning an electrical post in the bowels of her former house. True to his promise, Hermann had done the job without even one electrical glitch. The kitchen had functioned beautifully for the first time since Bruno moved in. The stereo went on without turning anything else off, and the lights in the bathroom worked. The extra cables and wires were discreetly hidden, as was Hermann. Come to think of it, thought Bruno, everything about the evening was perfect. Ms. Halstead surely knew some very influential and cultured people who would be interested in art and antiques. And, yes, he had to admit, he felt good in her presence, especially now that the evening was slowly coming to an end.

For the first time he noticed that the music gave a peculiarly poignant cast to the night cityscape. Why hadn't he been aware of it before? For some reason it was easy to remain immobile and to allow the old woman to guide his thoughts and emotions.

Halfway through the movement, she began to speak in a low, sonorous voice. He turned toward her, but her raised right hand admonished him to turn back and continue looking out the big bay window. He obeyed. The voice continued—a trained voice, a new voice, yet unmistakably hers. A transformed voice with an altered volume, pitch and timbre. He continued to watch the city as the fog slowly consumed one building after the other, and he gave himself to the stentorian lullaby of her voice: "How sweet the moonlight sleeps upon this bank!/Here will we sit and let the sounds of music/Creep in our ears: soft stillness and the night/Become the touches of sweet harmony."

7

MYRTLE DID NOT MAKE it to breakfast in The Pines's dining room the morning after her dinner with Bruno. Instead, to deal with the lingering effects of the wine the night before, she slept in and made herself some toast and coffee in her kitchenette. She luxuriated in thoughts of the wonderful evening with the gallant Italian gentleman in her beloved Russian Hill home, convinced now that the house couldn't have a better new owner. She was also convinced she and this handsome man had the beginning of something true, quite beyond the business that had brought them together initially, something with the potential for genuine closeness. Just how that was to be defined, she didn't know. She prided herself that she had no illusions. She was old enough to be his mother, well grandmother—*hélas*. But, on the other hand, why should something as trivial as an age difference constitute an impediment to the meeting of true minds and kindred spirits?

By lunchtime she was ready to face the world. Just as she was about to leave for the dining room, the phone rang. "Hello? Hello? Anyone there?" There was no answer. It was the anonymous caller.

"Oh, it must be you, silent one. I hope you are well, but I'm afraid I have no time to talk to you at the moment. I've made a late start today and I'm just on my way to lunch. Can't be late, you know. But if you are feeling lonely and wish to call again, I'll try to select a good poem or perhaps a prose passage for next time. That should help bolster your spirits."

No response.

"Well, as I said," Myrtle continued speaking into the receiver, "I've got to be going. So, good-bye for now."

After she hung up, she transported herself to the elevator and descended to the dining room. She was in sufficiently good spirits to greet Mr. Seward, the maître d', in a friendly way. As he ushered her to her table, she deigned to grant a nod here and faint smile there to various residents who were already seated at their meals.

From a far corner, Jack Peterson noticed Myrtle's entrance and watched her progress in his general direction. Most of the intervening tables were already full, and as Mr. Seward ushered her ever closer, the ex-lawyer seized the opportunity. He jumped up and pulled back a chair for her, as if they had planned to lunch together.

It worked. Myrtle Halstead allowed herself to be seated opposite Mr. Peterson, who said, as he pushed the chair in underneath her, "What a pleasure to have lunch with a lovely lady. I was afraid I'd have to dine alone." Then he bowed slightly from the waist and said, "Jack Peterson's the name. Jack Peterson, Esquire."

"Well, how do you do, Mr. Peterson Esquire," she replied with an inscrutable smile and a hint of condescension. She had noticed the Colonel Sanders lookalike from a distance, and now she detected the slight Southern accent in his voice as he took his seat across from her. She was still in a sociable mood from the previous night. "Have we met before, perchance?"

Jack Peterson informed her that although they had never been introduced, he had been at her January Reading Roundtable presentation and had been very impressed. So much so, he continued, that the following meeting, about Tom Mann's *Death in Venice*, had been a letdown, since she wasn't there.

"Ah, you must mean, *Tohhmas Mahhnn*," she corrected him, by emphasizing the long *o* in the author's first name, and by uttering the *ahhh* in his last name to demonstrate the difference between the German and American pronunciation of the letter "a."

The waiter arrived to take their orders. Ms. Halstead wanted menu A today, no perhaps B would be better. But could she have the Salisbury steak rather well done, please? And she'd prefer mashed potatoes—without gravy—to the rice, if possible. Fine. Then, she'd like to have both vegetables, that is, the zucchini from A and the squash from B, and she'd have a glass of 1 percent milk, instead of the usual 2 percent—be sure it's not that undrinkable nonfat, if you please. Calcium, you know. But she would also like iced tea but hold the lemon. She'd decide about dessert later. Jack Peterson ordered menu A.

Ignoring the German pronunciation lesson, Jack told Myrtle in his drawling manner that not only had the Roundtable's leader been pretty weak, well down-right boring, ma'am—and he sensed that she, like he, probably preferred to call a spade a spade rather than to beat around the bush—but the Venice story hadn't exactly turned him on.

Ms. Halstead squinted critically at this sleight to the greatest German author of the twentieth century. Who was this mere mortal with his hackneyed clichés and bumpkin's accent to criticize a Nobel Prize winner?

Mr. Peterson proceeded. The way he saw it, this old Aschenbach fellow had it coming. "First he goes to Venice, I mean Venice, Italy, you know, during some kind of epidemic." He interrupted himself to ask, "You know the story, don't you, ma'am?"

Myrtle's green-eyed squint narrowed at this question and the incipient furrow in her brow deepened. Her very nod should have told him that her knowledge of this work and its author was in every way so superior to his, that anything he said now would not only be superfluous but perhaps inflammatory, and certainly held against him. But he continued, undaunted.

"Well, there's at least a serious public health hazard there, in those dirty, smelly canals and all. You can just imagine. So, the prudent person would have turned right around and gone back home, where he came from, assuming there was no plague or epidemic going on at home. Second mistake: the guy's obviously a weirdo—no family, no kids, all alone—and he develops an unnatural attraction for this good-looking young boy with the funny name. Downright revolting, isn't it?"

Myrtle was about to roll her eyes, but the cottage cheese and Jell-O appetizer arrived at the moment, so she simply smiled at the waiter and began to eat. At least, he hadn't said, "ain't it?"

Since he had such a good listener in Myrtle, Jack ignored his broccoli soup and went on to explain Aschenbach's third mistake—lack of discipline. Old Aschenbach couldn't control his fatal attraction, and, as a result, dyed his hair—"Totally out of character for such an old codger, pardon the expression." At this, Jack ran a hand over his own full head of hair.

This gesture was, of course, not lost on Ms. Halstead, to whom it revealed the unjustified pride of a foolish person. Yes, for a man of about seventy-five, as she assessed him to be, he definitely had a substantial head of silver-white hair and a ridiculous waxed moustache. But this was about all that could be said for him. No, she ruminated, you could also say that through cultivating these physical features, as he obviously did with expensive shampoos, conditioners, rinses, and trips to those salons where gay men commanded outrageous prices from the affluent but vain elderly—in so doing he lined himself up with the likes of the third-rate actor that this imbecilic country elected to its highest office. And if that's *what turns you on*, then there's little hope left for this one-time great nation, and its decline was assured. Yes, she had to admit there was more one could say about this table partner—*à quoi bon*? Now she noticed on the two smallest fingers of both of his hands he wore four diamond rings set in silver, shiny as chrome.

"Well, and then," he continued, "the writer gives it all away in the end. I mean this Aschenbach character up and dies, right there in Venice. With that title, anyone with half a cabbage brain could see it coming!" Jack twisted one of his rings so that the diamond faced up again, and took his first bite of salad, well satisfied with his first literary exposition for the benefit of a renowned expert.

Myrtle noted a parsley shred stuck to the wax on his moustache, and waited to see whether or not he would continue. She knew it would be futile to attempt to refute the abysmal literary ignorance this man exhibited. During her teaching career, she had learned to recognize the culturally talented students during the first class. Much in the way some musicians were endowed with perfect pitch, some people were born with a gift for aesthetics and literary appreciation that involved a depth of both intellect and emotion that separated them from the Philistines. No amount of instruction could evoke this talent where it didn't exist; only the gifted could truly profit from instruction in the literary arts. Mr. Peterson did not belong to this elite.

The waiter brought Ms. Halstead's Salisbury steak and Mr. Peterson's chicken, and it was clear she could go on eating while he dominated the conversation, well, *fatuous monologue* would be a more appropriate term. She was grateful for one thing: she could relax. All too often her random table partners at The Pines expected her to carry the conversation, and this one had killed all desire on her part to engage in a dialogue. She preferred to remain the passive recipient so as not to waste any intellectual energy on a hopeless case.

Mr. Peterson cut a bite of chicken, and before placing the fork into his mouth, assured Ms. Halstead there was a *good news* side of this story.

Myrtle looked up accommodatingly as if to ask, "And what is that?"

Jack proceeded to tell her about the remarkable coincidence in all of this. The fact was, as he was sitting in that particular Roundtable discussion, it occurred to him the author's name, Tom Mann (he insisted on his casual, colloquial version) bore a remarkable resemblance to the name of an ex-client, Tommy Manchester, who had lived in Venice, California, when he (Jack) practiced law for many years in LA. Now she would understand the *Esquire* in his name, he added, while sliding a hand through his silver hair.

"Anyway, Tommy Man-chester—get it, ma'am? ha, ha—broke his back due to the negligence of an apparel manufacturer. You see, at a party, he tripped on a bootlace, fell down some stairs, and fractured his spine, all because the boot company had failed to provide a written warning of the hazards of using their products without stringing and tying up the laces." At this, the shred of parsley slid off his moustache and fell into his lap.

Myrtle's brow furrowed to its deepest depth, her eyes rolled toward the heavens and she almost dropped her fork at this sudden jolt of recognition. She, Myrtle Spencer Halstead, who had trained young minds for the theater, and who, in overcoming life's adversities through hard work, individual initiative, and sacrifice, was dining with a personal injury lawyer, a veritable ambulance chaser. Memories of the Great Depression rushed to mind. She had supported her poor mother who had been abandoned by an unfaithful, alcoholic husband, a preacher by profession, the monstrous hypocrite! Singlehandedly, she had worked her way through UC Berkeley by cleaning houses. Starting with her first teaching job, she had saved every possible penny, and with the first little lump sum she gathered together, she made a down payment on a modest, run-down house she renovated herself on evenings and weekends. By hit-and-miss, and by observing the workmen she was forced to hire for the bigger things, she learned basic handyman skills—painting, papering, and minor repairs. Sometimes she paid tradesmen by tutoring their children. By God, she had made it the honorable way, the hard way. Thus, only with a supreme effort did she manage to contain her composure by uttering out loud, "O nation miserable," and immediately resumed eating.

Jack studied her a moment, and then, convinced this constituted a verbal expression of sympathy for his ex-client's tale of woe, swallowed another bite of chicken and went on.

"Yes, ma'am. At the outset it seemed like a terrible tragedy. A healthy young man, a fine physical specimen, I must say, laid low in a hospital bed, with an uncertain future. Would he ever be able to walk again? Well, thanks to God and his excellent doctors, he recovered. And—this is the climax of the story—thanks to the generous settlement I won from that irresponsible apparel manufacturer, the boy was able to attend a good university and go on to medical school, where he finished with honors and an MD behind his name. You see, the settlement gave him a new lease on life. Last I heard he was an eye doctor at the UCLA Medical Center."

Jack paused to take another bite while Myrtle devoured her vegetables as fast as possible, having decided to forego dessert in order to escape this character. People could ruin your day, and Jack Peterson, Esquire was another proof of that. She also didn't want this encounter to totally erase the aura of the exquisite night before.

"Well," he said—he just didn't stop!—"I think someone"—he said this with a knowing look at her—"someone could write a modern-day story about Tommy Manchester in Venice. It could be uplifting, downright inspirational, the opposite of that sickly little novel, or novella, or whatever they call it, by that depressing German author. I'm sure you could do it. What do you think, Ms. Halstead?"

Myrtle raised her eyebrows. She had the good breeding not to utter her thoughts, but thoughts she had about this ludicrous proposal, and they came to her straight from the Immortal's pen: *O illiterate loiterer!/. . . this proves that thou canst not read.*

Her favorite dessert had already been placed before her, and, having gained on him while he was busy talking, Myrtle changed her mind and was able to finish her apple crisp topped with Dream Whip after all. Now, breaking her policy never to use the vapid phrase, she said "Have a nice day," and excused herself from the lunch table.

8

IT HAD BEEN A couple of weeks since her lunch with Jack Peterson when Bruno De Carlo invited Myrtle for lunch at a Chinese restaurant on Clement Street. She had the sense their relationship was taking on a meaning for him and a kind of regularity. She had called him after the dinner party at his new house, and he had called her during his return flight from his latest trip to London, Paris, and St. Moritz. Over hot-and-sour soup and spring rolls, and without waiting for any encouragement on her part, Bruno reported in detail about his *soirée* at the Beattys' and his latest antiquarian acquisitions from an auction at Christie's, London. There he made the acquaintance of an old count from Luxembourg who promised to entertain him in his Andalusian castle on his next European sojourn. What was more, during a visit to the Clignancourt flea market at the northern edge of Paris, he had picked up a rare wood carving, probably part of a triptych, maybe even a genuine Riemenschneider. At this very moment it was being analyzed and appraised at Butterfield's in San Francisco, and he was hopeful of making a handsome profit.

At this moment the black case at Bruno's side made a peculiar beeping sound and a red light lit up. This startled Myrtle, who was suspicious of her companion's latest, state-of-the-art mobile telephone. She distrusted any gadget more recent than the answering machine, and certainly wouldn't have tolerated a similar high-tech interruption from anyone else. But what could she do? He always had it with him. He answered the thing, and it was an art broker in New York, something about the Riemenschneider. Bruno shrugged an apology toward Myrtle and, receiver to his ear, got up with his black case, walked toward the corridor where the restrooms were located, and talked business, pacing in the dim light across from the dining room. Ms. Halstead could hear his voice waft in and out of audible range. When he returned to the table, he smelled of smoke.

Over Peking almond duck now, Myrtle told Bruno she was rereading Thomas Mann's *The Magic Mountain*, and expounded at length on the crucial meaning of Hans Castorp's dream in the *snow* chapter for the protagonist's development, his *Bildung*. To the extent Bruno leaned forward as she spoke, she felt she was making headway in her campaign to make him a man of culture; he was surely picking up something of value from her, because those soulful, brown eyes reciprocated with a gamut of meaningful looks.

As for his state of mind, Mr. De Carlo listened to the detailed discourse of his friend . . . acquaintance . . . tutor?—he couldn't decide how to categorize her—caught between two competing thoughts: on the one hand, he should really read this book, this *Magic Mountain*; he would definitely buy himself a copy before week's end; and, on the other hand, there surely must be some way to catch the waiter's eye for the bill, without her noticing a lapse in attention. He had to be at Butterfield's by 2:30 at the latest. A curator from Chicago would be at the auction, and he'd learned in an antiquarian shop in Verona that this man was one of the world's experts in woodcarvings. That the broker in New York was interested was another sure sign.

After Bruno left her at The Pines, Myrtle ascended to the twenty-fifth floor in the elevator and unlocked her apartment door in time to answer another anonymous call. She told the caller to please hang on while she put down her purse, looked for her reading glasses, got seated in her easy chair, and opened the *Magic Mountain* directly to the *snow* chapter. When she was settled and had caught her breath, she gave a short introduction to the life and works of Thomas Mann; then she proceeded to read the protagonist's terrifying and ambiguous dream vision. She admonished the caller to understand Mann's message as one that ultimately rejected the fascination with death in favor of an embrace of life. She hung up with the impression the silent caller had been particularly attentive.

Three weeks had passed since Myrtle last heard from Bruno. It was not unusual for him to be out of town in New York, Paris, or Rome, but why hadn't he called after their Chinese lunch? After all, she, in a fit of generosity, had picked up the tab, even though he had invited her. Well, maybe he'd unearthed a real find in Leningrad or some precious religious icons on the black market and was involved in complicated customs negotiations. Or maybe his ailing mother in Tuscany had taken a turn for the worse. That must be it. Not that she missed him or gave him a second thought. She had plenty to do, even though she had to stop driving because of the worsening cataract in her left eye. The Pines, the finest life-care residence in the city, offered a wealth of activities and programs for its residents; they had a rather adequate library, and she had vowed to reread Joyce's *Ulysses* by the end of summer, despite the bad eye, and before the surgery she hoped to schedule for September. She also decided to sort out her closets and give all superfluous items she had saved from recent decades to the Goodwill. Yes, she would finally impose order and efficiency on her twenty-fifth-floor apartment. She had no time to be lonely. The daily chores were almost overwhelming—checks to be deposited, bills to be mailed, tax documents to be gathered for the estimated taxes, correspondence, phone calls. People took up a great deal of time—her cousin Clara's visit every other Friday morning, the Reading Roundtable, her brother Frank's phone call from Illinois every Sunday afternoon. On top of all that, Mr. or Ms. Anonymous called about once a week, and she was having a difficult time choosing and explaining excerpts from Joyce's *Ulysses* that would be intelligible to someone who gave you no feedback.

Around 11:00 A.M. Myrtle descended to The Pines's Level A where her mailbox was located. As usual, the area was full of grey-haired women and an occasional elderly gentleman exchanging daily pleasantries.

"So glad to see you up and around again. Ella's still in the infirmary with the bladder problem."

"What? She slipped into a coma?"

"Will you be at the memorial service for Mr. Feinstein?"

"It's a blessing after all that suffering."

"Tonight's travelogue is on Austria?"

"No, Australia."

The last boxes were still being stuffed while the residents with last names earlier in the alphabet pulled out their mail. Those with the largest stacks proudly complained of so much to do, while those with only a few pieces of junk mail tried to hide the lack of interest the outer world took in them by disappearing quickly into the building's vast expanses. Myrtle looked through her mail in the elevator: *junk, junk, bill, bill. What's this? A postcard!* Her heart quivered, and she took hold of the handrail to steady herself as the elevator stopped at the fifth floor, and her favorite nurse entered with a cheery, "Good morning, Ms. Halstead. How you doin' today?"

"Oh, fine, just fine, Irene."

Irene pushed the button marked 19 then bent down and picked up something off the elevator floor, something Ms. Halstead had dropped.

"Hmm, looks like somebody's lost a postcard. Let's see," she said examining it, "Looks like Egypt to me. Here's a man sitting on a camel with a pyramid in the background."

By the time Myrtle realized it was her postcard, Irene had already turned it over and read the address, and who knows what else? Postcards were fair game for curious eyes. "Oh, it's yours, Ms. Halstead. Guess you dropped it here in the elevator."

Myrtle's outstretched hand was already demanding it back, and Irene handed it to her with the comment, "What nice handwriting! And what a handsome man in the picture!"

The wink of Irene's eye accompanying this remark may have been lost on Ms. Halstead, with her cataract, but Myrtle suspected Irene, by reading the card, had pried more deeply than she should have into her personal life, and it irritated her.

For her part, Irene noticed the trembling of Ms. Halstead's hand as she took back the postcard and thought she had best accompany her to her room. So when the door opened at the nineteenth floor and Myrtle asked her why she didn't get out, Irene told her she also had to go see Ms. Michaels at the end of the twenty-fifth floor, so she might as well keep her company all the way to her apartment. She'd stop on the nineteenth on the way back down. No problem. Really.

Normally, Myrtle enjoyed talking to Irene, but at this moment her presence was a burden. She was virtually unnerved by the prospect that anyone might even approach her refuge, her *ermitage,* uninvited. What she wanted was to close the door to her apartment as fast as possible, sink into her easy chair by the window, turn on the light, don her reading glasses, and devote the next half hour to the intriguing card.

On the elevator landing Irene slipped her strong, brown arm underneath Myrtle's frail, white arm as if they were buddies out for a friendly stroll, and Myrtle was helpless to prevent it. As they entered the hallway, Irene pared down her own vigorous stride to match Myrtle's slow and tottering pace, and the two women advanced down the long corridor toward room 2510. Myrtle was overly conscious of all the ramifications of this encounter, and she suffered from her own sensitivities. She was wise to these subtle tricks of the geriatric helper's trade. That good-natured supporting arm was not a sign of friendship but was there to prevent a stumble and a broken hip. It was also a sign of the physical superiority of youth, and Myrtle knew the slow pace Irene now took on was affected; it was a condescending accommodation to her own increasing debility. This stroll was almost unendurable!

Irene waited while Ms. Halstead fumbled for her keys. When the un-grateful old woman finally stepped inside her refuge, she uttered a sarcastic, "Have a nice day."

For the nurse's benefit, Myrtle slammed her door shut. She was sure Irene had nothing to do on the twenty-fifth floor, so why hadn't she left her alone? Now, finally, she was free and safe in her own realm, where no one would disturb her. She locked the deadbolt and made an agitated but cautious beeline for her chair. With her glasses in place and her bright lamp adjusted for reading, she examined the postcard.

It was no ordinary card, that was certain. So, Bruno was in Egypt. Well, that explained his silence. He'd gone from a quick buying trip in Spain to northern Africa and ended up on a vacation in Egypt. And his handwriting was . . . well *nice* was hardly an adequate term. Myrtle tried to analyze it. Aside from his extravagant signature on real estate documents, it was the first specimen of his handwriting she'd seen. Now she noted it was definitely clear and legible. It was not exactly typically American, but rather more Eu-ropean. And it was neither masculine nor effeminate, and that was probably because of its European characteristics. So, it was definitely different and interesting—*no, you shouldn't say* interesting. Interesting *is such an insipid, semi-literate cliché. Let's say it's* . . . pleasing. *Yes, that's it*—pleasing.

She turned it over. By God, the photo on the card was of him on top of a camel! Was that possible? She hadn't seen such a card since the old days in the US when people turned their own photographs into postcards. It must have been a current Egyptian tourist gimmick, and what a nice idea. And he did it for her! This was the first and only picture she had of him! What had made him send her a photograph of himself? Did it suggest a new degree of intimacy in their friendship? One usually only collects photographs of one's closest friends and family. She must be getting through to him, becoming someone significant in his life. Even in an exotic, far-away place, having dined with artists and royalty, dealt with curators and billionaires, he had remembered her. She was having an impact on him!

How handsome he looked straddling that homely beast. The light-col-ored stones of the pyramid rose up behind him in the distance and the en-tire upper horizon was clear, azure sky. His wavy black hair was longer than usual—probably no time for a haircut on his busy schedule—and ringed over the collar of his white shirt that was unbuttoned halfway down his chest to reveal a manly but not apish amount of hair. His sleeves were rolled up tightly, almost to the shoulders. No tattoos, thank goodness, and the bare arms' muscularity—she admired them now for the first time. Thanks to his natural, Roman pigmentation, his skin was tanned to a milk chocolate brown. She thought she detected the slight shadow of a beard. His face had the color of . . . *Agnolo Doni*. That was it! That's who he reminded her of, that explained her sense of *déjà vu* when she first opened the door to him on Greenwich Street—Raphael's portrait of Agnolo Doni: the handsome face, the masculine crease in the chin, the Roman nose, even if it was from Raphael's Florentine period. Bruno's grace atop an awkward camel saddle revealed a relaxed confidence in his body and position in life, something he was earning with his hard work. And although the ubiquitous sunglasses hid his eyes—of course, he had to protect them from the desert sun—she knew the hint of crow's feet hidden behind them would give enormous character to his face. He would age into an even more beautiful and distinguished paragon of manhood if fate granted him the long life he deserved. One day, she flattered herself, she might also take credit for instilling some of the depth of character that would eventually become his features.

Up until now, she had difficulty recapturing in her mind the very agreeable features of his face. She knew he was handsome, and she did know what he looked like, but when she closed her eyes and tried to visualize the exact look of his eyes, or his nose, or the curve of his mouth, or his teeth when he smiled, or those tiny, incipient crows' feet, or the exact hue of his skin, she had to admit she couldn't do it. The more she tried to focus on these traits, the more fluid they became, the more they eluded her and faded away beyond her visual grasp, leaving her frustrated. Now, she was happy to have received this gift she could examine whenever she wished. And he would be back—by God, next week if the card was right—in San Francisco!

9

ON HIS WAY BACK from Egypt, Bruno stopped to see his mother, Esperanza Maria Dicarlomini, in the Tuscan village of Monteriggioni. She was leaning out her third-floor kitchen window, between the dishtowel and pillowcase that were hung out to dry, when she saw the taxi approach down the narrow street. She cursed to herself. Her sixth sense told her it would be her profligate wretch of a son who had refused to marry the mayor's daughter, fled to America, and only came to visit her when he wanted money. Insatiable, that overgrown child of hers. And then he would have the nerve to criticize her for hanging her wash out the window and tell her once again to get a washer-dryer. *Well, too bad*, she thought, as she hung out her flannel pajamas to sway in the breeze.

After her husband's premature death, and after she recovered from the surprising shock of the enormous estate he had left her—having hidden his wealth from her throughout their marriage—she set up all three of her children with trust funds that produced handsome incomes. Her two good daughters had thanked her. But what did her ungrateful son do? Ask for more! Not that she couldn't afford it, but wasn't she generous to a fault already? She had given him 266,000,000 lira two years ago, and 800,000,000 lira last year, not to mention the monthly trust checks. But *basta*, now. She was tired of his demands. After all, she lived a simple life and didn't flaunt her wealth. She had calluses on her hands, while his hands were smooth as silk. And furthermore, a man should earn his own money. And she couldn't tell whether he did or he didn't. The shame of it! Thank God his father didn't know how she kept giving him more and more. The disappointment, yes, even dishonor, in having raised such a son had contributed to the early death of poor Lucio. She was sure of this. And Lucio had left her to find husbands for their two daughters, good girls, both of them. It had not been easy to find husbands for such good girls anymore, and her son had been no help in this matter. Life had been hard, and the malevolent neighbors who envied her and whispered put-downs behind her back, just didn't understand. Here she was, alone at sixty-five, and in two minutes this excuse for a son would knock at her door and expect her to cook up a pot of spaghetti Bolognese like a typical Italian mother. Then he would tell amusing stories and wait for exactly the right moment to ask her for a handout.

Well, to hell with it. This is not how Lucio and I raised him. If he's hungry, he can take me out to lunch.

"Mamma!" cried Bruno when Esperanza opened the door. He engulfed his wiry little mother in both arms, and things went downhill from then on. Over lunch—she insisted on the best restaurant in Pienza, fifty kilometers away, and he had to reorder a taxi and pay for that, too—she spun out her tale of woe.

"Bruno, your sister, Magdalena, your very own sister—if you can believe that a sister of yours would do this to her poor, old mother—she leaves her three-year-old son, Franco, every Thursday morning with me here. Your nephew, you know? Do you ever take a present to Franco, your nephew? No, you don't. Anyway, she expects me to babysit until 2 P.M. Can you believe this? And after I raised all three of you, my own bambinos, you included, with no help from anybody. I'm old, Bruno. I'm tired. I don't want to raise more kids. Believe me, three babies of your own are enough.

"And that's not the worst, Bruno—your older sister, Estrella, it's unbelievable. I'll cry if I tell you this. Estrella's husband, Emilio, the no-good, homebreaker, is having an affair with the podiatrist's wife in Siena, that bleached blond harlot, and everybody knows about it. It's a scandal and a dishonor to our family. It's an affront to the memory of your poor father! I tell you, I can't bear it! Estrella calls me three times a week from Siena and talks my ear off. But what can I do? What can I tell her? I'm here all alone, with no one to advise me.

"I'm old, I'm tired. Why doesn't the world leave me alone? Haven't I done enough, already? When do I get my rewards? We used to go on these nice summer vacations—me with Estrella's family—to Sardinia. Everybody treated me with respect. But that's out the window, now, like Estrella's marriage. It was the one time in the year I looked forward to. I just don't know, Bruno. What will become of us? Do I deserve this in my old age?"

Bruno listened carefully to his mother and assessed that in actuality, she was fine. The first year after his father's death had surely been difficult. His mother had withdrawn from the world and seemed inconsolable. But she gradually recovered from her grief and began to take part in village life again. She had plenty of friends in Monteriggioni, and she went to market and church regularly. And the attentions of the handsome village widower, Paolo Garibaldi, were not altogether unwelcome to her. Besides which, his mother was very rich, by Bruno's calculations, and judging by the trust fund at the Banco d'Italia which had been sending him and his sisters large monthly checks for the last ten years. Bruno knew she had taken a correspondence course in English and that in the last few years she had accumulated stacks of *The Wall Street Journal* and *Forbes Magazine* in her bedroom. Not to mention the touch-tone phone with automatic dialing and built-in fax and answering machine, the computer with modem on the big new desk, and a fireproof, locking file cabinet that was always locked.

After his father's death, Esperanza had sold off the extensive vineyards she learned her husband had secretly owned. Unbeknownst to her and her children, they had been in Lucio's family for generations. On the road to Monteriggioni, Bruno had seen the new wind surfboard factory and soft drink bottling plant that had been erected where his father's oldest vines had grown. A definite loss for Chianti, but surely a financial gain for his mother. But just how wealthy she was, he couldn't say—she hadn't traded in her village lifestyle for anything ostentatious. Like a peasant, she persisted in hanging her laundry out the window for the world to see. He believed she refused to buy a washer-dryer precisely because she knew how much her fluttering laundry irritated him.

After an expensive lunch, Esperanza insisted the taxi take the long way back to Monteriggioni, the scenic route. *The taxi fee was brutal*, thought Bruno as he paid it and realized this was not a propitious time to ask for more money. Well, maybe in the morning she'd be in a better mood, and if not, it could wait till the next trip. He had thirteen months left on his option for the villa near Nîmes.

Toward evening, Esperanza went on the attack about Bruno's personal life. Why wasn't he married? Who were his friends? Why hadn't he married Julia, the mayor's daughter, when he'd had the chance?

It was bad enough she was unapproachable about money, but why did she have to torture him about the distant past? For example, he couldn't have married the mayor's daughter way back when. He was only seventeen. And moreover, that little slut had been pregnant. Not by him, but by that scoundrel, Giuseppe Busculoni. Well, Julia miscarried already in her eighth week, lucky for her, because the adults never found out. But Bruno knew she was below his dignity, below his ambitions.

Now his mother tried to pry into his current sex life. It was a source of constant consternation that her son couldn't satisfy his sex drive on the average twice a week with a faithful Italian wife. Once, he had tried to argue his celibacy was a way to preserve himself, body and soul in the manner of a priest—pure, unsullied, unspoiled, and clean—for the ultimate union that he had not yet found. After that explanation she hadn't talked to him for six months, and only through the most delicate and diplomatic maneuvering had he won back her relatively good graces. She put him in a double bind. He certainly couldn't tell his mother his sex life was rich and varied, that it sported a variety of colorful partners, even of the same sex once in a while. Moreover, he'd mastered the art of masturbation, and in fantasy, too, he was near genius. He had stacks of erotic literature to rival his mother's financial literature. Many of these magazines and books, esoteric European, Indian and Persian documents, could someday be sold to a collector of erotica for good money. But that she wouldn't understand either. "California lifestyle" was a term of which she was deeply suspicious, as well as of the suggestion that nowadays in California people got married much later in life, or not at all. In sum, although he knew his masculinity was perfectly intact, even abundant, he couldn't convince her of anything. Again, it was hopeless. He was a sitting duck to her stream of rebukes that continued unabated until they both grew tired after dusk.

In the evening, Esperanza made some instant coffee and put out a piece of stale pastry, but she made no effort to whip up a pot of spaghetti or some veal scaloppini. Bruno told his mother she really should buy a washer-dryer, and then both mother and son went to bed hungry.

In the alcove on his lumpy old childhood mattress, Bruno examined the pictures on the walls: near the window, the majestic, antlered stag snorting white puffs of condensed breath from his nostrils in a romantic, wintery mountain landscape; on the wall opposite his bed next to the mirror, the Jesus with a crown of thorns and blood droplets on his forehead with hands pressed together in prayer, his eyes gazing heavenward; and finally, the portrait, which hung right above his bed, of a benevolently smiling Pope John XXIII in bejeweled, silk regalia with a pearly, peaked cap on his head. Good God, what kitsch! He would gladly have helped get her some decent art and furnishings for her home. But she never took his advice.

Amidst troubled thoughts and the musty curtains of his childhood, Bruno De Carlo finally fell asleep in Monteriggioni. The following evening, he arrived in San Francisco at 8:55 P.M., Pacific Daylight Time.

Bruno felt lousy, down. He couldn't shake off his jet lag. He kept waking up in the middle of the night and mulling over the trip. He filled his Renaissance travertine ashtray—the teak-ivory Balinese ashtray was already overflowing—with Gauloises stubs. Not that it hadn't been profitable. The tapestries in Spain had been a steal, and he had already found an eager customer in New York who would pay a ridiculously high price for them. The treasure house in southern France was still there, waiting for him. But how was he going to get the $500,000 he needed from his mother? It would become apparent to the Beattys within a year or two whether or not he was someone to be taken seriously. They knew the difference. He could not expect them to simply tolerate him forever as a quaint, token Italian count of unknown origins. He'd have to reveal some substance, sooner or later. The situation rankled him.

Two-thirty A.M. He wandered through the living room into the kitchen and poured himself a glass of Pellegrino. Then he returned to the living room and put some music on the stereo—one of Myrtle's tapes. At least the electricity on the entire main level seemed to be working. It had been a good decision to give Hermann a set of keys and permission to work while he was gone and stay in the basement whenever he wanted. After all, he was perfectly quiet and seemed to enjoy the challenge of putting the house current in order. Besides, he only wanted to be reimbursed for materials. This was something positive. But Bruno quickly reverted to fretting about the trip, and he dropped an inch of cigarette ash onto a white flower in his fifty-year old Bakhtiari. He kicked at it to make sure it didn't leave a burn mark.

It was not just the financial problem, although that would have been sufficient, but there was his mother's general reproach about his personal life. And indeed, despite his self-flattering rationalizations about his celibacy, his affairs and his autoerotic practices, he knew somewhere, deep down, she was right. She might not know the specifics, but he had to admit his sexual behavior was sometimes reprehensible. He reproached himself for having seduced the Beattys' pretty but superficial daughter, Crystal, in a Cairo hotel after he'd hitched a ride from Madrid to Egypt on their private jet. After they climaxed together, he'd had a violent sneezing fit that made his nose bleed and made her mad. And worse, there was the memory of that unsavory little episode in the Sahara with the sixteen-year-old camel driver, whose bottom front teeth were missing, with whom he had smoked some hashish. Then the night in a tent with him and two of his twelve-year-old Bedouin friends, who performed nasty things on each other. Mind you, he didn't touch them; he only watched what they did—for a fee, of course. Then, while he stepped out of the tent to take a leak, they stole his cash and disappeared into the desert. Not that the money was a great loss, but if his mother knew of these escapades . . .

On top of it all, he had broken his vow to swear off marijuana, so he felt thoroughly sullied and disgusted with himself. Here now, in the cool darkness of the San Francisco night, he realized he craved the type of companionship that would confirm to him he was not the shallow and dissolute wretch he feared himself to be.

10

SEVERAL DAYS AFTER THEIR encounter in the elevator, Myrtle ran into Irene near The Pines's administrative office. With a laugh and a broad smile, the nurse blocked Myrtle's slow forward motion through the hallway. Myrtle felt guilty for having slammed her door on Irene but hoped she wouldn't have to confront her own bad behavior so soon. But now the nurse stood solidly in front of her. Maybe Myrtle could pretend nothing had happened. Maybe Irene had forgotten the incident. Irene was faster on the uptake with a jovial, "Mornin', Ms. Halstead. How you doin' today? And how's that handsome honey of yours, Bruno, from Egypt? Wooeeee! That's some good lookin' dude if I ever did see one! You take care now, Ms. Halstead."

Irene winked at her, pinched her on the cheek, and managed to slip her sizeable figure past Myrtle without upsetting the old woman's balance. She was gone before Myrtle had time to say hello, let alone utter an apology.

By God, just as I suspected—she did read the card!

This realization momentarily arrested Ms. Halstead in her tracks. But Irene had skillfully forgiven Myrtle's nastiness without her having to make the effort, so she too forgave Irene's minor indiscretion. After all, Irene had entered the elevator innocently enough and had seen the card on the floor. When she picked it up, she was only doing her job, and of course she couldn't have known to whom it belonged until she read it. Myrtle came up with several reasons to excuse any possible mistakes on the part of good old Irene. She even allowed a smile to cross her face and concluded, *Yes, to be fair, Irene is a gem of a human being—and a good worker. I'll have to put in a good word for her with the administration. After all, she's trying to raise her poor little boy singlehandedly, and that's got to be a hard job these days with all the drugs and violence in the schools. My heart goes out to all the good, decent Negro folk like Irene, because it's that criminal element that gives them a bad name.*

Myrtle's thoughts were all tolerance and liberality now, and she had to check an impulse to hum out loud. She greeted several residents warmly as she made her way back to the elevator, oblivious to their *What's-gotten-into-her?* looks. Today was a lovely day. The Pines employed such wonderful help. Irene, though in her quaint dialect, had the underlying refinement of soul and good taste to notice the aesthetic beauty of her friend—*handsome honey*, she called him. Of course, she also called him a *dude*, and here Myrtle concluded that that term was neither complimentary nor derogatory in Irene's dialect, but rather a neutral designation for a male human being. Irene even remembered Bruno's name from having read the card. Well, even in a photograph seated atop an absurdly ugly camel, he was unforgettable. Surely, none of the other female residents of The Pines had such an extraordinary friend, let alone a *handsome honey* who was almost a dead ringer for Raphael's Agnolo Doni! She could well afford to greet these pedestrian mortals with more generosity, and she vowed to do so from now on.

Back in her easy chair, Myrtle tried to concentrate on *Ulysses*. She was two-thirds of the way through, but the words *handsome honey* kept insinuating themselves into her thoughts and interrupting her concentration. Finally, she set the book down, picked up the postcard on the end table, and studied it. Then she closed her eyes with the intention of deciding just how their relationship should be defined. *Handsome honey* certainly would not do. What about *friend*? *Acquaintance*? *Adopted spiritual son*? *Beau*? *Gallant*? She liked the old-fashioned terms. *Swain*?

The phone startled her. "Bruno," She gasped. She was immediately out of breath and her mouth dry. Fortunately, he carried the conversation long enough for her to regain control over her wildly pounding heart. He had been in Spain, Tunisia, Egypt, and finally, Italy, to see his ailing mother. Yes, she had received the card. She grasped it now and looked at those sunglasses as he spoke to her. Yes, she was well. Her eye was not much worse, but eventually she'd need surgery. She was deep into *Ulysses* and would tell him about it at their next rendezvous. Rendezvous—she had never used this term to characterize their meetings—they had always been *appointments* or *dates*, which could be interpreted either way. *Rendezvous* sounded more serious, and she worried how he would react.

Yes, he wanted to see her. He would be in town for several weeks. Lunch? Dinner? What did she prefer? She couldn't believe what came out of her own mouth now as she suggested dinner at her place, in her *ermitage*, at The Pines. She had always wanted to meet him elsewhere. She didn't even like him to pick her up or deliver her back to this home for decaying relics, elegant though it was. But suddenly it didn't seem to matter. Irene might catch a glimpse of him, and she would see he was far more handsome in reality than in the photograph, or than even Raphael's Agnolo Doni—she now had the habit of leaving the book on Renaissance art open in the library to that page for the edification of anyone else who might chance to glance at it. Now, Margery or Herb, who alternately manned the front desk, would see her *swain*—that was it!—when he came to call, as would some of the other old bores; they would know that this remarkable man was calling on Ms. Halstead, and that, my, didn't she know fascinating people!

Then they would be alone in her apartment. It was nothing to be ashamed of, on the twenty-fifth floor with its spectacular view of the most beautiful city in America, the Golden Gate Bridge and the bay toward the north, with her French seventeenth-century etchings and the genuine early Chagall on her walls, with her books—that is, her library—and with her sterling silver. After all, she had decorated her apartment with only the finest items she had cherished over the years. He, as a dealer in art, would appreciate this. She would buy a dessert—one of those delectable cakes from Fantasia, and the wine—the same Chianti Classico. If he could just pick up some French bread and bring some of his famous penne, they could enjoy a private potluck, and he could tell her about his travels, and she would explain the stream-of-consciousness form of *Ulysses*. Next Wednesday evening? By God, he agreed!

Wednesday, and Ms. Halstead was in a hurry. Up at six, she'd been the first one down to the dining room and had to wait interminably—four minutes and twenty-three seconds—for it to open and for Mr. Seward to seat her. She glared at the next people to enter the room, diverting them away from her table. She wanted to eat quickly and alone in order to get to Fantasia as soon as it opened, and after that, to Safeway. The last thing she wanted to do was to talk to any old people in their petty pace. She hadn't any time to waste today.

She ate breakfast by herself—one soft-boiled egg, six-and-one-half minutes, please. She always ordered it this way, but she was once again convinced they left it in seven minutes or more. What do you expect in a mausoleum like this? A glass of grapefruit juice, oatmeal with raisins—it came without raisins, but she had no time to send it back for raisins.

The service these days! If it were not for the likes of Irene, one would have reason to despair.

And one slice of honey wheat berry toast.

It was, of course, too light, and not wheat berry but plain wheat, but again no time. And what should have been margarine was most certainly butter—bad for the cholesterol level—but what could one do? America was an empire in decline. And growing old was fraught with an endless string of minor indignities. She should have made her own breakfast in her apartment. Well, at least it was over now, and she could get on with it.

Down at the reception desk, she approached Herb.

"Herb? Could you order a taxi for me, please?"

"Oh, good morning, Ms. Halstead. How are you today?"

"In a hurry, thank you."

Herb got the hint and picked up the phone.

"I'll get that taxi for you right away, Ms. Halstead."

Myrtle hovered over him as he dialed and waited for an answer.

"You might want to have a seat in the lobby, Ms. Halstead. I'll take care of the taxi for you." Herb looked up at her, holding the handset to his ear.

Myrtle didn't budge. She was determined to monitor Herb's conversation with the cab company. It had once happened to Mrs. Brubaker that the taxi ordered at the desk went to The Shores, not The Pines, and Mrs. Brubaker was late for an appointment. That was sometime before Herb was hired, but you never knew.

"That's all right, Herb. I'm quite comfortable here."

Besides, the lobby was deadly, Myrtle reasoned. You were easy prey to anyone who might walk by with nothing better to do than to demand your attention and waste your time. As long as she stood at the counter, she didn't feel like she was wasting time. Finally, Herb had someone on the line.

"Good morning. The Pines. Could you send us a taxi right away, please? Yes, on Sutro Street. Thank you." Herb looked up at Ms. Halstead. "They'll be here in about six minutes, Ms. Halstead."

"Thank you, Herb."

He had done it right—The Pines, not the Shores. She had heard it. But she still didn't want to sit and wait in the lobby, so an awkward silence ensued. Myrtle should have asked Herb how he was, but today she was too preoccupied. Herb tried to make small talk.

"I guess you're looking forward to getting rid of that cataract, so you can get behind the wheel again?"

By God, he wants to talk about my cataract, on a day like this!

It was the last thing on Myrtle's mind, although it was the reason for ordering the taxi at this moment.

"Yes, that's true," Myrtle answered perfunctorily, but then decided it would be better, indeed, to retreat to the lobby and take her chances with passersby.

Seated in an easy chair, she felt in her left coat pocket to make sure the two dollar bills for the cab driver's tip were there. Then she opened her purse and made sure for the third time that she had her wallet, the plastic bag bound by a rubber band that contained her cash, her keys, her scarf (not her good scarf for the evening, of course) and her net-bag, oh yes, and her list: cake at Fantasia and Chianti from Safeway, where she'd also stock up on some staples—a box of Kleenex, a bottle of Maalox (extra strength) a can of condensed milk, and her special, sinful little treat, a bar of Ghiradelli chocolate that she allowed herself once a month, although the price had gone up to $1.89 during the last year.

Five minutes after she sat down, Myrtle was ushered into a blue-and-white cab outside the entrance to The Pines by a Chinese taxi driver, whom she couldn't understand. He, however, managed to understand her. He opened doors for her at Fantasia, pushed her cart around Safeway, and, upon their return an hour later, even carried her bags into the The Pines's lobby—where she remembered to hand him his tip. Myrtle believed she was a keen observer of human nature. But she found the look he gave her at the sight of the two dollar-bills inscrutable.

At 5:00 P.M., with preparations for the evening complete, Myrtle finally sank into her easy chair, tired from the day's activities, and began to anticipate with pleasure the arrival of her swain—she could never reveal this charming little anecdote involving Irene to Bruno. Or could she? She fell asleep over this pleasant reverie and was awakened two-and-a-half hours later by the telephone.

"Herb? Yes? What? A Mr. De Carlo is downstairs? Already? Why he's not supposed to come till 7:30. What? It is 7:30?" Myrtle looked at her watch and had a hard time focusing her sleepy eyes on it. Indeed, it might be 7:30, and it was definitely twilight and not late afternoon light anymore that entered through her north window. Herb wanted to know what to do with him.

"Well, of course, I'm expecting him," Myrtle told him proudly, as if it were the most natural thing in the world for octogenarian ladies at The Pines to entertain dashing, young Italian counts in their apartments in the evening. She hesitated only a second and said, "Send him right up!"

Myrtle calculated it would take him about seven minutes and thirty seconds to arrive at her door, if the elevators were running at the usual evening pace. So, she would have just enough time to make it to the bathroom and touch up her lipstick and tie the blue-and-white silk Lapidus scarf she'd ironed yesterday around her neck. She couldn't rise out of her chair too fast, however, if she wanted to avoid feeling lightheaded, and then she didn't dare move too quickly across the living room toward the bathroom if she wanted to retain her balance. Her heart was racing wildly.

"Steady now, steady girl," she admonished herself.

In the bathroom, having applied her lipstick and freshened up, she arranged the scarf around her neck and adjusted her navy-blue dress on her body. Fortunately, she had put it on this morning. Her golden linen suit might have been a better choice, but there was no time. This dress was more flowing and sensuous, better for an evening affair. Thank goodness she dressed properly every morning before breakfast, so there was no need to race now. She smiled and studied her face for an instant in the mirror. Ignoring the fault lines age had carved into her features, she decided she looked fine. The doorbell rang, and she left the bathroom before any critical reflections could insinuate themselves into this magic moment.

Bruno entered her apartment hidden behind bundles of food and flowers with an air of *abbondanza*. He set everything on the floor and kissed Myrtle on the left check, and then on the right. Then he took her hand, pivoted her toward her north living room window, and pronounced, "What a view! Magnifico! I had no idea!" and launched into a steady string of superlatives about her one-bedroom apartment such as she had never heard before. He insisted she tell the story of every exquisite item on her walls—her shelves, her books—but of course, first, he must unpack, and they must share a glass of champagne and a toast. But before that, the flowers—an ostentatious bouquet of long-stemmed irises, much too large for any vase she possessed. Well, no matter, he would put them in the sink. Well, no, better in the bathtub, because they would need the kitchen sink. Flowers, after all, are only symbolic among friends. The important thing was they were finally together again after such a long absence. But he had something else, before the toast, and he pulled out two long, white candles—for atmosphere. This very special dinner deserved candles—did she have some holders to put them in?

Well, of course, Myrtle had some very special sterling holders, which, by the way, would certainly be of professional interest to Bruno—a pair she'd bought in 1937 for $400 at auction, whose value had surely grown astronomically in the meantime. She had shown them to no one, but this was the appropriate time to bring them out. Mr. De Carlo offered to help her retrieve the candlesticks from a dusty old box, high in a bedroom closet. No, she didn't need his help to reach, but he noticed she was not altogether steady on her stepping stool, and she had to struggle to get at them. When they finally emerged from the box, they were badly tarnished but more magnificent than expected. His admiration was genuine. And he guessed right—they were English, and early nineteenth century was close, very close to their manufacturing year of 1810. He did seem to know his trade, she noted to herself.

Myrtle twisted the candles into her candlesticks. Then Bruno retrieved a bottle of Veuve Clicquot from his shopping bags. He removed the cork, poured the champagne, and clinked Myrtle's bubbling glass with a wink and a toast, "To us . . . and to the finer things in life!"

By 10:45 P.M. the two friends were seated on the couch facing the north window, Fantasia's remaining chocolate crumbs on dessert plates on the coffee table in front of them. The candlesticks had been moved to this table, and Myrtle was bringing to a close a wide-ranging exposition that cleverly linked German romanticism, the surrealism of Magritte, and stream-of-consciousness techniques in James Joyce. When she finally finished, after 11:00 P.M., the attentive Bruno—Myrtle believed she had never conversed with a better listener—looked soulfully into her eyes, took her hand into his own, and held it silently for an unforgettably long minute.

Suddenly the phone rang—not Bruno's mobile phone, which he'd left next to her front door, but Myrtle's apartment phone. By God, no one called at this late hour! It rang again and Myrtle realized she would be slow to rise from the couch. Bruno must have noticed and offered, "Shall I?" nodding toward the phone.

"Yes, please," said Myrtle, hastily, annoyed at the interruption but too curious to ignore it.

Bruno stepped over to the table next to the easy chair, lifted the receiver, and said, "Hello, Ms. Halstead's residence . . . Hello? Hello? This is Myrtle's apartment. Would you like to speak to her? . . . Is anyone there?" He put his hand over the mouthpiece and said to Myrtle, "No one answers. What should I do?"

"Oh, it must be my anonymous caller. He's never called this late. But he's harmless. I've been reading *Ulysses* to him. Just tell him I'm busy and to try again some other time." She was anxious to return to the mood before the call.

Bruno did as he was told, hung up the phone and returned to Ms. Halstead on the couch, who seemed not the slightest ruffled by the call. Nevertheless, the interruption had broken the spell. Besides, Bruno was tired and ready to leave. To create a smooth transition he voiced a request, "Do one more thing for me, my dear lady, before I depart. Recite me a poem, please, while I close my eyes. Your favorite poem by Shakespeare, and when you finish, say no more. I will say adieu now, my friend. It was an enchanting evening. When you finish the poem, I will vanish."

Myrtle gladly fulfilled Bruno's request, but not immediately. She surprised him by now pulling out from under a decorative couch pillow a long green cashmere winter scarf with two thin golden stripes running its length. Without a word she slowly, ceremoniously, placed it over her swain's head so that the ends rested on his shirt. She patted those ends gently against his chest and gave him a knowing look—which he couldn't decipher. Bruno realized the scarf would be warm against chilly nights and that its color resembled the unique pale green of his friend's eyes, but that this color wouldn't coordinate with any of his clothes. He also realized he was meant to keep it, and Myrtle made no attempt to explain why. Satisfied, she leaned back in the couch, faced the window, and delivered a moving rendition of sonnet XXIII. This completed, Count De Carlo kissed her hand, picked up his jacket, and departed with the scarf around his neck.

Myrtle couldn't sleep. For the first time in years she left the dishes for the next morning. There would be plenty of time for such mundane tasks the following day. However, in the middle of the night, after she had only tossed and turned thinking of every nuance of the evening and then rethinking them over again and again, she thought that decision had been a mistake. She should have done them anyway, because it might have calmed her down. But now it was 3:10, and although she was too awake to fall asleep, she was tired enough not to want to get out of bed.

An extraordinary evening. He had never looked so handsome—all dark blue this time—suit, shirt, and tie all dark hues. How creatively stylish, this young man. What natural grace and beauty. So at home in his body. He must be San Francisco's most eligible society bachelor. He must have hundreds of opportunities. And yet he spent the evening with me! The entire evening—from 7:30 till 11:15 P.M., until after that stupid phone call. Let's see, that's three and three-quarters hours. And what conversation! And the looks, the little gestures—the greeting: two kisses, not just one, but one on each cheek! He kissed my hand when he left and looked so sad. Maybe it was the phone call. Maybe he suspected I have a boyfriend. Should I have explained when I said *he* that the anonymous caller could just as easily be a *she*, that I was just using the conventional masculine pronoun for both sexes? Was he jealous? And the most extraordinary of all, why did he request that I recite a poem before we parted? He must have noticed it was a love sonnet, the way he sighed with eyes closed. So, what was the implication? Is not the desire to listen to poetry a kind of confession of love? Just the type of thing lovers want of one another? Of course, I'm not a fool. I know I'm just an old lady who sold him a house. And yet, for eighty-five going on eighty-six I'm not exactly an old hag. After all, I have an anonymous admirer who calls regularly and listens to what I have to say. And someone with a good visual aesthetic sense, as Bruno certainly has in his profession, will know I was a beauty in my youth. Should I have been more forthcoming? Is he awake now? What is he thinking? Perhaps he's just another smooth operator with a hidden agenda. No, his eyes are truthful.

Myrtle's ruminations gave her no peace. Should she have recited sonnet XXIX, LVI, or maybe CIX instead of XXIII? Something less suggestive than XXIII? How did he feel about her? Were his feelings sincere, whatever they were? And had the anonymous caller interrupted something significant he might otherwise have said? She reproached herself for not having unplugged the phone. But that was against The Pines's safety regulations. She would have to reprimand Anonymous for the inopportune call the next time he or she called back. Toward dawn Myrtle Halstead fell fitfully asleep amidst the chaos of her thoughts of Bruno De Carlo.

11

It was evening of the longest day of the year on Russian Hill, and Hermann Wittgenstein sat at the desk in Bruno's office off the living room making an inventory of its contents in a spiral-ringed notebook. He took a break and twisted the ponytail at the back of his neck as he reread the postcard Mr. De Carlo had sent him from a mountain resort in the Pyrenees. Hermann didn't expect his good-hearted landlord back for several weeks. All the curtains were drawn, but bright lights were shining on his painstaking work. In fact, the electricity at 999 Greenwich Street was now in perfect order. Bruno had called Hermann a shedder of light. And since Hermann had done all of the work *for love*, as he frequently reiterated, plus reimbursements for materials, Bruno invited him to move into the basement permanently, or at least indefinitely. Hermann told him he was trying to save money and gladly accepted the offer. He was the model of discretion and reliability and thus a good person to watch the house when Bruno was gone. Both men were happy with the arrangement. It was working out beautifully.

Hermann had made his way methodically through each room of the house. Now, his surveillance took in his landlord's desk that was in disarray, you might say *disheveled* if all those papers had been hair. But this was nothing new to Hermann. He had been well-trained as a *Stasi* in East Berlin to go through desks worse than this one, to glean out the necessary information, and to leave them in the exact same order or disorder in which he found them, with not a clue that they had been scrutinized. He was an expert, too, in the art of opening mail and resealing envelopes so no one was the wiser.

Now he was about to do an inventory of the bottom drawer. It was all he could do tonight, if he were to do it right. He had already filled up nine notebooks on De Carlo's life—not only on the electricity that served his house, but on his clothing, down to the brand of underwear, his cosmetics, medications, his favorite brands of deodorant and shaving cream, both American and European; his favorite magazines; the titles, authors, and publication dates of his books—not too many in Hermann's opinion—the pots, pans, utensils, and appliances in his kitchen; the service and mileage record on his 1970 red Thunderbird, when the next smog check was due; an inventory of his tapes, records, and CDs; the scientific names of his five indoor plants. Thus, Hermann Wittgenstein already knew a great deal about Bruno, including the odd fact he sometimes kept company with the octogenarian woman who sold him the house. But he expected this desk would provide the puzzle's centerpiece. He knew from his East German secret police training that in cases where time was irrelevant you could afford to leave this to the last, to do the more marginal things first and work up to the crucial documents and clues to a person's life. The everyday items and bits of information gave you the fuzzy picture, which became more and more focused and finally crystallized through the documents you inevitably found in the desk—finances, correspondence, and the like. The desk corrected any mistaken interpretations you might have gleaned from the more trivial evidence, and the desk usually revealed important secrets, if there were any.

Bruno's bottom drawer was full of old postcards and letters. A mess. By the time Hermann went through the first batch of cards and made notes of their senders, dates, postage, and contents, it was 10:30 P.M. He thought he should go to bed but decided to open just one of the letters before he did so. There would be plenty of time to do the entire desk before De Carlo's return.

He picked up a turquoise-colored envelope and found a photograph folded into a typed letter—from a distant cousin of his landlord who had married an American woman and had two children by her. The letter's contents proved insignificant. But the photograph showed these same children and their mother, all three blondes, sitting at a picnic table in a park. He gasped. They could have been his own wife and children. Memories of the family he left behind suddenly welled up—little Bert, his delicate son, so unlike himself; Sabina, his strong and good-humored daughter; and Gaby, his intelligent, no-nonsense wife, whom he loved more than anyone in the world and yet had abandoned. As he stared at the picture, he felt a terrible pang of despair, as if nothing made sense.

His escape from East Germany came about during a freak opportunity the night he inspected the border near Duderstadt, east of the West German town of Göttingen—an exception to his usual duties in East Berlin. His cousin, Klaus, was stationed there, and he, Hermann, had helped get Klaus the position when he joined the State Security Police, the *Stasi*.

It was a moonless, overcast, dark night except for the border lights. It was freezing outside, and Klaus's fanatical compatriot, Stefan, was in the john at the moment he and Klaus finished inspecting a Polish sausage truck and allowed it to pass. Hermann made a spontaneous decision based on the calculated risk that Klaus would not shoot to kill. He simply ran after the slow-moving vehicle and never looked back. Fifty yards from the final barrier he caught up with the heavy vehicle on the asphalted no-man's strip as it rolled over the next-to-last speed bump. The first shots were fired as he jumped onto the back bumper and clung to the heavy door lever. They whined over the top of the truck. Stefan must have reappeared.

Thank you, Klaus, for waiting as long as you could . . . and for missing.

He knew they wouldn't fire after the Polish vehicle cleared the last bump. He trembled for fear and excitement while the truck rumbled over it into the West.

It had been a spontaneous act. He hadn't planned it. Hermann only knew he hated the country he lived in, hated his despicable job, and that his wife felt the same. He had discussed escape with Gaby many times, but they feared it was hopeless. She had once said, *If you ever can, do it.* And he had said, *If I ever do, I'll work till I die to get you and the kids out too.* That was all they'd ever said about it.

Hermann had been in San Francisco over a year now. He had found a job with the Strom Electric Company, which was owned by a German American. Now, thanks to Mr. De Carlo, he had a free place to live. He could save most of what he earned for the day his wife and children would join him in the West. And he was maintaining the skills that might help facilitate their escape from East Germany, once he could formulate a plan. Bruno was a good object to practice on. It was harmless. Besides which, if he didn't stay focused on something, he would go crazy for anxiety and loneliness. He examined the photograph again—he didn't have a single picture of his own wife and children in East Berlin, and he hadn't received direct word from them since his escape.

Late in the night at 999 Greenwich Street, San Francisco, California, seated at the desk in the brightly lit room of an art dealer, a large German man holding a photograph of strangers placed his balding head onto his strong arms and wept.

12

Midsummer. Myrtle waited impatiently in the eye clinic at St. Theresa's to meet Dr. Manchester, the ophthalmologist who would remove the cataract in her left eye. Her regular eye doctor had diagnosed her problem but, as he no longer performed operations, he referred Ms. Halstead to Dr. Manchester—a new colleague in the same department. A nice young man and an excellent surgeon. She would like him.

The soft, canned waiting room music irritated her. She couldn't concentrate on the pocket volume of Shakespeare's early history plays. Mr. or Ms. Anonymous had called this morning as she was trying to get ready for this appointment. Another inopportune call, and she had let him or her have it. It was bad enough to call and not identify oneself—it showed a lack of courage and character—but it was worse to exploit her time by listening to her read from the world's finest literature and expecting her to provide instruction in literary analyses, in effect, profiting from her expertise without the slightest respect for the time of day. It was definitely unacceptable, furthermore, to call someone of her advanced age after 10 P.M., not that anything indecorous was happening the night he or she called, and the man answered. No, that was a perfectly legitimate friend who happened to be of the male sex, whom she had every right in a free country to see at whatever time she wished without answering to anyone, least of all to an anonymous caller. And this morning she had no time to talk, because she had an important doctor's appointment regarding delicate elective surgery she was contemplating, and he or she should realize you can't expect to interrupt the lives of busy people at will like this. Before she hung up, she advised him or her to limit calls to the hours between three and five in the afternoon, when he or she would only interrupt, at the worst, her afternoon nap.

Here in the doctor's office, Myrtle realized she was not only still rankled by this call, but she was nervous. She tried to calm her nerves through distraction, by focusing on the woes of others that were far more catastrophic. Thus, *The Tragedy of Richard III*, the great play about that treacherous villain, depicted woes of such magnitude that her little cataract paled in comparison. She never went to a medical appointment without a good book because waiting rooms were notorious for insipid reading materials. One would think when health problems reminded people of their mortality, patients would wish to read something more uplifting to fortify their spirits. But no, the masses always went for superficial forms of entertainment. The three other patients with whom she shared the room confirmed this truth. They were all reading popular magazines, except, of course, for the child, too young to have been introduced to the benefits of the written word, who was crawling around at the feet of the woman reading *Woman's Life*. Moreover, all three adults seemed blissfully oblivious to the dreadful *muzak* bombarding their auditory senses from hidden speakers.

While Myrtle tried to concentrate on that lump of foul deformity, the Duke of Gloucester, as he performed his loathsome verbal manipulation of Lady Anne, in anticipation of wreaking havoc on the kingdom, these insidiously penetrating musical tones, surely selected to lull the patients into a false sense of security, crossed the threshold of her audible field—her hearing was still sharp—invaded her consciousness, and annoyed her. One might even say they terrorized her, like those phone calls. Good God, the insults one must put up with every single day! It was nigh unbearable. She shut the book on her lap and closed her eyes, but then the music had its way with her brain, forcing it into that mindless world of cliché-ridden adolescent emotions of first love and betrayal. This was no help in combating her own anxieties about this doctor's visit. Dr. Steinberg, a man of great wisdom, had assured her this other ophthalmologist was good, but the responsible patient must decide for herself. And who knows? These days hospitals were full of incompetent help. You never knew who might be handling you. Anything could happen. Why, Mr. Newcomb, who had resided on the fourteenth floor of The Pines, had filed a malpractice suit against a urologist at St. Theresa's two years ago, and now he—Mr. Newcomb—was dead, without the lawsuit ever having been settled. Surely, another sign of the times.

Her heart beat faster as she considered the dire possibilities, the unknown risks to which one submitted oneself when one visited a physician.

Her palms grew moist. She opened up *The Tragedies* again to the first act of *Richard III* with renewed determination to be brave. But despite the fact she read and reread the lines, she couldn't make it to Gloucester's monologue at the end of scene ii with any retention of what she had read. If they took her blood pressure, they would detect her anxiety—these strangers, who might look down on her for it, not knowing she was a woman to be reckoned with. Another minor indignity in the daily stream. But then, on the other hand, perhaps this wouldn't matter to them—to medical professionals who were always taking blood pressure and had no personal interest in her as an individual. Probably they saw her as just another pair of eyeballs, faulty eyeballs. She tried to calm down with these rationalizations. The musical pabulum droned on, and the crawling toddler ran a toy dump truck into her foot. She pretended to ignore the collision and picked up *People Magazine* from the table next to her.

"Myrtle Halstead."

She looked up to see the nurse, chart in hand, who had entered the waiting room and called out her name.

"Here, young lady," replied Myrtle, and the nurse approached to see if she could help her up. Myrtle refused her assistance. She had her cane today, and she had her own method of rising slowly from chairs and sofas that were too low and too soft.

The nurse ushered her down the hall and into a dimly lit room, where she seated her in the examination chair. She relieved Ms. Halstead of her cane but gave in when it became clear that this patient would not be parted from her purse. After asking her a few questions, she left her to wait for Dr. Manchester, who would be with her shortly.

Ms. Halstead surveyed the room for telltale signs of Dr. Manchester's incompetence. Well, she had to admit, the room was very neat and clean, rather simple and subdued, tasteful pictures on the walls; good grey carpeting, nothing objectionable—professional looking, at least. But looks could deceive. Then she spied the diplomas on the wall to her right, close enough to read if she squinted. In mahogany frames, they were placed near the window that looked out toward The Pines—placed as if he wanted his patients to be impressed with his credentials. Let's see, *Thomas K. Manchester, MD, University of California at Los Angeles . . . 1978 . . .* a gold seal . . . *Magna Cum Laude . . .* governor's signature, and so on. The other diploma, also from UCLA, indicating a residency in ophthalmology, dated 1979. Why, she wondered, did this information seem familiar to her? What bell was trying to ring in her memory bank?

A knock at the door and Dr. Manchester entered as Ms. Halstead said, "Come in."

A pleasant young man—too young and inexperienced, probably. Straight, sandy brown hair, smooth-shaved, neat white coat with his name over the left pocket in blue stitching. Grey slacks, black shoes. A polite greeting, friendly, businesslike . . . no, it couldn't be!

"Excuse me for being so forward, doctor," Myrtle began before he had a chance to introduce himself. "But before you start, you've got to satisfy my curiosity on one point, if you don't mind."

"Yes, I'd be glad to, if I can," he replied, noting her commanding voice.

"Well, I reside at The Pines, you know," she nodded in the direction of the window and thereby at the building across the street, " . . . and I met a rather peculiar, perhaps even unsavory character there—an ambulance-chasing lawyer, by profession—who told me a quite incredible story about a former client of his who years ago broke his back and eventually went on to medical school."

The fact that Dr. Manchester's eyes widened with surprise at this was not lost on Myrtle; neither that he seemed visibly taken aback.

"And, I would never waste your time with this, if it weren't for the fact that the young man's name was the same as yours—Thomas Manchester—I saw it on your diplomas. Just an odd coincidence, I'm sure. There must be a thousand Thomas Manchesters who happen to be physicians."

"Jack Peterson?" The ophthalmologist exclaimed. "Are you talking about Jack Peterson, Esquire?" The pitch of his voice rose noticeably.

"Yes, precisely!" Ms. Halstead replied with equal surprise.

"He's alive?"

She nodded and watched in amazement now as this Dr. Manchester turned away from her, went to the window, and looked out at The Pines— she mentioned that he lived on the fourth floor, opposite the emergency entrance. Now he peered down in that direction, and his shoulders quivered, she thought. She wasn't sure. He remained silent with his back to her, as if trying to conceal his feelings. An embarrassing amount of time passed before he turned back to face her, composure regained.

He looked at her chart now and then up at his confounded patient.

"Ms. Halstead, I want to be frank with you from the very start. Despite whatever opinions you may have of him, Jack Peterson virtually saved my life back then. Before my accident, I was heading off the deep end of drugs and delinquent behavior. A bad peer group, you know. It might seem an un-likely story to you—tripping over the boots and all—but it's true, and when I lay in the hospital, I thought I'd ruined my life. But then Jack Peterson came along and performed a miracle that guided me toward the right choices. Jack's settlement paid for the training that enabled me to help others now for the last ten years. You have every right to choose a different doctor, but I believe I might be able to help you."

At this moment, the voice, Myrtle's ever-reliable instrument at difficult junctures during her long life, failed her for the first time. She couldn't remember when a person younger than she had dared contradict her opinions, observations, or assertions. It was too extraordinary. And never had a physician displayed such emotions in her presence, in what should have been a professional situation. She had no adequate reaction for his explanation—an incredible mixture of clichés and sincerity, of pain and sentimentality. Whatever it meant, this situation was not good for her nerves! The rules of decorum and doctor-patient conventions had gone awry in a confused mess of assertions and misunderstandings. Suddenly, she felt old. She had turned eighty-six, recently. She was the recipient of anonymous, menacing phone calls. Her foot had just been struck by a dump truck. She slumped a bit in the examining chair. She looked away from Dr. Manchester, lost and more anxious than ever.

A kind man, Dr. Manchester perceived her distress. He regretted having contradicted this elderly patient. He approached her now with a benevolent, reassuring look and changed the subject. He told her about his career move from UCLA to Chief of Ophthalmology here at St. Theresa's in San Francisco. A wonderful city. She had lived here a long time? Well, she was very fortunate. She had good taste. He knew of The Pines's excellent reputation. The finest retirement residence in the city.

Ms. Halstead was grateful that he took up the parole and turned the extraordinary exchange back toward the familiar, the expected, and therefore manageable rhetoric. She began to sort out the confusion in her mind. She felt a bit guilty about her own derogatory remarks now that the truth of the incredible story was confirmed. She should have been more cautious than to express herself so frankly to a stranger. She knew from Shakespeare's tragedies that to express one's disdain openly could be a fatal error. And it was essential she assess this complex situation rapidly and come up with the right decision. She had a real medical problem, a bad cataract in her left eye, and an incipient one in the other eye. If she neglected them, what good would Shakespeare do her? This doctor had a good reputation in his field. An excellent reputation, in fact. Obviously, he had not dealt with Jack Peterson in a long time. Perhaps it didn't matter to her cataracts that the lawyer was an impossible boor, and that the ophthalmologist was too young and anguished at the time of his accident to be a good judge of character. Why destroy his illusions now?

He had given her the chance to drop the issue of Jack Peterson. Yes, San Francisco was a wonderful city, she would be glad to give him some tips, to fill him in on its history—anything he wanted to know. Moreover, she was glad to see some excellent new blood at St. Theresa's, she was quite impressed with his credentials—UCLA was internationally known for medical excellence.

He smiled tactfully, continued the chitchat, and took her blood pressure. She submitted graciously, and equally graciously, he refrained from comment as he wrote the figures down in her chart. Then he performed a thorough examination of her eyes, discussed the cataract operation in detail, and answered all her questions to her satisfaction. She noted he took his time with her. Thus, she became thoroughly reconciled to his treating her, convinced, in fact, that her shrewd assessment had led her to the best eye doctor in the city. She would settle for no one else. The surgery was scheduled for September.

13

Bruno had checked on the villa near Nîmes again, outside the village of Cabrières. It was overgrown, but securely locked up, with no signs of vandalism. Perfectly safe, his real estate agent in Nîmes told him. And Bruno assured the agent that he would have the $500,000 (about three million francs) before the option ran out. Then he took the train to Italy and stopped in Monteriggioni on his way to an art exhibit in Naples. He wanted to surprise his mother.

As the taxi pulled up to number thirteen in the narrow Via della Enigma, a light shone out of the third-floor kitchen window, and Bruno hoped that he might be in time for a late dinner of his mother's famous tortellini romano or maybe her clam linguini. But no amount of bell ringing, door pounding, or calling up to the bright window roused a response.

With two heavy suitcases, he walked to the café in the village square to call his mother. But her phone was constantly busy. Nobody in the café would say why. When he asked why the widow Garibaldi wasn't there at the café that evening, they only shrugged and smiled. Later, from his hotel in nearby Colle di Val d'Elsa—the taxi cost him another minor fortune—when she finally answered her phone at 10:30 P.M., he thought he heard the rustling of sheets and the whispers and suppressed cough of a man in the background.

His mother's questions seemed breathless and impatient. Was he married yet? Were his monthly checks arriving on time? Well, good. Wasn't he a fortunate boy to have such a generous mother? Nice of him to call. She hung up!

Bruno sank into his bed with a frustrated groan. She could obviously read his mind and knew he was after more money. She was avoiding him, her only son, who had persuaded a thousand women to do his bidding. In a year his option to buy the French villa with the invaluable Roman mosaics would run out. He'd have to turn the situation around in the next few months. He'd try again after Naples, and if that didn't work, he would have to think up a new scheme when he returned to San Francisco.

14

THE TESTS COMPLETED, MYRTLE lay in her hospital bed on a late afternoon in mid-September, waiting for her cataract operation the following morning. Up to a certain age, most cataract operations were done on an outpatient basis, but she was all too aware that at her stage in life, the risks increased even for this *routine procedure*, and that was why they were keeping her in the hospital overnight. She tried to reread *Hamlet*, but became stranded at the "To be or not to be" soliloquy. Would she still *be* tomorrow? Or would she die? Would something go terribly wrong during the operation? Something unexpected?

Dr. Manchester had told her there was nothing to worry about. St. Theresa's was a fine hospital. The operation would be painless, and there was nothing unusual about her particular cataract. It would be a breeze, and she should do very well and be pleased with the results. So, why was this overnight stay necessary?

She was nervous and *Hamlet* wasn't helping. The violent drama was obviously the wrong choice of literature. She was irritated with this text and with things the doctor had said. Why, for example, had he said she *should* do very well? Why didn't he say, "You *will* do very well?" Yes, she could die tomorrow morning, in one of those freak, one-in-a-million accidents. A major earthquake could jolt Dr. Manchester's laser hand and send a deadly beam straight through her brain.

At this moment, the devil himself entered in his white coat with a cheery, "How are you, Ms. Halstead?"

The strain in her, "Oh, fine, doctor," told him everything he needed to know about her anxieties, not to mention what the nurses had already said. He glanced at the paperback that lay on her chest.

"Hamlet? What a wonderful way to prepare mentally for an operation. You know, I've had a few very extraordinary patients who have been able to manage their preoperative anxieties in this way, with a kind of verbal—spoken or written—therapy. Of course, these are only the exceptionally intelligent patients. Not everyone can do this. By the way . . ." Dr. Manchester interrupted himself while he produced a container of pills out of a coat pocket and took a capsule and the cup of water from her table and offered them to her. "Could you please take this now and the other one when the nurse wakes you in the morning?" He placed the container on the night table. "It's the last step in your preop preparation."

Grateful for the young doctor's wise perceptions about her anxiety management program, she swallowed the pill without comment, and the doctor continued.

"I don't bother even bringing this up with most of my patients, but I'm sure you're someone who can understand how helpful it can be to focus consciousness away from the self and onto problems in the world, where things are usually worse than one's own situation."

"Well, yes, Dr. Manchester," Myrtle agreed readily. She was eager to please him, to get on his good side, so that he would take special care not to kill her the following morning. She had made the admitting clerk read St. Theresa's disclaimer form out loud to her before she signed it earlier in the afternoon. So, she had it in writing that complications including death were within the realm of possibility. "By the way, doctor, I'm sure," she lied now, "our mutual acquaintance, Mr. Patterson, has many fine qualities about which I'm ignorant only because I don't know him well enough."

"Do you mean, Mr. Peterson? Jack Peterson?"

"Oh, well, I guess so. Mr. Peterson, then, if you wish."

"Well, yes, indeed." Dr. Manchester seemed surprised and encouraged by this unsolicited concession. "Qualities that stem from an early tragedy in his life, to tell you the truth."

"Tragedy?" said Myrtle, clutching *Hamlet* closer to her breast and recoiling from the utterance of such a word in her hospital room. Furthermore, Jack Patterson, or Peterson, or whatever his name was, did not seem a person worthy of the term, *tragedy*. On the other hand, it occurred to her that to feign interest in him might be the way to endear herself to her potential executioner. Thus, she clutched *Hamlet* more tightly and turned on her imposing voice now as she uttered, "What do you mean by tragedy?" in such a way as to encourage Dr. Manchester to please explain in detail.

Dr. Manchester knew it would take about ten minutes for the tranquilizer to take effect on Ms. Halstead. This was the last patient on his rounds, so he could spend some extra time with her, to reassure her, to build up her confidence, and to tell the story of the person who had turned his life around. And who knew? Maybe if she knew more about the lawyer, the two old people might get better acquainted and thus be less lonely over there in their retirement home. He might be doing a good deed. "Well, it's kind of a long story," he began tentatively.

"Yes, yes. I've got all night," quipped Myrtle, as if she were impatient that he should get on with it.

"Well, you're right about that," laughed Dr. Manchester. "I've certainly got a captive audience in you."

Even Myrtle laughed a little at her situation and herself and said, "I'm all ears."

"OK, then. The story begins the summer after Jack graduated from Rice University."

"That's a relatively decent university," Myrtle interrupted already, "although it can't compare with the University of California."

"No, you're right again," agreed Dr. Manchester. "But then, Jack grew up in Texas, so it was a logical choice. Anyway, what happened was . . ."

Although she tried to listen, all Myrtle registered before she fell asleep were a few disconnected words: Big Island, Suzie, first love, volcano, earthquake, lava, and burned foot.

The operation was a success, just as that fine Dr. Manchester predicted, or rather *a piece of cake*, as the nurses taught her to say. The morning after the doctor's visit to her room, Myrtle was given a series of eye drops and wheeled into an operating room where her head was immobilized. An anesthesiologist told her he was going to give her something that would make her feel good, and he did. At some point they gave her injections around the eye that didn't bother her in the slightest. At another point she heard a sucking sound. Then things went dark for a short time until her new lens was inserted, and the light returned. From time to time she heard Dr. Manchester ask someone to hand him this or that instrument. Before she knew it, she was back in her hospital room. She spent the rest of the day explaining to as many nurses as possible, how her operation had gone. The following morning, Dr. Manchester removed her bandage, and immediately she could see better than ever, at a distance, out of her left eye. Aside from a little redness and puffiness, that was it.

Bruno was back from his latest sojourn in Italy and London. Marsha Kaiser noted his presence at the Beattys' weekend soirée and his attention to their daughter, Crystal, in her gossip column in *The Chronicle*. At The Pines, Myrtle managed to read this report with her right eye with a certain amount of jealous skepticism. Her left eye was doing well, and soon she would get new glasses. She looked forward to reading normally again—even though she set the newspaper down with the thought that you couldn't trust 90 percent of what was in it. Still, she expected, based on Marsha Kaiser's column, Bruno might call any day.

From the lamp table next to her chair, Myrtle picked up a bundle of photographs in a plastic bag encircled by a rubber band. As she struggled to separate the rubber band from the bag, it broke with a snap against the top of her left hand. She rubbed the offended spot for a moment, annoyed the sting would evoke another unsightly blue-black bruise. Because her skin was so thin, tender, and mottled with age, it could ill tolerate even minor physical insults. Moreover, she'd have to leave the rubber band wherever it fell. She might not find it even if she looked, and she didn't want to risk getting down on her hands and knees. However, she'd gone to the trouble of getting these photographs down from the cupboard in the closet last night, so she might as well make use of the brightest time of day to look at them.

Ever since she received Bruno's photo-postcard from Egypt, she debated whether or not she should reciprocate by giving him a photo of herself. Of course, she didn't want to give him a recent picture. Well, to tell the truth she didn't have many recent photos. Since Robert's death, it had been a rare occasion when anyone had taken her picture. But she had good photos of herself from her youth, when she'd been a beauty. As a twenty-year-old student, she'd played the lead role in Euripides's *Medea* to a packed audience in the Greek Theater at UC Berkeley. At first, she didn't want the role of a woman who kills her children, but she accepted it in good conscience when she learned the infanticide was not a part of the original myth—wherein Medea was actually an imaginative, visionary healer—but a later perversion of it. She went ahead and made it into the triumph of her college acting career, and the zenith, unfortunately, of a lifetime acting career that never materialized. The Great Depression intruded upon her hopes; financial necessity forced her to work for a living, first in a modest, one-room schoolhouse in California's Central Valley. Later, she made a move back to her beloved San Francisco and a better position at the state university. She supported not only herself, but also her abandoned mother and two younger siblings until times improved, and they finally became independent. For years, she saved and invested every extra penny—wisely—in real estate. Not a bad life's script, she mused to herself, trying out a term Dr. Manchester had employed recently.

She sorted through a handful of yellowed black-and-white photographs curled at the edges, holding each one carefully up to her right eye, which, despite its incipient cataract, was still usable, more so at the moment for close-up objects than the freshly repaired left eye. She shifted in her chair to gain as much light as possible from the window and twisted the lamp to shine directly on the pictures. She enjoyed confirming a self that was part of her life in which she was supremely intelligent and attractive, immeasurably more attractive than the empty-headed Beatty daughter, who would never be anything but rich. She wanted to share this self with her swain.

Picture after picture showed her with her fellow drama students—Edward Sheldon, dead three years ago. Nellie Jones, what had become of her? Helen . . . what's her name? She knew her name; it just didn't come to her now. That whole scintillating drama class. And there was the one when they took their bows after *Medea*, with their unforgettable drama teacher, Professor Anton Cunningham. She remembered the hopeless crush she'd had on him that lasted until she met Robert, whom she later married. But where was the special photograph for which she searched? The one of her alone, leaning against the Greek column, right of center stage next to the potted palm?

Finally, she held it in her hand—the young woman she had been, more beautiful than she remembered. A laurel wreath on her head of rich, curly locks falling to her shoulders, she wore a filmy white toga over her graceful body with its slender limbs, one arm outstretched in a pleading gesture and eyes rolled heavenward as if to implore the gods to explain man's incomprehensible fate. The potted palm's sharp spikes cut up the neutral backdrop of the stage, and, together with the Greek column, seemed a symbol of the social conflicts that doomed mankind to tragic destinies.

Yes, this was the photograph she would send her swain. Taken at the dress rehearsal, it had appeared on the program, and Robert had claimed it struck him like a bolt of lightning and awakened love at first sight. Though it had aged, she decided, the photo still had a powerful aura. It was still her, her essence. Although it captured a specific moment in time, it still could be called Self and was, thus, timeless and universal. Why not mail it to Bruno?

15

RIGHT OFF THE FLIGHT from Rome, Signore De Carlo took a taxi to his home on Russian Hill to shower and change into his tuxedo, then straight to the dinner party at the Beattys'. The same taxi from the airport waited in Greenwich Street, double-parked next to a Strom Electric Company pickup truck, before whisking him up to the mansion in Pacific Heights. Through-out the dinner he was especially attentive to the long-legged Crystal, who was still furious at him for the seduction in Egypt in springtime and the subsequent neglect.

In truth, he felt sick with himself all evening. His option for the aban-doned villa near Nîmes would expire in less than a year, and if he didn't have the $500,000 in time, the deal would be lost along with his hopes to catapult himself into the truly Big Time. He would be reduced to a token, tag-along socialite, and for how long was anyone's guess. And he could never ap-proach the Beattys for a loan. They must never know his future depended on a paltry $500,000. Since all his possibilities hinged on getting this French property and announcing to the world the discovery of the ancient Roman mosaics, failure would be the end to life as he believed it should be.

Back home following the dinner party, his jet lag kept Bruno awake. In his silk bathrobe he smoked one cigarette after the other as he ruminated on these problems. It was 3:00 A.M. He hadn't slept in over twenty-four hours, and he felt queasy from the stuffed squid that lay heavy in his stomach. His dinner partner, Crystal, had punished him by refusing to eat. She was thin as a bird to begin with and feigned lack of appetite to make a statement. He had cleared the two original squids off his own plate—they were delicious, one of the Beattys' chef's specialties, but very filling. During the few minutes he had engaged in conversation with Mrs. Stillman on his left, Crystal had apparently done her dirty deed. When he turned back again to speak to her, he discovered that his plate contained one and a half more squid than he had been served, while her plate was empty! Gentleman that he was forced to be, he ate them with a smile.

Bruno stared at the burning candle on his coffee table and sipped some Pellegrino while a B-grade movie flickered on the television screen in the corner. His involvement with this Crystal was another of those many errors he regretted, the result of a careless indulgence in the moment at that Cairo hotel. If he'd thought for even an instant before, he would have realized that to have something with the Beatty daughter was not necessarily a way to strengthen the contact with that family, so important for his future. Rather, such an illicit liaison had a greater potential to ruin everything. Now he was forced to humor her along and to keep up a front with her parents. He'd have to figure it all out later, but in the meantime, he absolutely needed money. When he called his mother from Naples, she had put him on hold while she talked to a broker in Frankfurt, and then his hotel had cut off his line. Every time he tried to call her back her line was busy. She had taken the receiver off the hook in order to avoid him. He was sure of it. So he gave up without attempting another visit. Nothing was coming together as it should.

He wasn't going to be able to sleep, so he extinguished the candle and turned off the television. He pulled on some jeans, a sweater, and a parka, and he wound the green and gold scarf Myrtle had given him around his neck. He descended to his garage with the hope his car would start. The first few times he had left 999 Greenwich Street on longer trips, the battery went dead and the car wouldn't start when he got back. But this time, Hermann had offered to disconnect the battery during his absence and reconnect it before his return.

Voilà! The powerful V-8 of his Thunderbird roared to life. He backed it out into the street and descended through his neighborhood and up the hill to Coit Tower. Here such a thick fog obscured the view to the point where he had to turn on the windshield wipers. He headed back down to Bay Street and decided to go out toward the Marina, close to the water where he could see the Golden Gate Bridge. But again, the fog was so dense he kept going rather aimlessly—past the villas and mansions of Presidio and Pacific Heights, up to Twin Peaks, and down again through the Haight Ashbury toward the heart of the city. He turned right or left randomly and entered a number of streets that seemed new to him. Having made a left off an unknown street, he found himself descending Webster and noticed a familiar landmark—the neon sign of the emergency entrance to St. Theresa's Hospital. So that must be The Pines on his left. Yes, of course. That's where Myrtle lived.

He pulled over to the curb about fifty yards from the emergency entrance, got out of the car for a smoke, and pulled the scarf tighter around his neck. He looked up toward the top of The Pines but saw the uppermost floors were shrouded in mist. *Old people rarely suffer jet lag*, he thought. The only light on that side of the building came from a fourth-floor window.

Bruno rubbed a cigarette stub into the sidewalk with his toe, got back behind the wheel of his red Thunderbird, and glanced at his watch—4:30 A.M., Pacific Daylight Time. He really ought to go home. The emergency entrance was quiet as he drove by. Somehow, he got going the wrong way on Gough Street, and before he realized it, he had reached Fulton. Then he might as well go via the Civic Center and Market Street. He liked this route, but he locked the doors. This neighborhood could be dicey. It was best to take precautions.

The area around the Civic Center—the Tenderloin and its seedy streets and denizens—held a certain fascination for Bruno. In direct proximity to the high life that took place in and around the elegant, but faux-European structures that housed the opera, the museum, and the city hall, a chaotic nocturnal population of drug addicts, prostitutes, and homeless lived out an underclass life. Here clumps of humanity lined up for meals in front of Glide Memorial Church and slept in doorways and parks, their stolen supermarket baskets loaded with the detritus of civilization. Clandestine objects were exchanged between dirty hands; suggestions of unhealthful sex were all-pervasive. No one could ever know this—he could never admit to the Beattys, nor to Crystal, nor Myrtle, nor his mother—how that mysterious, seamy side of human existence attracted him. But there was no harm in simply having such an academic interest, was there?

He cruised the worst area—Turk, Eddy, Jones, Leavenworth. At Golden Gate and Taylor, several people slept under the Golden Gate Theater's overhanging marquee. He made a left onto the one-way Taylor Street, where twenty or thirty feet away from the sleepers, a dark, slight, male figure urinated against the building. Then it turned toward Bruno's classic T-Bird as it rolled up the street in the middle of three lanes. The thin black man in grimy clothing approached the car. From behind the wheel, Bruno saw the man rub his crotch. Then he saw that his fly was open. Was the zipper broken, or did he just forget? The character fixed a pair of twinkling but bloodshot eyes on Bruno, extended his left hand, and moved his index finger in a beckoning, *come here* gesture. His lips seemed to be mouthing some words Bruno couldn't understand. Should he speed up and leave this netherworld and its strange messenger? A conversation with him might wake up the sleeping crowd, and then what? What did the man want?

The black man mouthed some words again; his finger wagged insistently, and a smile crept across his face, revealing a spread of crows' feet around both eyes and a set of bad teeth. The smile was so peculiar, it paralyzed Bruno. He pressed the brake but left the Thunderbird's motor idling. He could switch his foot to the gas pedal if he needed to make a quick getaway. The black man reached the passenger side of the car and moved his lips again. He was whispering. Why? He didn't want to wake the others? He leaned on the passenger side now. Bruno perceived something trustworthy about the smiling countenance. "Son," the old man whispered, "my son, why hast thou forsaken me? You knows Ol' Black Donald haves what you likes."

Bruno thought maybe these puzzling phrases constituted a pimp's offer for one of the toothless women in the pile of people under the theater entrance. Or maybe for the derelict's own favors. In fact, the man rubbed his front right pocket now with the beckoning hand over a lump in that pocket. He still made no move to close his zipper.

"Only a hundred dollars for Ol' Black Donald, my son," the man whispered imploringly and continued to rub the dirty pocket. "I guarantees it. You ask them." His bloodshot eyes rolled momentarily toward the sleepers, as if they would witness and guarantee the advantages of his deal. "My son, my son," he continued with religious fervor, "you knows Ol' Black Donald don't give you no shit. He gives you freedom! He gives you liberation! He gives you what you wants." Ol' Black Donald rolled his glazed eyes toward the heavens now and clasped his hands together. "Ol' black Donald guarantees it. Do not forsake Ol' Black Donald."

Now the vitreous eyes focused directly on Bruno, and they seemed to sparkle and blind him to the dilapidation of the rest of his appearance. At the same time Bruno realized his pulse had risen and that it was time to get the hell out of there, he felt weak, almost helpless against this apparition's cryptic arguments. He wanted to look away, but Donald's hypnotic gaze immobilized his eyes. Indeed, he sensed his vision slipping somehow deeper into unfathomable depths. Now his confused brain asked him, what harm could it do to help out the poor old bastard? Here he was, down on his luck, out on the streets. It's a form of charity . . .

As if he could sense his John weakening, Ol' Black Donald shuffled swiftly around to the car's driver's side while holding out an arm to keep the car stopped. He talked incessantly. "You just try it once and the One will makes his face to shine upon thee, my son. No obligation," and he began to extract the lump from out of his pocket while Bruno pulled a crisp, new one-hundred-dollar-bill out of his wallet. At the same moment, Ol' Black Donald placed a crumpled wad of toilet paper, which was wound around the mysterious prize, into Bruno's left hand. For a moment Bruno hesitated. It seemed that the wizard was giving up his prize too easily. Maybe a ten-dollar-bill would do; probably he wouldn't even notice the difference. But the wiry man immediately snapped his bony fingers with a sharp, loud crack that startled Bruno into compliance. He extended the bill toward Donald who snatched it with magical swiftness. Bruno didn't see where it went. In any case, it was time to disappear now, himself. But Ol' Donald had gripped Bruno's hand and held onto it. He put his head almost inside Bruno's car and smiled solemnly. Bruno suddenly realized whom he looked like—the framed color photo of the pope in his bedroom in his mother's house in Monteriggioni! The nose, the crow's feet around the eyes, and the benevolent smile were the same. Based on physiognomy, Ol' Donald was a thin, black incarnation of Pope John XXIII, the photo negative of the portrait that he had known since his childhood.

Now Ol' Black Donald did something extraordinary. He pulled Bruno's left hand out the window and raised it high in a kind of victory sign before releasing it. Then with his own hand, he slowly drew some kind of pattern in the air toward Bruno's car suggestive of a medieval heretic priest conferring an esoteric blessing onto one of his cult members. At the same time, in an intimate, soft whisper he said, "Don't forget Ol' Black Donald, my son. Do not forsake him. You come back, now, and Ol' Black Donald gonna give you what you wants." The last words were spoken so softly that Bruno could barely hear them. Nevertheless, they were both enticing and unnerving.

As the first light appeared toward the east, Bruno gunned his Thunderbird north up Taylor, left on California, and right on Larkin till he reached Greenwich and the world of Russian Hill, where he lived. He puffed on the inch-long, half-smoked treasure he had just purchased for one hundred dollars. The crumpled length of toilet paper in which the reefer had been wrapped lay on the floor of his red convertible. His Italian heart was pounding. His right hand steered and worked the cigarette. With his left hand he rubbed his own hard-on through his slacks. He thought, *by God, this is smoother than the best dope in Egypt. I'll sleep like an angel.*

And until early that afternoon, he did.

16

THE PINES SIERRA LOUNGE, halfway through the November Reading Round-table meeting. Heavy grey clouds moved slowly across the sky outside the large windows, but the drought continued. It refused to rain. Jack Peterson, Esq. sat in the chair next to Myrtle Spencer Halstead and insisted on holding his translation of *Madame Bovary* right under her nose. He repeated certain comments of the speaker, Madame Françoise Hayes—that Myrtle had heard perfectly well—into her ear. *The people who have nothing worth saying talk too much*, Myrtle thought. And others—like the silent caller, who had shown his or her intelligence and good breeding by accepting her criticism and adjusting to her preferred hours of three to five P.M., and who was currently listening to a short course on the Spanish classic, Cervantes's *Don Quixote*—didn't say enough. She felt the readings and the telephone relationship were mutually beneficial, despite the caller's total reticence. She had come to accept his or her silence for whatever it meant, and in return she was free to express her thoughts openly and to limit the length of the calls. She didn't know their origin, but they were all at the caller's expense.

Seated next to Jack now, she regretted her decision to bring her cane along this morning, because the sight of it in her hand, when she happened to enter the same elevator as he had, apparently incited the ex-lawyer's do-gooder instincts. He had not only seized her bag and insisted on carrying it but had also latched tenaciously onto her free arm. The cane must have made her look more helpless than she was, and she wished there had been a discreet way of whacking him in the shins or on the head with it as he led her down the hall to the Sierra Lounge.

That they would run into each other at The Pines from time to time was inevitable. She couldn't stay locked in her *ermitage* just to avoid him. But this situation, where she was doomed to sit next to him for two hours, aroused feelings of claustrophobia, and she had a hard time concentrating on the speaker. And, worse, he had insisted on seats in the front row, where everyone could see them. Somewhere, it was probably the fault of that good Dr. Manchester, who must have contacted his old benefactor by now. And they had probably talked about her.

Happy for the opportunity to be close to Myrtle for two full hours, Jack Peterson thought how fortunate it was they lived in the same life-care community and both enjoyed his new-found hobby—literature. Future serendipitous encounters like this one were thus assured. Moreover, the fact his old client—his optimal client, Tommy Manchester—had saved the eyesight of his impressive companion in the very hospital that housed the emergency room across from which he lived, this was likely a sign of divine providence. Dr. Manchester had contacted Jack several weeks earlier with the good news of his move from UCLA to St. Theresa's and promised to have lunch with him. Jack recalled the emergency room had given him a good feeling from the outset, and now he felt pride in having played a crucial, if indirect, role in Myrtle's successful operation. This fact would certainly bring them closer together. One day, he decided, all three of them—Jack, Myrtle, and Dr. Manchester—should eat together in the dining room.

Jack pulled on his moustache and turned the pages of *Madame Bovary* enthusiastically to page 112 and the part about the risqué carriage ride through Rouen. He pushed his copy closer to Myrtle's visual field, where she could appreciate all his pen markings and annotations and winked at her. She in turn crossed her arms over her chest, pointed her legs away from him, and placed her cane between their chairs. She didn't want to review this passage in Jack's presence. But now, *malheureusement*, she had to get through these two hours, and she might even have to combat any familiarity the ambulance chaser assumed because of her acquaintance with Dr. Manchester. It was an unwelcome social problem, and Jack might try to exploit it, right here during a meeting of the Reading Roundtable, an organization she had founded.

"Well, if I may insert my own two cents, here at this point, ma'am . . ."

By God, thought Myrtle, *he even has the temerity to interrupt today's speaker, Françoise Hayes, a native of Paris, with his inane comments on the great French classic.*

"I don't think we've considered the importance of the roles of medicine and sickness, of the imagery and symbolism and metaphors of operations and surgery and cures in this novel."

Mon Dieu! Myrtle wanted to shrink into her chair. *He's picked up some literary jargon and now he's trying to impress not only the refined former Parisian, but me, as well.*

Madame Françoise Hayes, a polite and gentle lady, yielded the floor to Jack, who produced a disorderly digression on the imagery, symbolism, and metaphors—he threw around these terms as if they were interchangeable—of things related to medicine. He discussed not only Monsieur Bovary's surgical profession and the fatal error of Hippolite's clubfoot, but the role of drugs, chemicals—to wit, the pharmacist—and poison, as if these things could explain the tragic outcome. Well, no wonder, thought Myrtle, if a person spends his whole life chasing ambulances, his spirit will inevitably dwell in the realm of medical waste. And to top it off, his drawling southern pronunciation turned *Yonville* into *Yawn-ville*, and *Rouen* into something approximating *ruin*, so that she would rather have listened to the sound of fingernails scraping across blackboards than to the opinions of this veritable Dulcamara of medical and literary charlatanism. It entered her mind for the first time that such a person might be hazardous to her health.

By the time he finished, poor Madame Hayes was thrown off track and never regained mastery over her presentation. Myrtle feared that Jack's continued presence at the Reading Roundtable might not only lower the standards but also lead to its demise. She had not wanted to make the effort again so soon after the surgical ordeal from which she had just recovered, but for the sake of culture perhaps she might have to consider scheduling her second Shakespeare presentation sooner rather than later.

When the Roundtable disbanded at noon, Myrtle could still not shake the tenacious lawyer. She had wanted to approach Françoise Hayes to thank her for her efforts and to commiserate about the problems one encounters when addressing *difficult* audiences, but with the *difficulty* in this case glued to her arm, she was prevented from doing so.

Jack, glowing from the attention he had commanded toward the end of the session, and convinced his analysis of Flaubert's novel—he accented the first syllable, *FLAW-burt*—had provided the intellectual climax for the session, wanted to extend the contact with Myrtle by accompanying her to lunch. It had been a long time since their first and very memorable meal together, he explained, and in the meantime, they had so much to talk about—a mutual friend in Dr. Tommy Manchester, in whose career he had played a major role, and her successful cataract operation. Not to mention his new hobby—literature! Good books! What a wonderful, small world! Fate had obviously brought them together. They were meant to be friends.

As he left the meeting with her, Jack wanted to tell Myrtle he had subscribed not only to the Book-of-the-Month Club, but he had begun to read the entire leather-bound *Harvard Classics* series in The Pines's library, and he would be honored if she would sometimes care to discuss Plato or Aristophanes or Cervantes or Milton, when he came to them in his reading program. He wanted to tell her that discussions that combined her literary training with his insights from the field of jurisprudence would be rewarding for both of them.

In front of her twenty-fifth-floor apartment—number 2510, he noted—Myrtle declined to have lunch with Jack in the dining room, saying she would prefer a peanut butter and jam sandwich in her own apartment. It had dawned on her that this literary imposter was perhaps the Anonymous caller. Any resident of The Pines could look up her phone number. Maybe *he* was exploiting her good will by listening to her discourses in order to enhance his literary pretensions and to impress her. *Quelle horreur!* She wouldn't put it past him.

Disappointed, Jack agreed the morning's intellectual exertions had surely been tiring, but he noted with pleasure that Ms. Halstead's cane brushed perceptibly against his lower left leg before she shut the door. A positive sign, a Freudian slip, he thought as he turned toward the elevator landing. An indirect expression of a desire for closeness. Yes, the cane's motion had an unconscious yet definite intent that was clear for a discerning mind like his to see. He whistled Frank Sinatra's "It was a Very Good Year," as he descended by himself to the dining room.

17

FRIDAY EVENING, AND HERMANN Wittgenstein stood in a long line to deposit his paycheck at the Wells Fargo Bank, Marina branch. He had saved exactly $7,326.17, and the sum was compounding at an interest rate of 6.75 percent. This constituted a small fortune in East German marks, especially if he could exchange it on the black market. And who knew how much more it would be by the time Gaby and his children were able to join him on this beautiful peninsula between the Pacific Ocean and the San Francisco Bay? By then they would have a cozy little apartment to live in, if all went well. He planned to tell Mr. De Carlo about the insulation and sheetrock he had installed on his basement walls, using mainly scrap materials he had salvaged from Strom Electric Company jobs. Sometimes he almost believed this would come to pass—that his family would join him in California. Things were changing in Eastern Europe. Amazing things had happened. The American President had gone to Berlin and challenged Gorbachev to "tear down that wall."

"Next, please!" Someone nudged him from behind, and Hermann realized a teller was calling him. Hermann advanced to the counter. When he left the bank, he got into Bruno's red Thunderbird. He had promised to take care of it. So, he had driven it to work and to the bank. Now he drove it back to Russian Hill. What a vehicle it was, with a powerful eight-cylinder engine! Maybe it guzzled gas, but this old 1970 model already had a catalytic converter and ran on unleaded fuel that was cleaner than even West German gasoline. His terrible Trabi back in East Berlin burned only part of the oil you mixed with the gas, of all primitive ideas, and spewed the rest back into the air as smoke—an ecological disaster zone of a vehicle. It wouldn't be allowed on the streets of California. Hermann had learned that the smog situation in Los Angeles had actually improved since the fifties, and that despite more people and more cars. But in Berlin? He shook his head thinking of the sickly green Trabant, for which he had scrimped and waited six years. To think Americans had produced a better car in the Model A Ford than his compatriots were still producing in the eighties with their sad excuses for vehicles. The shame of it! He sighed as he drove the Thunderbird into its garage and turned off the engine.

The next morning—Saturday morning—Hermann backed the Thunderbird into the driveway in front of the garage and began to go over it, his Thunderbird notebook—a red one—in hand. First, he raised the hood, checked the air filter and all the fluid levels; then he squirted some carburetor cleaner into the carburetor. He checked the tire pressure, including the spare in the trunk, and made a quick comparison with other readings and their dates. Then he noted down today's date, mileage, the fact the flywheel belt was loose, and the tread on the right rear tire was wearing unevenly—maybe because of a bad shock absorber or wheel bearing. Then he prepared to clean the vehicle.

After he removed the contents from the trunk, he was about to take out the floor mats when he found a longish piece of crumpled white toilet paper on the floor. It had an unusual smell, and when he found a hand-rolled cigarette stub in the ashtray, instead of emptying it, he made a note in the red notebook and went back upstairs into the house and retrieved two zip lock baggies and a pair of tweezers, and brought them back down to the car. Picking them up with tweezers, he placed the toilet paper in one baggy and the cigarette stub into the other. This was not his landlord's usual Gauloises. He would examine the items more closely later. Now, with a flashlight, he looked under the seats, through the glove compartment, and into every other corner of the T-Bird. Finding nothing else unusual, he vacuumed the interior, cleaned the dashboard and inside windows with Windex, brushed off the convertible top, and washed and waxed the exterior. He stood back and admired his work.

Pedestrians smiled and pointed at the vintage Thunderbird as Hermann drove it over to Jack in the Box on Lombard Street, west of Van Ness, for a quick lunch. He wolfed down three Chicken Supremes, two jumbo fries, and a large Diet Coke, as he was anxious to get back to the Italian's desk and the disturbing contents of the baggies that awaited his analysis and registration. Something was wrong in his landlord's life. There was evidence for that. What it meant, he didn't know, but he needed to pursue it. Now was the time to do so, while Mr. De Carlo was away.

Toward 6:00 P.M., Hermann scratched the bald spot on his head and twisted his ponytail. Various colored notebooks were open on the floor behind the desk chair where he sat. Notations had been made in the *Personal finances—Italian Trust* notebook, the *Business: Art/antiques* notebook, the *Taxes—California & IRS* notebook, the *Taxes—foreign*, the *Personal letters* notebook, the *Travels* notebook, and the *Social life* notebook.

This evening he had begun a new notebook; he labeled it *Theories/ Conclusions*. So far, he had only entered a few words, no full sentences, just: "drug problem/hash; sometimes (?)"; "personality: not married, jetsetter, playboy, high society"; "relationships: many women, including old!—M.H.—warum?"; "name: 'De Carlo' or 'Dicarlomini'??"; "money: rich (Italian checks, mother); sells antiques"; "southern French villa—$500,000 = 3,000,000 francs—warum???"

Hermann doodled with these notations while he speculated on how they might hang together. In East Germany it had been easier to profile people you spied on and come to definitive conclusions about their lives. Here, everything was so different, so mixed up, so much more complicated. There were no clear lines to peoples' lives, and no clearly defined objectives to direct this particular search. He had learned a lot about America, but he realized at least half of what he had learned in East Germany was wrong. Well, no, it was true too: all the bad things you could say about crime, poverty, and American television were true, in a way, but whenever you found some truth, the next day you'd find out the opposite was also true in America. There were so many different people here and they all lived together, sort of, but not really, and they were all open and friendly, but then again, not really, and life was very superficial, but then again very difficult, so Hermann wasn't sure if he would ever understand it all. But one thing he was sure of: he liked it better, and it would be almost perfect if he could only get Gaby and the kids here.

Now he concentrated on his landlord again and on his own notes. What brought an aristocratic Italian all the way to San Francisco? Why did he become an American? How did he get into the social world's highest echelons? Why didn't he get married? Did he do anything besides buy and sell art and antiques on all his trips abroad? Why did he keep seeing the old woman who sold him this house?

The pieces of the puzzle didn't fit together. But did it really matter? It was a challenging game, to be sure, a good exercise to keep his police skills honed. And it satisfied his need for predictability and security. But ultimately, maybe he was wasting his energy. More important, Hermann reminded himself, was to develop a plan to get Gaby and little Bert and Sabina out from behind the Iron Curtain and to a new life in California. If they could only see him now—in this great house in the fabulous city by the bay and the Pacific Ocean with the bridges, the sea gulls, the fog horns. A pang of guilt rushed through him when he thought of drab, gray Berlin. He was so lucky-unlucky to be here.

He had had no direct contact with his family since his escape; the only messages ran through relatives in Bremen, who were not always reliable. His family was well; presumably they were waiting for him—to return? to rescue them?—and they knew he was living in San Francisco. Would they look up pictures of the Golden Gate Bridge in library books? Would they watch *The Streets of San Francisco* on television? He worried incessantly they might think he had forgotten them, abandoned them, or maybe that Gaby had found another man. No, he would go crazy if he thought of this possibility. This communication barrier was so inhuman, so humiliating, so wrong! At the moment, the best he could do was hope. Hope and work and save. And plot and plan.

He needed more money, and when he had it, he would have to go back to West Germany and find a way to communicate with them and smuggle them out, maybe meet them somewhere in Czechoslovakia or Hungary or Rumania. Recently, some people had escaped to Austria in a hot air balloon. There were cracks in the border, and he would find them. But it would take time, and he needed more money. And it would be dangerous.

He fantasized that he was his landlord and could fly to Budapest on a small jet; he would meet his family in a fine restaurant and drive them by limousine to the airport where the private, corporate jets had a separate terminal, where VIP passports weren't always checked, where customs were sometimes waived, where the rich and famous simply stepped into airplanes that flew them into free countries beyond the political barriers that divided the suppressed masses of the world.

A large, blond German man roused himself from his late-night reveries on Greenwich Street. Slowly, he stood up and walked over to the window that faced southeast. The lights of the city were magical. No fog tonight. No rain either. He sighed and reached into his pocket to get a Kleenex with which to wipe a tear. There he found not only the Kleenex but also the miniature screwdriver and the tiny electronic device he intended to install in his landlord's telephone. He blew his nose, returned to the desk, unplugged the phone from the wall, took it apart, and installed the gadget Bruno would never see. It would not record his landlord's calls, but now, if Hermann happened to be at home when Bruno used the phone, he would be able to listen to the conversations from his own phone in the basement. This would certainly shed some light on his landlord's mysterious life.

18

ON THE FOURTH FLOOR of The Pines, Jack was asleep. He had attended the New Year's Eve party but left after it became clear Myrtle was not coming. Now it was almost midnight, and he was in bed dreaming about a fiery arbitration session that erupted into a shouting match—which woke him out of his slumber. A noisy commotion came from outside where an ambulance was arriving at St. Theresa's emergency room. Jack sprang out of bed and went to the window, his heart racing.

By God, there were two ambulances—one of the sirens was still winding down—and a police car. The activity was frantic, with orderlies, nurses, IVs, stretchers, two hysterical family members (it seemed)—one hanging on the arm of a policewoman—walkie-talkies, and everyone on the run. This was serious, something major.

Jack's heart continued to race. His natural instincts made him want to get showered and dressed in suit and tie and head down there with his briefcase, right into the middle of the turmoil. That's what he would have done in the old days. He would have been there from the start, annoying the medical staff perhaps, but assuring the victims that whatever the contents of their tragedy, there was hope in this difficult hour to be found in the realm of jurisprudence. He would tell them that although the legal system couldn't always cure what ailed the body or soul, nevertheless, the potential compensations it held out could be converted into a better future. His message was often the only bright spot they could cling to during such a desperate period.

It would be senseless, of course, to get showered now and descend to St. Theresa's. He was retired. He was seventy-five years old and lived at The Pines. No one wanted him in the hospital. The exclusionary tactics of younger members of his profession were one of the reasons he finally gave it up. Their discrimination came so naturally to them they didn't even see the prejudice in it. But this was a battle he had chosen not to fight. Now others, younger men, and maybe some women, would contact these victims with offers of help, but few would be as effective as Jack had been. *No way,* he thought. *Such a waste. All my knowledge and experience.*

He went to his refrigerator to get some milk for hot chocolate. He didn't need to pursue this thought; he knew where it led. He'd thought it many times before. It was what people said when an old person died, especially an old person who had been an expert in some field, a specialist: all that knowledge and experience, accumulated over a lifetime—gone. The implications were that younger people just didn't have that kind of wisdom, that with the death of an accomplished elder, something was irretrievably lost to the world. The death of that particular grey matter extinguished a whole useful universe that could no longer be tapped and exploited. To compensate for such a loss the younger generation had to work very hard and very long to reach the same level of expertise, if they ever did. There was something terribly wasteful about the life cycle—death and rebirth. But what could you do?

Mug of hot chocolate in hand, he returned to the window. One ambulance and the police car were still there. He could still sense the impulse to dress and descend, to join the scene, to partake in the messy, wrenching human tragedy. But now, even as he philosophized on the significance of all these things, a vague new thought—at first just a sensation, really—began to enter his consciousness slowly, subtly, so that he couldn't yet articulate what it was.

This was life, this was the normal cycle, after all, that he should be here, old, widowed, in a retirement home. At some point he would die. But, on the other hand, right now he was still alive. He was *only* seventy-five, one might say—not that old nowadays. People were living longer and healthier lives thanks to modern medicine. In fact, he was slim, his blood pressure normal, no evidence of disease; just look at his spectacular hair! He ran a reassuring hand over it. If he still wanted to go down there to that emergency room to help those poor souls in their hour of need, and if he was indeed a repository of a certain kind of useful knowledge—maybe even wisdom— then perhaps there was something else to be done, there might be other ways to pursue happiness and achieve satisfaction in old age.

Carrying his mug, Jack wandered around his apartment, immersed in thought. He sat down on his sofa and raised the mug to his lips. But without taking a sip, he set it back on the coffee table, because his thoughts turned to Myrtle. She was an inspiration. And he was sure she was not uninterested in him. There was that brush of her cane, after all, when he escorted her to her apartment after the November Reading Roundtable. These things weren't without meaning, even if the perpetrator wasn't consciously aware of them—he knew that much about psychology. And she would have noticed his interest in literature. She had listened so intently that time over lunch to his analysis of *Death in Venice*.

Something in this recollection arrested the forward motion of his reveries. He sat for a minute, his mind a blank. Like the minute of respectful silence during which a special person is honored, Jack's mind experienced a moment as a *tabula rasa*, as if the hard disk of his brain had momentarily been erased in preparation for the creative inspiration that was about to enter it. His cerebral cortex temporarily on hold, he was receptive now for the rush of energy this tumult of thoughts and emotions was about to generate into an original, creative idea.

Shortly past midnight on the The Pines's fourth floor, a retired lawyer sprang up from his living room sofa and said out loud to himself, "That's it! That's *it*! Yes, that's what I'll do." *I'll write a book, a novel, not just an anemic novella, like that German writer, but a real long novel, maybe two hundred pages, about Tommy Manchester, by God. That's it! It will be inspirational. It will help people. I've got the perfect working conditions right here in my apartment: my window onto Sutro Street for inspiration; Ms. Halstead for literary consultations, twenty-one floors up in this very same building; the Reading Roundtable, for continuing literary education; and last but not least, my own world of experience to draw on.*

Propelled by his inspiration, Jack paced between his living room and kitchen, and, at 1:00 A.M. on January 1, 1989, he sat down on his sofa with a ballpoint pen and some sheets of white paper. He placed the paper on an issue of the *American Bar Association Journal* he pulled out from under the now-cold mug of hot chocolate and wrote seven words on the top sheet: "Resurrection in Venice by Jack Peterson, Esquire."

19

By mid-February, a rumor had sprung up at The Pines that something was wrong with Jack. On the morning of Valentine's Day, someone dared ask Myrtle, as she picked up her mail, whether she happened to know if Mr. Peterson was indisposed? He hadn't been seen in the dining room for weeks.

Myrtle didn't know, of course, and had she not been in such a good mood, would most probably have told the questioner that she, frankly, couldn't care less. But discretion caused by high spirits prevailed, and she couched her ignorance in a polite fashion and went about her business. By God, she had significant things to think about today. Count De Carlo was to be her dinner guest tonight—for the first time, in The Pines's dining room, and on Valentine's Day! She'd had her hair done yesterday, and now she was performing the daily tasks early so she'd have time to prepare, intellectually and spiritually, for the evening she anticipated with so much pleasure.

From the mailboxes she went to the in-house store and bought a bottle of Calistoga Water and some Maalox tablets. Then she went up to the library to return the copy of Chekhov stories she had finished reading. She left it on the return table, chose a new book, and then pulled out the large, thick volume on Renaissance art and set it down next to the reference dictionary and opened it up to Raphael's portrait of Agnolo Doni. As she emerged from the library, she bumped into Irene and, as a result, dropped her next reading project, Dostoevsky's *Idiot*, onto the floor. The kind nurse bent down and placed the book back into Myrtle's hands.

"Say, you're lookin' good today, Ms. Halstead!" Irene greeted her tactfully, diverting attention away from the matter of the dropped book. "Who does your hair, honey? It sure looks great!"

"Well, Shirley does—you know her, I'm sure." Myrtle was glad to accept the compliment from Irene, because she positively wanted to look good for her swain tonight. She was well aware of Irene's interest in her *handsome honey*, and she felt a special intimacy with her now that made her want to communicate her delicious secret to the nurse. She had long since forgiven her the indiscretion about the postcard from Egypt. "You know, Irene," she began tentatively, and then she surprised herself by blurting it all out. "I've got a dinner guest tonight. My Italian friend is coming to dinner."

There, she'd said it. No reason to be shy about it. After this evening, after Bruno had graced The Pines's dining room with his exquisite presence, everyone would know anyway. So why try to hide it from so dear a person as Irene? Indeed, Myrtle was proud of it. She wanted to show him off. She wanted all the plebeians to know that she knew and entertained people of such . . . distinction.

Irene broke into a wide grin and chucked Myrtle under the chin. "Ooooweeee, Miz Halstead! Now that's something! That's mighty fine! You have a good time now, just let those good times roll, girl!" Irene patted Myrtle's arm in good-bye and was gone down the hallway, shaking her head. Myrtle thought she heard her say, "Hot dog!" to herself before she disappeared around the corner.

Myrtle waited at the elevator landing and saw in the mirror behind the flower vase, that she did indeed look good. Her green eyes sparkled below her delicately arched eyebrows. The hairdo was becoming, and she certainly didn't look eighty-six. She smiled into the mirror, trying to fashion the smile with which to greet Bruno when he arrived that evening.

At 7:00 P.M. the dining room was still full, though some diners had finished and were about to leave. Most residents arrived between 6:00 and 6:30. It was unusual to arrive at 7:00, although dinner was, officially and occasionally, served until 7:30. On the right arm of Count De Carlo—strapped over his other arm was a black mobile telephone case—Myrtle's entrance had the intended impact on her fellow residents. As Mr. Seward led the couple to a table at the far southeast corner, they traversed the entire sweep of the large space. Ms. Halstead had planned it this way; she had reserved this particular table in advance with Mr. Seward, informing him in a confidential manner, that it was to be a "special occasion." On the way to their table, Ms. Halstead held her head high and treaded slower than usual. The diners to whom she granted, in the manner of the queen of a minor principality, a slight smile here and a brief nod there, noticed her posture was unnaturally erect.

The table was perfect. Mr. Seward had even arranged for a candle in the middle—a white one. Having placed his telephone under the table, Signore De Carlo preempted Mr. Seward in pulling back the chair for his hostess. He then produced from some unknown hiding place a single, long-stemmed red rose. Mr. Seward signaled a waiter to bring a vase for the rose and wished them a "pleasant dining experience." Bruno then pulled what must have been a rare, antique, silver cigarette lighter from a pocket of his black, doubled-breasted, Italian-cut suit, and lit the candle while he smiled at Myrtle. He would like to have lit up a cigarette, but he felt that to do so would somehow violate the dignity of this special relationship. His elderly acquaintance should not know that he smoked, and his wayward impulse sent a twinge of guilt through him. Smoking, moreover, was forbidden in The Pines's dining room.

Myrtle smiled back at Bruno and at the same time stole a glance into the room to see how many diners would be impressed by the sight of her table. Horrified, she noticed that a man seated against the wall four tables away had just dropped a bundle of white paper—single sheets—onto the floor. That man was Jack Peterson. *Grace à Dieu*, as he stooped down to pick up his papers, his back was turned to her. But Myrtle's disquiet increased as she realized his table companion was her eye doctor. Please God, if you exist, don't let them see me and want to address me. Not tonight!

Thomas Manchester had already recognized his cataract patient, Ms. Halstead. He was ready to come greet her when his host dropped his manuscript, obliging the doctor to squat down to help pick up the scattered papers.

Myrtle glanced again in their direction and could see that as the two men crawled around near the kitchen entrance, Jack Peterson's mouth continued its unceasing palaver about whatever inane topic he was forcing upon Dr. Manchester. His ravings may well have had to do with those papers, for all she knew, and she counted on the lawyer's hyper-loquaciousness to keep them occupied throughout the dinner and thus prevent a meeting and a ruination of this very special evening with her swain.

Since it was the first time she had hosted Bruno in The Pines's dining room, she was nervous about it. The kitchen was reputed to be the best of any San Francisco retirement residence, and tonight it was preparing a special menu for Valentine's Day. Of course, it couldn't compete with a *haute cuisine* San Francisco restaurant, Bruno's own home cooking, or a charming potluck in her apartment, for that matter, but here they were freed from the necessity of preparing food and could devote their full time to each other, to profound communication. She imagined that the depth of their conversation, indeed, their very presence would radiate a magical aura throughout the dining room.

Myrtle adjusted her chair and turned her head to block Bruno's view to the extent possible from the embarrassing crawling men nearby. She reached out her braceleted hand to touch Bruno's forearm in thanks for the beautiful rose.

"How lovely!" she said. "How thoughtful. Now, do tell me about your trip. And how's your poor mother doing? Better, I hope."

At that moment the waiter arrived. Myrtle recommended the New York steak, medium-rare—the beef could be trusted. But she changed her mind and ordered the swordfish herself. The sherry consommé was a good starter, and the eggplant parmigiana would be a welcome side dish to the frequent broccoli on the menu. Was he aware of broccoli's anticarcinogenic properties? The rice pilaf was inedible, so she insisted they both order baked potatoes, but without the baco-bits—they were fake, she informed Bruno. Part of the general decline of American civilization, *hélas*! And the Caesar salad was consistent and reliable, but it must follow the entrée, not precede it, please.

Bruno acceded to Myrtle's culinary desires. He was much too accustomed to the two- and three-star restaurants of France, to the fine restaurants in this city, and to the dinners at the Beattys' to expect anything of this dinner as far as the food was concerned. But that didn't matter. What did matter was she accepted and took him seriously. Unlike his mother, Myrtle respected him. Of course, she didn't know much about what he actually did, but she had an innate faith in him. Unlike Crystal Beatty, Myrtle wasn't angry with him. He hadn't made any promises to the old woman—explicit or implied—that he couldn't fulfill, and she had made no excessive demands on him. On the contrary, she seemed satisfied with an occasional phone call or postcard, with a little attention. When he spent time with Myrtle, he knew it pleased her, and far from the world of drugs, sexual deceptions, and financial ambitions, this relationship made him feel good, almost clean and innocent. He was aware it was Valentine's Day. The impulse to smoke had passed, and he resolved to do a good deed.

The consommé arrived lukewarm at their table. The duo consumed it, however, Myrtle slurping softly. Bruno invented some news about family troubles—his sisters in Italy and their broken families. And how this weighed on his mother, already in delicate health: her gnawing diverticulitis that the Italian doctors couldn't control; the distressing skin cancer; the painful gall bladder operation last year complicated by the weak heart. Yes, it could happen at any moment, despite the best doctors in Italy. He just didn't know how long he would have his dear, old mother. Why had fate handed his poor old mother such trials?

Myrtle was touched by the boy's deep concern for his long-suffering mother. To bolster him, as her swordfish arrived and his steak—it was more medium than medium-rare, but Bruno didn't mention this—Myrtle reached for the bottle of Chianti Classico she had brought along in her handbag for this special occasion. With some difficulty, she extricated the green rubber band from the plastic Safeway sack she tried to keep hidden, extracted the bottle from this same sack, and placed it on the table. She asked him to un-cork it with a corkscrew she pulled from the same bag; she didn't want any more attention than necessary from the waiters. Now, having recognized his need for moral sustenance and courage due to his family problems, she launched between bites into an account and analysis of Prince André's suf-fering and death in Tolstoy's *War and Peace*. There was always help for life's trials to be found, she explained, in great, classical literature. He should seek consolation there more often. She could always tell him where to turn.

Just as she finished her lecture, the waiter bothered them again for their dessert orders.

"Pardon, Ms. Halstead, but would you like moose ow chocolate. . .?"

"Young man," Myrtle interrupted immediately, "you mean *mousse au chocolat*," demonstrating for him the correct French pronunciation.

"Uh, sorry ma'am." He tried again with a "*mousse au* chocolate," but forgot not to pronounce the final *t*.

"*Mousse—au—chocolat*," Myrtle repeated with emphasis and waited for his correction.

His face red, the waiter shifted his weight and tried a third time: "*Mousse* ow *chocolat*." Now everything was right except that he reverted to his original pronunciation of *ow* for *au*.

Myrtle sighed and gave Bruno a knowing look. For his part, the Italian-American, having drunk three-fourths of the rather good Chianti himself, wouldn't have been so strict with the shy Hispanic waiter. But on the other hand, Bruno was more or less captivated by the personality (or was it the learning? or perhaps the voice?) and yes, the *wisdom*, of this very worth-while companion. When he suddenly caught himself wondering what she must have looked like as a young woman, he immediately censored these thoughts and deflected them back in a platonic direction. She was certainly different from anyone else he had ever known. And perhaps others should be more respectful as well. Somewhere he regretted the lies he'd told her about his mother, but then he rationalized that Myrtle would have no way of knowing the truth.

"Well, besides the *mousse au chocolat*, is there another dessert?" Myrtle questioned the waiter.

"Uh, yes ma'am."

"Speak up then. What is it?"

"Uh . . . uh, it's . . . uh."

Either he had forgotten or was too embarrassed to admit in front of this impossible witch that he wasn't sure how to pronounce *crème brûlé*. But Myrtle had not only read it on the menu; she also knew from experience that whenever *mousse au chocolat* was one of the choices, *crème brûlé* was the other. Since her phonetics lesson was having no discernible effect on this poor immigrant from south of the border, she cut it short to save valuable time with her swain.

"Well, permit me to inform you, in that case, young man, that it's *crème brûlé—crème . . . brûlé*." She pronounced it slowly for his edification but didn't wait for him to repeat it. "That's what we'll both have. Two *crème brûlées*, if you please." She would have liked to add *s'il vous plait* but restrained herself.

Now Myrtle leaned toward her table companion to explain the *mousse au chocolat* tended to be too sweet but that for some unknown reason the *crème brûlé* was consistently excellent. Bruno nodded and smiled. At the same time, the intimidated waiter dared utter one more word.

"Coffee?"

Without looking up, Myrtle simply waved a *no* in his general direction. By chance, her wave was sighted four tables away by Jack, who at this moment, a thick manila envelope in hand, was leaving his table with Dr. Manchester. He interpreted Myrtle's flap of the hand as a friendly sign of greeting.

After retrieving the pages of the first draft of his novel from the dining room floor, he and the good doctor had discussed Ms. Halstead's presence, but decided not to disturb her while she obviously hosted her out-of-town nephew or similar relative, during his rare visit to San Francisco. She was so lonely, after all, and had so few visitors, that they would exercise the good taste not to bother her and run the risk of detracting from this rare treat. Besides, Jack did not want her to inquire about the contents of this envelope that she would have noticed by now. His novel was to be a surprise for her. He was elated, however, that she had waved at him, and left the dining room in high spirits, resolving to speak to her again at the next Reading Roundtable meeting.

By the time Jack and Dr. Manchester were safely gone, two *crème brûlés* had arrived for Myrtle and Bruno, who were alone in The Pines's dining room. The white candle had six inches left and several streaks of dribbled wax congealed to its side. Waiters cleared tables and lay down new tablecloths for the next morning's breakfast. A vacuum cleaner hummed over the carpet at the far end.

Bruno was positively soothed by the pronouncements of Myrtle's authoritative voice, which had convinced him of his special worth. The fact she chose to direct such lengthy and elevated discourses at him implied he possessed exceptional qualities and sensitivities. If these qualities were not yet fully realized, they were nevertheless there, at least as potentialities he could develop. His mother would never understand this finer side of him. But this unique relationship with Ms. Halstead affirmed him deep down as a person. Here were no suspicions, no doubts, no put-downs. This woman appealed to the uncommon, the highest in him, which was yet to be. She exacted a kind of purity, invoked a realm devoid of vices. Didn't it prove he wasn't the cad, deep down, that Crystal Beatty—and a whole string of other women he could name, but would rather forget—thought him to be?

He *could* appreciate the finer things, if only given a chance. He was sure of it. He would start here in California, far away from his native Italy and his mother, who stymied him at every turn. He would devote at least one part of himself to this relationship with Myrtle, to the concept of something good, positive, inviolable. He would not have to give up his financial ambitions. On the contrary, if all went well with his deal to purchase the southern French property with the Roman mosaics, he would be able to integrate both pursuits—financial and artistic—into a harmonious whole and a life of integrity and substance. With wealth he would have the leisure to read the great books to cure his dilettantism and acquire true cultivation, something for which everyone had respect, and which went beyond any superficial trappings fame and fortune alone might bring. Yes, he had a respectable, even a dignified future.

He would go buy a copy of *War and Peace* tomorrow. Really, he would. He would devote an entire hour to it tomorrow afternoon. He would stop smoking, or at least reduce his cigarette consumption. And he wouldn't smoke while he read. He would be able to discuss it, at least the first volume, with Myrtle when he returned from his next European trip.

Suddenly, Bruno leaned forward in his chair, eyes wide open.

What was it, Myrtle wondered, this sudden look of surprise?

Bruno realized how late it had grown and that he had an appointment with Ol' Black Donald at 10:00 P.M., sharp. He would have to hurry to get Ms. Halstead back to her apartment, and to excuse himself in time to drive down to the Tenderloin.

Now he leaned forward and looked directly into her eyes. The candle flame flickered in his dark pupils and his look penetrated into Myrtle's soul.

He took her hand and lifted it so both their elbows rested on the table like two arm wrestlers.

He said, "My dear, dear Myrtle, if only you were twenty years younger and I twenty years older . . ."

Instead of finishing the sentence, he kissed her hand, like a Viennese gallant, and without releasing it, slipped out of his chair and pulled her up from hers and fluidly led her out of the dining room, and, arm in arm, up to her apartment. Nothing more needed to be said, and nothing was said when he parted from her at her apartment door at 9:38 P.M.

20

AT 10:02 P.M. A blazing red Thunderbird rolled around the corner at the Golden Gate Theater. A cigarette stub between pressed lips, its driver worried he was late as he looked for a scruffy, wild-eyed black man. But there was no one there, either in front of the theater or in the door's alcove on the east side of the building. Bruno surveyed the street and spied a dark green Jaguar half a block down on the other side facing the wrong way, its parking lights on. This seemed suspicious, maybe a police decoy? He'd better leave.

As he drove up Taylor Street he looked inside the Jaguar, where the interior light was on. At the wheel sat an elegant woman of about sixty—he could spot a wealthy socialite a mile away. This was no police decoy. Sitting next to her in the expensive car was Ol' Black Donald. As if this were the most normal situation in the world, Donald pointed at Bruno and waved him to come back. Bruno noticed his heart racing at the odd sight. His first impulse was to disobey Donald, and he drove slowly on by and turned left onto Turk, thinking he'd better take off and forget this appointment. Maybe he even knew this woman, or she him. What if she were a friend of the Beattys? But then, how did she know Donald? He also thought of what Donald had said to him—that he had what Bruno wanted. What could that be? He was sure it meant more than just a joint of hash. Donald exercised a strange pull on him. Why couldn't he resist?

At a snail's pace, Bruno drove all the way around the block, thinking alternately yes and no, until he found himself headed back toward the

Jaguar. Now Ol' Black Donald stood in the middle of the street. His eyes were penetrating even at a distance, and a wiry left hand ordered Bruno to park at the curb on the opposite side of the street. As Bruno moved into position, the Jaguar's engine and lights came to life. With his right hand, the black man made an extraordinary and complicated beatific blessing over the dark green vehicle that was ready to pull away. Now he pointed with his right index finger at its driver, whose window was open so that Bruno could see her. At the same time, he pointed his other index finger at Bruno as if to join them in a secret pact. Bruno looked at the face of the woman, who made no attempt to hide her countenance. On the contrary, the interior lights of her Jaguar were on, and she looked straight at him as if she wanted to expose her soul. And in her sad eyes Bruno took in more genuine fear and misery than he could stand to encounter. Despite her high station in life, some terrible thing, against which she had no protection, had befallen her.

Shocked by the stranger's expression, Bruno averted his eyes as the Jaguar slowly pulled away and disappeared into the night. Ol' Black Donald approached Bruno's window, saying, "Hey man! Howzit goin', brother?"

He was scruffy as ever, but through the vulgar exterior the facial features of a thin, black Pope John XXIII shone so beatifically that Bruno trusted this dark enigma had his own best interests at heart. Bruno hoped, however, Donald wouldn't want to get inside his Thunderbird.

"It's good, man, so good," Donald began a monologue of puzzling remarks in a casual tone that suggested whatever he said was perfectly self-evident and intelligible. He went on as if he and Bruno were good old friends and there had been no gaps between the three or four meetings they had had. "Yes, the One provideth for his chillen, man. It's the time, man, oh yes, and so good." His voice rose now, in enthusiasm. "And it will be, yes, yes, for each and every one. At the right time. From the One and only One. It's so good, yeah, yeah. Oh, Lord."

Bruno wanted to say something. He wanted to ask Ol' Black Donald why he, Bruno, was here with him at all, whether he understood what was going on. But, of course, that was absurd. Who was the woman in the Jaguar, and what did she have to do with him? That was a reasonable question. But he was paralyzed, as if caught in the inexorable logic of a nightmare. Donald scratched his crotch and rolled his eyes crazily toward the heavens as if invoking a covenant with mysterious, unseen powers. Bruno thought he was either strung out on something or enjoying an ecstatic moment of transcendence of an order he, Bruno, could not understand. Donald began to quiver—his hands, his arms. Soon his shoulders shook, and his body trembled. "How good, how good. The One provides for his chillen, and Ol' Donald gonna hand it on now, to Mr. Abbondanza, here."

Donald must have read Bruno's personalized license plate. *By God, he can read,* thought Bruno, *and he pronounced the Italian correctly.*

"Yeah, yeah. Praise the One for Abbondanza, for I gots what he wants."

Now Donald looked Bruno in the eyes. And Bruno realized the black man wasn't old, as he had assumed. Behind the unwashed face and the stubbly whiskers, his skin was smooth. Donald was grungy but middle-aged. His eyes were bloodshot, and as he leaned down toward Bruno's face behind the wheel, Bruno could smell an odd combination of musty, unwashed clothes, alcohol breath, and a faint scent of French perfume, which he must have picked up in the Jaguar.

What was it? What did he have? Bruno sensed that this time it might be something more than the usual smooth reefer, or the miraculous dash of white powder that had earned Donald several hundred-dollar bills. *If so, let's have it, so I can get home, away from this surrealistic scene.*

He pulled a hundred-dollar bill out of his wallet and asked if that was enough. Donald ignored the bill and continued to rave, "Yes, I gots it, and now you's gonna get it. It's what you want, ooo-eeee!" he added with a high-pitched screech and rolled his eyes upward again so only the reddish whites showed. Now he made several more ritualistic hand signs which suggested to Bruno that Donald might begin to lose control, so he started his engine, which prompted Donald to slam his right hand down on the Thunderbird's roof above Bruno's head.

"Oh ye, oh ye, oh ye, oh ye, oh ye of little, little, little, little, little," Donald uttered reproachfully, and Bruno suddenly felt ashamed for his impatience. "Slowly, my child. The One provides for ye, oh ye, with what you wants!"

Now Donald leaned back from the window and stood up very straight, at attention. His eyes focused intently on Bruno, he slowly pulled various ratty layers of shirts out of his pants. Then he pulled the lot of them up to expose a skinny abdomen, and the corner of an envelope that he drew out from a spot over his sternum. Now he handed Bruno the clean, light grey, business-sized envelope made of high-quality paper, slightly scented with the same perfume Bruno had detected on Donald's person. Bruno accepted the envelope and saw it was blank and sealed. He wanted to ask Donald about it, but Ol' Donald's pope's gaze commanded silence, and now his arms gestured Bruno to move his vehicle away from this sacred spot and be gone. Donald said not a word more. Bruno obeyed, and as he turned left at the end of the street, he looked back to see Donald standing erect in the middle of the street, both arms raised in the air as if to signal a heavenly touchdown.

Hermann had fallen into a deep sleep in his basement dwelling at 999 Greenwich Street when, shortly before midnight, someone pounded on his door. Disoriented, he threw off the blankets, pulled himself up off his cot, and lumbered toward the door. This was unusual. No one aside from his Italian landlord had ever knocked on this door, and that only once, and never at this time of night. As he approached, he heard the unmistakable voice of Mr. De Carlo calling, "Hermann? Hermann? Are you home? Wake up! Hermann?"

"Yes, I am in here," Hermann replied. "Just one minute, please." Hermann switched on his porch and interior lights and opened the door.

"Hermann! I'm so glad you are home." His landlord's agitation was obvious. "I need your help." Without an invitation, Mr. De Carlo walked right into Hermann's partially remodeled basement apartment, exhaled a cigarette, and said suddenly, as if surprised at himself, "Oh, I'm sorry to bother you, Hermann. It's late, I know."

In his pajamas Hermann assured him it was all right, wondered if it had something to do with this apartment, and offered his landlord a seat on one of his wooden crates.

Mr. De Carlo sat down on a crate with a pillow on it but got right up again since he couldn't explain what he wanted to say without moving about. He had to fly to Europe on the first flight out in the morning, he had very urgent business, actually in southern France, well he had to see a doctor in Montpellier, but no, not because there was anything wrong with him, but it had to do with business and his very future, virtually a matter of life or death, and could Hermann please take care of things, including his Thunderbird while he was gone, and he'd really appreciate that, and again, he was sorry to wake him up, and now he had to go pack and try to sleep for a couple of hours before calling a taxi. Pacing, he dropped an inch of cigarette ash onto Hermann's cement floor, spewed out his garbled message at break-neck speed, and brandished a clean, light grey, business-sized envelope made of high-quality paper that had been torn open and seemed to give off a perfumed scent. It must contain a significant letter, thought Hermann, who reassured Mr. De Carlo he would take care of things. And he offered to drive him to the airport, to save time and money.

The landlord accepted immediately. Glancing at his watch, Bruno wished Hermann a good sleep and agreed to meet at 5:30 in the morning, ready to go. He dashed outside and back up into his house. Hermann swept up the cigarette ash and emptied it into a garbage can outside. He left the door open a minute to clear the air before settling back down on his cot, content to note his landlord hadn't objected to the major changes that had taken place in his basement over the past several months; in fact, he seemed not to have noticed them.

To his surprise, before he fell asleep again, Hermann heard the triumphant sounds of the last movement of Beethoven's *Ninth Symphony* wafting down through the ceiling. He knew which tapes had come via the gift subscription to the music club from his landlord's old lady friend, and that up until now his landlord had not opened most of their cellophane wrappers. But the Italian had chosen this moment in the middle of the night to break open Beethoven's *Ninth Symphony* and had turned up the volume of his stereo. What was going on with his landlord? He hoped he'd find out more on the way to the airport. Later, when he woke once at 3:15 A.M., Hermann opened his basement door and looked around. His landlord's house was lit up brightly, and its occupant seemed to still be moving about. And he was replaying the *Ode to Joy*.

For a man who hadn't slept, Bruno was very cheerful as Hermann drove him to SFO early the next morning. Mr. De Carlo didn't allude any further to his urgent business in Europe, but insisted Hermann drive him in his Thunderbird. After all, "You like the T-Bird, don't you, Hermann?" Bruno inquired.

"Yes, Mr. De Carlo, sir. Yes, I like it. It is a very fine car, very strong and heavy. Not like German cars, that fall apart easily."

"That's strange. Don't you think Mercedes and BMWs and even Volkswagens are good, strong cars, too?"

"Oh yes . . . well, yes. I think so, too, yes. Those German cars are strong and good, too, I think. Yes, you are right. Of course." Hermann realized he'd almost given away to his landlord the fact that he was from the other Germany, the communist part behind the Iron Curtain where cars had cheap, ugly fiberglass chassis that fell apart on impact and no emissions controls. He didn't know what his landlord would think. If he knew, maybe he wouldn't want him in the basement anymore. So, he added, "But I think I like American cars very much, like this one. I like the color, and so do other people. They smile at it, you know?"

"Yes, I know," said Bruno, and smiled at Hermann.

"Yes. So, it is very much fun to drive in it." Hermann was glad to have brought the conversation back to the Thunderbird.

"I agree. And since you take such good care of it, I want you to drive it every day while I'm gone."

"Every day?"

"Yes, it's good for it, you know. I don't want it to get rusty. Will you promise?"

"Well, yes, sir, Mr. De Carlo, pal, if that is something that you want."

"Yes, I insist, Hermann, and furthermore you have to promise to do something else for me, something important. Will you promise?"

"Well, yes. OK. If it is important for you, I promise so. If it is not important, I also promise so."

When he got out of the car at the airport, Bruno handed Hermann an envelope and instructed him to open it and dispose of the contents after he was gone but before he returned from Europe. Hermann had to promise again, and he did. Bruno told him it would bring good luck. Then he grinned broadly, waved, and vanished into the international terminal.

When Hermann arrived early at the Strom Electric Company in the Mission District, he parked the Thunderbird in the yard at the back and opened the envelope from his landlord. This envelope was unlike the envelope De Carlo had held the night before. It was just an ordinary white business envelope, no scent. But inside were five one-hundred-dollar bills.

21

For the Easter Roundtable meeting, Myrtle put on her beige raw-silk suit with the broad collar and a long strand of cultured pearls. Everyone came to this meeting. It was the year's high point—not necessarily of a literary nature, but it was nevertheless one of the few social events offered at The Pines which Myrtle anticipated with pleasure. The program was always followed by a special members' luncheon served in the penthouse Sierra Room, and this year she had been asked to select the taped background music, which always accompanied the lunch. While past precedent had favored forgettable program music, she knew this year's lunch would be graced by the sounds of Bach's *Mass in B Minor*, the greatest choral work in the history of Western music.

As she made her way to the meeting, other members greeted her with respect. Most knew about her acquaintance with a dashing young Italian count with whom she had dined some time ago—rumor had, in the meantime, solidified his aristocratic status, and she was not one to contradict this belief—and they could only speculate as to the exact nature of their relationship. No one was bold enough to ask.

The program was led by the current assistant chairperson, Sarah Crawford, the well-liked widow of Nigel Livingston Crawford, a Stanford scholar of international repute who had developed a public television series on comparative European literature and culture that rivaled Kenneth Clarke's earlier programs on art history. Following her husband's fatal heart attack a year ago, Ms. Crawford had carried on bravely. Everyone was moved by her courage to offer a program on notable medieval women writers and the theme of Easter, accompanied by slides of European castles and fortresses. Myrtle nodded and smiled knowingly at Sarah's accurate information and insightful commentary and afterward asked the only informed question about the relation of Eleonor of Aquitaine to the troubadours of Languedoc.

Myrtle was pleased to note the repellent Jack Peterson had not shown up for this special Roundtable, and that she could answer the few questions she received about his whereabouts with a disinterested, "Who? Oh, yes, Mr. Peterson. I have no idea," as if she had forgotten who he was and wouldn't have noticed if he had vanished altogether. She retained a gnawing suspicion he might be the anonymous caller to whom she was now reading selected Goethe poems, in both the original and in English translation. She was relatively sure, however, the ambulance chaser would not have had the patience and good taste to appreciate them, nor the self-control to listen without interrupting her.

The program came to an end with a warm round of applause for Ms. Crawford, and Myrtle was gratified to hear the opening strains of the *Kyrie Eleison* fill the Sierra Room as the audience started to move toward the tables and the special lunch. She was not particularly religious, but Easter carried pleasant echoes from her childhood, and she appreciated, even at her age, its symbolic message of renewal. Besides, the religious music of the world's greatest composer was simply divine.

Ms. Halstead was seated at the head table along with Madame Fran-çoise Hayes, Ms. Crawford, and Ms. Isabelle Gillette—those who played prominent roles in the organization. Soon she was enjoying the prime rib. She even indulged, uncharacteristically, in a glass of red wine for lunch, giving herself to the festive mood of these spring rites.

Between the main course and dessert, the chairperson, Mme. Hayes, rose to the podium to make some announcements. She ended them by acknowledging their founder, Myrtle Spencer Halstead, and thanked her for her continued support. These remarks evoked a warm round of applause, so that Myrtle felt moved to smile and nod, and even to wave her hand at the audience. At this moment, glowing in the warmth of the wine and recognition, thinking of her Italian friend, and feeling life still offered grand moments, she, and everyone else, heard a door at the back of the hall bang open. All eyes turned toward the disturbance, which appeared in the person of Jack Peterson, Esquire, who quickly made his way to the head table, waving a piece of paper and smiling at the entire world, but especially at Myrtle.

Jack briefly greeted Ms. Halstead, touching her forearm in an intimate gesture Myrtle found so unwelcome she quickly withdrew it and placed it under the table. With the other hand she picked up her salad fork and resolutely speared a piece of lettuce. Oblivious to her reaction, Mr. Peterson moved on to Mme. Hayes. A few steps back from the microphone, he conferred with her and showed her his piece of paper. Poor Mme. Hayes, who didn't know any better, quickly returned to the microphone.

"Ladies and gentlemen," she began. "May I please have your attention again? I've an unexpected announcement to make, which will be of great interest to this gathering. I have just been given the pleasure of informing you of the good fortune of one of our members, Mr. Jack Peterson, a new member this year to the Roundtable, that surely brings honor to our organization."

She cleared her throat and glanced at the smiling Jack Peterson, who in turn glanced toward Myrtle, who focused exclusively on her Caesar salad and crunched away with a vengeance.

"I'm sure you are all familiar with the name, Schreiber & Sons," Mme. Hayes continued, "the New York publishing house. Well, our own Mr. Peterson has just been awarded a sizable advance for the novel manuscript he recently submitted to them." Gasps and murmurs of surprise ruffled through the crowd. Mme. Hayes smiled at Mr. Peterson when the murmurs died down and added, "Perhaps that explains why we have missed him at several recent meetings." She glanced back down at the piece of paper in hand and said, "Mr. Peterson's novel, entitled, *Resurrection in Venice*, is scheduled for publication this fall."

Mme. Hayes improvised now to make something of this significant literary event for The Pines. She reached for the wine glass at her place and turned back to the microphone. Raising the glass, she said, "I'm sure I speak for the entire Reading Roundtable in expressing our heartiest congratulations, Mr. Peterson, and in proposing a toast to the success of your book."

Glasses were raised, clinked, and emptied, and applause louder than that which had sounded for Ms. Halstead broke out. Mme. Hayes asked a waiter to arrange another chair and place setting at the head table for Mr. Peterson.

The baked Alaska arrived, but Myrtle hardly had the strength to lift her spoon to her lips. She could barely hear the strains of the *Pleni sunt coeli et terra gloria dei* anymore. The harmony of the sublime moment was shattered. She suddenly felt old and tired, as if the efforts to keep on striving were no longer worth it. What did it matter that she had founded this group with Shakespeare in mind? Or that the world's greatest music was playing in the background? No one was listening to it. They were all talking about this dreadful lawyer, this uncultured boor and the silly book he had allegedly written.

Ms. Crawford was the first to sound the alarm. Ms. Halstead had slumped in her chair. The baked Alaska bowl had tipped over at her place, and red cherry sauce had run down the front of her beige suit. People rushed to help. Jack and a waiter helped lay her down on the floor. They ordered another waiter to call the infirmary about the medical emergency. Jack knew something about emergencies and saw right away that this was not a heart attack. Myrtle had merely fainted, obviously from excitement.

22

His landlord had been gone for a very long time, and Hermann thought about him as he plastered over the sheet rock in his basement apartment. Never in his life had anyone given him a gift of that size—five hundred dollars! He tried to figure it out in West German currency. Maybe eight hundred German marks nowadays. And in East German currency it would constitute a small fortune, and more on the black market. Even here in California five hundred dollars was a handsome sum for which he would have had to save a long time. And this came with no strings attached, so far as he knew.

He had promised to *dispose* of the envelope's contents to do his landlord *a favor*. So, he disposed of it by depositing it into his account at his bank in the Marina, where he now had accumulated a total of $8,904.26. What a wonderful bonus. And what did it mean, that it would bring good luck? It already was good luck in itself.

For a moment, Hermann felt happy to be in America, to have a good job at the electric company, to have money in the bank, to have a free apartment and a generous landlord. If only Gaby and his children could be here with him, and not in East Berlin. He would take them for a ride across the Golden Gate Bridge in the red Thunderbird with the top down. And they could all take care of Mr. De Carlo's place and do whatever they could to repay his kindness. These thoughts brought tears to Hermann's eyes, and he had to wash the plaster off his hands before he could get some toilet paper to dab his cheeks and blow his nose.

Out of respect for his landlord's generosity, Hermann had refrained from his usual surveillance ever since his departure. He had simply stacked the mail without steaming open any envelopes or taking any notes. He had watered plants and cleaned up the kitchen, run the dishwasher, and put away the dishes without checking any drawers. But temptation was finally overcoming Hermann's restraint, because this time when Mr. De Carlo left town things were left in an unusual disarray. Not only had the landlord left a mess in the kitchen, but the whole place was a pigsty, as the Americans said. Clothes were strewn about the bedroom, ashtrays were overflowing with butts, his desk was a terrible clutter, and half the drawers had been plundered and abandoned in a state of chaos. Why?

Something must have happened in his landlord's life. This trip was different. For one thing, it was too long. Hermann suspected it had something to do with the subtly scented envelope the night before his departure when Mr. De Carlo knocked at his door and attempted in an erratic way to explain this trip. What could that be?

Hermann finished plastering around dinnertime. Then he cleaned up and drove to the Jack in the Box on Lombard. He ordered two double steak burgers, a large order of fries, a jumbo Diet Coke, and a cherry tart, all of which he ate at the restaurant. Then he drove back to 999 Greenwich Street. He watered the plants and decided to check out the stack of mail first. Nothing unusual there—just the familiar bills, statements, and advertising. He didn't even bother opening their envelopes and left them on the coffee table. He felt strongly that the desk and the mess Bruno had left in his office could provide some information. Of course, if he went through it, he would have to recreate the same exact disorder, so as not to arouse suspicion. On the other hand, since De Carlo entrusted the house to him, it might not look out of place if he voluntarily straightened up and stacked up some of the papers and openly told him so, when he returned. He could say he had wanted to dust and vacuum.

As he mulled over the most efficient approach, Hermann's eyes landed on an item sticking out among others in the wicker wastebasket next to the desk. The corner of a light grey envelope, which, as he bent down for a closer examination, looked like the same one Bruno held in Hermann's basement abode, the night before he left for Europe. Making a mental note of its exact location in relation to the desk, Hermann lifted the wastebasket and placed it in the middle of the living room carpet, where he himself sat down. Then, he methodically removed the items and papers that lay on top of this envelope and placed them in a neat row for easy viewing. None of these papers would have come from this envelope. None had the proper two folds one would expect in an 8.5 x 11-inch sheet of paper intended for a number ten envelope. In fact, nothing in the wastebasket was made of the same fine-quality paper. With the entire contents of the wastebasket spread out in front of him, it became clear whatever had been in the envelope was not there now. Bruno must have disposed of it elsewhere or taken it with him. But, and Hermann thought this was crucial, the envelope, which he now held and examined from every angle, contained doodles on the back, made with a fine-tip, blue felt pen, of the sort his landlord always used, and in his unmistakable Italian hand. This was key, he was sure of it. It was just a matter of interpreting these notes and doodles. The most prominent of them was the figure $500,000.00, followed by two exclamation points. This figure was underlined three times and the numbers had been written and then retraced several times, so that that item stood out. Then came the words, "Prof. Charpentier, Montpellier Med Center." Farther under this, at an angle in the corner appeared: "Make delivery to Donald. Think of code name—Call Jaguar." Now several words were crossed out: "Jag, Golden Gate, Life Insurance, Hermann, Myrtle." Then one was left: "code: MH." In the other corner: "life or death" and again "$500,000.00," this time not so pronounced. Several houses or mansions were sketched on the envelope, as if they floated in billowy clouds, and surrounding them more large exclamation marks.

By God, this was something! Hermann returned the papers spread out on the floor in front of him to the wastebasket in the reverse order from that in which he had extracted them. All save the significant envelope with these astonishing doodles that he decided to photocopy the next day so he could study it at leisure. After it was copied, he would return the envelope to its place between the bank statement envelope and the unopened Police Charity envelope.

As he fell asleep on his cot in the basement, Hermann mulled over the notes and symbols on the envelope and tried to find a common thread, a meaningful pattern. He wished now that he had listened to more of his landlord's phone conversations, but since installing the bug, he had rarely been at home at the right time to intercept calls, and the few he had overheard had been harmless—with his travel agent, with someone from the Opera Guild who wanted money, and with Myrtle, his old lady friend.

"Hello."

"Hello, dear. This is Myrtle."

"Yes . . . who?"

"Why, Myrtle."

Silence.

"Myrtle Spencer Halstead."

The voice was remarkable, thought Hermann, who had picked up the phone in Bruno's house the following afternoon, just after he deposited a light grey envelope covered with doodles back into the wastebasket between the bank statement and the Police Charity envelope. Normally, he wouldn't have bothered with his landlord's phone calls when he was out of town. But at this moment, he happened to be there, his landlord had been gone for a very long time, and, on an impulse, he picked up the handset when the telephone rang. What harm could it do?

"Oh, yes, ma'am." Hermann replied. He realized this had to be his landlord's old friend and the former owner of this house. For her part, Myrtle assumed she had reached the wrong number and was about to hang up.

"Yes, ma'am, you are Mrs. Halstead, I think so, yes. And I think you want probably to talk to Mr. Bruno, yes? But I think I must say to you that Mr. De Carlo, he cannot talk to you because he is in Europe, I am very sure. And I think he will not be back for some weeks."

Silence.

Hermann continued, "And I think I can say to you that I am Hermann Wittgenstein, electrician, and I look after this house, Mr. De Carlo's house, when he is not here."

"Yes," replied Myrtle after a pause. "Mr. De Carlo has told me about you, and I'm pleased to meet you over the telephone."

"Yes, oh yes, ma'am, I am too pleased, thank you."

"You're welcome. You have confirmed, Herr Wittgenstein, what I assumed, namely that Mr. De Carlo is in Europe. As you may know we are acquainted, and normally he contacts me rather regularly, but it has been quite some time since I last received a card from him—from Geneva—and I just thought I might call to see if perchance he had returned."

"Oh yes, I understand you, and yes, he is not returned, like you say to me, but ma'am, Mrs. Halstead, I am very happy to tell him you called when he is home here, and some things you want to tell him? Yes. I will do this, and I hope you are in very good health, and can I do some things for you also, maybe? If you say to me if you have some things, and I am very glad to do them, too. And also, do you speak German, ma'am?"

"Why do you ask?"

"Well, because you pronounce my name just like a German person would—Herr Wittgenstein."

Myrtle liked his directness, if not his English syntax.

"Thank you, young man. Yes, I do, or I should say I did years ago, but my German has grown rusty from disuse. *Ich weiß nicht was soll es bedeuten,/daß ich so traurig bin;/ein Märchen aus alten Zeiten . . .* (I don't know what it means that I am so sad. A fairy tale from very long ago. . .)."

"*Ach,* that is my Grandmother's *Lieblingsgedicht,* her favorite poem!" Hermann blurted out, interrupting her voice at the beginning of a German rendition Myrtle selected from her foreign language repertoire. Shrunken as it was over time, it still included some classic French and German poems and Italian quotations. "That is a very beautiful poem of Heinrich Heine about the Loreley on the Rhine River," Hermann continued, "and a very sad poem, and you speak it very, very well in German, ma'am, Mrs. Halstead!"

For twenty-seven minutes now—Hermann had noted the time on his watch when he picked up the phone—Myrtle, flattered by Hermann's compliment, told the German immigrant various things about the house he was living in, about his landlord, about her current residence at The Pines, about old age, literature, and the state of the nation. She threw in a German word or phrase whenever she could, pleased at the chance to utilize bits of her passive knowledge that otherwise went unappreciated. She ended her monologue with a performance of the entire Heine poem.

After hanging up, Hermann felt the need to get out. He descended to his apartment where he grabbed a jacket. He locked the house, backed the Thunderbird out of the garage and drove over to the Panhandle. Halfway through Golden Gate Park on the way to the ocean, the sunshine disappeared when a wall of ocean fog so thick he had to turn on the headlights enveloped him. He parked at the Great Highway and walked down to Ocean Beach. Normally, you could see the Cliff House from here, but now it was obscured by a dense grey veil.

Hermann zipped up his jacket, pulled the collar up around his neck, and trudged through the sand toward the water. The waves were furious and threatening. Their spray blended into the fog, which hampered the long-distance views Hermann had hoped for. Aside from a sleek Doberman Pinscher and a yellowish Golden Retriever that wandered around near the waves, Hermann seemed to be alone on the beach. The dogs ignored him as he passed by them moving south, head down against the wind.

He found himself thinking both of his grandmother in Leipzig and of this old American woman, Ms. Halstead, who quoted Heine's classic lines on sadness—*Traurigkeit.* She had kept him on the phone a long time in the same way his grandmother latched onto anyone she happened to encounter to combat loneliness. Certainly, Hermann himself had learned more about sadness and loneliness since the night of his escape than he ever wanted to know. And he had to fight back tears now, as he felt sorry for all three souls—his grandmother, Ms. Halstead, and himself. He dug a Kleenex out of a pocket of his jacket and blew his nose as he slogged along.

Eventually he turned around and headed back up the beach thinking about Ms. Halstead's relation to his landlord. Or his landlord's relation to her. There was something strange about it. He understood what she wanted from Mr. De Carlo—an ear to listen to her, someone to take an interest in her. But what did he want from her?

Suddenly the Golden Retriever emerged out of nowhere, bounding past Hermann in a rapid, diagonal trajectory at water's edge. No owner in sight. A few seconds later the Doberman shot past from behind, close to Hermann's legs, startling him by his even greater speed and splashing his pants with saltwater. Both dogs barked excitedly and threatened to disappear in the fog ahead of him. For some reason Hermann didn't want to lose sight of the two vigorous animals. He started running after them, slowly at first, but then faster, as if chasing them, or perhaps, something else altogether. He could barely make out the dogs ahead, but he could hear their barking, and he ran as fast as he could through the retardant sand as if he needed to reach something just beyond his grasp. He hadn't exerted himself like this since the night he ran after the Polish truck at the East German border, and now it felt important to move forward, to speed up, to fight against the wind, fog, and spray. For a while, the dogs stayed ahead of him, guiding him. Then suddenly, when he had almost caught up to them, they turned west and plunged headlong into the waves in some incomprehensible canine ecstasy. At this moment something dawned on Hermann. He stopped abruptly and watched the dogs frolic crazily in the waves for a few seconds. Then he thought, "The envelope! Those doodles!"

Turning on his heels, a large blond German left two dogs splashing at the edge of the Pacific and transported himself as fast as he could through the softer sand that hampered his every step as in a bad dream, across the beach back to the parking lot. Overheated and panting, he unzipped his jacket. Where was the T-Bird? Fog obscured everything except dim outlines of large objects that constituted parked vehicles. He ran one way and then the other. Finally, a reddish object emerged that turned into the Thunderbird. He got in and drove back to 999 Greenwich Street as fast as safety allowed.

Hermann pulled the light grey envelope out from between the Police Charity envelope and the bank statement, where he had deposited it before Ms. Halstead's phone call. He could have studied the copy he hid in the basement, but since his landlord was gone, he might as well study the original again. He sat down in the desk chair and took his time to scrutinize in great detail every mark, word, and symbol etched in his landlord's hand on both sides of it. Finally, the picture started to emerge. The evidence was all there: Mr. De Carlo was waiting for Ms. Halstead to die! She was the code name: *MH—Myrtle*. And he was going to cash in on her *life insurance*, which must amount to $500,000.00. And so the five hundred dollars Bruno gave to him, *Hermann*, crossed out in the scribbles, was just a symbol of this dishonorable, yes, diabolical plan, a spontaneous gesture based on his own selfish, even evil expectation of good fortune, which was in turn based on the poor woman's *life* or (in this case) death. Yes, the pieces fit. He would then buy a *Jaguar* or even a new house or an old villa, like the doodled ones floating in the sky, when he had the money. But what did *make delivery to Donald*, written in the far-left corner of the envelope, and the pharmacy in Montpellier have to do with all of that? Well, perhaps he planned to marry the old woman and collect the life insurance after her death. Some gold-digging people were not beyond exploiting the elderly in this way. Hermann had heard about such things since arriving in this country. And if this Myrtle was already in poor health, then he might not even have to murder her . . . with drugs . . . from France! *Gott im Himmel*, there were a number of possibilities, all of them criminal, none pretty!

Hermann dropped the envelope onto the desk and leaned back in the chair. Of the hundreds of people in East Germany he had spied upon for the state, he'd never seen anything like this, and the ugly revelation hit him like a ton of bricks. With East Germans, you spent untold hours sifting through banal evidence, but their life stories invariably added up to nothing more than insipid, everyday drudgery, punctuated at most by an occasional unhappy love affair or an illness. The discrepancy between the government's suspicions and the voluminous research efforts into spying on its citizenry, and the unearthing of any significant revelations, was enormous. All the wasted man-hours trying to document what everybody already knew—everybody hated the government. In fact, ironically, the most remarkable lives were the ones like his, which were so perversely devoted to examining and recording the minutia of all the other dull lives. It had been crazy, Hermann concluded, as he ruminated on his past. But now, maybe, just maybe, his training and this exercise in surveillance would finally yield something significant.

Hermann rose from the desk and walked to the east window. He looked out and saw the fog had not yet reached the East Bay. Downtown Oakland, even though he knew it was a dangerous place at night, looked like a twinkling golden gem. He paced in painful confusion. On the one hand, Mr. De Carlo had been so good to him, a real benefactor. He'd always paid promptly for the electrical materials. He was cheerful. He let him drive his

Thunderbird and live in his basement. He'd given him five hundred dollars. He trusted him with the keys to his house. If he were really up to something evil, would he let people into his house where they might find the evidence? This last fact made no sense to Hermann. He assumed that here in America, wealth, status, accomplishment, even good looks, like Mr. De Carlo's, were the outward signs of moral worth, personal order, and discipline. His landlord had the trappings he admired and wanted to emulate. He believed with his start in America, even he, Hermann Wittgenstein, already stood on the first rung of a social ladder that would lead higher toward achievements one could rightfully be proud of. What if he were wrong? What if it were all an illusion? What if America was fatally flawed, as badly as East Germany, just in different ways?

Hermann paced, hands in his pockets. He jingled the keys to his apartment in his left pocket and the keys to his landlord's house and car in his right pocket. Nobody in East Germany would give his keys to a stranger or semi-stranger. And no one would let a stranger into their house or apartment unless they had to. Everyone was too afraid of being monitored, even by his or her own family members. But here was someone who trusted him enough to expose him to his personal life. And, actually, it was he, Hermann, who was abusing this trust. If his landlord learned of his suspicions and they were proved wrong, it could mean mortifying shame and personal disaster. De Carlo would throw him out. He would lose his basement apartment, not to mention the Italian's good will and generosity. Maybe Mr. De Carlo would sue him or inform his employer. He had heard of such things. It could ruin his start in the New World.

But, on the other hand, if he sat by and allowed a helpless old woman to be exploited or even murdered for her money, what would that mean? He would be an accessory to a crime. He would have to do something.

23

LATE AFTERNOON. MYRTLE SAT in her easy chair and dropped her note pad and the heavy volume of Shakespeare's complete works onto the floor with a thud. She placed her pen and glasses on the end table, sighed, and closed her eyes. She was weary but satisfied. Her second program on "Love and Age in Shakespeare" was ready, and it was magnificent. It would focus on *King Lear*, but the sonnets would play a major role. The passages for oral citation were excellent and calculated to move her audience. Moreover, they were perfect for her voice. She had already read them out loud and would practice each day before the meeting, maybe on the mystery caller, whom she halfway hoped might call this May afternoon. At any rate, she had plenty of time before the summer solstice, when the program was scheduled. She knew as much about love, including its perils and glories, as anyone else, probably more.

But she promised herself this would be her last such presentation. The effort extracted its pound of flesh, because she gave her all. A half-hearted performance would not be worthy of her talents or the subject's dignity. She would summon her energies this one last time, but then it would be up to the others, the younger ones, to carry on, if they could and would. Since her fainting spell during the Easter Roundtable luncheon, precipitated by that annoying imposter, Jack Peterson, she had not been quite the same. She wondered if she hadn't suffered a little stroke. Dr. Adib of The Pines's own infirmary had examined her and diagnosed a harmless, temporary loss of consciousness, but could one really trust such a superficial diagnosis? He hadn't bothered with any tests, and she couldn't help suspecting that all-too-frequent attitude, even among medical professionals, that if you're that old, what do you expect?

She was eighty-six, on the other hand, and she was beginning to feel old, she had to admit. Moreover, she hadn't heard from her friend, Bruno, for an interminably long time. She had talked with his houseboy, Hermann, on the phone, and had learned Bruno was still in Europe, for an indefinite period. But in the past, he had always called or sent a card. This degree of neglect was unusual. It was partly his silence which prompted her to agree to give her second Shakespeare program in June. Not that she wanted to do so this soon, but she knew the deadline was good for her, since it forced her to keep her mind occupied.

Not that she had ever lacked discipline. She had worked hard all her life, and in her old age, she had kept up with her personal finances and correspondence meticulously; she still spoke with her accountant on a regular basis, she took her phone calls dutifully, even the silent ones, and she entertained Clara every other Friday in her apartment. She read the *New York Times* and *The Chronicle* every day, not to mention her own literary reading program she'd pursued long before she moved to The Pines or dreamed of founding the Reading Roundtable. But still, in the midst of this busy, regulated existence, she caught her mind wandering off to the subject of Bruno De Carlo rather often, and she found her disappointment with the daily mail and the silent telephone had become depressing. She lifted the receiver and confirmed the dial tone was functioning, but today even the anonymous caller failed to call.

As she grew drowsy in her easy chair, she imagined Bruno coming to the Roundtable meeting unannounced, entering through the door like a miracle as she began her program. He would sit down quietly in the back while the awed audience took note of his presence. He would be mesmerized by her voice as it inspired everyone to tears with the depth of sentiments communicated in a profound, aesthetic experience. At the conclusion of her triumph, he would come forward to greet her, and kiss her hand for all to see, and accompany her to lunch in the dining room.

At the same time Myrtle dozed off to sleep, Jack sat on his couch in apartment 4002 with a mug of hot chocolate on the coffee table in front of him. With the help of a long letter from Martha Gonzales, his editor at Schreiber & Sons, he finished the corrections in his novel, *Resurrection in Venice*. He would return them to Martha, who would later send him the galley proofs. They would be able to get the book in print by the fall. Jack liked Martha, who had corrected his grammar, style, spelling, and syntax, improved the structure, form, pacing, characterization, and plot, and given him lots of good suggestions about cutting here and adding there, all of which he had taken. Martha told him she would be happy to work with him on his next book—it was important that author and editor develop a good working relationship—and Jack was all for this. He and Martha had already discussed several ideas for a second book, and her company had high hopes of grooming Mr. Peterson into a major, best-selling author.

Wasn't life wonderful? And hadn't he made a wise decision to join the Reading Roundtable, and to stick with it even through the boring sessions? To not drop it in favor of the checkers club? Why, this decision had changed his life and given him a new direction and purpose. Who would have thought that in his golden years a whole new world of books and a new profession as a writer would open up to him? Life was an amazing adventure!

His corrections completed, he set his red pen down on the low table. He took a sip of hot chocolate and sat comfortably back in his sofa. He lifted his legs, placed his feet on a stack of magazines, and ruminated on the felicitous sequence of events that had brought him to this unexpected peak in his life: his long and successful career, his client, Tommy Manchester, his move to The Pines, his attendance at the Reading Roundtable, and last but not least, his friendship with the group's remarkable founder, Myrtle. Yes, indeed. Of all the links in this wondrous chain of events, he was convinced Myrtle was the most important one. From the moment he first heard her inimitable voice reciting Shakespeare, he had been hooked. Though he was not conscious of it then, it was still true. He owed his current good fortune to her. So, shouldn't he try to repay her in some way?

Jack got up and sauntered back and forth in his living room. He went to the kitchen and poured more milk in his mug, got down the Hershey's chocolate powder, mixed a heaping teaspoon with the milk, and heated it in his microwave for a minute and a half. Mug in hand, he walked back toward the window and then aimlessly around the apartment again, while he pondered the question he had just posed to himself. It had really started with that dreary *Death in Venice* story by that German writer who wrote those endless, drawn-out sentences that were so hard to digest. Any reader, especially a smart one like Myrtle, would appreciate a clear and simple prose style—as Martha Gonzales had characterized his own—and be inspired by the happy ending to his story. Myrtle, who understood literature so well, would obviously be proud to be associated with his book.

As he moved about now, he felt another new idea coming on. And just as he sat down again on the couch, it came. He sprang back to his feet and said out loud, "Eureka! That's it! That's what I'll do. I'll dedicate my novel to her! There it will be in the front of the book, for the entire world to see— an acknowledgment during her lifetime, for as long as she may live, and a memorial preserved in print for untold generations of posterity, after she is gone." He tried it out and liked the ring of it: "To Myrtle Spencer Halstead, my literary muse."

24

THE VISIT TO MONTERIGGIONI proved a crucial turning point. On Tuesday morning, June fifteenth, Bruno Dicarlomini waylaid his mother, Esperanza, in the bakery, so that she was forced to talk to him. That evening he drove her all the way to Siena in his rented Alfa Romeo for the finest three-star dinner possible in *La Jardinetta Marcellina*, off the Piazza del Campo, that enormous, curiously sloped square where they ran those crazy, two-minute *Palio* horse races. Why his mother loved the Piazza del Campo so much and why she always attended that ludicrous horse race in the sweltering heat of summer—in fact why all the traditional Tuscan hype over it—he didn't understand. Grown men in the different neighborhoods of Siena spent all year perfecting flag-twirling techniques to show off on this day—flag twirling! What Italians wouldn't do to attract attention. He had to shake his head whenever he thought about it. He had taken these quaint, local customs for granted in his youth and liked them. But now he even avoided the Italian cafés in San Francisco's North Beach. Bruno preferred sitting in a jet plane or in his red Thunderbird with the top down any day. Now, however, without flinching, he walked his mother across her favorite piazza and down a side street. In a flower shop he bought her twenty-four red roses. Then he ushered her like a princess into the elegant restaurant. After they were seated, he presented her with an antique ivory cameo worth a modest fortune. Flinty-eyed, she examined it carefully on all sides. Then she squinted at her son and said, "The answer is no."

Well, he had to know this. He had succeeded in making the initial contact with Dr. Charpentier in Montpellier; and he still had to pick up the drugs from the pharmacy. All systems were go for the drug plan. But he wanted to check out his mother one last time. She was his backup. If she came up with the half million dollars, even at the last moment, it was the safer, the legal, and therefore preferable way to go. Even before he had a chance to order dinner for them, he had his answer. This option was hopeless.

He knew he'd had too much to drink, and some idiot in a BMW from Rome almost ran them off the *autostrada* on the way back to Monteriggioni. He spent a bad night on the lumpy mattress under the pope's picture, and in his dreams the pope told him personally that he must abandon this particular avenue of pursuit. He must give up begging his mother for money.

He woke the next morning with a splitting headache. His mother made him some instant coffee and some dry toast with nothing on it. She intended to go to the bakery later. While he packed his things in his childhood room, the pope's picture caught Bruno's eye. It was momentarily illuminated by a bright sunbeam that streamed through the window, from which he had pulled back the heavy curtains. He sat down on the bed, leaned closer to it and confirmed how similar it was to the face of Ol' Black Donald in the San Francisco Tenderloin, except for the skin color. In the light of day, this countenance appeared somehow different, and it suddenly struck him as new and providential. He remembered his dream, and the more he stared at the photograph through his headache, the more the pope's eyes seemed to take on a kind of glaring life, to penetrate into his mind and take hold of his actions, just as his black counterpart in San Francisco was able to do. Now the benevolent face in the picture told him to go ahead with the alternative deal, the drug deal, to embrace it without hesitation if he were not to lose all hope of buying the decaying French villa with the Roman mosaics. Time was running out, after all, the pope told him.

Bruno blinked and closed his eyes, to make sure the image and its message didn't change. When he focused again on the picture, he was sure of it; the pope was guiding him; he had given him a sign. He felt relieved. It was decided.

No one witnessed the forty-two-year-old Italian-American, Bruno Dicarlomini, as he stood up in his old room on the Via Enigma. Facing an old photograph of Pope John XXIII, he made a quick sign of the cross—something he hadn't done since he was a boy—in a salute to this mysterious omen. But then, as if to say goodbye to the old gesture, he followed up with a number of improvised new hand motions that broke away from orthodoxy into brave, new, uncharted territory.

As he drove northeast out of Monteriggioni with the top down, and headed toward *la Provençale*, the highway along the Mediterranean and the Côte d'Azur, that would take him in two days' time to his rendezvous with a pharmacist at the Montpellier Medical Center, Bruno's headache lifted and he sensed a new feeling of liberation, of cutting ties, of independent resolve; you might call it . . . maturity. He would stop begging from his mother. Either this unconventional plan, offered to him by fate and Ol' Black Donald, would work, or, if it didn't, he would accept his station in life, but devote more effort to the finer things in any case—the things Myrtle had introduced to him. That same night, June 16, 1989, Bruno extinguished his cigarette in a hotel room in Cannes and opened an English version of the first volume of Tolstoy's *War and Peace* that he had purchased the previous week in Rome. He began to read.

Two days later, Bruno realized there was no other way. He had the drugs from Montpellier, but to fly back to San Francisco on a commercial flight was too risky. They might search his luggage. The drug-sniffing dogs might be on duty. He didn't know whether or not this stuff was anything dogs could smell, but he couldn't take a chance. He knew the Beattys were leaving on their private jet from Marseilles the next day, June nineteenth, and he had to hitch a ride on that plane. Then, when they taxied into Butler Aviation at San Francisco airport, he would be home free. No one would bother these passengers about the contents of their suitcases. And then he would earn the reward upon which his future depended.

Such were his thoughts as he drove from Aix-en-Provence to Marseilles. Everything was set except this last step. He would have to sleep with Crystal Beatty again. He regretted having to sacrifice himself in this way—he'd probably start sneezing again and get a nosebleed when she had those endless orgasms—but it was for a good cause. She was his ticket onto that airplane. Her parents liked him but had grown wary of his attentions to their daughter. He would have to win them back via her. And he would make it up to her afterward, somehow.

Bruno arrived in Marseilles toward late afternoon and checked into a hotel. He knew the Beattys would be leaving Marseilles Airport early the next morning, but they would be eating in *l'Escale* if tradition prevailed. They always did. And there would be time to take Crystal out on the town and perform his persuasion in his hotel room, after dinner.

At 7:50 P.M., Bruno was seated in the elegant, three-star restaurant at a table by himself near the window, but central enough so anyone entering the room would see him. If his hunch was right, the Beattys would arrive at eight o'clock sharp. He ordered an aperitif, and took his time studying the menu.

Emitting the scent of *Dark Waters* cologne that had driven Crystal wild in Cairo, he wore a stunning, charcoal silk suit by Lagerfeld with a wine-red tie and a matching handkerchief visible in his breast pocket. He had spent two hours in an outdoor waterfront café, so his already ruddy complexion had taken on a vibrant tinge. Glass in hand, Bruno now rehearsed a sad air to correspond to the story he was fabricating for the Beattys' benefit about his ailing mother, when they would meet—*quelle surprise!*—in this fine Marseilles restaurant, the evening before they all had planned to return to California!

Bruno finished his aperitif as the seventeenth-century Louis XIII mantle clock on the sideboard to his left chimed 8:00 P.M., and the American billionaires, Harold and Saundra Beatty, along with their beautiful, slender daughter, Crystal, were ushered into *l'Escale* in Marseilles.

25

It was extraordinary. What did it mean?

His landlord would be home sometime today—June 20, 1989. Bruno hadn't told him when, so Hermann couldn't pick him up at the airport. And now, this telegram Hermann had just pulled out of another number 10-size, light grey, high-quality envelope he had steamed open. It was identical to the one with the doodles in Bruno's wastebasket. The envelope had been mailed to Bruno's address, but it had no return address. The telegram inside was from Marseilles, France, and addressed to an "Old Black Donald, c/o General Delivery, Rincon Annex, San Francisco," and it read: "MH: YES! Return SFO 6/20/89. Meet what time? Write to 999 Greenwich. Abbondanza." This was the telegram. Then someone in elegant American handwriting—female, he thought—had written below this message on the telegram: "Rendezvous same place, 6/21/89, 12:01 A.M. (midnight), sharp. Bring MH." Hermann believed he noticed an almost ineffable, perfumed scent as he copied down these unsettling messages, folded the telegram, returned it to the envelope, and carefully sealed it. He watered the plants and checked out the house to ready it for the Italian's return. Then he descended to his basement lodgings to study his notes.

His landlord had obviously sent a telegram to someone for whom he was going to smuggle drugs from France to San Francisco. That much was clear. Why a drug dealer would have such elegant handwriting and take the trouble to use perfumed stationery was beyond him, but this was such a strange country. What bothered him was he feared the poor old lady, Myrtle, was a pawn in this scheme and would become an extortion victim, to the tune of $500,000! And in spite of De Carlo's seeming gentility, Hermann couldn't exclude the possibility that diabolical conspirators might murder her for her money. He'd watched enough television by now to know nothing was impossible in this country, for good or for evil. He decided to wait up all night for his landlord's return and to follow him to the mysterious rendezvous. The Thunderbird was waiting for Mr. De Carlo in the garage.

Before he began his self-appointed watch, Hermann entered his landlord's house again and took the heavy brass poker from the fireplace. He carried it out to the Strom Electric Company truck and placed it under the seat—in case things got out of hand, and he had to step in to protect Ms. Halstead's life.

26

It worked like a charm. Bruno stepped off the Beattys' jet at Butler Aviation at 10:05 p.m. With layovers in the Azores, Charlotte, and Denver, he thought they would never get there, but it had been worth it. No customs, no immigration here or at the other American airports. The goods were in the second suitcase he carried in his right hand. He declined the Beattys' offer of a ride in their chauffeured limousine and hailed a cab. Crystal glared daggers at him when they parted, because he'd sneezed during her orgasms the night before, read *War and Peace* all the way across the Atlantic, and slept between Charlotte and Denver. He planned to make it up to her later. He deposited his precious, uninspected cargo on the back seat of the cab, and climbed in next to it.

The taxi whisked him to 999 Greenwich Street, where he paid the driver to wait a half hour until he could get something from upstairs and come back down and make sure his car started. He impressed the importance of this on him with a fifty-dollar bill.

As he approached the stairs, Bruno glanced down the side of his house and saw a light was on outside Hermann's basement dwelling. He certainly didn't want to see Hermann now, so he tiptoed up to his front door as quietly as possible. Inside, he set down his suitcases and opened one of them to reassure himself it was still filled with boxes of drugs from Montpellier. Then he went to the stack of mail Hermann had dutifully organized by weeks on his coffee table. If the plan was working, Donald would have picked up his last telegram day before yesterday at General Delivery, the Jaguar woman would have met with him that evening, and one of them would have mailed him a note in a fine grey number 10 envelope confirming the exchange of *MH*, their agreed-upon code for the drugs the Jaguar woman needed, poor thing, that would earn him the money he needed—the $500,000 that was his key to life on an authentically grand scale.

The correspondence he sought lay on top of the most recent stack of mail—the fine grey envelope with the weak but unmistakable scent. Now he saw the Jaguar lady's cultivated handwriting below his own telegram. A brave soul, this socialite, thought Bruno, and lucky for him that money was no object for her. He hoped things would work out for her, too. If she survived her illness with the help of these drugs, which were illegal in the United States, maybe they'd meet someday over dinner at the Beattys'.

Suitcase in hand, Bruno locked his front door and walked carefully down the stairs so as not to arouse Hermann. He went back to the taxi and pointed to his garage door on the other side of the house. He instructed the driver to pull up to the corner of Greenwich and Hyde and wait and see if he saw a red Thunderbird back out and drive off. If so, he was free to go. If the Thunderbird didn't start, the taxi would have to drive him somewhere else. With fifty unexpected dollars in his pocket, the driver was happy to oblige.

Despite two bright lights, two cups of coffee and his best efforts, Hermann had fallen asleep. Now he woke up with a start and glanced at his watch. *Verdammt nochmal!* It was already past 11:30. Where was Mr. De Carlo? Quickly, he called his number upstairs. No answer. He grabbed his keys and ran outside and up the stairs to his landlord's main entrance. The porch light was on. He rang the bell and knocked loudly. No response. He entered and immediately knew his landlord had been there while he overslept. A suitcase lay unopened on the living room floor, and the fine grey number 10 envelope was gone from the coffee table. Hermann had blown it. He ran back down the stairs and around the other side of the house. Sure enough, the garage door was open, and the Thunderbird gone. He looked up and down the street, and the only vehicle he saw was a yellow taxicab that turned right at the end of the block and disappeared out of sight. Damn it! He had screwed up. If he'd done this with an assignment back in East Berlin, he would have been in a Stasi slammer. Maybe he was losing his touch. Now events would run their course beyond his control, and he feared for Myrtle.

He went back upstairs to his landlord's living room and decided to check out the unopened suitcase. He went through Bruno's personal belongings. Nothing out of the ordinary, except for an English paperback translation of Tolstoy's *War and Peace*, volume one. That was curious. An old photograph was used as a place mark. He opened the book to this spot and was amazed to find it full of underlinings, exclamation points, question marks, checks, and notes in the margins—all in his landlord's handwriting! And the notes went all the way up to page 482, out of 712 pages. This was something new. But more amazing was the old photograph—black and white but yellowed with age, it showed a young woman with curly shoulder-length hair wearing a bizarre costume consisting of a laurel wreath on her head and a peculiar, light-colored, loose-fitting dress. One arm was outstretched, and her eyes rolled backward in a weird expression. It must have been a kind of carnival costume, thought Hermann, and the party seemed to have taken place in a large ballroom supported by fake Greek columns and decorated with prickly potted plants.

He tried to decipher the writing across the bottom of the picture. It was difficult to read, because the handwriting was shaky, like that of an old person. "To B De C from MH-Medea." MH? By God, it was she, a photograph of the old lady when she was young! How did his landlord happen to have this? Why would she have given him such a silly-looking picture of herself in this carnival outfit? And what did *Medea* mean? The word made him feel uneasy. Didn't Medea have something to do with Greek mythology? With battles? Or dead children? He tried hard to remember. He must have learned this ages ago in school. In recent years his reading always had the point of political analysis, and little to do with mythological allusions. This, at any rate, was surely a bad omen.

Now Hermann studied the notes in the margins of *War and Peace*. Very often reference was made to "Myrtle" or "MH," as in "ask Myrtle" or "discuss with MH," and these were invariably located next to a number of lines of text or a paragraph that was underlined or marked with a horizontal blue line, made with a felt-tip pen. By God, this was a new clue! His landlord had a growing record, tape, and CD collection, but this was the first evidence he took even the slightest interest in literature. What could it mean?

Dumbfounded, Hermann looked out the window toward the fuzzy lights of downtown. It was growing overcast. It even began to look like rain, but that made no sense in early summer. None of this made sense. The pieces of the puzzle didn't want to come together. If anything, they seemed to be moving farther apart. In East Germany, literature was seen as a powerful political force and tool. Literature and writers were both respected and feared, because words could change things. Look what Marx's *Das Kapital* or Hitler's *Mein Kampf* had done to change history. So, it had been important to control what was printed, to find out what was read, and to monitor those who wrote, in order to protect the system.

Hermann understood all the good arguments. But as he held *War and Peace* in his hands and looked once again at the peculiar photo of the young

MH, he recalled one of the lowest points in his Stasi career—the two years he had organized the surveillance of Wolfgang Ziermann, a young dissident writer whom the regime had deemed dangerous. Ziermann was too popular to throw into prison, so the government declared him unworthy of GDR citizenship, banned his books, and exiled him to the West. Hermann had helped in the electronic bugging of his apartment as well as the gathering of 13,000 pages of information on him by the time the writer left in 1983. Of course, this collection mill didn't stop at that point, but continued through the work of East German spies in the Federal Republic and the Stasi at home. This process would still be going on at this moment. What a terrible waste! Hermann knew these writers led the most miserable, banal lives of all the citizens they tracked. They rarely left their houses because, of course, they sat all day at broken down typewriters, if they were lucky enough to own one, and typed all day. Lacking typewriters, the poor slobs wrote with pens on cheap, gray, recycled paper. They didn't really do anything. They just invented fictions for the most part and wrote them down. And most of them were careful not to think up or at least not to write down anything too imaginative, so as not to annoy the government. Then, if and when they did leave their apartments, they generally went shopping in ill-stocked stores or frequented cafés with stale air where they talked to friends about their dreary lives or about more imaginary things. Generally speaking, they were pale-skinned caffeine or nicotine addicts, either too thin or too fat; they smoked and drank too much and they frowned even more than the general populace. Boring, as the Americans would say.

But this one dissident writer really got to him. When one of the Stasi literary experts in charge of Ziermann's case fell ill, Hermann had to replace him in analyzing the writer's works. In this capacity Hermann had to read everything Wolfgang Ziermann had written. To this end his training in electronic surveillance was no help. Neither was the crash course in socialist literary censorship, which left him feeling ill-prepared for Ziermann's works. He knew he was supposed to maintain an objective distance from whatever message was being promoted, and to keep in mind a long list of socialist requirements for good writing, but the more he read, the more inadequate he felt. Hermann came to believe Wolfgang Ziermann was smarter, more intelligent than he was. Ziermann's texts were subtle and complex—so much so that he often couldn't decide whether they were good or bad, according to government guidelines. He felt inferior to Wolfgang Ziermann but couldn't admit it to any of his comrade-critics. He didn't really want this job. He preferred electronic surveillance any day.

At one point, Hermann found himself copying down by hand, due to circumstances beyond his control, a poem aimed directly at him, or so it seemed. The gist of it was that it was the Stasi itself, which insured Wolfgang Ziermann's own immortality as a poet and writer. No matter what else happened, they, the Stasi, would record him for posterity; they had deemed him important; they, by harassing him, had made him interesting to the world; they insured his voice would be heard, especially after his exile, both there, in the East, and in the West—where he would enjoy a better life. And Wolfgang Ziermann even wished the Stasi well in its endeavors.

Oh, the shame of it! To be forced to write down these lines that ridiculed his life and job! This poem, at least, Hermann had understood perfectly. It was ironic, even paradoxical, and unbearable, because Wolfgang Ziermann was right. The writer had captured the absurdity of his life and occupation, and he was right. History would someday vindicate Wolfgang Ziermann but not Hermann in his mean little occupation. That was two years before Hermann's escape in 1985, and that encounter with literature had had an impact on him.

A glance at the ludicrous MH photo suddenly brought Hermann back from his nocturnal cogitations. He examined its backside and found nothing on it. He looked once again through his landlord's suitcase but came up with no envelope in which it might have been sent and no other clue as to the incomprehensible document's meaning. Maybe it wasn't significant? Maybe he should just forget it all and go to bed. But what if his landlord were now on his way to murder MH with French drugs?

Hermann bolted out of 999 Greenwich Street and jumped into the Strom Electric Company truck. He knew Ms. Halstead lived at The Pines on Sutro Street. Fourteen minutes later he entered the retirement home's outdoor parking lot and was relieved to see only three cars there—and no red Thunderbird. But then, maybe his landlord had already picked her up and left for their rendezvous with death? He persuaded the night guard to let him in as far as the desk—it had to do with an urgent matter of vital concern to Ms. Halstead. He absolutely had to call her from the desk. There was no time to waste.

Herb was in charge at the reception desk. He told the large, blond German this was very unusual, having unannounced visitors, but Hermann insisted he just had to speak with Ms. Halstead on the phone about an emergency. Since the armed guard was right there in case anything out of the ordinary should happen, Herb dialed Ms. Halstead's room and gave the receiver to Hermann. When Ms. Halstead finally answered with a surprised tone—no one called this late at night—Hermann spoke very slowly in German to her, so that Herb would not understand their conversation. He learned that Ms. Halstead was alone, sleepy, and irritated. But she lightened up at the unexpected opportunity to practice German with Hermann, who appreciated her competence sufficiently to address her in this foreign language. She was particularly pleased at the news that Bruno was back in town and might try to contact her soon. No, she assured Hermann, in English and German both, he had not called her or contacted her for a long time.

After she hung up, Myrtle wondered why Hermann told her not to worry as long as Mr. De Carlo didn't contact her until after tonight, because then everything would probably be all right and under control. At first, she thought of her reliable adage that you couldn't trust 90 percent of what you read, or 80 percent of what people tell you. Did this communication belong to that 80 percent? It was late and probably the poor immigrant was intoxicated and raving and therefore unwilling to speak in his flawed English. But then, on the other hand, there was the remote possibility she might have misunderstood his German; hers, after all, was rusty. She resolved to get out her old German grammar tomorrow for a brush-up review. Yes, it might be her fault. To err is human, after all.

Herb was relieved when the mysterious German conversation had ended. He made a mental note to ask Ms. Halstead the next time he saw her when and how she had learned German. He was more relieved to see the large Teuton leave the building. The guard told him later, however, that the Strom Electric Company pickup had left The Pines's parking lot only to restation itself across the street. Herb and the guard kept a close watch on it throughout the night. They were ready to call the police at the sign of anything unusual.

Notebook and brass poker ready, Hermann kept watch in the Strom Electric Company pickup outside the entrance to The Pines all night, to make sure no red Thunderbird tried to enter the grounds. By eight o'clock the next morning he was satisfied the danger had passed. Bleary eyed, he drove off and went to work.

27

At the same time Hermann arrived at The Pines to protect Myrtle, Bruno drove slowly toward the Tenderloin. The timing was perfect. Underneath his excitement he was jet lagged. He knew he was operating on nervous energy, so he'd have to be careful. It had been a long flight, and before that, a long night with Crystal Beatty, followed by his sneezing fit. In the middle of the night, he had to get up, his nose bleeding, to drive her back to her parents' hotel near the Marseilles Airport, where she slammed his rental car door shut. In the morning he had to return the car and pretend to be well rested when he boarded the Beattys' private jet, having accepted their generous offer of a free ride back to California. Now, as he drove down Jones Street, he thought about the crazy BMW from Rome on the *autostrada* and vowed not to get into an accident between here and the Golden Gate Theater. He couldn't allow the police near his Thunderbird. He slowed down to a snail's pace, but then he thought, no, it would be a mistake to drive too slowly—that could arouse suspicion. He glanced back at the suitcase on the back seat. Maybe he should have put it out of sight in the trunk.

Well, too late now. Just drive normally, he told himself. *Don't draw attention to yourself. It will be over in a few minutes. Then life as it was meant to be will begin.*

One minute after midnight on the morning of June 21, 1989, two cars entered Taylor Street, one from Golden Gate, and the other from Market. One was an elegant, dark green Jaguar, the other a 1970 red Thunderbird, in

mint condition. A bedraggled black man in tattered clothing with a countenance resembling Pope John XXIII stood in the center lane of the three-
lane, one-way street. Both his arms were held high as two sets of headlights
approached in the parallel curb lanes. He waved at them as if directing two
jumbo jets into parallel gates. When the vehicles stopped next to him, the
Thunderbird's driver emerged rapidly and handed the black man a grey suitcase he took from his back seat. As the driver got back into his Thunderbird,
the black man bore the luggage of hope to the back of the Jaguar and placed
it in the trunk. After he closed the trunk, he received two envelopes out of
the driver's window. He stuck one of them through the neck of his sweater
and placed it against his torso behind various layers of clothing. The other
he handed to the driver of the Thunderbird—a light grey number 10 envelope that emitted the scent of fine perfume.

The black man resumed his position in the middle of the street, equi-
distant between the cars, and began his arm motions again. Both vehicles
now pulled away, as if propelled solely by his gestures. Within two blocks
the cars had vanished in different directions. But the black man's arms were
still raised toward the cloudy, dark heavens as a much-needed summer rain
began to fall.

28

At nine o'clock, after six hours of blissful sleep, Bruno entered the downtown office of Wells Fargo Bank just as it opened. He asked to speak with Mr. Rodriguez, his personal banker, and during the next half hour Mr. Rodriguez arranged for Mr. De Carlo's $500,000 bank check from Security Pacific to be deposited into a three-month jumbo CD that would earn Mr. De Carlo some nice interest income. Business concluded, Mr. Rodriguez shook Mr. De Carlo's hand and accompanied him to the front door of the bank. There he shook his hand again, patted him on the shoulder, told him to have a good day, and encouraged him to call or drop by—any time at all—if he could be of any help, whatsoever, in the future.

Outside the bank, Mr. De Carlo noticed for the first time that it was raining. How unusual for early summer, but wonderful! Then he realized he was wearing his good, dark brown Balmain suit and the gold Yves St. Laurent tie. He had dressed up in honor of this significant financial transaction. Now he wanted to protect this elegant outfit from the elements. A man of his stature shouldn't be seen in a crumpled suit. He backed up to the bank's front door under an overhang, and within seconds, Mr. Rodriguez was there again at this side asking him if he could be of any further assistance. Could he perhaps call a taxi for Mr. De Carlo? The taxi that had brought Bruno to the bank had disappeared, so that, yes, if he would be so kind.

Mr. Rodriguez thanked Mr. De Carlo profusely for the privilege of being of assistance, any assistance whatsoever, and was about to bound back into the bank when an empty taxi happened by and their waves succeeded in hailing it down. Mr. Rodriguez ran to open the taxi's back door for Mr. De Carlo, shook his hand, and patted him on the shoulder again as he climbed in. Before he closed the door, he started in again on offers of help. But by then the taxi driver had started to pull away from the curb and Mr. Rodriguez was forced to run a few steps along the curb and slam the door shut so his precious client would not fall out. Mr. De Carlo nodded and waved, and Mr. Rodriguez waved back and watched the taxi until it disappeared into the one-way traffic going south on Montgomery Street. He thought he had never seen a more beautiful male specimen than this Mr. De Carlo. And he was rich, to boot! He hoped he could be of some assistance, any assistance whatsoever, to him in the future.

As they joined the traffic in Montgomery Street, the taxi driver asked his well-dressed customer where he wanted to go. By God, Bruno had to think a minute. Where did he want to go this morning in the rain? Everything he could do for the moment to ensure a bright future was done. Despite the long trip yesterday, he felt absolutely tremendous, on top of the world. No point in going home. Anything there could wait. What he needed now was someone with whom to share his exuberance, someone who would appreciate his accomplishment. Someone who might even be proud of him.

The taxi had to stop for the signal at Montgomery and California, where Bruno spied the flower stand in the plaza of a skyscraper. "Wait here a second," he told the taxi driver. "I've got to buy some flowers." He jumped out of the taxi and dashed over to the flower stand through the rain, which had slowed to a drizzle. There he purchased twenty-four red roses, the best they had, for Myrtle Spencer Halstead.

He ordered the driver to go to The Pines. He had never dropped in on her unannounced, but he couldn't imagine his visit would be unwelcome. He'd been gone a long time, but wondrous things had happened. He might take her out for lunch—to celebrate his good fortune. But not only that, he was halfway through *War and Peace*, and he wanted to tell her that it was, indeed, an amazing work of art. He knew now what his aging mentor was all about.

When he spoke with Margery, The Pines's receptionist on duty, he was informed Myrtle was not in her room.

"It just so happens she's presiding over a program of the reading club up in the penthouse Sierra Lounge, sir."

"Is that open to the public, by any chance?" he inquired.

Margery knew the handsome Italian was a friend of Ms. Halstead and noted the bouquet of roses under his arm. Although The Pines's events were intended for the residents, friends of residents were always welcome, so she took the liberty to invite him to attend this function.

"I'm sure no one would mind, Mr. . . "

"De Carlo," Bruno filled in.

Margery wanted to correct herself now, and say, "Count De Carlo," since she had heard about his aristocratic status. But she was trained in discretion and said, "If you would just sign the guest register, and then take the elevator to the top, the twenty-sixth floor, and go down the hallway, you'll find the group in the lounge on the left. The meeting has probably just started."

"Let this sad interim like the ocean be/Which parts the shore, where two contracted new/Come daily to the banks, that, when they see/Return of love, more blest may be the view;/Else call it winter, which being full of care/ Makes summer's welcome thrice more wish'd,/more rare."

The inimitable voice swelled to resonant heights in the middle of Sonnet LVI, then faded away to a whisper at the end of the couplet. Myrtle lowered the eyes she had raised toward the overhead lighting fixtures during her impressive program-opener and directed them critically toward the slight disturbance she had just heard. A door had opened at the back of the Sierra Lounge. She had nothing but disdain for latecomers, and particularly those who dared exhibit such mediocre behavior when she was speaking. She already suspected whom it might be and was mentally prepared for Jack Peterson, Esquire to barge in and make some nonsensical remarks during the question period, or even try to interrupt her delivery. She had even readied a few devastating Shakespearean quotes, which were far too subtle for him to comprehend, with which to answer him. After all, this was to be her ultimate performance, so she had prepared for all eventualities.

All eventualities, except for the arrival of Bruno at the back of the room, in an elegant, dark brown suit and a warm gold necktie, and with an enormous bouquet of red roses in his arms. By God, it was he! Myrtle's composure was momentarily ruffled as she realized her wildest fantasy, one she had dismissed as childish—the one about his attending this meeting—was coming true before her eyes. There he stood now, grace incarnate, in the flesh, close to the door, like an expression of some mysterious but luminous cosmic harmony, smiling at her.

Other eyes in the audience turned back to see what had happened, and whispered comments were exchanged. Myrtle gripped the podium for support, took a deep breath, exhaled slowly, and tried to compose herself. She had had her hair done yesterday. She wore her subdued green Chanel suit with its loose jacket and flowing skirt and the spectacular green and black silk scarf from Saks. She reassured herself that she looked smashing. A flush of pride, confidence, and pleasure crept over her. Her swain spied a seat at the back and quietly slipped into it. Subtly, she nodded her acknowledgment of his presence and felt a surge of invigorating energy, a compelling sense of harmony, come over her, a sense that Dante's eternal light was reflecting in on itself and on this hallowed space, on this summer solstice. The presence of her swain would be her muse, her source of inspiration for the next hour. She would perform for him with the same energy, brilliance, and subtlety of histrionics she had employed in her portrayal of Medea in the Greek Theater many years ago, at the apex of her acting career.

Now she launched into her program with an analysis of *King Lear*—interspersed with readings of pertinent passages—including the false concepts and perceptions of love that informed the king's flawed and aging mind. She explicated the tragedy based partly on the infirmities of old age and partly on the anomalous concepts that informed the ideology of the king's generation over against the younger one. She showed how, through understanding of his own fatal flaw and through suffering, Lear came to understand and embrace the higher—yes, the highest—concept of love in the form of *caritas*, or charity.

Myrtle devoted about twenty-five minutes to *King Lear*. All the while, Bruno sat with twenty-four red roses in his lap, gracing the olfactory senses of those seated close to him. He was entranced. He realized there might be some kind of kinship between the enormous fates described in this Shakespearean tragedy and the profound historical and equally tragic fates described in the Russian novel he was reading. Moreover, the importance of his own fate seemed to have grown in stature, at least now—*nel mezzo del cammin*, in the middle of his life—that it had taken a radical turn for the better. His future was assured; and this impressive woman was his invaluable mentor. There would be much to talk about over lunch.

But Myrtle did not stop with *King Lear*. The theme was love, and it was equally important to explore the implications of this subject in the early tragedy of love, *Romeo and Juliet*, with which the audience might be more familiar than the later piece from Shakespeare's tragedies of the third period. Now she explained why not only the generational conflict between age and youth contributed to that tragedy, but also the universal yearning for a love that transcended the grave. Myrtle read now some of the most beautiful love passages in the English language, so that tears welled from many an eye in her audience. For half an hour she read and expounded on the idea of *Liebestod* or *l'amour et la mort* and its implications for Western literature and culture, and for our personal lives. Brilliantly she made the link to *King Lear* and its tragic, transcendent view of love, and explained these various aspects as complementary to each other, as necessary parts of the larger whole that constituted the basic thrust of our very beings. She soared now to the heights of her forensic and intellectual capacities. She outdid herself, and in a moving and emotional conclusion, she paraphrased Prospero's epilogue from *The Tempest* to thank the audience for their attention and to announce this would be her last such performance.

The perfectly modulated voice uttered its final words so quietly the next step would have been a whisper. All ears in the audience, even those with hearing aids, heard them perfectly, however, because the room was so quiet, you could have heard a rose drop. Myrtle willed this tangible silence to continue for a full five seconds more. Then she finally lowered her eyes and said, "Thank you very much."

Thunderous applause broke out. Thunderous, at any rate, compared to anything that had ever been heard in the Sierra Lounge. Even the applause at the announcement of Jack's novel had not been as loud, Myrtle noted with satisfaction. She nodded twice with her head, as the elders rose to their feet, grabbed canes or chair backs to prop themselves up, gripped each other's arms, and yet managed to clap as vigorously as a younger audience at La Scala, or so she imagined. It was a moment of unadulterated happiness. Even the Countess Olofsky pulled herself into a standing position and managed to flap her gloved hands together several times. Myrtle knew there would have been shouts of *brava* if the audience hadn't been so old and timid. As she moved toward her chair to sit down, the applause didn't diminish. But she had no encore for them. They, too, knew this was the end.

While people continued to clap, Ms. Halstead's magnificent young friend—the Italian count—made his way toward the front of the room in his tailored European suit, spreading the aroma of the fresh roses he bore in his arms. The count bowed as he approached his lady and bestowed a gallant kiss on her hand before handing her the flowers. The spectators witnessed the unfolding of this fairy tale, as the young man picked up her bag, offered his strong arm, and the two of them walked in triumph out the door of the Sierra Lounge like royalty taking leave of their adoring subjects.

29

ONE EARLY AFTERNOON IN mid-October Myrtle sat in her easy chair at The Pines, an open book on her lap. She removed her reading glasses and placed them on the small table next to her. She couldn't concentrate anymore. Her mind kept slipping away to her swain. Why hadn't he called? There had been the attention surrounding her triumph in the summer, then two lunches and one visit. After that, silence. It didn't feel right.

Most likely, he was still in Europe in the ancient villa he had purchased in southern France. But for such a long time? She didn't want to count the weeks, and yet time passed quickly at her age, and she wished there was some way to slow it down. *Die Zeit ist ein sonderbar' Ding*—time is a curious thing. This morning she heard an excerpt from Strauß's *Rosenkavalier* on the radio and found herself changing the station. The aging *Marschallin's* poignant lines were too depressing. It was no longer her favorite opera. She had loved it in her youth, when she could afford a detached attitude toward the inevitability of aging, but now time was gaining on her. When would it overtake her? The *Marschallin's* anxieties had become all too real. Good God, she reminded herself, she was already eighty-six. She'd had a cataract operation—something old people did. How had it come to this? She'd always tried to appreciate each moment, each phase of her life, as if by concentrating on them as they occurred, they would move more slowly. She knew her human life was but a moment in eternity and had decided early on, out of gratitude, never to wish any moments, however difficult, to pass. She had done well in this. Yes, she'd savored or at least tried to value every moment, the pain as well as the joy. She'd never been bored, and yet, it had still moved so incredibly fast! Here she was, eighty-six years into her existence, and who knew how many more years or even days would be granted her? What was the saying? *Tempus Fugit Velut Umbra?*

She closed her eyes and conjured up the inscription chiseled into the entrance to the old walled city of Concarneau in Brittany she'd seen long ago: *Le Temps Passe Comme l'Ombre* (time passes like a shadow)—weathered but visible in both Latin and French underneath a sundial on the stone wall across the moat. What year had that been? The sight had impressed her as a young woman on one of the many days the sun had been hidden behind the clouds over the land of Cornwall and the Arthurian legends. Thus, it had seemed to her that nature refused to cast the shadows necessary for this sundial to indicate the time—so that to suspend time might occasionally be possible.

This positive twist in her temporal musings brought Myrtle back to the thought of Bruno. She wasn't sure why he'd purchased a domicile in southern France, since Paris would have seemed the logical place to locate for his kind of business. But then perhaps he could store more art objects in a large villa than he could in the limited space of a Parisian apartment. He had said something about mosaics in regard to the villa, which he hadn't clarified. She wished he would contact her. He had only sent a few postcards, saying he would explain everything later, that indeed, he had a big surprise that she would hear about soon enough—one that would make her proud of him. What might that be? Maybe he'd found a woman, a fiancée, and he was reluctant to tell her. Maybe he didn't want to hurt her feelings?

This thought immobilized Myrtle for a moment. But then she rejected it. No, he was much too busy for that sort of thing. Not that it couldn't or wouldn't happen someday. She expected it. He was too attractive a bachelor for it not to happen. She was prepared for it, she assured herself. She had no illusions. But now she simply couldn't entertain the thought of another woman, besides his mother, in the life of her swain.

She searched her memory for other possible explanations for the long silence. Had she said something offensive? He was such a sensitive person, and becoming more sensitive all the time, with his growing appreciation for literature. He had made such perceptive comments about *War and Peace*, particularly about the ending where Tolstoy explains the impossibility of sorting out the complexities of a battle or, for that matter, any historical event. Perhaps he was having difficulties, suffering from insurmountable complexities in his own life. In which case, she should have been more observant and aware of his needs. But then, how could she know? He couldn't fault her for not knowing something he failed to communicate. But then, perhaps she should have simply asked? Go straight to the source if you want to know the truth.

She knew Bruno's number by heart, and while she didn't expect him to be home, there was the slim possibility he was back in town and just hadn't had time to contact her. She reasoned that she virtually never called him at home, perhaps only twice or three times during their entire friendship, because she didn't want to impose on him. But if he were at home, and if there was something weighing heavily on his heart, he should be able to tell a friend and thereby unburden himself. She wouldn't be intrusive; he could trust her. And she had the strength to share his burdens, if he would just avail himself of her support.

She really didn't expect an answer after the fifth ring, and she was irritated that a man with a mobile phone had apparently failed to turn on his answering machine. But suddenly a voice was there.

"Hello. Mr. De Carlo's residence."

"Well, is this not Mr. De Carlo himself?"

"No, ma'am, this is Hermann. Hermann Wittgenstein." Hermann recognized the voice and knew immediately to whom it belonged. "Is this you, Mrs. Halstead, ma'am?"

"Oh, yes, Herr Wittgenstein, of course! We haven't spoken to one another in some time. *Wie geht es Ihnen*?"

"*Danke, sehr gut*, thank you. And I should say to you that my landlord, Mr. De Carlo, you will probably want to know, is now in Europe. I expect him not to return here for some weeks."

Hermann was curious to talk to this lady again, this "MH," whom at one point he presumed to be in mortal danger in his landlord's plot. And now, over the phone, she seemed perfectly well. Following the night he had overslept, missed out on his landlord's drug deal, and kept watch at Ms. Halstead's retirement home, Hermann's investigations had come to a standstill. He was stumped. His interpretation of the mysterious messages had obviously been wrong. Where did this old woman fit into the picture? Would he ever understand her role in his landlord's life? He was happy, at any rate, to know she was well, especially since she reminded him of his grandmother.

"Well, yes, I'm fine for someone of my age, Herr Wittgenstein. We have never met face to face, but you know I am an *elder*, as we say, but I have good eyesight, thanks to the skill of the best ophthalmologist in the Western United States, and I remain quite busy. As a matter of fact, it's something of a coincidence that you answered the phone, Herr Wittgenstein, because I was just reading poems by your great German poet, Goethe."

She reached down to pull the volume up off the floor, and Hermann thought from the sounds of rustling and grunting that perhaps she was fainting or suffering some kind of attack.

"Hello? Hello there, ma'am. Are you there still? Are you all right? Hello?"

"Yes, quite all right. I was reading poems, as I was saying. One of my favorites is the *Erlkönig*. You know it, I'm sure, *nicht wahr*, young man?"

"*Aber, ja*," said Hermann, relieved the old woman was back and willing to speak in the language he hardly used, but sorely missed.

Without even asking, Myrtle started in on a passably good reading of Goethe's *Erlkönig*, but before she finished, she heard strange noises, like sniffling, in the receiver. Ignoring these sounds, she continued to the end of the poem. By the time she finished, they had stopped. In fact, the end of her rendition was met by silence—as if this German immigrant had been the anonymous caller. She didn't want to be the first to break the silence; after her efforts, he should say something first. As the silence continued, she considered the possibility that he suffered from some psychological or emotional disorder. When the silence became unsustainable, Hermann ended it by breaking down in sobs.

Well, this was a great compliment, thought Myrtle. She had been so effective that even her rusty German had moved him to tears. He was different, this boy—a truly sensitive soul!

"Now, now, Herr Wittgenstein. I'm sorry if I upset you."

"No, no, ma'am. You didn't," Hermann managed between sobs and nose blowing. "It is the poem that makes me sad. I am sorry. I just am too sad, all of a sudden, when you read this poem. You have a good voice for reading German, and you, see, I uh, I uh, thought of my son and daughter, and uh . . . uh . . . they are so far away."

Knowing he was a poor immigrant and suspecting his children were in the old country, Myrtle hinted that money wasn't everything and that airplanes and credit cards could get you anywhere.

"Yes, I know, ma'am, but you see, ma'am, they are in . . . *East* Germany. I have not seen them for three years, my wife, too. I have escaped. But they are not allowed to leave."

East Germany?! Now Myrtle was speechless. By God, this was something new and interesting! Something Bruno had not told her.

"Herr Wittgenstein, how extraordinary! I had no idea," Myrtle exclaimed with the full resonance of her voice. Then she lowered it to a more confidential tone. "I certainly appreciate that you've trusted me with this information. You know I have some German blood in my ancestry, and I've traveled to Germany in the past, long before the Iron Curtain divided it. But I've never had the opportunity to speak to someone from East Germany."

Myrtle hesitated for a moment and then continued.

"Perhaps you find this a bit forward, but I would be more than happy to continue this conversation in person, if you would be willing to indulge the curiosity of an old woman. I assure you I am thoroughly discreet and only wish your best. It just so happens that I am free for the rest of the afternoon, and if you could come over to The Pines on Sutro Street, we can continue our discourse in private, undisturbed."

Now another silence came from Hermann's end. He was confused. At the same time something in MH's confidential tone evoked the unpleasant memory of the secret surveillance training he had received from his Stasi superiors in the course of his dreary career, he was also attracted by the invitation to talk to someone about his life, about his Gaby, Sabina, and Bert, and he wanted to say yes.

Myrtle realized he was uncertain.

"Herr Wittgenstein. I know from your landlord that you are a highly skilled electrician, and you would also be doing a good deed for a senior citizen, if you could take a look at my little Chinese lamp. It's been flickering of late, and, of course, I'll be glad to pay you if you can fix it."

Hermann Wittgenstein entered The Pines twenty minutes later. His first visit to the reception desk had been at night, and he'd been too excited to notice his surroundings. But now he realized he'd never seen such an elegant palace for old people. He left The Pines five hours later, having repaired a Chinese lamp—for free—having learned not to say *pal* to people—you addressed with *sir* or *ma'am*—and having related his life's story to Myrtle. It was dark when he stopped at the Jack in the Box on Lombard Street. Despite the cup of Jasmine tea and three tea cakes he had received from Ms. Halstead on flowery, gold-rimmed china, he now consumed three double cheeseburgers, two orders of onion rings, a jumbo Diet Coke, and a piece of apple pie à la mode. He drove home in Mr. De Carlo's Thunderbird and slept like a baby for ten hours.

30

ON AN EVENING IN late October, an Alfa Romeo convertible raced up the narrow Via Enigma with the radio blasting Verdi arias by Pavarotti and the driver yelling, "Mama, Mama. Come out! I'm here. Hurry up! Come on down!"

Bruno had been driving all day from Cabrières in southern France and now he honked several times—something rarely done in this quiet village. Several people opened their shutters, leaned out their windows, and cursed at the disturbance. When they recognized the profligate Dicarlomini son, they reproached him for being crazy. Bruno laughed and waved to all.

"Where's my Mama?" he cried and jumped out of the convertible with the motor still running and pounded on her door. Three floors above him a window opened, and Esperanza looked down critically at her son.

"What's the matter with you, Bruno? Have you gone crazy?"

"Yes, Mama. And I'm taking you out to dinner now in St. Gimignano. To the Palazzo. Hurry up and get ready!"

This was strange. He didn't want her to whip up some tortellini with basil pesto and some tiramisu for dessert? He wanted to take her to the Palazzo, her second favorite restaurant in Tuscany? He was not polite, submissive, or fawning in tone, as he usually was on a begging expedition. What had gotten into him? Esperanza's boyfriend, the widower Garibaldi, was in Assisi for the weekend visiting his daughter, so she had nothing better to do. Besides, she loved the rack of lamb with polenta in the Palazzo.

Fifteen minutes later she descended to the street wearing an old brown dress, a gray cardigan, and a string of white pearls. People surrounded her son, and children clambered over his rented Alfa Romeo. Bruno laughed and talked with the villagers as if he were Pavarotti on a home visit after an international tour. It was so unlike the son she was used to, so . . . Italian. She felt a momentary flash of pride that her son was the center of this positive attention.

"Mama," he cried when he saw her. He rushed over and kissed and hugged her off her feet. Then he shooed the children from the car, ushered her into it with a flourish, and bounded over the door into the driver's seat like an athlete. He gunned the Alfa Romeo down the cobblestones and waved at the villagers in their wake.

Through colorful autumn hillside vineyards crowned by rows of cypress trees, Bruno talked all the way to St. Gimignano. He was ecstatic. His mother hadn't seen him like this since he was thirteen, having shot the winning goal for his soccer team—one of the last worthwhile things he'd accomplished that she could recall. He talked about San Francisco, about a Russian author named Tolstoy, about someone named Myrtle, about art and Roman mosaics and about a piece of property in France. He had driven all day and wanted to celebrate with her—why and what she wasn't sure. He talked so fast. Sometimes in English and sometimes in French. He seemed to forget she didn't know French, could read some English, but only spoke Italian. He didn't ask for money; he didn't even hint. He said she must eat the best things on the menu. She looked forward to the lamb.

At the restaurant she got her wish—herb-crusted rack of lamb grilled over a wood fire. He ordered the most expensive menu and also two bottles of French wine she'd never heard of—Chateau Latour de Pauillac 1961—that obviously cost a fortune. Even with all her money, she would never dream of spending over a million lira on something that could be consumed so rapidly. On the other hand, the wine went very well indeed with her succulent lamb. In fact, she willingly drank most of one of the bottles, which she found exceedingly smooth, almost oily, fruity yet smoky, like nectar for the gods, like nothing she'd ever drunk before. She found herself liking her son.

Toward 11:00 P.M., Bruno demanded the bill. Esperanza thought her stolen glance must have been mistaken. No dinner for two could have that many zeros in the sum. Well, it was his problem. He laid down an American Express card insouciantly and then ushered his mother into the hotel lounge and turned on the television.

"We're going to watch the news now, Mama."

The waiter brought him an Armagnac from 1946, the year of his birth, and for her an espresso with amaretto cookies. What were they celebrating?

The news began. A scandal in the Italian parliament. A Mafia assassination in Naples. An earthquake in Japan, and a major archaeological find in southern France, in the village of Cabrières, near Nîmes. Bruno pinched his mother's arm and pointed to the screen. There he was in front of a large, overgrown stone villa being interviewed by French television reporters, translated into Italian.

"Yes, we found the mosaics and the Roman baths during renovation work. Apparently from the fourth century, AD. Quite extensive judging by what we have uncovered so far. Totally unexpected. A major treasure of antiquity."

"That's you?" Esperanza exclaimed in a skeptical tone, but loud enough to indicate she was paying attention. Bruno held his finger over her lips while the commentator went on to explain how the interviewee, an Italian-American from California, just happened to be an art expert in antiques and antiquity. Otherwise, the find might not have been appreciated. He just happened to buy the villa as a vacation abode, but of course, now he realized its enormous significance to the art world. A discovery as significant, perhaps, as if an unknown Beethoven symphony or Shakespeare tragedy had been unearthed. The Italian-American looked forward to working with the curators and archaeologists who would be flying in from all over the world to evaluate the find and to plan extensive excavations. It would, of course, be restored to the French nation as part of its *patrimoine*, and it would make an immeasurable contribution to the overall cultural heritage of Europe.

By God, thought Esperanza, her son, Bruno Dicarlomini, her bambino, was the center of attention on television—Bruno descending into a cellar, Bruno pointing out mosaic tiles, Bruno explaining this and that. He was treated like an expert, like someone worthy of respect, like a scientist with a breakthrough discovery, like someone important and famous. It dawned on her that she hadn't thought of him as *her bambino* since he was thirteen years old. It also dawned on her that his discovery might make him rich, too. Even richer than she was.

The son drove his mother home through the Tuscan hills in bright moonlight. He turned the radio down and drove slowly because he was drunk, and because he was happy. He had much to live for. He desired a long life. He no longer needed to beg from his mother. He could treat her like a grown-up son should. She could be proud of him, of something he had accomplished. But not only that. The discovery was also an enrichment for him. The mosaics would assure his rightful place at the Beattys' dinner table, and more important, they were aesthetically beautiful in and of themselves. He was fascinated, too, by what they represented, by their place in history and Western civilization. He would learn Latin. He would read Horace,

Catullus, and Caesar. He would read the Greek dramatists and thinkers—
Aristotle, Sophocles, and Aristophanes—who influenced the Romans and
in turn European civilization. He was beginning to realize all these things
were linked together and were intrinsically valuable. There were worlds of
knowledge, worlds of the mind and intellect that contained possibilities and
riches, and he was only halfway through his life. He would have time to
devote to these things, time to read, learn, and grow.

When they reached the door of Esperanza's house, Bruno was reluctant to stay overnight. Normally, he wanted to sponge a free night off of
his mother's hospitality. Now, he wanted to go to a hotel. Esperanza had a
struggle to convince him to stay. She promised him she'd make her special
strawberry pancakes for breakfast. She hadn't done this in years, but now she
wanted to do something for her son, the son with the new self-confidence,
this son who might turn into marriageable material after all, who might
even provide her with more grandchildren.

Because it was so late already, Bruno consented to stay at his mother's.
He'd have a long drive tomorrow—back to southern France.

His mother put clean sheets on his bed, apologized for the poor mattress and promised to buy a new one. She fluffed up his pillow, brought
him a bottle of Pellegrino and an extra blanket. She asked him if there was
anything else he wanted. Then she kissed him goodnight and left the room.

Five minutes later she was back in her nightgown and bathrobe. She
opened his door without knocking and found him standing in his pajamas
looking at the pope's picture that hung near his bed. "Bruno," she demanded, "where did you get the money to buy that big old villa with the Roman
mosaics in France?"

Holy Jesus, thought Bruno. *Here she goes again.*

He should have known she wouldn't hesitate to pry into his personal
affairs the second she got wind of anything suspicious. After all, he'd been
hounding her for money for a long time, and she hadn't budged. But now
she'd seen his treasure house on television and had put two and two together.

He looked at his wiry little mother with her arms crossed over her
chest and knew there was no use deceiving her; she would eventually torture
the truth out of him. There was no use even trying to put her question off
until morning. He might as well get it over with.

Bruno turned on a second lamp, pulled on his velour robe and sat his
mother down on his lumpy bed. He lit a cigarette, picked up an ashtray and
began his story, walking back and forth in the small room.

Esperanza didn't interrupt her son as he spun his tale of faraway places
and strange events—of a wealthy American woman in San Francisco, about
sixty years old, maybe older, who was ill with a type of breast cancer, and

of a French drug called RU486 that was effective in treating her form of the disease, but was forbidden in America because it could also be used to perform abortions. Did she follow him?

So far, so good. Esperanza believed in papal infallibility, but she was no fool. Respectable Italian women had abortions all the time. She had had one a year after Bruno's birth, and she had recently accompanied her daughter Estrella to the doctor, after she learned about her husband's affair with the podiatrist's wife. The Italian doctor had used the same French drug, and Estrella's abortion had been a lot easier than her own a long time ago. And if that drug also helped cure cancer—well, then it was one of God's latest miracles, and the current Polish pope and the American President must have been too busy to keep up on the latest developments from the Head Office. It was a just a problem of a time lag.

Bruno continued. The Jaguar woman, the wealthy American who is ill, well she owns a Jaguar, you know, a British car?

Yes, Esperanza knew what a Jaguar was.

And the woman's daughter is dying from AIDS from a tainted blood transfusion. The mother, that is, the Jaguar woman, wants to save or at least extend her own life in order to see her daughter through her final illness. And, well, Bruno was asked by an elderly American named Donald, a, uh, pharmaceutical expert, to do them a favor—Donald and the Jaguar woman—and pick up the medications for the woman on one of his trips to Europe.

Why didn't the Jaguar woman do this herself?

Well, she can't leave her sick daughter. And she was afraid to take the risk, because the medications are not yet legal in America.

How did Bruno know Donald?

Well, what did that matter? He knew lots of important people in San Francisco through his art and antiques business. He'd even had dinner several times at the Beattys'. Did that name mean anything to her?

Yes, she squinted her eyes and nodded.

And why didn't this pharmaceutical expert—Donald—pick up the medications for the Jaguar woman in France?

Well, Donald doesn't travel. He's somewhat infirm, and he's tied down by his own small business that he runs singlehandedly. He has obligations to local clients who depend on him. He's very conscientious. And he's a very spiritual man, too. In fact, his face is practically the spitting image of our Pope John XXIII.

Bruno flicked an ash into the ashtray and approached the bed where his mother sat attentively at the edge and made her turn around to regard the pope's picture. They both took a good look at it while Bruno straightened its frame, which hung slightly crooked on the wall.

Bruno started to back away from the picture and his bed, but his mother raised her hand and gently took the ashtray and cigarette out of his hands and set them down. She stood up, faced her son and placed his right hand directly over her heart and spoke to him.

So, her son, Bruno Dicarlomini, took the risk for the Jaguar woman, and she paid him enough money for him to buy the French villa? Was that true?

Right.

And he thought it would help save her life? Was that true, too?

Yes. He nodded and studied her face as tears welled up in her eyes and rolled down her checks. He felt her flat chest heave under his hand. Now she released the hand that she held on her bosom and pronounced, "I'm proud of you, Bruno, my son." Then she gave him back the ashtray and cigarette and left his room.

When the door closed, Bruno went to the window and looked out at the tiled roofs and the Tuscan landscape beyond. Clouds moved across an almost full moon, and he could just make out the row of seven tall cypress trees on the far hill that would border rows of grapevines in the daylight.

This is peace.

He yawned and, realizing he was tired, threw his robe across a chair and examined the pope's picture once more. With a slight smile on his lips, he improvised a creative gesticulation for its benefit. Then he got into bed, turned out the light, and fell asleep.

31

MYRTLE DIDN'T WANT TO attend the Halloween Roundtable Meeting that afternoon. She didn't like the idea of mixing high literature with this pagan folk custom that had become so crassly commercialized. Besides, she woke up with a headache and felt out of sorts. After breakfast she forced herself to read *The Chronicle*, but an article in the Arts section that announced the speaking tour of senior citizen and ex-attorney, Jack Peterson, a San Francisco resident, whose first novel, *Resurrection in Venice*, was climbing up the best-seller list, increased her discomfort.

Good God, she thought, *the public is lapping it up.*

Several days ago, she had even seen him on television, on some insipid talk show, when she was trying to tune in to the MacNeil/Lehrer Report. There he'd babbled one inanity after the other in front of the entire nation, live. Thank goodness the silent caller had phoned and interrupted her viewing, proving, to her relief, he or she was not Jack.

Now, as she set down the newspaper, her headache intensified at the thought that the mediocre man might also attend this Roundtable meeting dedicated to the Gothic novel, a genre unworthy, for the most part, of the rubric literature. No, she definitely didn't want to go. But she had promised both Mme. Hayes and Mrs. Crawford she would, as they absolutely needed her input about important business, and they had even changed the date and time just to accommodate her.

She tried to read a couple of short stories by Mark Twain for an hour, thinking lighter fare might ease her headache, but if anything, by the time she entered the elevator to ascend one floor to the Sierra Lounge, it was worse. She even felt slightly dizzy as she took her seat and ignored several people who tried to greet her.

Mme. Hayes called the meeting to order and Ms. Gillette, the secretary, read a report about the last meeting. Two people commented on the report, and then Mme. Hayes discussed *old business*.

Myrtle looked at her watch and couldn't read it at first. Her eyes didn't want to focus. She raised her arm to put it in a better light. With some effort she determined fifteen minutes had already passed with irrelevancies about which no one asked her opinion. She also realized her headache seemed to be concentrating itself in a sharp pain behind her right eye. She decided she had better return to her apartment to take an aspirin. As she began to make motions to leave the room, Mme. Hayes spoke to her directly.

"Oh, Ms. Halstead, I hope you can stay just a few more minutes. The very next item on the agenda concerns you directly. I'm so sorry you've had to wait so long."

"Well, just a few more minutes, I suppose. I'm afraid I'll have to depart soon, however." She sat back down.

"Thank you so much. We'll try to make it short. Mr. Peterson?" She called out Jack Peterson's name, looking toward the back of the room. Oh God, not him, too! Myrtle had not seen him until this moment and was not pleased to think her presence was desired for anything in which he was involved. But now she had agreed to wait just a few more minutes.

Jack strode to the podium like a young stallion, his silver hair streaking forward, or so it seemed to those who were no longer swift of foot. He thanked Mme. Hayes as he took the podium and thrust a new copy of *Resurrection in Venice* above his head, as if it were a Wimbledon trophy.

"Madame Chairman, Madame Vice Chairman, Madame Secretary. Honorable Guests, and in particular, Madame Myrtle Halstead."

He bowed toward her. Myrtle shut her eyes in hopes that the pain in her head would subside, and also to shield herself from the sight of the unbearable one.

"I have the privilege and unprecedented honor today to address this most illustrious group, The Pines Reading Roundtable, of which I have been a proud member ever since I took up residence in this fabulous community.

"I hold now in my hand"—he pumped the hardback copy above his head again—"the tangible evidence of the amazing transformation in my life that I owe to this super organization. I'm sure you don't want to listen to some long-winded lawyer talk your ear off, ha ha, so I'm going to recommend only that you read the book, the inspiration for which dates back to the Ides of March meeting last year that many of you attended. I'm sure you'll all agree with me that that was some prophetic date! Now, many of you can say, 'I was there too!'"

He paused, as if to give the audience time for the profundity of this revelation to sink in.

"You will find my *Resurrection in Venice* to be the upbeat answer to Tom Mann's dismal *Death in Venice*. Reading his story will get you down, but I can guarantee mine will inspire you and make you feel good. Since I promised to be brief, I won't read any excerpts now, but, of course, you are all invited to my public reading and signing next Tuesday afternoon at 3:00 P.M. at Post Street Books—ask the desk for the bus connections. But in lieu of that and to express now, publicly, my true emotions and gratitude at this momentous occasion, I will simply read you my dedication."

Jack opened his book to the page following the title page, cleared his throat, bounced a knowing look off Myrtle, and read out loud, "To Myrtle Spencer Halstead, my literary muse."

All eyes focused now on the eighty-six-year-old woman in the front row as she opened her mouth as if to laugh, jerked her head backwards, slumped sideways toward her neighbor, slipped completely off her chair and fell to the floor.

By God, she's fainted again, thought Jack. *It's the excitement.*

He took action immediately.

"Everyone remain calm," he cautioned the audience in a loud voice. "Mme. Hayes, you call the infirmary and have them send a nurse and gurney up right away."

Jack had the presence of mind to remember his book and stepped off the podium, hardback copy in hand, to approach the figure crumpled on the floor. He set *Resurrection in Venice* down next to Myrtle and carefully rolled her unconscious body onto her back. He noticed the distinct smile her lips formed even in this compromised state. Other observers claimed later, however, that her expression had been, rather, *macabre* or *grotesque*.

32

HERMANN WAS WORRIED. HE had called three times yesterday, November first, the day they had agreed upon to arrange another meeting, but Myrtle hadn't answered her phone. Today he finished with a job at 2:10 P.M. in the outer Mission, so he decided to drive by The Pines and drop in on her.

At 2:35 P.M. the large workman entered the lobby. Margery at the desk remembered him and that he had visited Ms. Halstead several weeks earlier to fix her Chinese lamp. Where Ms. Halstead dug up this assortment of male friends—the Italian count and now this burly German in the overalls—Margery didn't know. But then it was a free country, and Ms. Halstead had a right to associate with whomever she pleased, even if she was a distinguished and ancient lady. Normally, however, visitors to The Pines were better dressed than this man.

"Excuse me, ma'am, but I have tried to call Ms. Halstead on the telephone and did not reach her yesterday. More than once. Three times, I think. And so, please, could you call her now for me?"

"You are a friend of Ms. Halstead's aren't you?" Margery inquired.

"Yes, ma'am. A friend," replied Hermann.

"Well, I'm sorry, sir, to have to inform you that Ms. Halstead is across the street in St. Theresa's hospital in a coma."

"In a coma?" Hermann wasn't sure of the word for a moment.

"Yes, I'm afraid she suffered a stroke yesterday and hasn't regained consciousness."

"She is not conscious?"

"No sir, I'm sorry. I guess you didn't know."

"No, I did not know that. I want to talk to her. She told me to call her yesterday, and then she did not answer."

"Well, you can't talk to her now, because she's in a coma."

"But . . . how is she otherwise? I mean if she is unconscious now, she can still wake up and be all right. Is that not so, ma'am?"

"Well, I don't know. The doctors say her condition is guarded and her prospects uncertain at the moment. At her age . . . well, you never know."

The German workman turned away from Margery, stuck the baseball cap with the lightning bolt logo that he had been holding into his left hip pocket and drew a long handkerchief out of his right hip pocket. Then he began to blow his nose and wipe his eyes. When he regained his composure, he turned back and said, "But I just two weeks ago repaired the Chinese lamp of Ms. Halstead. She was working beautifully."

"Oh yes, I know about that. She told me," said Margery. "In fact, the lamp was turned on in her apartment when we entered it after admitting her to St. Theresa's intensive care ward."

Hermann sobbed again. Margery stood up and leaned over the desk to pat down the blond hairs that stood erect on his strong forearms and to reassure him.

"There, there," she said. "Why don't you go see her? She's right across the street, and, you know, even comatose patients know if someone is there. They can hear you and feel your presence. You can talk to them. She will probably enjoy your being there. It will do her good."

"I will take the lamp to her," said Hermann.

"Oh, I'm sorry, but I'm afraid we aren't authorized to remove anything from her apartment as long as she's . . ."

"She loves her Chinese lamp, and I will turn it on by her bedside in the hospital."

Hermann didn't seem to have understood Margery but fixed her with an unblinking gaze as he related his idea.

Margery sat back down and looked around the reception area as if in search of advice. She wrinkled her brow, rubbed her nose, and finally dialed a number.

"George? Margery. You're in the garage? Could you come up to the front desk, please?"

George appeared in a few minutes and Margery stepped aside and spoke to him in a whisper. After George disappeared, Margery asked Hermann to follow her out the front door and around the corner of the building to a service door. She instructed him to wait there until George reappeared.

He would have something for him in a plastic bag that he could take over to St. Theresa's. She pointed the way for him, and yes, he could leave his Strom Electric Company truck parked in The Pines's parking lot as long as he liked.

Hermann explained to the nurse on the fourth floor at St. Theresa's that he was a friend of Myrtle Halstead. He showed her that he just had a little Chinese lamp in the plastic bag. He explained that in a coma she couldn't see flowers, but that she really loved this lamp.

Room 409 was too dark, indeed, he thought. How did they expect her to wake up in such a dark place? He plugged the small lamp into a wall outlet and set it on her night table, so that the light illuminated her face.

"Hello, Ms. Halstead," he said bending over her bed. "I am Hermann, Hermann Wittgenstein, the electrician. Your friend. I tried to call you yesterday, but you did not answer, so I found out you moved over here. I brought you your Chinese lamp. She now is working fine, and she will give you more light here in your room."

Hermann picked up Myrtle's limp right hand in his right hand, brought the Chinese lamp closer with his left hand, and ran her hand over its polished wooden base. He held her fingers to the switch and said, "When you wake up, you can turn it on and off, how you like, with this switch. Remember it?"

He returned the lamp to its stand and Ms. Halstead's limp hand to her body, then said, "Now I must go back to my truck across the street for some tools and things, but do not have any worries, because I will come back in ten minutes."

He put his hand on Ms. Halstead's cheek and noticed her mouth formed a slight smile.

When Hermann left St. Theresa's at 6:15 P.M. that evening, room 409 was equipped with a small Chinese lamp, four new track lights on rheostats and timers that lit up the room brightly during the day and went out automatically at night to help Ms. Halstead get the idea when she should make an effort to wake up and when it was OK to sleep. When the nurses saw the new installation and the distinctly happy expression on Ms. Halstead's face, they didn't touch anything.

Hermann entered room 409 again four days later. Now, a strange man with silver-colored hair was seated in a chair close to Ms. Halstead reading to her. He held a hardback book in such a way as to benefit from one of the bright track lights, but the Chinese lamp had been turned off and placed on the floor behind the nightstand. Right away Hermann noticed that the corners of Ms. Halstead's mouth were turned down.

Hermann set down a cardboard box full of electronic equipment and asked the man what he was doing here. But Jack Peterson held up a warning hand to him and continued to read a few more lines. Finally, he stopped and said to Ms. Halstead, "Well, that's the end of chapter 8, Myrtle. Great stuff, isn't it? I can tell you're enjoying it, and I'll be back to give you the next installment day after tomorrow. No, wait a minute; I've got a reading that day. We'll have to make it . . . how about next Wednesday, in the afternoon? Sorry to make you wait so long, but just hang in there Myrtle, my muse. Jack will be back, ha, ha. Let his story be your inspiration to get over this thing soon. I'm sure you'll be snapping out of it by the time I've finished reading to you. Why don't you aim for that? OK, old girl? So we can celebrate. Well, see you later. Looks like you've got another visitor. So, bye for now, and have a nice afternoon."

Jack rose from his chair, his book firmly in his left hand, and extended his right hand out to Hermann.

"Howdy, pardner," he said. Hermann gave it a bone-crushing shake. Jack winced and said, "Glad to meet you. I'm Jack Peterson, Esquire, author. Maybe you've heard of me or my book, *Resurrection in Venice*?" He held out the copy for Hermann to admire.

"Did you turn off that Chinese lamp?" Hermann said, glancing in its direction behind the nightstand.

"Oh, that God-awful thing? I put it down on the floor so she wouldn't have to look at it when she wakes up."

Hermann seized the book from the man's left hand, dropped it on the floor, and stepped on it hard enough to break its back.

"I am sorry, Mr. . .., " he said as he leaned down, picked up the smashed book, and handed it back to Jack Peterson, who backed out of the room, his mouth open.

Alone with Myrtle, Hermann set the Chinese lamp on the nightstand and turned it on so its soft glow shone on her face. He sat down next to the comatose woman, took one of her hands into his own and announced, "I am Hermann, Ms. Halstead."

Then he got up and talked to her while he set up a CD player that would automatically play Mozart piano concerti three times a day. By the time he was finished, it was clear the corners of her mouth had turned upward.

On November 9, 1989, Hermann got home late to his basement apartment on Greenwich Street. He'd eaten at Jack in the Box and spent the evening with Ms. Halstead at St. Theresa's. Her color and breathing seemed better to him. He thought she squeezed his hand occasionally when he talked to her. He read newspaper articles out loud about the big changes in East

Germany. People were streaming out of the country via Hungary and Czechoslovakia. He had told her all about Gaby, Sabina, and Bert. He was gaining hope that he might see them again, after all. Ms. Halstead seemed interested in this. He could tell. Hermann thought she was getting ready to wake up.

At home, he turned on the television and went to bed. He was about to fall asleep when the eleven o'clock news report came direct from Berlin. The Wall was open! Hermann sat up, wide awake, turned up the volume, and stared at the screen. People were dancing on top of the Berlin Wall. On top of The Wall! West Germans pulled East Germans up onto the wall—and vice versa. They popped corks, squirted each other with champagne, and drank deliriously. Hermann rubbed his eyes. Cars, stupid little Wartburgs, Ladas, and Trabants full of East Germans, drove slowly, for the first time in their lives, through the checkpoints to the west side of the city. Embarrassed border guards and police stood by watching awkwardly, their purpose in life having ended. Pedestrians streamed past them while West and East Germans greeted the compatriots from whom they had been separated for twenty-eight years. Strangers embraced on the streets, former enemies hugged and slapped each other's backs. The border was open!

Hermann watched and watched. He went through all the channels and tuned in the radio to gather all the news he could. Incredible! What did it mean? He wanted to call someone—Ms. Halstead?—and tell her the good news, but it was too late at night, and Ms. Halstead couldn't answer her phone. But then, it wouldn't disturb her either. At midnight he dialed her number at the hospital, just to give her the sense that something exciting was happening. To his surprise someone said, "Hello, Ms. Halstead's room." Hermann's heart skipped a beat.

"Hello? Uh, excuse me, I thought Ms. Halstead is asleep."

"Well, yes, she is asleep. She's in a coma . . . Is this Hermann?" The night nurse recognized his accent.

"Yes, ma'am. Are you Nurse Fortunato?"

"Yes, Hermann. We're in Ms. Halstead's room, because we think she might wake up."

"Oh yes! I think that, too! This afternoon I thought already that. So, will you tell her please, that I am calling, and tell her that I am seeing the news, and guess what? The Berlin Wall is opened up, and German people are drinking champagne on top of this wall."

"Well, yes, Hermann. We'll definitely tell her. And that's wonderful news. And we're happy for you. So maybe you can tell Ms. Halstead in person at your next visit."

"Oh yes, ma'am. I will. I will come there tomorrow for sure, and I will bring some newspapers and read her all the news from Germany."

"Good. I'm sure she'll enjoy that Hermann. But you better get some sleep now. It's late."

"Yes, OK, ma'am. I will and thank you and good night to you."

It was after midnight when Hermann fell asleep, the TV still on, at the same time Bruno's plane, which had been delayed, touched down at SFO.

33

IN THE MORNING BRUNO stepped outside 999 Greenwich Street to check his mailbox and take a breath of Pacific air at the same time Hermann stood downstairs at the corner of the house in his bathrobe watering potted azaleas and rhododendrons.

"Hermann, hello!" Bruno called out, cheerfully.

Hermann jerked his head around, startled, and watered his foot.

"Scheiße!" he said under his breath because he'd been lost in his thoughts prior to the interruption. He had no idea his landlord was back. Laying the hose down at the base of a hedge, he said, "Hey, hello there, Mr. De Carlo, pal. I mean, sir. Sorry, sir," and approached him. "So, you are home. I am glad of that. Did you have a good trip?"

Hermann spoke in rapid, short phrases as he approached Bruno, who met him halfway down his front steps. Hermann sounded nervous or excited to Bruno.

"Yes, excellent. Would you like to come up a few minutes for a cup of coffee?"

"Well, yes. But no, I cannot right now, I am sorry, because I have to go see someone. Well, actually, someone you know her too, sir. You know, I am her friend, too, now, Mr. De Carlo. I mean Ms. Halstead, your friend, she is now my friend, too, and I promised to tell her about the Berlin Wall today, that is coming down in Germany. Maybe you know about it already? But, well, she is, Ms. Halstead is in a coma at the hospital."

"What? What did you say? Are you talking about Myrtle Halstead, at The Pines?"

Hermann nodded and saw how his landlord's face underwent a sudden transformation. The broad smile turned into a worried look, and the ruddy, dark complexion suddenly lost its color, as if he had turned into a sickly, pale Scandinavian except for his wavy black hair. In short, his landlord looked shocked, and Hermann spontaneously took his arm in case he was going to collapse. Indeed, his landlord sat down on one of the steps and dropped his head, so Hermann tried to reassure him.

"Mr. De Carlo, I must tell you not to have worries, because Ms. Halstead is much better already, and the nurses thought she might even wake up last night. I have been seeing her often. And I promised to go see her today. So maybe you want to come, too?"

Hermann's words seemed to help Bruno, who now asked questions. When did it happen? What did the doctors say? When had he seen her last? Hermann told him all he could, and then they agreed to meet again in twenty minutes and drive to the hospital together. Bruno asked Hermann to drive them in the Thunderbird. He didn't feel like driving.

Hermann turned off the water and went back into his apartment to dress. He was so nervous he ended up wearing unmatched socks. Everything was happening at once. The Berlin Wall had come down! He would soon be reunited again with Gaby, Sabina, and Bert. Ms. Halstead was going to wake up from her coma, any time now. And on top of that, his landlord had returned. Somehow, he hadn't expected that, either. What should he say to him?

In the meantime, Hermann knew Mr. De Carlo had done no harm to Ms. Halstead. His suspicions had been unfounded, his investigations wrong. His landlord was obviously shocked and sorry to hear about her stroke. As far as the $500,000 and the mysterious French drugs went, well, maybe he, Hermann, didn't need to know what those doodles on the envelope meant. Maybe, it wasn't any of his business. Maybe it was time to forget his old East Germany Stasi profession forever.

On their way to St. Theresa's, Hermann felt the need to confess. At the very least he owed his generous landlord an explanation for his acquaintance with Myrtle. So, he told Bruno how he'd just happened to answer her call by a fluke that day she had talked so long to him. When his landlord thanked him for answering his phone and even encouraged him to answer it in the future, he sighed in relief and went ahead and let out the whole sad story—his escape from East Germany, his hopes for a reunion with his family, and finally, how he fixed Myrtle's Chinese lamp and set it up in her hospital room. Well, damned if Bruno didn't commiserate with Hermann about East Germany and approve of everything Hermann had done!

When Bruno and Hermann entered Ms. Halstead's room at St. Theresa's, Scarlatti harpsichord music from Nurse Fortunato's boyfriend's CD was playing in the background. Ms. Halstead wasn't awake yet, but the nurses all agreed she'd moved more often, twitched her eyelids, squeezed their hands, and looked happier than before. Hermann spoke to her first and told her he'd brought her friend, Mr. De Carlo, to see her. He held his landlord's beautiful bouquet of roses close to her face so she could smell them even if she couldn't see the flowers. Then he put them in a vase and left the two of them alone. He promised to return in the afternoon.

After Hermann left, Bruno pulled a chair close to Myrtle's bed. He held her hand while he told her about his luck in discovering Roman mosaics buried underneath his villa, and what they meant to the international art world, and their implications for his future and fortune. But he emphasized that was not the most important thing for him. Rather, it was their intrinsic aesthetic and historical value he appreciated most, thanks to her. He thanked her for opening his eyes and heart and mind to art and literature. She'd had a major impact on his life, which had changed drastically for the better. He would always be grateful to her. His own mother in Tuscany was better, she should know, by the way, but she, Myrtle, was his beloved teacher and spiritual mother. As he told her these things, Bruno could tell Myrtle understood him and was happy for him. It seemed to him she squeezed his hand and smiled ever so slightly, in defiance of her coma.

When Hermann returned to the hospital, his landlord was gone. But Mr. De Carlo had left him a note instructing him to take the T-Bird and meet him for dinner at Stars near the Civic Center at seven that evening. Ms. Halstead's right hand clasped Bruno's note on her chest, and Hermann was convinced she was aware of delivering it to him when he took it. She seemed in a good mood, and he told her about images from Berlin on television and read articles to her from *The Chronicle* and *The New York Times*. He kissed her forehead and left her in time to go home and change before meeting his landlord at Stars. He was convinced that Ms. Halstead squeezed his hand as he said good-bye.

Hermann had never been in such a beautiful restaurant. He moved down a mirrored corridor full of plants and palms potted in brass containers past a well-lit, busy kitchen with a young, ethnically diverse army dressed in white preparing food. When he reached the end of the corridor a chic woman with shiny blond hair said, "Good evening, sir. Do you have a reservation?"

"Uh, no. Well, maybe. I do not know, ma'am. I am here to meet my friend, well, uh, landlord, at seven o'clock."

"Well, perhaps there's a reservation under his name?"

"Perhaps. Yes. Maybe you are right."

"Well then, what is his name, sir?"

"Oh, it's Mr. De Carlo."

"Ah, Signore De Carlo?" A smile spread over her face, and she addressed Hermann cordially. "He's already at your table. Just follow me, sir. May I take your coat?"

When Hermann gave her his jacket and she led him through the restaurant, he was pleased to note it was not too dark, like the two steak houses his Strom Electric Company boss had treated him to, the ones where you needed a flashlight to read the menu and to see what you were eating. The ceiling of this one, as a matter of fact, was covered with twinkling, star-shaped lights that mimicked a starry dusk. While the canopy of this fantastical sky grew darker throughout the evening, the stars shimmered with greater intensity, creating a vibrancy to the ambience—an effect that remained below the level of consciousness of most diners, but which impressed Hermann no end.

As they approached the table where Bruno sat waiting, the maître d' said to Hermann, "We'd like to offer you an aperitif on the house. Would you like our special *Kir Royale* or would you prefer something else?"

Mistaking *aperitif on the house* for something like *scotch on the rocks*, Hermann answered, "I'll uh have the operative on the house."

The dark-haired woman winked at Bruno as she showed Hermann to his seat and said, "We'll bring you a Kir right away, sir. And I wish you both a *bon appétit* and a splendid evening with us here at Stars."

In a few minutes, Hermann received his first Kir Royale and liked it very much. He also enjoyed his chilled appetizer of oysters with the long French name from Tomales Bay. He enjoyed it, that is, after he figured out which piece of cutlery to use on it. It wasn't too difficult, because his landlord picked up the stubby little three-pronged fork they brought with the oysters, and Hermann followed suit. Hermann had never seen so many sparkling glasses at one place setting before or experienced so many changes of plates and cutlery during a dinner. He decided the wise course would be to not eat anything until Mr. De Carlo took the first bite or sip. He was glad Bruno ordered the same things for both of them.

Bruno was amused that Hermann watched him throughout the meal and copied his every move. He also sensed Hermann's intense observation seemed to pose other, more important questions. During his absence, after all, Hermann had become attached to Myrtle, and he was probably curious about his, Bruno's, relationship to her. He didn't know what Myrtle had told him before she suffered her stroke. One thing was certain: unlike Myrtle's relation to Bruno, she would not have been training Hermann in the interpretation of lyric poetry or Renaissance drama. Bruno smiled at his own thought and noticed Hermann smiling back.

Bruno didn't mind telling Hermann about his good fortune; in fact, he wanted to. Myrtle's coma felt like a family crisis, and Hermann seemed like a part of his small American family now. For some reason, this morning on the way to the hospital, Hermann had given him a rambling but intimate confession about his wife and children in East Germany and about how he'd gotten to know Myrtle. He had seemed plagued by guilt over things that were either misfortunes or harmless coincidences.

Poor guy.

Well, he possessed a genuine goodness of heart and he, Bruno, was lucky to have found him, lucky he did such a thorough job rewiring his house, and lucky he took such good care of it and his Thunderbird. Moreover, he, Bruno, would soon be rich and famous beyond Hermann's ability to imagine. And, even better, he had a new avocation—literature—that would enrich the rest of his life. Bruno needed to share this news with someone. Crystal Beatty was out of the question, at least for the moment. He had told Myrtle at the hospital, but in her present state, she constituted an under-responsive listener. He'd already told his mother as much as she could understand. Beyond that, there was Hermann. So, Bruno raised his red wine glass—they were working on their cheese plate now—and said to Hermann, "I'd like to propose a toast to our mutual friend, and my spiritual mother, Myrtle. That she may return to health and continue to inspire us to make her proud."

After Bruno took a sip, Hermann did, too. Then the German dabbed the corners of his eyes with his handkerchief and tried not to cry. Bruno moved quickly on to the next topic.

"I'd like to toast something else as well, Hermann. You may think this strange, and I'm only sorry our friend can't be with us at this dinner to share my satisfaction, but I told her about it this morning at the hospital, and I had the feeling she understood me."

"Oh, yes, Mr. De Carlo, sir. I know she understands. Everything you say. I've been telling her all about East Germany and other things, and it makes her happy to listen. I am very sure."

"Yes, Hermann. By the way, why don't you call me *Bruno*? It's OK with me."

"Oh, thank you, sir, Bruno."

"Anyway, Hermann, it may seem strange, but I want you to drink with me to my own good fortune."

"Oh yes, I am very happy to do that! Yes, of course, Bruno, pal, sir, I mean pal!" said Hermann, without knowing what Bruno meant, but feeling assuaged that everything in his world seemed to be working out so well. He already had his red wine glass to his lips when Bruno interrupted to explain why they were toasting.

"You see Hermann, you've told me about your life, and now I want to tell you what's happened in mine." He set his wine glass down on the table and Hermann followed suit.

"You see, by a series of circumstances I was able to buy an old villa in southern France that turned out to contain, buried underneath it, mosaics from the early Christian-Roman era that are very, very valuable. That's why I've been gone so often and so long. The property cost only five hundred thousand, but the mosaics are worth many millions, no one knows exactly how much yet. Remember the five hundred dollars I gave you once?"

Hermann's jaw remained slightly ajar as his landlord explained to him a three-way financial partnership involving pharmaceuticals that profited him $500,000 and helped out two other deserving San Franciscans, one of whom was a wealthy woman with a dying daughter. He'd gotten to know her through his contacts in San Francisco society because of their mutual interest in fine automobiles—his Thunderbird and her Jaguar. Anyway, he'd bought the villa with the $500,000, and he'd given Hermann the five hundred dollars as a gift when this windfall came through, and to ensure that his good luck would continue—a kind of superstition.

"So, Mr. De Carlo, sir . . ."

"Call me Bruno."

"OK, sorry, Bruno. So, uh, this woman who drives a Jaguar is not Ms. Halstead, I mean is not a relative of Ms. Halstead?"

Bruno realized the wealthiest person Hermann had ever met was probably Myrtle. *By God, he must think I borrowed money like that from her! Well, Hermann doesn't know much about money, what a relative thing it is, what a trifling amount that is compared to what I'll be making. As a matter of fact, Myrtle's money never occurred to me. And, of course, now it's irrelevant anyway, along with my mother's money or anybody else's.*

Bruno smiled reassuringly at Hermann. "No, there is absolutely no connection. What Ms. Halstead means to me has nothing to do with money."

Hermann's right hand still gripped the stem of his glass as he scrutinized his landlord. The former secret policeman had learned to detect lies on faces, but the countenance of the handsome, dark-haired Italian-American across from him was pure innocence. Indeed, the gold candles on the far side of the orchid in the middle of the table was close enough to Bruno to cast a particularly appealing warm glow on his face. By God, this cleared up his last doubt—about the $500,000 and the drugs. He had been dead wrong to suspect his landlord. Mr. De Carlo was not only handsome and rich but also good! He had come to America, worked hard, had some luck in business and made it big. And he was generous, too. Just like this country. When he glanced around the restaurant, it seemed to Hermann as if everyone in it was beautiful or handsome or distinguished. All were well dressed and smiling with the benevolent magnanimity befitting a chosen people elevated out of the commonplace into a privileged existence directed by a higher power. Well, maybe that went too far. He reined himself in from these far-reaching speculations. Maybe he was intoxicated from the food and that really good wine from France. But what a crock they had been fed back home, when they were told Americans only went around exploiting everybody else. In truth, it was the GDR that was mean and stingy, because *everybody* was so damned poor.

Though immersed in these thoughts Hermann noticed his landlord move his glass up and down and then sideways in an attempt to capture his attention. It was almost as if Bruno had made a kind of religious gesture to focus back on their little celebration. And the candles' reflections seemed to set his glass sparkling. His landlord then smiled and winked at Hermann with such clarity and brightness in his eyes that Hermann now banished forever all doubts and suspicions. Maybe he didn't understand everything about his landlord, but Hermann decided once and for all that he understood enough. He raised his glass and clinked it enthusiastically against Bruno's, and said, "Here's to you, pal, Bruno."

Bruno said, "And here's to you, Hermann, my friend."

34

AT THE SAME MOMENT Hermann entered Stars Restaurant near the Civic Center, Myrtle woke up from her coma at St. Theresa's. Albinoni was playing in her room, her Chinese lamp shone light on a beautiful bouquet of fragrant roses next to her bed, and she felt luminous and ethereal. She was well aware of where she was and that the Berlin Wall had opened up. She was also aware that her swain, Bruno, who had left her these flowers, had discovered Roman mosaics in his southern French villa that would bring him fame and fortune in the international art world. All these things seemed wonderful to her—and wondrous. How good it was to be awake again, as if after a hundred-years' sleep. She savored these lovely moments, this heavenly state of consciousness for a long time, reflecting on its meaning. Unconsciousness had been peaceful and semi-consciousness delicious, and she had never imagined she could feel quite like this—clear-headed, at peace with the world. Happy. Yes, this was happiness. How extraordinary it was that life had granted her a reprieve. She was back. But for how long? And for what purpose? She had to make use of her time.

Suddenly, she heard a familiar voice in the hallway. Ms. Fortunato, the night nurse, who must just be arriving, and . . . oh no, not him. But it was unmistakably the voice of Jack Peterson who asked Ms. Fortunato, "Well, is the old girl awake yet?"

She couldn't hear the nurse's answer, but Jack Peterson confirmed, "Well, if anything will wake her up, this will. I'm going to read her the last chapter of my book, *Resurrection in Venice*. Don't you love that title? You haven't bought a copy yet? You should really listen too, you know. Well, I know you've got other work to do, but when you get time, they've got it at Harold's Books, just a couple blocks from here, on Buchanan Street. You should really do yourself a favor and get a copy."

Myrtle knew what to do.

When Jack Peterson entered her room, her eyes were closed, and the corners of her mouth turned down, an expression Jack knew was only a result of her comatose condition, during which she couldn't express her true emotions and pleasure at his presence and with his readings. He just knew that his company did her good, and that his uplifting story buoyed her spirits. It had to. Proof came halfway into the chapter, when he crossed his legs. He noticed one of his shoelaces was untied and when he bent over to tie it, the plastic water pitcher on Myrtle's bedside table fell onto his shoulder, spilling water onto his clothes and his book, which he'd set on the floor. Myrtle's hand had moved back to her chest—he'd seen it out of the corner of his eye—but not to the same place as it was before. She had moved! She wasn't awake, but she had definitely reached out to him! She had only missed and spilled water on him, because he'd been tying his shoelace at the moment. It was a sure sign. She loved his book. She was literally moved by it. She must love him!

35

BRUNO HAD TAKEN A taxi from downtown to Stars, but when they left the restaurant Hermann drove them both back to 999 Greenwich Street in the Thunderbird. After he parked the car in the garage the two men stopped at the base of the front steps, and Hermann thanked Bruno for the dinner. Hermann had never eaten in such a fine restaurant with such good food and wine. And how happy Hermann was for Bruno—they were friends now; he could call him *Bruno, pal*—that he had found Roman mosaics in his French house that would make him a multi-millionaire. They shook hands and slapped each other's backs. As he was about to climb his steps, Bruno said, "Look, Hermann. A half moon," and pointed east.

"Yes," said Hermann. "It's beautiful tonight, very clear. You know there will be a heavenly display later. I heard it on the radio. I think I might be watching it, maybe."

"How sweet the moonlight sleeps upon this bank . . ." said Bruno.

"Uh, what?" Hermann looked at him quizzically.

"Nothing. I think I'll listen to some music before going to bed."

"OK. I think I will watch the news about what's happening in Berlin, before I see the heavenly display. Good night."

As Bruno ascended his steps, Hermann unlocked his basement entrance. When he turned the television on to watch the eleven o'clock news, Hermann's head swam with the day's events—Ms. Halstead, the restaurant, Bruno's house in France—but what he saw on the screen amazed him more

166

than anything else. The concrete wall that for twenty-eight years had seemed indestructible had become porous in the last twenty-four hours. Berliners, from both sides, were streaming unchecked back and forth through the openings. People were hacking holes in the concrete, and no one was stopping them. The enormous, delirious street party that began the night before was still going on. He watched in fascination as Trabis loaded with excited revelers continued to putt across the borders while their occupants yelled and waved to cameras for the world to see. At 11:20 he spied a green Trabi with a familiar dent in the right fender. A woman drove while a boy and girl held a sign out of the back window toward the television cameras that read, "Hallo Hermann! Hallo Papa! California here we come!"

While Bruno slept at 999 Greenwich Street, a blond German with arms as strong as a wrestler stood smiling at the heavens in the parking lot at Twin Peaks next to a pickup truck with *Strom Electric Company* written on both doors. While a motley crowd of San Franciscans *ooed* and *awed* as they watched a shower of meteors race across the night sky at midnight, the German watched with them through eyes blurred by tears of joy.

36

AFTER JACK LEFT HER room in his damp clothes, Myrtle needed to act fast. He had stayed so long reading his terrible book to the bitter, happy end, that he had almost destroyed her good mood. The imbecile didn't even get the hint when she knocked the water pitcher down onto him. She examined the roses now and her Chinese lamp and then located the nurse's call button. A light went on when she activated it, and almost immediately she heard footsteps approach and Ms. Fortunato's excited voice say to a colleague, "She's awake!"

"Ms. Halstead?" she said, bending over her elderly patient and picking up her hand. "This is Nurse Fortunato, you're in the hospital. You've been asleep for a long time, but everything's going to be all right. Can you say 'hello?'"

"Yes, of course, dear. Hello, Ms. Fortunato, and thank you for your good care. But now I need your help with something."

"Yes, Ms. Halstead. Shall I straighten your pillows or give you a sip of water? I see your last visitor must have knocked your water pitcher off the nightstand."

"No, I did."

"Well, Ms. Halstead, that would be quite an accomplishment," she said, and Ms. Halstead saw the wink she gave to the nurses' aide who began raising the head of the bed and straightening her pillows. Ms. Halstead didn't want to take the time to explain her motivations to Nurse Fortunato or to risk being thought disoriented by the coma, so she didn't insist.

"Well, maybe I just dreamed I did, when I heard the pitcher fall down."

Nurse Fortunato smiled and said, "Now, you shouldn't talk too much, Ms. Halstead. You don't want to strain yourself." She tried to stick a thermometer into Ms. Halstead's mouth, but the patient refused.

"No, please, let's wait for my temperature. I'm sure it's all right, and I need your help with something very important before we do anything else."

"Oh, of course. We'll bring the bedpan right away, ma'am."

"No, no, Ms. Fortunato. That's not necessary. Please bring me a blank piece of paper and a pen. And do you have a photocopy machine at the nursing station? Yes? Good. Go now, quickly, for the pen and paper please. I've decided to give a gift to Hermann. You know him? Yes, he's a very nice man, and he will soon be reunited with his family. He's going to need some money."

"Now, now, Ms. Halstead. You've been in a deep sleep for quite a while. We need to take things slow and easy at first. Let's do that tomorrow."

"Oh, no! This can't wait. Surely, it's not too much to ask you for pen and paper, is it, since I haven't made many demands on you these last days?"

Nurse Fortunato rolled her eyes at her colleague and said, "Wow!" under her breath as she left to get a pen, paper, and a clipboard. In the meantime, the aide called the night resident, wiped up the spilled water, brought a fresh pitcher, and placed it next to the roses. Soon Nurse Fortunato and the resident arrived, and they and the aide watched in amazement as Ms. Halstead wrote in a bold hand and explained in lucid English that she was creating a codicil to her Last Will and Testament directing $200,000, which otherwise would have gone to charity, to the blond German with the pony tail and bald spot. A second codicil, she added, would give $35,000 to a nurse named Irene Sanders at The Pines.

"Now, young man," she addressed the resident physician, "would you please read out loud what I've written? And speak up, so we all can hear you. I'll need two of you to sign as witnesses." Myrtle flapped the papers insistently toward the doctor who, surprised by the strength and tone of her voice, grasped them and stared at them for a moment. Then he glanced at Nurse Fortunato and the aide who looked on with expectant attention. Myrtle said with insistence, "Please, let's get on with it."

Now the doctor began to read, then raised the volume of his voice on a hand cue from the patient. The nurses listened with the reverence a congregation might afford a silent prayer at church. When the physician finished, Myrtle smiled with satisfaction and thanked him. She had detected no errors. Then, at her request, the two women signed the paper that also attested to the soundness of her mind and to the lack of coercion. Finally, Ms. Halstead instructed the women to make photocopies and send them both to her lawyer and to the trust department at her bank. Only then did she allow them to take her temperature and blood pressure and enter them on her patient's chart. Her caretakers advised her to take it easy after all the exertion. She agreed and they left the room.

Myrtle fell again into a deep sleep, and at midnight she took leave of this world, the corners of her mouth turned up.

Three days later, after Margery informed Pacific Bell of the death of its customer, Myrtle S. Halstead, the phone company closed the account and stopped service to her number. Now, the anonymous caller, who had repeatedly called the number for several days in vain, called again for the last time. Man or woman? Young or old? Immigrant or native son? Had he or she profited from these calls? Would he or she miss them?

Instead of hearing the voice he or she had hoped for, instead of hearing readings and commentaries on Shakespeare and the world's great literature, this caller heard a recorded message that the number was no longer in service. Thus, Myrtle's voice *answered* the silent caller with silence.

37

IT WAS A BRILLIANT morning when a sober group of people boarded the Elysian Foundation boat near Pier 39—Bruno, Hermann, Jack, Dr. Manchester, Myrtle's second cousin, Clara, Margery from The Pines's reception desk, and nurse Irene Sanders, as well as Mme. Hayes and Mrs. Gillette from the Reading Roundtable—to accompany Myrtle's ashes to their final destination, west of the Golden Gate Bridge. Prudently, Myrtle had arranged for this outing over a year ago, everything except for Jack's presence, which she, reduced now to a bag of ashes in a plastic box, was unable to prevent.

The weather was wonderful—clear, sunny, fresh, but not too cold— and the boat sailed first under the Bay Bridge to give her friends a magnificent view of the city, before turning around near the Alameda air station and heading back under the bridge and around the north side of Alcatraz, under the Golden Gate, and out into the Pacific. Margery tried to calm an emotional Irene, who, recovering from injuries sustained in the Loma Prieta earthquake, was seated in a wheelchair sobbing audibly into a handkerchief between exclamations of, "Glory, hallelujah!" Mme. Hayes, Mrs. Gillette, and Clara sat on deck at the stern with floral wreaths from The Pines and the Reading Roundtable. Dr. Manchester stood with Jack near the starboard prow, where the latter held a copy of *Resurrection in Venice*. He tried to fight back seasickness while he rehearsed the passage he intended to read when the Elysian Foundation poured the ashes into the ocean. Bruno and Hermann remained below deck inside. Bruno drank a cup of coffee and tried to console Hermann who began to cry when he picked up the brown plastic box labeled, *Myrtle Spencer Halstead.*

"It is really heavy, Bruno," he said, choking back tears. "I did not think she was so heavy, like this, I mean her ashes. She was such a good person. And so generous to me. I miss her so much. She should now be here, with us. It is not right. Now I cannot do some things to pay her back." He broke down in tears and sat down on a bench, clutching the plastic box in his strong arms.

Bruno sat down next to Hermann and patted him on the back.

"Look, Hermann. Listen to me. We all miss her. I miss her, too. She gave me a lot, too—a whole education in things that money can't buy and that changed the direction of my life. I needed that change of direction, just like you needed the money she's leaving you."

"It is so much money!" Hermann sobbed, almost angrily. "Two hundred thousand dollars. It is too much. I do not deserve so much."

"But Hermann, I'm sure she had more money than that, and you were one of the few people who did anything for her. And you have a family now to take care of again. When you fly to Germany next week to see them, you'll need money, and if they move to California, you'll also need money. Ms. Halstead knew all of that, I'm sure."

Hermann quieted down as he thought of his upcoming reunion with his family. Suddenly his future had opened up. His world was full of brave new possibilities that nearly overwhelmed him. He bit his lip and Bruno put an arm around his shoulder.

"Look at it this way: she was old, she lived a full life. Remember what the nurse told you? How very happy she was when she wrote the codicil? It gave her pleasure to do that for you, and she died content. We're young . . . well, middle-aged. Our lives have new directions, and we have responsibilities. She wanted you to have that money. And I'll loan you whatever you need until it's transferred to your bank account." Bruno could see Hermann was going to burst out in sobs again and said, "If you promise to stop crying! Get a hold of yourself, man. This is a piece of good fortune. Get used to it."

"Yes, yes. I know. Now it is for happiness I cry, too, pal. Let me cry today. I am so happy and sad at the same time, and I have so much things to think of. After today, I promise I will not cry again till I see Gaby and Sabina and Bert in Germany."

"It's OK. It's even good for you. I don't really mind. But remember the best thing you can do for Ms. Halstead is to use her money for yourself and your family and to not forget her. As a matter of fact, I have a feeling she will be with us for a very long time."

It was time to go up on deck. The ocean was rougher now that the Elysian Foundation boat had passed under the Golden Gate Bridge. It was colder, too, as they approached the mile limit, after which it was legal to scatter ashes over the ocean. The coastlines north and south and the bridge joining the two sides were imposing, almost majestic. The boat idled its engines and the Elysian man held the box near the boat's edge. Margery and Mme. Hayes each said a few words about their departed acquaintance.

Irene managed to say, "Glory, hallelujah," before dissolving into tears.

Hermann said, "Thank you for everything, Ms. Halstead, very much. I miss you very much," and then wept all over again.

Bruno read lines from *The Tempest*.

Declining to say anything, Dr. Manchester remained respectfully silent, while Jack, despite a very queasy stomach, started to read a passage from *Resurrection in Venice*. But the water was so choppy that the Elysian man started to pour the ashes overboard before Jack got very far. Most of the ashes fell into Pacific waters, but a strong gust of wind blew a fine white cloud of Myrtle Spencer Halstead into Jack Peterson's face, tickling his nose at first, but finally choking off his voice. Book in hand, he couldn't stop coughing as he disappeared below deck for the remainder of the trip.

Irene's wheelchair was locked and fastened to a post, and the others on deck hung onto the railings so as not to lose their footing. One after the other they tossed their flower wreaths onto the water in the direction of the ashes. The wreaths bobbed on the choppy surface and floated off. The boat shifted into gear and made one wide circle around the spot where the ashes had been poured. As it turned slowly back toward the Golden Gate Bridge and San Francisco Bay, Bruno and Hermann remained on deck and continued to look west. All they could see receding in the distance were bright flowers floating on blue waters.

PART 2

The Mission

Training—training is everything; training is all there is to a person. We speak of nature; it is folly; there is no such thing as nature. What we call by that misleading name is merely heredity and training. We have no thoughts of our own, no opinions of our own; they are transmitted to us, trained into us.

—Mark Twain

Prologue

March 21, 2008, Good Friday, 6:00 A.M.

IN HIS BEAUTIFUL CEO's office at De Carlo & Wittgenstein on Treasure Island, Bruno hadn't slept all night. Instead, he intermittently paced between the potted ficus tree and the north window or sat in his hi-tech, ergonomic desk chair while recollecting his two-year friendship with Myrtle Spencer Halstead. She had wielded enormous influence on him. She had improved and molded him into a person with serious interests and values that went beyond his ambitions then, and even now, two decades later, beyond the parameters of his enormous success in the art world. Because of her, the masterworks of literature had had a humanizing effect on the flighty and unreliable personality he possessed when they met. He came to love, more than any other novel, the great morality tale of *Les Misérables*. But now he wondered if his admiration for the fictional story of Jean Valjean's heroism and self-sacrifice translated into the courage required in his real life to take on the daunting task for which the CIA had chosen him—to mentor Adolf Hitler's identical twin brother. Following his all-night ruminations, he still felt uncertain.

Mr. De Carlo left the building at 6:15 A.M. and drove his wine-red Maserati out to China Beach. He parked and pulled out of the glove compartment the green scarf with the two gold stripes Myrtle had given him long ago. Ever since she placed it, like an Olympic medal, around his neck that evening in her apartment, he took it with him whenever he could, as a talisman—not that he wore it often. Now it didn't matter that it didn't go with his exquisite charcoal silk suit. It would feel warm around his neck on this chilly morning.

As Bruno walked down the path to the empty beach, he breathed in the fresh ocean air. The water was calm, the waves small. First, he walked southwest until the cliffs stopped his progress. Then he walked northeast along the shore until he came to a breakwater of boulders that jutted a good distance into the water. Bruno stepped up onto one of the large rocks and decided to adjust the scarf that was too loose around his neck. He pulled it off and intended to fold it carefully lengthwise and rebind it more securely, when, startled by the sound of a foghorn, he dropped his arm and loosened his grip on it. At that moment a large black dog, probably part German shepherd, charged past him from out of nowhere, snatched the scarf in its mouth, and plunged headlong into the water.

Bruno yelled at the dog—to no avail. He turned around to look for its owner, but the beach was empty. He watched the dog frolic and swim well beyond the end of the breakwater before returning to shore without his scarf. Pausing next to Bruno, the black dog shook itself and showered his pant legs with saltwater before charging back up the hill pursued by Bruno's curses.

Bruno was struck by a sudden pang of sorrow and despair. He looked out at the Golden Gate Bridge that seemed to come into existence in the expanding light of morning, and then across the water to the impressive brown cliffs of the Marin Headlands. It was in these waters that Myrtle's ashes were scattered twenty years ago. How could he be so careless as to lose this tangible memento she had left him? He felt like a clumsy fool. Ashamed. Full of frustration, he scanned the water's surface where the dog must have abandoned the scarf and took a few tentative steps forward on the rocks closer to the water. Nothing. The water on his pants had soaked through to his skin. He felt numb and cold.

Bruno was about to turn around when something stopped him—an object that seemed to appear on the surface of the water. And it might be green. Or gray? He squinted and it seemed to drift nearer. Yes, it was coming closer. No, it can't be. By God, he could make out a dolphin with his scarf in tow!

"*Mamma mia!*" he exclaimed.

There aren't any dolphins in these waters. This is impossible! Am I dreaming?

He shut his eyes for a moment, but when he opened them it was there again. The sea creature was definitely approaching the breakwater on which he stood. Spontaneously, Bruno waved at the dolphin, thinking to himself, *This is crazy! This can't be happening!* But the dolphin with the scarf securely in its jaws answered his wave by leaping into the air, so that the wet ends of the scarf sailed at its flanks almost like wings. Then it dove under water in a joyful display of physical prowess.

Oh no, it's lost.

But the smooth gray mammal surfaced again, this time very close to the breakwater. The animal held its long smooth snout and the scarf up toward Bruno in a gesture that beckoned the human to venture out to meet it.

Despite his various talents, Bruno feared water and didn't know how to swim. The rocks on which he stood were slippery and dotted with barnacles and mussel shells. The ocean swells seemed larger now. They splashed against the boulders and flung spray into the air. Bruno took a couple of steps before hesitating again when his left foot slipped precipitously.

I can't risk it.

The dolphin took another dive and resurfaced again with the scarf. It came closer still to the end of the breakwater, but Bruno realized it couldn't venture in further without grounding itself in the shallows. Instead, it held up the scarf and rocked its head from side to side as if to say, "Look, I'm doing all I can!"

Torn between his fear and the beckoning sea creature, Bruno hesitated.

It's just a scarf. It's old. Myrtle will never know. I'm cold and wet. This is dangerous.

But then, looking carefully at the rocks, he calculated that if he could just move about three yards further, over a few more boulders, he might be able to reach the scarf. But he couldn't do it standing up.

Bruno lowered himself carefully onto his buttocks and from a sitting position edged his body forward by shifting his hips and legs from one position and one boulder to another. With trembling hands, he grasped whatever firm or jagged surfaces, even clumps of barnacles or mussel shells, that presented themselves.

As the man approached it, the dolphin made a third dive, reappeared, and swam as close to the end of the breakwater as was safe for it. It raised itself as far out of the water as it could and extended its snout toward Bruno's right hand, which he, in turn, stretched as far over the water as possible without losing his balance and falling in, until Bruno held the scarf that the dolphin released to him.

His clothes torn and hands scratched, Bruno sat for several minutes breathing heavily, the scarf, now heavy with sea water, spread over his thighs. He watched the dolphin swim immediately into deeper water before leaping into the air once more in a twisting salute before disappearing into its underwater world. In return Bruno improvised a bold, flourishing salute with his right hand in that direction. Then he half-crawled, half-scrambled back to the shore. As he walked across the sand with the scarf over a shoulder, a beam of sunlight lit up the north tower of the Golden Gate. He no longer felt cold.

1

When Hermann Wittgenstein's pager beeped on April 20, 2008, it startled him, and he spilled coffee on his necktie and slacks.

"*Scheiße!*" he exclaimed under his breath as he grabbed some tissues from the polished granite dispenser and rose from his expansive rosewood desk at De Carlo & Wittgenstein's art and auction house. He turned off the pager and dabbed at his spotted clothes. He pushed his chair back from the desk and looked at the blotches. Annoyed with himself, he hoped they would dry before he reached the airport. There was no time to go home to change clothes. He'd been in a meeting with his boss, Bruno, that had run past 11:30 A.M.

Now he pressed the intercom button and asked, "Gaby, *kommt der Flug rechtzeitig an?*"

The familiar, calm voice of his wife at the reception desk answered, "Yes, Hermann. The flight's on time, at 1:05 this afternoon." Then she whispered with a slight reprimand in her tone, "Hermann, *Du sollst doch Englisch sprechen!*"

Yes, of course, he should speak English. But she must know how nervous he was. He had to meet Adolf Hitler's twin brother at San Francisco International, Air France flight 300 from Paris, and he had been thinking about it in German. Even though he knew that this Hitler only spoke French and some broken English, it was hard not to think about a close relative of Adolf Hitler in German.

As he traversed his spacious office toward his private restroom, he glanced out the window and marveled momentarily at how much San Francisco had changed since his arrival in the mid-1980s, when the Mark Hopkins, the Pyramid building, and Coit Tower were the outstanding skyline features. The new millennium had added gleaming towers of tinted glass, which made him almost nostalgic for the San Francisco that had originally welcomed him. Not everything had changed. Foghorns still sounded when the fog rolled in, and tourists still crowded Fisherman's Wharf, except for those that drove to Napa to taste wine these days.

In the restroom Hermann peered in the mirror and practiced the greeting he would use at the airport, "Bonjour Monsieur Lamour! *Bienvenue en Californie! Comment allez-vous? Je suis* Hermann Wittgenstein, *de l'entreprise* De Carlo & Wittgenstein."

He hoped, of course, Jean-Louis Lamour would understand he was just trying to be polite. He even hoped Hitler's twin would know German, as irrational as that thought might be; it just didn't seem possible that he didn't. He also hoped the twenty-one-year-old would be too tired from the long flight to talk very much. He would suggest he take a nap in the backseat of the Mercedes. He had instructed the company's chauffeur to program some music in the car's audio system—Wagner, Beethoven, Liszt, Debussy, Ravel, Edith Piaf, country Western, the latter just in case he was curious about American music.

Hermann was prepared to talk with him about the reception and exhibit at De Carlo & Wittgenstein of his earliest *boulist* paintings, completed during his late teens in Colombières-sur-Orb. Beyond that he wouldn't know what to say. He wished Bruno would have met this plane, or anyone else in their firm. At the very least, he wished *he* could have driven the car so he would have something to do. But now Donald Washington was the executive chauffeur, and it was Donald's job to drive.

The first time Donald donned his white gloves, tailored chauffeur's uniform, and cap, he had himself photographed in front of the company's fleet of Jaguars, Mercedes, and BMWs in front of the extravagant Gerard Kerry-designed headquarters on Treasure Island—which rivaled the Sydney Opera House and the Bilbao Guggenheim in its quirky architecture. Donald had a good eye for a photo op, and a framed copy of the photo ended up in Bruno's office next to photos of Myrtle, an old stone house in southern France, Bruno's mother, and even a picture Pope John XXIII—a gift Mrs. Dicarlomini had sent her son for his fiftieth birthday. From then on Donald insisted everyone stop referring to him as "Ol' Black Donald." Now, it was "Donald" or "Mr. Washington." Untalented though he was, Donald loved to drive, just as much as Hermann did. Normally, Hermann didn't complain. After all, he was a partner in this hugely successful art and auction house and making so much money it would be ungrateful to whine about the infrequent downsides of his work, but this particular task upset him. He asked himself what Myrtle would have thought but drew a blank.

2

HEAVY TURBULENCE OVER HUDSON Bay shook Hitler's identical twin out of his slumber in a center seat of the first-class compartment on Air France flight 300 from Paris to San Francisco.

"*Merde*," he said out loud, causing Latrone Sanders, the CIA agent next to the righthand window to glance over at this passenger whom he was trailing on this important and sensitive mission, and to check his electronic gadgetry. There was nothing any of them could do about the turbulence but wait it out. Sanders knew that clear air turbulence, where fast-moving meets slow-moving air in the jet stream, could suddenly plunge an aircraft hundreds if not thousands of feet down, and normal turbulence, if severe, could rip apart even the largest jumbo jet. There were forces of nature, he mused anxiously, that were stronger than any structure or object that man could build. He had been a child when the Loma Prieta earthquake struck in 1989. He had been listening to a James Brown tape on his boom box when he was supposed to be doing his homework. His mother, Irene Sanders, a nurse at the Pines, had come to his room four different times to tell him to turn it off. Finally, she screamed at him that he was becoming a good-for-nothing disappointment, and that Ms. Halstead would be ashamed of him. That was designed to make him feel exceptionally guilty. Next, she said if he didn't shut it off by the time she counted to five, he would be sorry forever. Then she started to count, "One. Two. Three. Four."

Latrone didn't know what his mother would do that would make him sorry forever, and he actually did feel guilty. Moreover, he really did intend to turn it off on the count of five. But just as he reached for the off switch and his mother began to yell out the word "*five*," he was knocked off his feet by the earthquake. It was precisely 5:04 P.M. on October 17, 1989, and their rented house in Santa Cruz split in two at the threshold to his bedroom where his mother stood, and his mother disappeared under an avalanche of collapsing building materials as the "*five!*" she began to call out transformed itself into a scream of terror that sounded like "*Eeeeeeooooww*" before it was extinguished under the pile of rubble.

Stunned, Latrone found himself sitting on the floor, which continued to bump and sway to the soulful wailings of James Brown while lamps and books crashed down around him. His bedroom was the only part of the house that remained more or less intact.

It had been a defining turning point in Latrone's life. Although his mother was able to attend Ms. Halstead's funeral a month after the earthquake, she was still in great discomfort. During her slow convalescence she and Latrone were forced to move in with Irene's sister in San Jose for six months. During this period Latrone became a different human being—cheerful, and a model student, whose only ambition was to make his mother proud.

Once Irene Sanders was well again, she purchased a condo in East Palo Alto with her inheritance from Myrtle. There she supported herself and her son with disability checks and money she made caregiving homebound seniors. Latrone finished high school and attended Santa Clara University on a scholarship and part-time work. Then he passed the government exams and joined the CIA in Washington, DC where he was building a career.

Now, if this plane made it from Paris to San Francisco, he would visit his mother on his days off and tell her stories about his job that would make her smile and pinch him on the chin and say, "Miz Halstead would be so proud of you."

But Latrone had serious doubts he would ever see his mother again. The turbulence was such that he worried about the airplane's tensile strength. After all, it was a European Airbus, and several of them had crashed in recent years. Maybe it was poorly built like their rental house in Santa Cruz. That house had been constructed before the stricter codes and wasn't close to being earthquake-proof or even earthquake-resistant. There was a big difference between those terms if you were talking about an earthquake of six or seven on the Richter scale, or one that was eight or nine, or even ten. After all, a ten *was* possible. And nothing man-made would withstand that kind of force. And it was really the same principle with aircraft. What's more, there had been an uptick in cabin injuries during the past three years involving unbelted passengers who had received brain injuries from hitting the ceiling during sudden turbulence. Damn! He wished he weren't so afraid of flying. He couldn't stop thinking about the dire possibilities. He hated this part of his job.

The more Latrone contemplated these terrifying risks, the more his bowels wanted to move, but the captain had put on the fasten seatbelt signs and warned passengers over the loudspeaker to refrain from moving about the cabin. Latrone always admired the passengers with the guts to defy the captain's warning, and now he agonized between the growing urgency to get to a bathroom and the fear of being thrown against the ceiling of the cabin. They really should issue helmets on these flights, he thought. Then the risk of brain injury to passengers whose natural urges couldn't wait out the turbulence would at least be reduced. He remained in his seat wondering how long he could stand the anxiety.

In his center seat, Monsieur Hitler II, as Latrone thought of him, had had the presence of mind, or maybe just the dumb luck, to ring for a cabin attendant, order another small bottle of Veuve Clicquot, and have a quick flirt with the stewardess at the first sign of turbulence, before the captain ordered even the cabin attendants to remain seated with seatbelts buckled. Latrone was envious, since he wasn't allowed to drink on the job. *Shit*, he thought as the jumbo jet bucked and rocked at 39,000 feet.

After Jean-Louis downed the bottle of champagne, he adjusted his pillow and blanket on his already fully reclined seat, closed his eyes and grunted with contentment. He absentmindedly twisted one of the locks of his dark, stringy, shoulder-length hair around his index finger and then around the downward curl of the right half of his shaggy moustache, and thought about what his friend Gilles had told him about flying back in France.

Gilles was the only one of his friends to have flown on a jet airplane— a roundtrip from Montpellier to Corsica. When Gilles returned from his week in Corsica, he talked incessantly about those flights—on *Air Liberté*, forty-two minutes on the way down, and forty-seven minutes on the way back—the difference because of rain and side winds on takeoff.

Gilles had saved his boarding passes and ticket stubs. He had also kept the napkins and paper cups, in short everything with the airline logo he could stuff into his shoulder bag—even the little airline pillow—and shown it to Jean-Louis. He also described the exhilarating odor of jet fuel, the mighty whine and rumble of the engines, the jiggling and bouncing of taxiing, the surprising speed, the startling rattling noises during take-offs, the growl of the landing gear coming down, the enormous jolts of the landings on one wheel, the mighty G-forces that pushed you back into your seat, and most of all the tremendous turbulence taking off from Ajaccio on the return trip through driving rain and storm clouds that lasted for at least five full minutes, and how all of this was perfectly normal. Nothing to worry about. A plane could take all of that. That was what airplanes were built to do.

Jean-Louis recalled all the things his friend had said about flying, and profited not only from them, but also from the effects of the fine champagne. He realized the motions were not much worse than the bumping of the garbage truck he and another buddy, Pascal, used to drive through the winding roads around Colombières, so he was perfectly able to trust the integrity of this impressive machine, the likes of which he had never seen. As he grew sleepy, he imagined he was back in southern France on a warm summer day when he dozed in the garbage truck after drinking a glass of pastis. Pascal, unaware how short his life would be, would drive the hairpin turns up the Orb River Valley after stocking up on Berlou rosé at the winery in the mountains south of the Gorges d'Héric.

Latrone tightened his seatbelt even tighter and watched the peacefully slumbering Hitler twin. While the plane tossed and lurched nauseatingly toward California, he gripped the armrests and thought if he weren't black his knuckles would have been white.

3

JACK PETERSON, ESQUIRE, SAN Francisco's unofficial novelist laureate, stepped up to the telescope on his fourth-floor balcony. He removed its cover and swiveled it to point down toward St. Theresa's emergency room entrance to engage in some late-afternoon ambulance-watching. He had a busy schedule for a ninety-five-year-old, and he didn't feel guilty about indulging in some R & R. Not that he felt much different from seventy-five. His white hair was still magnificent, his physique slim. Maybe he'd lost an inch of height and added a few wrinkles, but his prostate operation had been a complete success, his novels were widely read, and next week Gloria Majestic would tape a television program on his life as an author in his suite at The Pines. Sure, he was getting on in years, but more and more people were making it to one hundred and five these days, so he could easily have ten years left. Wasn't life wonderful!

He did a few leg and arm stretches as he stood at his telescope and some thigh and buttocks squeezes for muscle tone as he looked through the lens. Nothing was happening, so he turned the telescope toward some other buildings. But even the windows with open curtains held little interest for him. Inside these homes and offices Jack could see people were engaged in humdrum everyday activities: working, eating, TV-watching, sleeping, lovemaking—no stories there.

At such moments, he wished he had moved up to the twenty-sixth-floor penthouse or even into Myrtle Halstead's apartment after she passed away. From there he could have seen the bay, the Golden Gate, Sausalito, Coit Tower, Berkeley, and the Bay Bridge—distant horizons and other perspectives. But he knew those sights and even the physical closeness to his literary mentor were not what he needed for inspiration. What he, Jack Peterson, author of six bestsellers, needed—and his formula always worked—was the view of the emergency room. When characters crossed the threshold into that traumatic and sacred space, they passed from everyday normalcy into new lives, lives that had been suddenly, catastrophically changed by fate. Entering there meant abandoning the familiar, moving into new terrain, new realms of psychological and physical woe, pain, and agony, but also of hope, struggle against the odds, courage, and finally, triumph. Adversity made winners of his characters. That's what his readers liked to hear. That's what he could write about. That's what inspired him.

Jack waited in the sunshine and paced leisurely on his balcony until his patience was rewarded with the wail of a siren. He quickly placed his right eye to his telescope as the ambulance, accompanied by a fire truck and a police car, rolled up to the emergency entrance. His hands trembled slightly as he focused in at the scene. This might inspire a story.

4

Hermann gave Gaby a quick kiss at the reception desk on the bottom floor of De Carlo & Wittgenstein's big office building next door to the warehouses and galleries on the northern edge of Treasure Island, and across the street from Weber Brothers new sound studio.

"*Ich werde gegen zehn Uhr zu Hause sein* (I'll be home around ten). . ."

"English, please, Hermann," his wife insisted in a low voice.

"Yeah, you're right, *Liebste*," replied Hermann.

Hermann and Gaby had spoken German at home, after work, when their children, Sabina and Bert, were growing up in the city, but the kids had resisted speaking German, making dinner conversations unpleasant. Gaby and the children had left East Germany back in 1990, a year after the fall of the Berlin Wall, and Hermann and Gaby didn't want their kids to lose proficiency in their native language. So, Hermann had the bad habit of thinking in German most of the time. At work, sometimes at important business meetings, he would forget to speak English and not realize he was going on in German to clients until they laughed or signaled they were not amused. Bruno had told him over and over to stick to English, because the more he used it, the more it would improve. Hermann knew Bruno was right, but he was often embarrassed, because he knew he still made mistakes. Of course, his English was much better than when Hermann first got to know Bruno and lived in his basement and fixed his electricity and called him "Mr. De Carlo, pal." He felt foolish whenever he thought about "Mr. De Carlo, pal," and hoped Bruno had forgotten about it. Myrtle, he knew, would be proud of how much he had improved, and he missed her. She was someone who would have been glad to correct his mistakes, and he wouldn't have minded, because they had had such a great relationship and she had reminded him of so much of his grandmother.

Gaby paged Donald, who was in the underground parking lot, to drive the Jaguar up to the portico, where Hermann ultimately met him. She was well aware how dramatically their lives had changed due to historical events. Soon after the Wall came down, she and Hermann had been reunited in a West Berlin hotel for the first time since his escape. They spent the entire night awake in bed in each other's arms. For the first two hours she reprimanded him for his escape and her terrible time since his departure. Then she apologized, since, after all, she had encouraged him to escape. Then Hermann described how lonely he had been in San Francisco, and how he'd become an electrician, lived in the basement of his boss's house before Mr. De Carlo became rich and famous, and how he'd met this wonderful old lady who reminded him of his grandmother and who had willed him $200,000, and how he would buy a house for them in the Sunset District, and how he sometimes drove a red Thunderbird around the city by the bay. They talked and cried and laughed all night long about their past, present, and future, and never got around to making love. The next day, Hermann saw his children again. They greeted him awkwardly with mixed emotions. But when he took them all out to a good restaurant and to see *Pretty Woman* in a West Berlin movie theater, they couldn't wait to move to California.

But that was two decades ago. A whole other life. Now Gaby was the receptionist for De Carlo & Wittgenstein. Not that she *had* to work. Her husband was a wealthy partner in this thriving art and auction house that had surpassed the local Butterfield's and Sotheby's in business and prestige. She and Hermann had a beautiful home in the Marina, much more elegant than their first house in the Sunset district. But after their children left home, she wanted to get out of the house, as the Americans put it. She spoke excellent English and loved the bright, modern, and spacious reception area in this wacky building with its wonderful views around the San Francisco Bay. She often thought back to her workplace in the shoe factory in East Berlin and shuddered. It had been so dark, dingy, cold, and unsafe. To be fair, though, she had had good woman friends; they had commiserated regularly during breaks and lunch and on the streetcars and in the cafes about their lives in East Germany, about the drabness of everything, about the regime's rigidity; they had complained about the difficulties of raising children and about the boorishness of their husbands who didn't share equally in the housework.

They enjoyed their solidarity, and they enjoyed complaining together. These had been warm, human relationships that she missed in America.

Back in East Berlin, their apartment had been cramped and ugly, but she knew all her neighbors by name and greeted them every day. Back then she chatted with her grocer and baker. In San Francisco, her house was large and comfortable, expensively furnished and beautifully landscaped, but she rarely saw her neighbors, let alone talked to them. She couldn't even talk to their gardeners and house cleaners, because they spoke Spanish. So, it was better to get out of the house and go to work where she could meet new people. Everyone liked her. Things weren't perfect, but they had worked out better than she could have imagined.

She looked through the big glass windows now and saw her husband, who, even in his tailored business suits, always managed to look ruffled, talking to the executives' chauffeur. Donald looked like somebody famous, but she didn't know whom. She knew Hermann would be trying to persuade Donald to let him drive the Jaguar, and the black chauffeur would be telling him that was *his* job. Neither she nor Hermann could fathom how Donald, so lacking in qualifications, had gotten his job, but Bruno had hired Donald years ago.

"Look, Hermann," Donald said, "you know you should be phoning people or texting people while we go. You know that, dude. Not driving, no way. 'Cause *I'm* the driver, man. *You* gotta concentrate on the important stuff, like this French artist, Jean-Louis, this Hitler clone or twin, or whatever he is."

"What?! How do you know *that*? Who told you that?"

Donald raised a bony finger and replied, "Well, shit! Like, you don' think somethin' like that can be kept secret from me, do you? From Ol' Black Donald? Come on, man. I know what's what. Donald knows stuff, you know." Donald jabbed Hermann boldly with his bony finger in the middle of his chest.

Hovering over him, Hermann gaped in disbelief. Then Donald smiled his inscrutable smile, and Hermann stepped back, realizing it wasn't Donald's fault he knew. Donald simply knew everything; it was an inborn talent, akin to perfect pitch, and a mystery. And Hermann knew Donald could be trusted with the important things.

But then he got annoyed all over again.

"Donald, what are you doing with this Jaguar?" Hermann said, looking at the dark green car at the curbside. "Why didn't you bring a Mercedes, or a BMW?" Hermann thought Hitler's twin would be more comfortable in one of the German-built company cars.

"Hermann, you not the boss. Mister De Carlo paged me to take a green Jaguar today . . . and *he's* the boss!" Donald stated this with authoritative emphasis and smiled to show he had upstaged Hermann.

Hermann glanced back through the windows toward Gaby to indicate his exasperation with Donald, as if she would know what they argued about. But Gaby pointed to her watch to signal the two men to get going. She saw her husband glance at his own watch and then saw how he and Donald quickly got into the Jaguar, Donald in the driver's seat and Hermann on the passenger side. Then she watched as the car ran up over the curb and bounced down into the driveway and disappeared.

5

BRUNO RECLINED ON HIS back in his twenty-five-thousand-dollar ergonomic leather executive's chair that was stuffed with NASA memory foam
to maximize back support and minimize pressure points. The attached
custom swing-arm stand for holding books and papers adjustable to the
optimal viewing distance supported one of the gold-embossed De Carlo &
Wittgenstein document folders visible to anyone in his office. He always
left one on top of whatever else he was reading, and as the intercom buzzed
now, he jerked with such a start that his copy of Cervantes's *Don Quixote*,
the Ormsby translation, fell off the stand onto his lap.

He pushed the intercom button on the armrest and Gaby's voice said,
"Sorry to disturb you, but it's Olaf Knudtson, calling from Washington."

"OK, put him on."

Bruno pushed the speaker phone button built into the marvelous chair
so he could talk to the CIA's biotechnology division chief while he set his
Cervantes volume back onto the stand underneath the document folder.

"Yes, how are you, Mr. Knudtson? We hope the weather has improved
in the East for you . . . Very well, thank you . . . El Niño has spared us this year
. . . Yes, we've received all the documentation and we'll keep you informed
by phone and email . . . Yes, of course I understand, Mr. Knudtson. And yes,
I can assure you we will adhere to the greatest secrecy. Only my partner and
I know about Monsieur Lamour's true identity. And you've probably seen
the file on him—Hermann Wittgenstein, my partner—who was formerly

an East German secret policeman? . . . Yes, that's right. He escaped in 1985 and emigrated to California where he had an uncle. Originally, he was my electrician. I've known him ever since then. He's totally reliable. So, we're well equipped to keep track of Hitler's twin and to promote him . . . In my opinion he's an acceptable, second-rate artist, and it's an advantage that he already has a bit of a reputation in the south of France. We'll be able to make something of this so-called *boulist* trend he started there . . . I can assure you he'll do so well in the art world in San Francisco he'll have no time for political involvement."

The call over, Bruno leaned back and thought about his history with Olaf Knudtson, who contacted him several years after Myrtle's death and at the beginning of his spectacular rise in the art world. Gerard Kerry's plans had been completed for his new postmodern gallery and auction house campus, and the ground on the Treasure Island site had just been broken. Out of the blue, Knudtson wanted his help to deliver an important piece of information to an Interpol contact in Istanbul. Stunned, Bruno had balked. What could the CIA possibly want from him? But then they told him the agency had tracked his harmless drug deal for the Jaguar lady back in 1989, and it was not too late to prosecute him. Knudtson assured De Carlo they had the goods on him. They hadn't pursued the matter back then because the Jaguar lady happened to be a "special friend" of the vice president of the United States, but Knudtson had kept an eye on De Carlo's international business travel and knew he had language skills, contacts, and cultural sophistication that could be useful. So, Bruno couldn't refuse this gentle extortion, and he subsequently played a role in several international capers for the agency, nothing particularly dangerous, thank goodness. What would have become of his business if he hadn't cooperated? Of his dreams? Of the fortune to which he aspired in the new world? Everything could have died on the vine.

It turned out he was successful on several minor missions. They hadn't been a lot of bother, and he had met some amusing characters. He smiled now as he recalled the memorable nights in luxury hotel suites and fabulous meals in Paris, Lyon, and Naples, not to mention that spectacular excursion flight over Mt. Everest on a nearly cloudless day—all on the government's dime. By now Olaf Knudtson trusted him and hoped he made the right choice in Bruno. Because this mission was not a minor one. It was unique, and it was major.

6

As FLIGHT 300 FROM Charles De Gaulle approached the Bay Area, Latrone stared out his window. He now wished he'd been seated in the middle of the plane instead. When you couldn't see out the window, takeoffs and landings were less terrifying because you couldn't tell how far you were from the ground or the water. All you could worry about were unseen private aircraft encroaching into the flight paths of scheduled airliners. Latrone knew this became more likely the closer you came to an airport, and that in general takeoffs and landings were the most dangerous flight segments, partly because of increased air traffic, and partly because, especially when you landed, pilots were tired and less able to concentrate on what they were doing.

Now, remembering what he'd learned in his stress-reduction class, Sanders inhaled and exhaled slowly a few times. He closed his eyes and tried to pretend he was snoozing in his office chair in Noe Valley. But when the wing of the mammoth Air France Airbus tipped suddenly, he opened his eyes with a start and looked out to see what had happened. He peered into the impenetrable fog of a white cloud and couldn't see a thing—not Mt. Diablo, not Oakland or Fremont across the bay, not any sailboats on the water underneath them. Maybe they weren't that close yet. They could crash into the bay without seeing it coming. Was the plane's altimeter accurate? If *he* couldn't see anything, would the pilots be able to see the runway?

The young CIA agent glanced resentfully at the center seat where Hitler's brother slept like a baby with a silly smile on his lips, oblivious to the imminent danger facing this aircraft, which might very soon slam into the water, crashing short of the runway.

Shit! We survive all that turbulence, we make it all this way, and then it ends like this—drowned in cold water and mud, twisted around metal airplane parts.

He recalled the infamous TWA flight 800 that exploded out of New York in 1996. *It* had been on its way *to* Paris. Now *this* plane was returning *from* Paris! And there hadn't been any major crashes at SFO for a long time, either. So, the law of averages, or maybe chaos theory, said it was time for something to happen again. And with his luck, it would happen now, on *this* jet, the one *he* was on, not to mention the uncanny character across from him.

To distract his mind, Mr. Sanders thought about his stupid mission—trailing the clone of Adolf Hitler! Well, actually, his twin. But then an identical twin was for practical purposes a clone, wasn't it? With the same monozygotic genes? Here we are, over a century after Adolf Hitler's birth. World War II is history, although people like to say history repeats itself, but that's only a cliché and not true. Similarities occur, but circumstances are always different. A second Hitler would never happen, especially here in America, and the government was spending unconscionable sums for the secret surveillance of this character.

Latrone glanced over at the subject he was tracking with the disheveled facial hair. Just look at him! Now he mulled over the details he had learned of the story of his origins—about the night Adolf Hitler's mother bore two babies, identical boy twins, back in 1889, in an Austrian brewery inn where the Hitlers rented rooms as boarders.

The midwife in attendance, herself barren and in desperate desire of a child, had not told Frau Hitler during her pregnancy that she suspected twins, and Klara Hitler's belly did not bulge more than many other pregnant women during her nine months of waiting. When Frau Hitler went into labor, the midwife was prepared. As soon as the new mother was delivered of the two sons, she gave Frau Hitler a whiff of something sweet to smell, which made her fall asleep. She quickly hid one of the infants in her brown canvas satchel and carried it down the back stairs to the inn's basement where its cries would not be heard. Then she raced back up, fetched Fräulein Müller, the apprentice midwife, who was heating water in another room, and handed the other baby to her, saying all was well. Frau Hitler was exhausted and asleep. She instructed

Fräulein Müller to clean the baby boy and lay it on its mother's breast as soon as Frau Hitler woke up. Then Hilde Neuhauser departed through the basement, saying she was taking the jar of preserved beets Frau Hitler had promised her. When the midwife left from the cellar door at the back of the inn, she carried her satchel close to her heart.

It was a bitterly cold night, unusual that late in April, with a carpeting of snow on the ground as Hilde began her trek to her house in the neighboring village. She took the longer route next to the river so that if the infant cried, the noise of the river would drown out the sound. Near the river she wouldn't encounter anyone this time of night. After thirty minutes she saw the lights of her village. The baby, well bundled in her satchel, was breathing peacefully. He had not cried, and she was eager to tell her husband, Franz, about their good fortune. She might have quickened her pace, when, in the darkness, she slipped on a smooth, icy rock. Her foot skidded out from under her, she lost her balance and fell in the direction of the river but was saved from sliding into the freezing current by a Linden tree, whose bare branches she was able to grab. For a moment she was glad she hadn't injured herself, but as she pulled herself up, she realized her satchel was gone.

"Mein Gott! Das Kind! Der kleine Bub'!" She wanted to scream, and without thinking she slid to the river's edge and plunged her hands into the current in search of the bundle. She waded several steps into icy water and peered desperately downstream, but it was dark, the river flowed swiftly, and beyond that point, it was deep, and she couldn't see anything. Struck, as if by lightning to her nervous system, she flailed wildly with her arms on the surface of the fast-moving water. Sobbing and wailing, she beat the water's surface with her hands, splashing herself. Despite the cold, she felt white hot with fear. What had she done?

As a half-moon appeared from behind some clouds, she turned toward the shore as if to search for a face that might help her. But there was no one, and what would she have said if there had been? In turning her body, she noticed a promontory of earth held together by mighty tree roots supporting a thick trunk and tall tree that jutted into the water and created a miniature inlet, rather calm, right at the bank, and that an object floated in it—no, two objects. She lunged at one of the objects and held up her satchel—empty—and flung it on the shore. Then she reached for the baby's body and grabbed it to her bosom. She shook it and pleaded with it—to cry, to scream, to breathe. But the baby was already cold and lifeless.

Hilde could see from the garden behind their house that Franz had left candles burning in the kitchen for her. He probably would have left soup on the stove, before he went to bed upstairs. She couldn't go inside until she hid the body. She couldn't bring it into the house because of the cats. She thought a moment, shivering and trembling now in her cold wet clothes. She looked around the garden and at their small pond. She pushed aside the bushes that surrounded it, bent down, and placed some round stones into the satchel where she had placed the baby after pulling it out of the current—carefully, so as not to scratch his now frigid, but perfect, innocent body. She didn't want to harm it in any way. She had wanted to love it, to suckle it, to raise it, the child she had always wanted and was not able to give to Franz. She would tell him in the morning. She would have to. He would know what to do.

Now she lowered the heavy bundle into the shallow pond. The water was dark from an accumulation of rotten leaves and organic matter. She saw that it sank gently under the surface a short way down and rested on the soft, muddy bottom, less than a meter deep. No one would suspect it or be able to see it even if the sun were to shine the next day.

The temperature dropped over night, and the next day Hilde and Franz Neuhauser's pond was frozen solid. But Franz devised a plan. Two days later, in the dead of night, Franz and Hilde were up with picks, axes, crowbars, and shovels. Franz had pulled the small donkey cart into the garden, next to the pond—ever so slowly so as not to make any noise—and shoveled it full of snow and ice and laid a net and coils of long, sturdy rope into it. In the cover of darkness, he and Hilde hacked at the ice near the edge of their pond. They hoped they wouldn't arouse the neighbors, most of whom were farmers who worked hard and slept well. Hilde worried it would never work; the ice was hard as stone. But Franz was a strong man, skilled and determined, a blacksmith by profession. Once they had managed to saw and hack a shallow rift in the ice, Franz was able to pry a large block that contained the satchel up from the pond's edge and lift it at an angle onto the ground. Together they were able to roll and pry it up a wooden ramp into the cart. Franz covered it well with snow and burlap. He spread several layers of canvas over the top and tied everything down to the cart and set out.

By the time Franz Neuhauser reached the end of the path leading to the glacier early the next afternoon, and the donkey cart could go no further, the block of ice had partially melted and was small enough that the contours of the satchel inside were blurred yet visible. Franz stared at it with sorrow in his heart—for his wife, the innocent boy encapsulated inside, for himself, and for the crime they were concealing. He had always been an honorable man, but he loved Hilda too much to see her imprisoned, and he knew how to hide their actions so that no one would be harmed and there would be no consequences. No one could possibly be hurt by his plan.

Now he tied together the block of ice and the sturdy metal box he had constructed the day before in his blacksmith's shop. He placed them into the net, slung the long ropes around his neck and started up the path in winter sunshine that glinted so brightly off the white snow that he had to squint. Several hours later, nearly exhausted from trudging up the mountain, he reached the edge of the deep crevasse in the glacier he knew so well from his childhood. The glacier and this crevasse had moved a short but noticeable distance since he left the village of his youth when he was eighteen, married Hilde and moved to the edge of Galgendorf fifteen years ago.

For several minutes Franz sat resting on a large rock that jutted out of the snow as he looked at the objects in the net. More ice had melted from around the satchel, enough that he imagined he could see the contours of an infant through the ice that still clung to the cloth. When tears began to stream down his cheeks, he allowed himself to weep out loud, alone as he was at the glacier. But he had to finish his task. He bowed his head and said a silent prayer, asking God's blessings on the baby—the son he would have loved and raised as his own—confessing his sins, asking forgiveness for his wife, and good health for the baby that survived. The light of day was beginning to wane; he needed to start down the trail. He carefully tied one end of the coiled ropes to the net, stood up and walked out onto a boulder that stuck out over the glacier's crevasse. For a moment he held the net and its contents close to his chest and suppressed a sob. Then he said out loud, "Auf Wiedersehen, armer Junge," and began to lower the net slowly into the deepest depths of the fissure, where the ice was a deep blue. He had prepared plenty of rope, and he had tied a heavy rock to the end of it so he could toss the rock in such a way that the rope end couldn't stick to an icy wall on its way to the bottom. Now he began to lower the bundle slowly into the frozen abyss, where it would rest, well hidden. When at last, with aching arms and burning palms, he only held the rock at the end of the rope, he tossed it a few meters away from the bundle and listened to see if he would hear it hit the bottom, but it disappeared without making a sound.

In 1987, the avid mountain climber and distinguished American scientist, Dr. Philip Seed, conducted research on cryogenics during his sabbatical at the university laboratories in Salzburg. One fine afternoon, when he should have been home with his highly pregnant Mexican-American wife, Carmina, who was due to deliver any day, he was hiking at the base of the Schreckensgletscher glacier when he spied some indistinct brownish objects lodged next to a boulder perhaps two hundred meters up a slope. He knew he ought to hurry home, but he couldn't resist taking a short detour up to the boulder to inspect those objects. After all, years ago this same glacier had afforded him a spectacular find—of a well-preserved frozen weasel, from the mid-sixteenth century according to the x-rays and carbon dating conducted on it. The find had made the newspapers in Salzburg and in the Italian Dolomites, where it came to rest in a local mountaineering museum, which credited Dr. Seed with the remarkable discovery.

Seed had always been inexorably drawn to the cold and to high mountains. A day without snow or a drink without ice cubes was a bad day for him. Thus, his natural proclivities overlapped with his professional pursuits. Arriving at the boulder, Seed found some rotten twisted rope, a shredded net, and a small metal box encased in a layer of ice, as well as a large chunk of ice with something frozen inside. It was probably another small animal—perhaps another find to impress the anthropologists. To lighten it he chipped some ice off the hunk with a hand pick and packed the objects into the large, empty backpack he always took on his hikes in perpetual preparation for another serendipitous encounter. He trudged back down the mountain, put the backpack into the trunk of his leased Renault, and drove to town where he parked near a Lidl grocery store in order to purchase some plastic bags. Outside the store he placed the now-dripping objects into the bags before taking them to his laboratory at the university.

Philip Seed thought again about his wife, but then he thought Women have babies every day, *and the frozen objects could constitute a significant discovery which could make the entire foreign sabbatical worth it.*

Once inside his laboratory, Seed placed the block of ice with the indistinct object into a large sink under a trickle of warm water. He placed the metal box onto the hard surface of a working counter and hacked away at it with pick and hammer to remove the remaining encrusted ice. When the box was freed, he examined it for a latch, edge, wedge or some mechanism by which it could be opened, but there was nothing. It appeared to be handmade, and the seam that separated the lid from the base of the box was soldered shut. He bent down to retrieve the electric metal saw from the shelves below the counter, plugged its cord into an outlet and attacked the box again. The motor and the blade spinning on metal made a loud, irritating, raspy noise, and the sparks that flew out from the saw showered down all around him. The cutting was slow and laborious, and Dr. Seed was careful not to damage whatever might be contained inside the box. He didn't hear the zaps and sizzles when some of the sparks landed in the sink, creating miniature lightning strikes in the tub and on the sack in it.

When the scientist had cut through two edges of the rectangular box, he was able with a screwdriver to pry it open sufficiently to pull out the papers he found inside. Amazingly, they were dry. The box seemed to be lined with something smooth. Was it lead? At any rate, the carefully folded sheets of paper had suffered no water damage, and the handwriting was as legible as if written yesterday. But they were dated April 22, 1889 and in the old German Sütterlin Handschrift. *Seed had studied German in the 1950s, and taught himself how to read the old-fashioned handwriting, so he could make out what was said:*

> You, the reader of this letter, will learn herein of the shame and crime of Franz and Hilde Neuhauser of Galgendorf, who were too weak and cowardly to confess to the authorities our terrible deeds. When you read this, we will long since be buried along with our appalling secret. My beloved wife, who was never able to bear us a child, was midwife to Klara Hitler, and took, out of love, one of Frau Hitler's twin boys, whom Hilde delivered into this world of sorrows the night of April 20, 1889, hoping that we might raise it as our own, for we dearly desired to have a child. With her skills as a midwife, my wife concealed the birth of Frau Hitler's second boy from the mother and stole him away from the brewery inn the night of his birth, leaving Frau Hitler and her other healthy son in the capable hands of Fräulein Margarethe Müller. Making her way home in the dark, my wife slipped, alas, next to the river, and the baby, concealed in a satchel, fell into the cold waters and perished. Why God chose to punish the infant for Hilde's crime, we will never know, and our guilt will torture us until the end of our days. I confess all of this to you, future companion in this veil of tears, whosoever you may be, if God wills that someone should be appraised of this terrible truth, because I am compelled to confess to someone or something, even if just to this piece of paper, what

otherwise will exist only in the troubled hearts and minds
of two unhappy people, until we die. May God grant us an
early death. May God grant Frau Hitler's surviving son a
long and illustrious life. And may God's eternal wrath slay
me if what I say be not true.

It was signed, "The most unhappy Franz Neuhauser,
Schmiedemeister of Galgendorf."

Three more sheets, in a clumsier hand, told the details
of the birth in the brewery inn and of the midwife's catastrophic trek home; they were signed, "Hilde Neuhauser."

No sooner had Philip Seed read these astonishing epistles than he
was startled to hear gurgling, cooing sounds coming from the sink.
He turned on his heel and literally leapt the three meters to the
basin to find a naked pink infant boy lying on its back, surrounded
by tattered fabric fragments. He was opening and closing his little
lips as if to lap in the lukewarm water that was trickling onto his
face from the running faucet. Philip Seed looked around wildly to
see if someone else had perchance entered the laboratory while he
was busy opening the metal box. But there was no one. He had the
presence of mind to stick the extraordinary letters into the breast
pocket of his jacket, and to turn off the faucet. He noticed that the
baby's umbilical cord was freshly tied and not yet trimmed, and
realized immediately, that if the letters weren't a hoax, the baby
must have survived drowning a century ago by the same mechanism, a kind of cryogenic sleep, that young children occasionally
lived through when suddenly plunged into icy water. Then, quickly
frozen in the Neuhauser pond and in the glacier's ice, it had moved
slowly down the mountain over the last century until he chanced
upon it. The sparks that landed on it in the sink must have sent an
electrical shock to its nervous system that reanimated it. It was all
too extraordinary! Philip Seed had to think fast. His wife would be
very angry with him by now.

When Dr. Seed reached their rented apartment in Salzburg,
Carmina Seed wasn't exactly angry. Lying in their bed, she was
in too much pain to sort out her emotions. Her legs were spread
wide, and a small head with dark wet hair was emerging from between them. She had managed to spread towels under her and on
the floor at the end of the bed to catch blood and fluids. Her water
had broken, and labor had begun immediately and dramatically.
Without thinking, Philip laid the glacier baby, or Adolf II—for
that is how he already thought of him—whom he had wrapped in
lab coats, down onto the towels on the floor below the bed. Then

he laid one hand on Carmina's abdomen and another under the small emerging head and said encouragingly, "Push Carmina, just a few more thrusts and you'll be there."

"What do you think I'm doing?" she snapped before letting out a cry. When her moans subsided, she said to her husband, "I've boiled the scissors on the dresser, over there. You can cut the cord with them, owww, damn it, Lord have mercy!" she cried in pain and pushed again.

Now the baby's head came out along with a gush of waxy white vernix that rained down onto the glacier baby on the floor. Philip put some pressure on Carmina's abdomen and pulled on the head, and he soon held a slippery fresh new baby boy in his hands. Then he had a flash of genius. Carmina had closed her eyes out of exhaustion and relief. The pain was over. Philip quickly cut his son's umbilical cord to the same length as Adolf II's and laid him down next to the glacier baby, whom he unwrapped and smeared with some of his son's moisture. He popped up and said, "Well done, good job, it's over," to Carmina, who glared at him and shut her eyes. Then he picked up a baby in each arm and kicked the lab coats out of sight under the bed. When one of the babies and then the other began to cry, Carmina opened her eyes in surprise and Philip announced, "Carmina, my sweet, we have twins, two healthy baby boys!"

At the end of his mental flashback, Latrone whispered, "Fucking crazy!"

He had had a couple of exciting assignments during his six years with the agency, but this one might prove to be the strangest, one he would have to keep to himself forever. He had sworn never to reveal the truth, even under torture. His thoughts were interrupted by the pilot's announcement of their descent into San Francisco; passengers were requested to return to their seats. Sanders still couldn't see anything out the window through the impenetrable fog. When they crashed near the end of the runway, at least his life would be over quickly, and he would never be tortured over that weird character. He glanced over at Hitler's brother again, who was yawning with mouth wide open and stretching his arms languorously above his head at the same time.

No manners, Sanders thought. *But what can you expect considering his origins?*

Agent Sanders knew Philip and Carmina Seed had custody of Hitler's twin for only one year. Within a few months of his find, and after returning from Austria to his laboratory at the University of California, San Diego, Seed had had the good sense to contact the CIA, and the CIA had had the good sense to vet Dr. Seed thoroughly and to subject his wife and him to repeated psychiatric examinations. Then the agency compared the baby's DNA to fragmentary Hitler DNA obtained from the Russian secret services. It turned out that Seed's story was true. The DNA matched. This *was* Adolf Hitler's identical genetic twin, almost the same as a clone. Although a sheep and some frogs had been cloned, cloning of an entire human being had never been done, so reanimation of the frozen baby was the only explanation. Then the CIA had had the good sense to devise a plan for the baby's life, which would prevent him from becoming a power-hungry dictator of a major world power. To this end they arranged for his adoption by a modest family in a southern French village where he could be raised a harmless peasant.

Before that adoption and during the child's first year with the Seeds, and without knowing why, Carmina thought the presumed twin was rather uncanny compared to his brother, whom they named Fernando. Before she knew about the mammoth deception her husband had perpetrated on her, Carmina would often argue with her husband that the boys didn't look alike. Alone, she would look at Hitler's twin, shake her head and exclaim, "There's something not right about him. He doesn't seem the tiniest bit Hispanic." Once she learned the truth about the baby's origins, Carmina Seed was not unhappy to relinquish him. Hitler's twin was then placed in the home of a jovial policeman and his wife, M. et Mme. Pierre Lamour in Colombières-sur-Orb, not far from Clermont l'Herault and within the boundaries of the *Parc naturel regional du Haut-Languedoc*. The Lamours spoiled and mellowed the boy with pastis, a liquor for which the young Jean-Louis, as they named him, developed an early and enduring affection.

Although he exhibited some talent for drawing, Jean-Louis was an undistinguished student and dropped out of school at sixteen. He continued to live at home and did odd jobs as a gravedigger, trash collector, and sign painter, all the time under surveillance by both the French and American governments. A curious turning point came in the fall of his sixteenth year when his best buddy, Pascal, was killed in a freak accident. As a speeding truck overloaded with wrecked vehicles rounded a tight curve in the Vallée d'Orb near their village, a smashed car fell off the top and onto the garbage truck that Pascal and Jean-Louis were driving to the dump. It could just as easily have crushed Jean-Louis, but the wayward wreck killed Pascal who had been in the driver's seat. Sitting next to Pascal, Jean-Louis was, miraculously, unscathed. Before he passed out from the shock, however, Jean-Louis remembered seeing Pascal's blood splattered in a broad ribbon of perfectly round droplets across the thighs of his own light-colored pants.

Sporting a four-day growth of beard and already tipsy from pastis—the only thing that blunted his sorrow—Jean-Louis attended Pascal's funeral at the little church above the main road. After the burial, Jean-Louis went to Lamalou-les-Bains with some friends and continued to drink all evening. He didn't know how he got home that night, and he woke up the next day with a massive hangover that apparently altered his brain—according to his French parents. From then on, he refused to work, and when he applied for disability from the French government, he received it. His facial hair grew uncontrolled, he chain-smoked, slouched, hung out with other idle youth at Lamalou, came home late, and took up painting in his parents' basement until three or so almost every morning. With watercolors on papers that he propped up on a couple of empty wine barrels, he at first painted red circles and spheres over and over again. His French mother had seen the round blood drops on his pants, but her adopted son forbade her to wash them. Instead, he stretched out the pant legs and nailed them into the mortar of the stone basement wall, as if for inspiration, near the wine barrels. Mme. Lamour thought that Jean-Louis's artistic hobby would help her boy work through his grief, but after two months of the same red circles, she wordlessly placed a bowl of greenish white grapes on a small plastic table next to the easel she bought for him and was pleased to note they had the desired effect. His paintings began to depict white grapes mixed in with the red spheres, and in time new colors and things appeared that no longer resembled blood droplets, which, however, retained spherical shapes or at least curved contours.

Some of Jean-Louis's unemployed buddies arranged for him to exhibit his paintings at the Lamalou casino during a summer festival—more as a joke than anything else. But when some tourists actually paid money to buy a few of them, the buddies told a psychologist at the Lamalou medical rehab hospital about Jean-Louis, and the psychologist persuaded him to give art therapy classes for some of the patients, especially the brain-injured accident victims. From there Jean-Louis's reputation as an artist spread eastward to the towns of Bedarieux and Clermont l'Herault and then to Montpellier. Somehow a gallery owner in Montpellier got wind of an unusual talent in the Languedoc and arranged to take him along with two other young artists on an excursion to visit Van Gogh's house at Arles and the Alyscamps—a Roman necropolis in which Lamour had expressed a morbid interest. That day marked a turning point from which Lamour increased the pace and scope of his productions of kitschy spherical Mediterranean landscapes—now in oils on canvas—as well as an intensification of his abstract tendency to round and curve the subjects of his paintings into circular shapes, in a sort of curved counterpart to the squarish objects in cubist paintings. At

least, this is what the gallery owner's friend, Bernard Delavigne, the art critic
from Aix-en-Provence, said when he first saw his work and jokingly dubbed
it *boulist* from the French word *boules,* meaning spheres or balls.

What dumb luck, Latrone thought—a thought that annoyed him so
mightily he temporarily forgot to be fearful of this flight, which was on
its final approach. He knew this second Hitler, or Jean-Louis Guillaume
Lamour, the name on his French passport, had a southern French accent
and knew a smattering of Occitan. Latrone also knew this character knew
a bit of English he'd picked up from American pop songs and movies. But
word had it he didn't care for the English language, and he had been a rather
docile baby with the Seeds, notwithstanding Carmina's somewhat alienated
feelings for him, and a sweet toddler with the Lamours, and a mediocre
teenager, undistinguished except for his painting. CIA agent Sanders had
no understanding of art, but he had read a lot of history on Hitler for this
assignment. When he looked over at him, it was impossible to distinguish
any familiar Hitlerian features behind all that dark hair on his head and face
and those ridiculous green-framed, tinted glasses he probably wore more as
a bohemian affectation than a necessity.

Mr. Sanders looked away from his charge and out the window again.
As he stared intensely into the fog, the engines suddenly dropped in pitch
for no good reason. He rubbed his wet palms on his pants. He squinted as he
looked down and now saw they were practically skimming over the water,
with no runway in sight! Any second they would hit the bay. He reached
down under his seat to feel for his flotation device. He lowered his head
between his knees and clasped it with both elbows over his frontal cortex
in preparation for the crash. He pictured his name on the sad list of those
killed, and the reporting of another major FAA investigation. He thought of
his poor mother, alone in the world once he was gone. At least she'd get his
government life insurance. He would quit this job if he survived this flight,
he promised himself.

As flight 300 taxied up to the Air France gate, the stewardess who had
brought Monsieur Lamour his champagne gently shook the shoulders of
this youthful first-class passenger who had fallen asleep again. She thought
he was unusually young for the first class. Most of her passengers were elderly or at least middle-aged. Young people generally couldn't afford first-
class tickets. But this scraggly character with the long stringy black hair that
fell over his forehead, the shaggy moustache and beard, must have been a
member of a rock band. There was something about his appearance that
seemed familiar. Probably she'd seen him on TV, but she couldn't place him.

Now, she had to do her job. "*Monsieur, excusez-moi, mais nous sommes ar-riveés à* San Francisco . . . *Monsieur, Monsieur?*"

Hitler's brother slowly opened his eyes and smiled into those of the pretty French flight attendant. He reached for her hand and said, "*Merci, ma petite. Vous êtes très gentille, même ravissante* (you are very nice, even enchanting)." Before he pulled off the airplane blanket, he regretfully tried to tame his erection and to focus on something other than the erotic dream he'd been enjoying before this awakening in California. Next to the right-side window, a CIA agent stalled getting his things together until Hitler's brother moved to debark. Then Agent Sanders followed the young French-man at a discreet distance through the jetway to the baggage and customs area. After they passed through customs, he would hand a computer disk to a Hermann Wittgenstein, who would be there with a chauffeur and a sign and exchange a secret hand gesture with his relief agent. Latrone would then grab a taxi to his mother's in East Palo Alto. His job would be done, at least for the time being.

7

BRUNO PRESSED THE HANG-UP button on his chair, which was designed according to cutting-edge ergonomic and user-friendly principles, then the *Gaby* button and said, "Please get Jack Peterson on the phone for me. He lives at The Pines."

He hadn't spoken to Jack in a long time and had put off this call as long as possible. Jack had almost desecrated Myrtle's burial at sea in 1989 by attempting to read from his hackneyed bestseller, *Resurrection in Venice*. Bruno had resented it in silence back then. In the meantime, he had noted Peterson's meteoric rise in the world of American mass marketing where art, craft, creativity, and knowledge counted for nothing, and the lowest common denominators of clichéd formulas, notoriety, connections, and handling were everything. He knew Myrtle had held the retired lawyer in contempt, and now he had to fight the temptation to insert a degree of condescension in his voice.

"Jack Peterson here!" a vigorous old voice shouted into Bruno's earpiece so loudly he had to turn down the volume. *He must have grown deaf.*

"Hello, Mr. Peterson. So nice to talk to you again. It's been such a long time."

"Yes, indeedy, sir. How's the auction business, these days? Those are quite some fancy headquarters you've got over there on Treasure Island. The next best sight after the Pyramid building, ha, ha."

Bruno knew Jack was lying. He would have no more appreciation for modern architecture than he had for good syntax.

"Fine, just fine, thank you." Bruno didn't want to talk to him longer than necessary.

"By the way," Jack said, "I picked up a painting from you about three or four years ago at auction. What a kick. An old Fauberge, or Faubourg, or maybe Farberge. I don't remember the painter's name at the moment. Anyway, got a bargain. Went one Sunday afternoon with a lady friend, ha, ha. It's hanging here in my living room—the painting, I mean, not the lady, ha, ha, ha, ha!" Jack's laugh grew louder the longer he spoke.

Bruno made a mental note to check the back records for Jack's painting—probably something thoroughly mediocre, if he judged Jack's taste correctly.

"Well, I'm pleased to know you're getting pleasure from the painting, Mr. Peterson. But you're probably wondering why I'm calling you today. Do you have a minute?"

"Yes, indeedy, I do. What can I do for you, my boy?"

"Well, De Carlo & Wittgenstein is sponsoring a major exhibit of a young French painter, Jean-Louis Lamour, next month, and I'd like to extend a personal invitation to you and a guest to the gala opening reception."

"When would that be, sir? I'd have to check it out with my secretary."

"The fifteenth of March, here in the auction house on Treasure Island. We'd be glad to send a driver to pick you and your guest up and take you home afterward."

"Well, that's right friendly of you, and I have a notion to accept right now. I'll have Linda—that's my secretary—firm it up with you after our conversation."

"Well, that's wonderful, Mr. Peterson. It will be nice to see you again. We'd like our artist to meet some local figures in San Francisco's cultural world. We'll have reporters from *The Chronicle* and *The Los Angeles Times*, as well as some other artists, literati, and society people. We want to make him feel welcome while he's here."

"How long's Frenchie staying in San Francisco?"

"A year or two, perhaps longer. He'll be an artist-in-residence and instructor at the New Age Art Institute in the Richmond District."

"New Age Art Institute, you say? I thought that new age stuff went out with Motown music."

"Well, you're right, Mr. Peterson, but the name stuck at this school, just the same."

"If I were teaching there, they could call it the *Old Age Art School*, don't you think, Mr. De Carlo?" Jack snickered at his own joke. "But then people might think it was a school for old codgers like me, ha, ha, ha." When his laugh turned into a cough, Bruno seized the opportunity to end the conversation.

"Let us know if you'd like to bring any writer colleagues or other, uh, celebrities, who are interested in contemporary art, Mr. Peterson. We'd be more than happy to expand our guest list."

"Well, that's right magnanimous of you, sir, and I surely will, if I think of anybody, that is. And I'll look forward to your opening, sir. And to the chance to see you again."

After Bruno had passed Jack back to Gaby to arrange details, he thought how unfortunate it was that Myrtle's ashes had failed to silence Peterson's hackneyed voice in one insipid novel after the other. During those same years, he, Bruno, had been building something positive—a successful business based on a new concept. Unlike Butterfields and Sotheby's, which catered exclusively to the rich, De Carlo & Wittgenstein welcomed all classes of clientele. They auctioned absolutely everything—from cheap flea market items to the finest art objects, albeit in three different categories. They displayed their wares in three adjoining cavernous auction galleries that contained Peets' cafés, wine and oyster bars, chic bistros, and bookstores with reading lounges where everyone felt welcome to stay as long as they liked. The appeal of the online auction business had waned after out-of-control Russian hackers kept attacking the websites and stealing users' identities. The economy had picked up, and De Carlo & Wittgenstein's had become the in destination for an outing. Browsing the preview items had become a favorite Bay Area pastime, and De Carlo & Wittgenstein's friendly staff would appraise any item, no matter how lowly, without appointment, for free, 24/7. Volume had become their success, but also their reputation for service, fairness, and honesty. And people all over the country loved to claim that they had been inside the outrageous Kerry buildings and had walked or jogged the path around its campus with the marvelous views of the city and the bay.

Two walls of the spacious reception foyer were covered with murals depicting the spectacular Roman mosaics Bruno had found in his southern French farmhouse in Cabrières that had catapulted him to fame in the art and antiquities world—the crucial stepping stone that had eventually brought him here, to these spectacular headquarters, and to social prominence, not only in San Francisco, but internationally. More important for Bruno, the Roman finds and subsequent wealth had bought him time to read. He never would have guessed how much that would mean to him back when he thought status and fortune were everything. Now that he possessed both, Bruno realized what Ms. Halstead had given him had been far more valuable—a love of books, good books, which made even the long flights he had made on CIA business more enjoyable. Last week, as a matter of fact, he caught himself turning down a dinner invitation to the Beattys' in order to stay home and finish reading Wallace Stegner's *Angle of Repose.*

Deep in thought, Bruno traversed his spacious office and headed for the restroom. He stepped into the hallway and was just about to enter his private bathroom when its door swung open, and Crystal Beatty emerged, tossing her head back and shaking out her long, straight, blond hair behind her ears. They startled each other.

"Oh, Bruno," she said, breathlessly. "I was just about to go over the vehicle depreciation numbers."

They had broken off their relationship some time ago—officially. Bruno had wanted his freedom more than sex with her, but she had clung to her accounting job at De Carlo & Wittgenstein to be near him. It irritated him that she used his personal bathroom, and that she hadn't given up on him, because he was beyond her. Not just because they were both too old. Age, of course, was a relative thing—he was sixty-two and she was only forty-seven—but somewhere along the line, on his road to achieving his goals, sex—at least with her—had receded in importance. Not that he was impotent. But, well, *she* just didn't do it for him, he decided. Maybe he'd get interested again, but he had been terribly busy building up this magnificent business and indulging in his new passion, and Crystal's persistence had been overwhelming and therefore simply not sexy, too obvious and therefore awkward. Now she was almost an old maid. She was insanely wealthy, with her family's money, but all she wanted was to land him. And he didn't need her money. Too much money, he had decided, was more burden than blessing. With her zillions, she never needed to work, but what did she do? Get an accounting degree. That way she could weasel her way into his company and be useful. She was good at her job, and it was disconcerting. Somehow, he couldn't shake her.

"Oh, that's great. Can you brief me on it at the next board meeting?"

"Well, I think we should do a one-on-one. It's kinda complicated. How about tomorrow at 4:30 P.M.?"

"Well, you'd better check with Gaby. I don't know my schedule exactly."

Crystal, of course, was way ahead of him. She had already checked with Gaby and knew Bruno would be free. She hoped she could occupy him until closing time when they might move seamlessly together out to dinner.

"OK. I'll let you know." She batted her eyelashes to which she had just applied fresh mascara in Bruno's bathroom, twisted provocatively around in her tight skirt, and headed toward Gaby's office. When Bruno entered his bathroom, he was almost knocked over by the lingering, cloying scent of her Lagerfeld *Parfum Fatale pour Femmes*, that was supposed to contain human pheromones. Whatever it was, he found it as annoying as the flecks of mascara and makeup smudges on his mirror.

8

HERMANN KNEW HE SHOULDN'T have, but he let Donald come into the waiting area outside of customs at the airport. He should have left Donald with the car in the parking lot, to protect it, and because he was the chauffeur. Then he should have paged him to drive the car around to the curbside as soon as he recognized Hitler's twin emerging from the customs' hall. But Hermann didn't want to meet the foreigner by himself. He had learned about Adolf Hitler in his youth, and although East Germans liked to blame the West Germans for Nazism, Hermann thought maybe all Germans shared in the guilt, even if Hitler had been Austrian. Hermann's father had hidden some Nazi photos and memorabilia in a suitcase in the basement of their home when Hermann was a boy, and the fact these objects were hidden made them ominous. Now, aside from the greeting Hermann had practiced over and over again in his mind on the way to the airport, he didn't know what to say to this special guest, and he was afraid people might recognize the dictator's twin and then something would happen—he didn't know what. So, both Hermann and Donald waited outside of customs.

Donald sat on a bench and Hermann paced. He checked the overhead monitor for the fifth time. The flight had landed; passengers were in the customs area and would be emerging any minute. He walked up closer to the large automatic doors where weary travelers came out in a gradual dribble—mainly Asians. But then some Caucasians emerged speaking French. He tried to look at the tags on their luggage. Were they Air France tags? He couldn't get a good look at them. A few more Europeans came out between the Asians, but they didn't say anything. Their tags were red, white, and blue. Finally, he screwed up his courage and asked a man and woman, "Are you coming from Paris on Air France?"

He got a blank look from them. Maybe it was jet lag. Then the man said, "*Excusez moi?*" as if Hermann had spoken to them in Martian.

"Paris? France? Gay Pareeee?" Hermann asked again, trying to make it clear.

"Ah, *oui, naturellement*. Yes. *Nous arrivons de* Paris. *Oui.*"

"Thanks," said Hermann and hurried back to Donald, who was almost asleep on the black vinyl bench. "Donald, his plane has arrived!" Hermann said excitedly and shook Donald's shoulder. "Come on, bring the sign."

Donald rose slowly from the bench because of his bad knees and brought the computer-made sign that read, "M. Jean-Louis Lamour," in big black letters. Centered underneath that were the names "De Carlo & Wittgenstein." Hermann thought he would surely recognize Hitler's twin, a.k.a. Jean-Louis Lamour, but Bruno had insisted he bring this sign and hold it up when the passengers got off the plane. Now Hermann told Donald to put on his cap and gloves, stand up straight, and hold the sign. They looked like a VIP welcoming party, Hermann in his expensive suit and Donald in his chauffeur's uniform, cap, and white gloves. And when Hermann realized several of the people waiting to meet passengers looked at them, he worried if they stood out, people might notice that they were meeting Adolf Hitler's carbon copy. Of course, Hermann was informed he would have a moustache and straggly long hair and would probably be wearing bizarre green glasses. Latrone had informed the CIA agents in San Francisco before the flight left Paris, and the CIA agents had informed De Carlo & Wittgenstein. But what if young Hitler had shaved his beard during the flight and removed his glasses? Then this man might look just like Hitler! As a matter of fact, he would *have* to look like Hitler, if he were his identical twin. Who else could he look like? Hermann suddenly panicked at this thought. Good God, every American knew what Hitler looked like. He'd been the biggest terror of the last century, and if Hitler were recognized right there at the airport, maybe people would start screaming. On the other hand, they might think they had wandered into a Hollywood film production. Anything could happen.

Hermann loosened the tie that suddenly seemed too tight around his neck and took the sign from Donald and fanned himself with it. "Maybe you ought to sit down again, Donald. This could take a long time."

"OK. You're the boss."

"And you can take off your cap and gloves, Donald. You may as well be comfortable."

Donald stuffed his white gloves into a hip pocket and removed his chauffeur's cap as he made a beeline back to the seat he had occupied before. Hermann moved away from the rail to view the emerging travelers from a distance. Now, most of them seemed to be from the Air France flight. Many spoke French, all had tricolor luggage tags on their suitcases piled on their carts. But to judge by their clothes, most of the first-class passengers were already out of the terminal. Hitler-Lamour should have been among the first-class passengers. Where was he?

Hermann went back to the overhead screen and checked for the sixth time. It indicated that Hitler's flight had landed and that passengers were going through customs. Soon this indication would vanish when the screen was updated. He looked around for someone to ask, and when he accosted a uniformed employee headed into the customs area, he was told he should check at the airline counter if he had an inquiry about a particular passenger. The employee couldn't tell him whether all passengers from the Paris flight had come through; it wasn't his job. But he assured Hermann it could take a long time and suggested perhaps the passenger was having trouble with his luggage.

Hermann was about to send Donald up to the Air France check-in counter when a racket arose from behind the customs doors—a howling, growling, and barking that grew louder and higher in pitch as the automatic doors opened and two uniformed employees came out carrying an animal cage that emitted the frantic sounds. A third employee pushed a luggage cart piled high with suitcases. A scraggly, long-haired Frenchman walked backwards and bent over in front of the cage, sweet-talking to it in French, and gesticulating to the officials to set it down. He carried an overcoat in one arm and a big cloth bag with a long strap over the other shoulder. His hair was dark and stringy, and he had a thick moustache with droopy handlebars that twisted into a ragged, three-inch beard. He wore odd, green, horn-rimmed, dark-tinged glasses. Hermann realized it must be him. Thank goodness he hadn't shaved. Jean-Louis Lamour took no notice of his surroundings as he fumbled with yellow-stained fingers to light a cigarette and was prevented by the certain gestures of the officials, who, over the Frenchman's protests, also refused to put down the noisy, agitated caged animal. They carried it all the way outside the terminal to the curbside with Hitler's twin shuffling and stumbling along in protest. Hermann and Donald followed in pursuit. Latrone Sanders, the CIA man who had followed the twin and the airport handlers at a discreet distance, now caught up with the San Francisco contacts and quickly extended his left hand toward Hermann. Hermann shook it with his own left hand, and Mr. Sanders quickly handed Hermann a computer disk that Hermann stuffed into a pocket inside his

jacket. Sanders then turned and walked away. Before he entered the terminal building again, the agent glanced back at the little group and shook his
head to himself. His job was over, and he headed for the closest restroom.

Donald held up the sign, but as he, Hermann, Hitler's duplicate, and
the two airport officials crowded around the cage, the Frenchman took no
notice of it, so intent was he on the liberation of his pet. The officials wore
thick leather gloves, and one, ready with a leash, kneeled down next to the
little door while the other unlatched the cage. When the door opened, the
barking and growling suddenly stopped, and the dog—now everyone could
see it was a shaggy, black miniature poodle—cowered in its cage, not daring
to come out. When one of the officials tipped up the back of the cage till the
animal slid out unceremoniously onto the sidewalk, the other grabbed its
collar and snapped on the leash. Then he handed the leash to the scraggly
Frenchman, and the officials, including the luggage cart handler, retreated
with the empty cage back into the terminal.

Now the stunned dog began yapping, barking, and running around in
circles on its tether, so that bystanders took notice. The poodle twisted the
leash around both Hitler's brother's right leg and Hermann's left leg, and it
nipped at Hermann's ankles and lifted a leg to pee on his Gucci shoes. Hermann moved his foot quickly enough to protect his shoes, but at the same
time dragged the little beast along with his leg. Hitler's twin in the meantime succeeded in lighting a Gauloise and taking a few long puffs. Then he
remarked casually to Hermann and Donald, "*Ce n'est pas grave. Ce n'est pas
grave. Ce n'est pas un chien mechant* (It's nothing serious, he's not a vicious
dog)." He seemed to acknowledge with these words, that they were the ones
who had come to meet him and his poodle.

Hermann tried to remember the French lines he had memorized to
say to M. Lamour, but realized he'd forgotten most of them. He held up the
sign and abbreviated the greeting by saying, "*Bonjour, sejour ici.*"

Lamour gave a squinty frown of incomprehension, stuck the cigarette
between his lips to free his right hand and extended it to Hermann who
dropped the sign. Hermann's face was red with embarrassment as he shook
Hitler's twin's hand. At the same time the little dog growled and began
clawing and scratching at Hermann's shoes. At this, Lamour dropped his
handbag, took the cigarette out of his mouth with his left hand and stooped
down to his animal saying, "*O la la, pas comme ça, mon Fisto, pas comme
ça* (Oh, la, la, not like that, Fisto)," and patted its head. He put the cigarette
back between his lips and succeeded in unraveling the leash from around
his own leg. Freed now from its master's leg, the dog did the same with Hermann's leg, which allowed it to shoot away from them, barking raucously in
ever-expanding spirals on the sidewalk. The closest bystanders edged away

from the little spectacle, so as not to be confronted by the out-of-control canine or tripped up by the leash that jerked along behind it. The racing black poodle had obviously never been inside a poodle salon in Paris, and in its hairy, bedraggled, and undisciplined appearance, it shared a physiognomic affinity to its master.

Instead of trying to control his hysterical dog, M. Lamour took the diversion as an opportunity to catch up on his nicotine habit. He released the cigarette stub dangling from his lips and lit another Gauloise. He took a slow drag and smiled at the ray of sunshine that had just penetrated through the fog to illuminate his dog at the curbside. Donald, in the meantime, seeing his boss was out of his depth, whipped out one of the white gloves from a hip pocket. As the poodle was about to race past them on one of its mad circuits, Donald flashed the glove in front of it. Though Fisto was nearly blinded by the long hair over his eyes, he saw enough of the white cloth to snap at it and clamp his teeth down on it, halting his frenzied forward trajectory. Donald now reigned it in with the leash and said, "Good dog, nice pooch, *bonjour*, atta boy, *oui, oui*, there now, hey man, *oh la la la la*, it's OK now," in a string of such calming admonitions that the dog, with its jaws locked on the glove, froze in place. In a minute the poodle let itself be picked up by the chauffeur.

Hermann ordered Donald to stay with Lamour and the dog, and he went to get the car. When he pulled up ten minutes later at the curbside, the poodle in Donald's arms was happily licking the chauffeur's ears and face, while Donald and Lamour laughed and talked, in what language, Hermann couldn't imagine, carrying on like old buddies.

Hermann loaded the Frenchman's luggage into the trunk of the Jaguar, and once everyone was inside, Fisto curled up on Donald's lap in the backseat. Donald spread the white glove over his knee, and the dog rested its head on it and went to sleep. Hermann moved the front passenger seat far enough forward so the Frenchman, who insisted on getting in back next to Donald, could stretch out his legs. Soon he too was snoring while smiling, and his head fell down onto Donald's shoulder. Hermann wanted to call Bruno to tell him they were back on Highway 101, but Donald advised him in a whisper not to, that he might wake the dog. Then he said to Hermann in a low voice, "The dude's cool, man."

As they drove north in silence, the entire French greeting came back to Hermann in perfect clarity: "*Bonjour Monsieur! Bienvenu en Californie! Comment-allez-vous? Je suis Monsieur Wittgenstein, de l'entreprise, De Carlo et Wittgenstein, je vous souhaite un très bon séjour ici* (Good day! Welcome to California! How are you? I am Mr. Wittgenstein of De Carlo & Wittgenstein, I wish you a very good stay here)." *Now* he could say it, damn it!

9

On Wednesday morning The Pines's lobby was crowded with elderly residents, many of whom had spilled outside into the front parking lot. Herb had to call for more help at the front desk and then went outside to persuade them to come back in. It was damp and foggy, and they might catch cold. Besides, the television crew would need space to handle their equipment. It would be dangerous with all that gear coming through, and The Pines couldn't allow the residents to block the entrance or be exposed to an unsafe situation. Herb greeted several individuals by name—"Good morning, Mrs. Morgan, Ms. Chambers, Mr. Greenblatt"—then he made a general statement to the small crowd desirous of catching a glimpse of the middle-aged, African-American superstar, Gloria Majestic, when she arrived to tape the program with the best-selling novelist and Pines resident, Jack Peterson.

"I'm sorry, but I have to ask you to go back inside," Herb began. "A large monitor will be set up in the dining hall, and starting at 10 A.M., you'll be able to see Ms. Majestic's arrival on the big screen. But we have to keep this area clear. The crew needs access to the front entrance. If you're going out today, please use the exit on the other side of the building. Remember, those of you who are current Reading Roundtable members are invited to attend the taping on the fourth floor in Jack Peterson's suite starting at 2:00 P.M. We ask you to be seated there by 1:30 so the show can begin promptly. So now, I'd appreciate it very much if you would kindly go back inside. Thank you for your cooperation."

Herb tried to herd the curious residents back in. They were out there much too early, of course. And it seemed they moved more glacially than usual, exaggerating their bad knees and hips as a stalling strategy in the hopes of getting a look at the television people who would be putting them and their retirement residence on the national map.

Blue-haired Ms. Samuels tapped Herb on his back with her cane and asked, "What time is Gloria Majestic supposed to arrive?"

"Ten-thirty A.M.," Herb replied, "if all goes according to schedule. You should be able to get a good view from the third floor, Ms. Samuels, if you just look out your window."

Ms. Samuels smiled and nodded. She had already invited several lucky residents from the upper floors down to her apartment for this event. Her living room had an excellent view of the front parking lot and main entrance. Miss Jorgensen, who had not been invited to Ms. Samuel's apartment said, however, loud enough for others to hear, she preferred a good seat in the dining room, because, just as with a sporting event, one would see better and sit more comfortably in front of a large screen.

Countess Olofsky piped up at Herb, "I've been a member of the Reading Roundtable ever since it was founded by Ms. Halstead."

"Well then, you should enjoy the taping of the live show this afternoon."

A few steps away one resident remarked to no one in particular, "But she'll sleep through it, just like she sleeps through everything else. They ought to let someone else take her place."

That evening the dining room was full and the decibel level higher than usual. The taping of her book program that was broadcast monthly on national television—this time featuring best-selling San Francisco author Jack Peterson and the elderly Reading Roundtable audience—went so well that Gloria Majestic decided to postpone her return to Burbank and stay on for dinner at The Pines. She ordered her crew to do some more filming of the Pines residents and to interview them about their lives. It had been less what Jack Peterson had said about his books or about literature that had piqued her interest than the fact she had been struck by this particular audience.

At The Pines she had noticed how very bright, curious, and perceptive most of the comments and questions had been. But she hadn't failed to see that one particularly distinguished, even aristocratic-looking old woman had slept through the entire taping, snoring so loudly at one point that they would have to do some sound editing. She had observed how embarrassed other audience members had been, and how they discreetly tried to wake her, and how it hadn't helped. She sensed that Jack Peterson, although she didn't think much of his books or the movie adaptations, had something admirable about him—a force, a personality, an ambition, a drive at age ninety-five, a will, an interest in life. On the other hand, she didn't understand why he chose to live in this old-age residence rather than a private mansion surrounded by servants he could well afford. To be sure, he had purchased and remodeled three adjoining apartments into a luxurious suite. When she asked him on the program whether he preferred to remain within a community of his peers, he had said that was only one reason he remained at The Pines. The major reason was his own little secret, but he would give her a clue.

Then he led her out onto his fourth-floor balcony where she couldn't fail to notice his telescope on its swivel mount. The television crew followed and filmed them as Gloria Majestic studied the neighborhood that consisted of typical city blocks with apartment buildings and a hospital. She was stumped for an explanation. Mr. Peterson didn't have the best view at this relatively low level, she thought, which must have been better on the highest floors. But this telescope must have something to do with his secret. When he encouraged her to look through it, she realized in horror that he could spy on people in their apartments. Was this man a geriatric voyeur? Was that his perverted secret? But his books didn't suggest anything untoward. And she had to be careful what she said on camera. She continued to peer through the telescope longer than good timing allowed, trying to think of what to say. When she finally stepped back, Jack Peterson, with a fatuous and knowing smile, swung his arm in a broad gesture that encompassed his entire balcony, including the telescope, and reiterated to her that the balcony contained the clue to his secret. Relieved to have thought up a solution for the cameras, Ms. Majestic grasped Mr. Peterson's hand and concluded one had to respect the secret of an eminent ninety-five-year-old writer, and perhaps look for the solution to the mystery in his next novel. Jack beamed into the cameras.

Gloria's producer loved the taping. It would make a great show. Ms. Majestic herself was impressed by it for different reasons. She had had a new insight. Having never concerned herself with old people before—busy as she was—she realized she tended to lump them all together under certain rubrics and adjectives—senior citizens, old ladies, old codgers, grandmas and grandpas, old geezers or lechers, has-beens, over-the hillers, Golden Agers. She realized she could easily continue to expand this list of terms, most of them derogatory, all of which she had employed—though not on camera, of course—and still did in her private life and thoughts.

On screen she had to be politically correct, and on her talk show she had ignored the topic of aging. There were hundreds more sexy topics to discuss, but her producer had persuaded her she could no longer ignore this Jack Peterson phenomenon in northern California on her book show. And the program had turned out to be an eye-opener. There were people here with all the attributes and emotions of younger people, both positive and negative, which were, if anything, intensified by their age. She couldn't get over the members of this "Reading Roundtable," as they called it. Were they ever sharp old cookies. Oops, there she went again with one of those labels. When she thought about it, she couldn't remember having ever received such intelligent, thoughtful, and perceptive comments, such critical feedback, including honest, insightful criticism of Jack Peterson's books, the very ones they were discussing, and about which *she* couldn't express her reservations on the air. The Reading Roundtable members had the audacity to speak the truth. Where did that freedom come from? She had read enough books and book reviews in the last fifteen years to know they were right on. There were differences in writers, and the best ones weren't always the most popular. At least she and her program had made some good writers popular. She was proud of this. But here were some of these elders saying the smartest things. Could that old cliché about the wisdom of age be true? Was there something here worth investigating? And who was that Myrtle Halstead they all alluded to?

Cameras were set up at different locations in the dining hall. Gloria Majestic was seated next to Jack at the VIP table along with a charter Reading Roundtable member, Madame Françoise Hayes, who at 102 was hard of hearing but still quick witted. Ms. Majestic had tired of talking with Mr. Peterson and spent most of the evening in animated conversation with the other women at her table. A microphone was suspended over the table while two cameras filmed the diners. Other cameras panned the room and focused occasionally on different tables to capture anecdotes and opinions.

Thursday morning Gloria Majestic flew back to Burbank with a lot of tape and a cluster of new ideas in her head. She also had an invitation from Jack to come back to San Francisco in three weeks to attend a reception put on by the prominent San Francisco art and auction house, De Carlo & Wittgenstein, for a young French artist. When told that other Reading Roundtable members would also be attending the event, she accepted.

10

JEAN-LOUIS LAMOUR WAS WIDE awake at 3:00 A.M. in room 302 at the Ritz-Carlton. He had managed to stay awake through dinner with Hermann and Donald in the elegant hotel dining room, where Hermann had insisted Donald accompany them. Hermann didn't want to put Donald's dinner on the expense account since Bruno wouldn't have approved, so he decided to pay for it out of his own pocket. Monsieur Lamour smiled to see the menu was in both French and English, and he ordered the same things for all of them in his southern French accent: the *foie gras,* the *langoustines,* the *escargots,* and the *prunes rôties.* He had grown up drinking pastis and table wines of the l'Herault, but he had heard enough about the champagne and Bordeaux regions of France to order a bottle of Taittinger champagne to start with and two bottles of Château Beychevelle, 1988.

By the end of dinner, Donald knew about fifty useful French phrases and tried to kiss Hermann's hand. Hermann decided to hide the receipt from Gaby. When they left the hotel restaurant, he also tipped the maître d' a hundred-dollar bill for feeding Fisto while they dined. After Hermann and Donald said goodnight to Jean-Louis in his room, Hermann had a word with Latrone Sanders's relief agent in the lobby, then he drove an intoxicated Donald and a whiny Fisto to Donald's Fillmore apartment. Hermann promised Donald he'd tell Bruno the chauffeur couldn't come to work the next day due to a cold. It was after midnight when Hermann made it home.

Hitler's twin brother was puzzled as he puffed on a cigarette at 3:00 A.M. in his room. He'd been sleepy at dinner, so why couldn't he sleep now? He'd slept from 11:00 P.M. till 2:00 A.M. But he'd been wide awake since then. He'd rarely lost a night's sleep before. In fact, he had a great talent for sleep. He was one of those lucky individuals who could fall asleep just about any-where and under any circumstances—in the garbage truck, in a noisy bar, at a loud party, at a movie. It couldn't be indigestion now, because the food and wine in America were good, better than he had expected and better than everyone back in Colombières had predicted. And everyone had said the Americans were uncultured and you couldn't trust them. But so far, he couldn't say. Americans had a hang-up about smoking, but the waiter spoke good French and Donald was a *cool cat*, a term he had already learned. And Hermann Wittgenstein wasn't a typical American. Jean-Louis figured Mr. Wittgenstein couldn't help it if he were a German, and uptight about every-thing, more so even than the Americans.

The only really bad thing about the whole experience so far was that Fisto was absent—Fisto who always slept with him at the foot of his bed. Toward morning, his little poodle would crawl up to the pillow and lick his master's earlobes until Jean-Louis cuddled him in the crook of his arm and both would fall asleep again. It was clear his dog wasn't welcome in his hotel room with its chandeliers, huge Chinese lamps and vases, and lavish bouquet of flowers, the scent of which overwhelmed him. He had moved the enormous bouquet in his suite into the closet, but the cloying odor of lilies and lilacs, roses, lavender, rosemary, and Scotch broom still penetrated the bedroom, so that he could only get rid of it by filling the room with cigarette smoke.

He flipped channels on the satellite TV and was pleased to come across a French channel with a rerun of *Questions pour un Champion* with the aging moderator, Julien Lepers. In Colombières, he could always fall asleep during this quiz program. But now, even this didn't work. Maybe he was suffering from jet lag, like Hermann had predicted. Jean-Louis crawled out of bed and took a hot bubble bath in the huge marble Jacuzzi bathtub.

Merde, he thought. *Fisto would have loved this. If they don't want Fisto here, I'm not going to stay here.*

After he dried off, he tried to phone Donald. He had numbers for Don-ald, Hermann, and Bruno in case of emergency, but at Donald's number he only got an answering machine message in English that was hard to under-stand. After the beep, he left a message: "Cool cat, Donald, *c'est moi*, Louis. I *manque* Fisto. *Merde! No dormir. Telephonez moi, s'il te plaît.*"

After he set down the receiver, Jean-Louis spied the small zippered bag that the pretty Air France stewardess had given him as he debarked the plane. He had forgotten about it and decided to inspect it now. He dumped its contents onto the bed. There was a piccolo bottle of Perrier-Jouet champagne with a screw top, a copy of yesterday's *Le Monde*, a CD of Debussy's *La Mer* by the Radio France Orchestra, a *Toblerone* chocolate bar, an extra luggage strap, and a cosmetic kit with toothbrush, toothpaste, razor, shaving cream, mouthwash, earplugs, facemask, comb, slippers, and a male perfume by Lagerfeld called *Fatal pour Hommes* that he opened up and whiffed. What an aroma! He'd never been one for aftershave or perfumes, but this was *tout-à-fait différent*. He couldn't stop sniffing it. He dabbed some on his body and set the open bottle next to the champagne on his bedside table. He propped the pillows up on the headboard, pulled the blankets up to this chest, and started to look at *Le Monde*. Every thirty seconds or so he picked up the perfume bottle for another intoxicating smell or took a swig of the Perrier-Jouet. In less than ten minutes he fell into a deliciously erotic sleep and dreamt of an unknown American woman with sexy legs and long black hair.

11

CRYSTAL BEATTY KICKED THE ivory-colored leather ottoman across the floor where it bumped into the dwarf kumquat tree in the corner of her office, causing its green leaves to shimmy excitedly. She tossed her head at the same time so that her long hair flew up and slapped her in an explosion of blond about the head. He had evaded her again. What else could she do? She'd worn a tight mini-skirt, black silk nylons, and spiked heels that hurt her feet. She'd spent twenty minutes doing her face, applying the pale blue eye shadow he'd once told her made her eyes look like daybreak. She'd worn a new perfume, and he still had an excuse not to go to dinner following their meeting on vehicle depreciation of their fleet of trucks and luxury cars. It seemed to her he hadn't appreciated her good accounting work. She'd done a meticulous job and had even researched the pros and cons of buying a corporate jet. Before she finished her presentation, Bruno claimed he had a physical therapy appointment for a pain in his shoulder. When she'd offered in a flirtatious way to massage it herself, his turndown was just too much. She had to find a way to get back at him. But what could she do?

She stomped over to her bay window and looked out at Alcatraz and the drab old prison buildings that continued to draw tourists despite their dilapidated state. The reception for this French artist, Jean-Louis Lamour, was coming up; Bruno wanted her there because of her name. She knew it because he'd also asked her to bring along as many of her family members as possible. This could be her chance for revenge.

12

THE NEXT MORNING, HERMANN left his car with the Ritz-Carlton valet and entered the hotel at 10:00 A.M. The late hour was designed to give the Frenchman time to sleep in after his long flight. Hermann was to take him to De Carlo & Wittgenstein and show him around. Then they would have lunch with Bruno. In the afternoon, Hermann would drive him out to the New Age Art Institute, where he was to be an artist-in-residence.

Jean-Louis was not in the hotel—not in his room, the breakfast salon, the massage parlor, or the hair salon. The CIA relief agent was clueless. Maybe Jean-Louis had slipped out when the agent was in the men's room. The Frenchman had not checked out, but his things were gone from his room. An empty piccolo bottle of champagne was at his nightstand, and although the room exuded a perfumed scent, the hotel's bouquet of flowers was in the closet. Hermann's only clue, when he, the agent, and the assistant manager searched the room, was the list of emergency phone numbers Hermann had given him. It lay next to the phone, and Donald's number was circled.

Sixteen minutes later, at the door of Donald's Fillmore flat, Hermann heard laughter inside over loud Thelonius Monk music. As soon as he knocked on the door, Fisto started to bark behind it. The laughter stopped, and then the volume of the jazz music dropped down low. Donald's voice called, "Who is it?" and Hermann answered, "It's I, Donald—Hermann. Open up, please, Donald, OK? Is Adolf there with you?"

Verflucht nochmal (Damn it)!

He'd been thinking in German again and used the twin brother's name. Bruno was right; he really had to stop that bad habit. What if Jean-Louis had heard it? Damn it again! He could kick himself!

"Yea, man. That little terrorist dog be here, and so's his master. But give me a minute so I can contain him before I open the door, so he don't bite your head off."

It grew quiet again inside, and it seemed to Hermann as if Donald were taking his time. While he waited, Hermann picked up some old advertising flyers that stuck out of Donald's mailbox slot and lay them in front of Donald's door. When Donald finally opened the door—only a narrow crack—Hermann thought he could smell marijuana. Donald was still in his pajamas. His hair stuck out in tufts, his breath was atrocious, and his eyes were glazed. *Good God!* Why Bruno had hired this character was beyond him. Donald wasn't even a good driver.

It was dark in Donald's flat, and from the outside landing and with Donald standing in the way, Hermann couldn't really see anything inside, but he could hear Jean-Louis's voice saying soothing things in French to Fisto, who continued to whine and growl. He was relieved to realize Jean-Louis sat far enough away not to have heard him say *Adolf*. And he had to be grateful to Donald for deflecting the name onto the dog. Donald wasn't stupid, Hermann had to admit.

Hermann leaned forward, but Donald made no move to widen the crack or invite him in. He just stood there in his thread-bare green and white checkered pajamas, a slight, disheveled, aging black man, smiling inquisitively at the well-dressed, massive Hermann, who wanted to get on with business.

"Well, what's he doing *here*?" Hermann whispered now to Donald.

"Just having breakfast, man. We eatin' breakfast. That's all."

"I mean, why didn't he stay at the hotel? It's one of the best in town. When did he come over here? He didn't check out or anything."

"Look man," Donald whispered louder back at Hermann. "You've got to understand, man. He's an artist, man. The dude's very cool. He missed his dog. You can't jus' take an artist out of his world like that, take his dog away and put him down somewhere else—plop, just like nothing's happenin'—in that snooty hotel, and then abandon him. He's a long way from home, man. Like he comes from the country near the mountains, a little village, and he don't speak the English language real good. You gotta realize, he's just not comfortable, not yet, anyways."

It seemed to Hermann that Donald spoke with great authority of things about which he knew little. Hermann was now convinced one or both of these new acquaintances had been smoking pot, and he also knew

Donald would have a perfect excuse if challenged—like marijuana was the best remedy for a hangover, and therefore a medical necessity. He would certainly have some doctor's certificate attesting to his medical need, and there would be no way to prove it wasn't authentic, so there was no use even asking. Donald knew all the angles, but Hermann didn't think someone who took drugs could be trusted as a chauffeur.

"Donald," Hermann spoke up, "I've got a job to do. Have you forgotten that I've got to get Mister Lamour out to the island by 11:30? Then we've got lunch with Mr. De Carlo. Could you please let me in?"

Hermann worried Monsieur Lamour was too precious an investment to let him run loose like this. If something happened to him, all the plans Bruno and the American government had for him could be in jeopardy. And what would happen then? Hitler's twin might get in with the wrong crowd, and who knows where that would lead?

"OK, OK, Hermann. But try to be cool. He just a young kid. He's sorta lost, you know."

Donald stood aside and let Hermann enter his flat. At the same time, Donald called out to the Frenchman, "Hey, *mon ami*, Louis. Hermann *est la*, ha, ha. Hold onto Fisto, man."

Hermann noticed Donald seemed already half fluent in French. Hermann bent down to clear the low threshold to Donald's flat. He'd sometimes picked up or dropped Donald off here, but he'd never been inside. It was dark, cramped, and strewn with an odd assortment of furniture the chauffeur must have picked up off the streets or, at best, purchased at a thrift shop. And Hermann slowly realized the darkness and an odd sense of closeness came from the fact the whole place was covered with rugs and carpet pieces—not just the floors but the walls and ceilings too, and several layers thick. You could never vacuum a bumpy, uneven floor like that, Hermann thought immediately. It looked to him more like Donald must simply have added a new piece of carpet or cheap bathroom throw rug to those already there whenever he wanted to cover up some dirt.

The carpets were of all different sizes and shapes—whole ones, pieces, remnants, and throw rugs—and they were distributed and attached to walls and ceilings in a haphazard-looking mosaic according to some strategy only Donald understood. It frightened Hermann. He thought of mental patients in padded cells and of judo students who could use the room for soft landings. He noticed how very colorful the random mixture of carpet remnants was, not just that they formed a crazy collage of forms, shapes, sizes, and textures. The place reminded him of underground caverns, because the carpet pieces were so poorly attached to the ceiling—simply tacked or nailed in with straight nails—that many of them hung down like stalactites in a grotto. Hermann was startled when his head brushed against one in the living room. He didn't know what to say, and Donald, who looked a little sheepish, offered no explanation. It was warm and sticky inside, yet dark and otherworldly; a place only a spelunker could love. Hermann also thought the carpeting must reduce Donald's heating bills.

Jean-Louis sat at a table topped with coffee cups, baguettes, smelly cheese, and smoldering cigarette stubs. Fisto sat up on a chair next to him and licked a paper sack with a red and yellow Poggi's Deli logo and the words, "We Deliver." The dog growled when Hermann said, "*Bonjour*, Monsieur Lamour."

"*Bonjour*," the Frenchman replied, hardly looking up. His entire face looked even more like that of his dog, Hermann thought. Lamour patted Fisto soothingly and reassured the animal, "*Ce n'est pas grave. Calme toi, Fisto. Oui, ça va, mon petit* (It's not serious. Relax, Fisto. It's OK my little one)."

"Mr. Lamour, I'm sorry I'll have to continue in English now, but I hope you had a good sleep?"

"*So la la.*" He buttered a piece of baguette and heaped some jam on it.

"Well, I guess you're glad to see your dog again."

"*Oui*, I love *mon petit chien*. I need him, and he needs me. I do not like being *sans lui*. It's a . . . *fidélité profonde*."

It was the most Lamour had said to Hermann. Hermann realized he understood the last two words—*fidélité profonde*—because they were like English—"fidelity profound"—a kind of deep friendship. He could understand, even appreciate that concept. It seemed like the first good quality he had noticed in the uncanny twin. But then, on the other hand, he didn't know whether Lamour had lapsed into French at the end because his English had run out, as Hermann's own English had done when he was first learning the language, or whether Adolf's brother simply didn't want to use it anymore.

"Well, we'll find you an apartment that accepts pets. But, you know, I looked for you at the hotel, and well, now I'd like to drive you over to Treasure Island, to De Carlo & Wittgenstein, to our galleries, to meet Mr. De Carlo. We'll have lunch there. And this afternoon I'll take you to your art school."

"*O, oui, Le Nouvelle Âge.*"

Hermann figured out enough French to realize this meant "New Age." "Yes, the New Age Art Institute," he replied. He didn't know what else to say and wished Donald were coming too. "Well, are you about ready to go?"

M. Lamour said, "OK, *d'accord*," and stood up, carrying the piece of baguette, sticky with jam, in his left hand and allowing crumbs to roll off onto the table and floor. When Fisto looked up at his master, Jean-Louis picked up his poodle with a great sweeping gesture of his right arm that made clear to Hermann that Fisto was coming, too.

Hermann admonished Donald to be at work tomorrow, and Donald told Hermann to bring M. Lamour back to his place tonight, in case he didn't want to stay at the Ritz. It would be cool. He told Hermann he had dog food here in his apartment.

Donald preceded Hermann, Lamour, and Fisto to his front door. When he opened it, the light streaming in made the mosaic of carpets all over the place look even more like trash than from the inside. All the dust and defects were highlighted in the light of day, and this same light glinted off many of the tack and nail heads that held the carpet pieces in place. It was too bizarre, thought Hermann, who shuddered to think what would happen if Donald someday struck an electrical wire in the walls with one of those nails. He would warn him about that later. He also wondered what Donald's landlord would say about the damage all those nail holes did to the walls, if he ever found out. He couldn't understand why Donald didn't at least buy some better furniture for his apartment, since he knew that the chauffeur received a much-too-generous salary from De Carlo & Wittgenstein.

"Hey, Louis, catch you later, *mon ami*," Donald said to Jean-Louis as he left.

As they gave each other a high-five, Hitler's twin said, "*À tout à l'heure, cool cat.*"

I don't get it, Hermann thought.

13

Bruno reclined in his splendid office chair reading the latest update to the dossier on Hitler's identical twin from the CIA that Olaf Knudtson had sent him via a secretly coded, encrypted email. Bruno had printed it out because he didn't like to read on a computer screen; he preferred sheets of paper he could hold in his hands. It was the same for books; he didn't like listening to audio books, and he disdained Kindles. He preferred to turn pages, to underline significant passages with a pen, and to write remarks in the margins. For him, a book remained sterile and naked without such markings. The Hitler dossier, clipped onto the bookstand of his recliner, was, of course, a government secret, and Bruno was an official secret government agent in this case, so he shouldn't have made a hard copy of the email. But he would shred the hard copy after he read it, and no one would be the wiser. Hermann was privy to the same information and had been vetted by the CIA, and Hermann was a patriotic, absolutely trustworthy German American.

The Hitler update reviewed some of the details about the twin's youth from age one to twenty-one in the Orb Valley—the period after Dr. Philip Seed and his wife relinquished custody of the baby to the American government, which worked together with French secret services to raise it in a Western, yet out-of-the-way environment. It included some of the French documents concerning the subject's upbringing that should help Bruno in his task of turning the young Frenchman into a successful and therefore harmless artist devoid of political interests.

When he finished reading, Bruno set the documents in his lap, closed his eyes in concentrated thought, and smiled. He had vacillated about this project but had finally overcome his doubts and was excited by it. Not by the money the CIA offered him, mind you. He didn't need money. He had arrived where he wanted to be, financially. Actually, way beyond it. He was sixty-two years old, entering the last third of his life, in good health, and enjoyed respect and connections; he was ready for a new project, one that would do some good, not just for himself, but for the society that had been good to him, and for the world, because, after all, it was the world, especially the *Western* world, that had brought him to the felicitous position he now enjoyed. If someone had cloned Adolf Hitler, the world would be rightly afraid. And in this case, if genetics alone determined a person's destiny, Jean-Louis Lamour, Hitler's identical twin, posed a serious threat to civilization. So, what nobler service could he, Bruno, perform than to detoxify, so to speak, a potentially evil dictator? To divert him from sinister ambitions and set him on a path whereupon anything he accomplished would be of little consequence to anyone, aside from a few wealthy art investors? Within the rarified air of that world, Hitler's twin would be safely beyond the reach of neofascist groups should his identity be leaked someday and racists decide to appropriate him for heinous goals. Bruno knew this extraordinary project, this unusual, unprecedented challenge, was made for his unique resources and expertise. He himself was someone who had moved beyond his own genetic heritage, his modest Italian childhood, and transformed himself in a different milieu where he became a new person. He wondered if the CIA fully appreciated that fact. They certainly couldn't appreciate Myrtle's role in his development. At any rate, he was still young enough to take it on, to accomplish one more *grand geste*. He might even make his mother proud again.

There had been a short period of time at the beginning of his meteoric ascent when his mother was proud of him. But it didn't last. Despite her wealth, she was probably too set in her village ways and mentality. But it rankled him. She refused to come to beautiful San Francisco where he could have shown her his adopted home and impressive business, where he might have convinced her there was reason to take pride in her son's accomplishments. Alas, she wasn't a Myrtle Halstead.

Bruno thought of Dante's *Divine Comedy* and of the dark forest in which he was lost in the middle of his life when he first met Myrtle. So much had changed since then. The French painter was at a similar crossroads in his young life, Bruno thought, and he envisioned him, not descending into the inferno of politics, but ascending into a paradise of fame, wealth, and insouciant happiness. In the manner of his mentor, Myrtle, and like Dante's Beatrice, Bruno, would accompany Jean-Louis on this quest. Unlike Beatrice, however, Bruno would operate in the background. He would discreetly manage his neophyte's trajectory so as to avoid all the darkness, turmoil, pain, and destruction his genetic double had unleashed during the previous century. He would render this Hitler's life safe, secure, and irrelevant. Yes, he mused, this was something he could do. The brave souls who had tried to assassinate the original Hitler had paid for their courage with their lives. But Bruno could neutralize this new Hitler without martyring himself or even drawing much attention to himself. The endeavor would even leave him time to indulge in his favorite activity—reading great books.

After agreeing with Olaf Knudtson to take on this extraordinary mission, Bruno had plunged into helpful new readings—sociological and anthropological tracts and treatises on multicultural experiences. Jean-Louis, after all, was the product of a foreign culture—French—totally aside from his genetic makeup. And he was coming to America, with all the concomitant problems of adaptation. How much had he been shaped by the environment of his youth, and how much by his genes? An age-old question.

Now Bruno opened his eyes, crossed his legs and picked up the definitive analysis of the classic native American novel, *House Made of Dawn*—about the postcolonial intercultural clash between the Native American, Spanish, and white American worlds—by the eminent French critic, B. Rigal-Cellard, and finished reading the last chapter. Rigal-Cellard deepened his understanding of the problems a stranger faces in adapting to American society. Like the "dis-abled" Abel, the hero in the Momaday novel, this Frenchman and Hitler's identical twin, Jean-Louis, came from such a modest, rural area of France, Bruno realized, he could be expected to encounter structurally similar problems. Bruno also knew this from his own experiences in Cabrières, which was not far away from the Orb Valley where Hitler's twin became Jean-Louis Lamour, and where Bruno had found the Roman mosaics that had made him famous.

He was beginning to feel sleepy when he set the Rigal-Cellard book down in his lap, lowered the back of his high-tech chair, stretched, and closed his eyes. His thoughts wandered to the latest analyses from the ongoing Seti project on the Internet, the government-funded microwave search for radio signals coming from distant reaches of the universe in the hopes of finding extraterrestrial life. What interested him about this was less the scientific endeavor than the discourse about aliens as the *Other*, the necessity of abandoning one's own Eurocentrism or Amerocentrism in favor of recognizing the validity of the *Other's* mentality, the alien's point of view, whatever that might prove to be. He thought Jean-Louis Lamour might not be good at this and would need a lot of patient, sensitive coaching.

Bruno had printed out hard copies of much of the Seti information off the Internet but was now too comfortable to pull them off his bookstand. The downside of his high-tech chair was its soporific effect. He was just about to doze off and he would have if he hadn't heard the restroom door close in the hallway outside his office. He quickly came to his senses, got up and stuck all the loose pages that had absorbed his attention into the book by B. Rigal-Cellard and slipped it under a stack of file folders on the corner of his desk. By then he thought he could smell Crystal's preposterous new perfume, and, forgetting to lock the door to the hallway, he quickly exited out his main door.

When Crystal knocked on Bruno's door from the hallway, where she'd just used his bathroom, there was no response. When she tried the doorknob, she found it unlocked. Bruno usually locked it when he left his office. So, he must be nearby and would be right back. She walked into the CEO's office and sat down in one of the chairs opposite his desk, swung her blond hair back behind her ears, crossed her silk-stockinged legs, and swung the top leg rapidly back and forth. After a minute or so, she uncrossed her legs, stood up, and walked toward the window behind Bruno's desk. As she passed the desk, she inadvertently brushed a stack of file folders onto the floor. A book with a stack of loose pages stuck into it, that had been hidden under the folders, fell into the wastebasket next to the desk.

Crystal got down on her hands and knees to gather up the file folders and the documents that had slipped out of them. She didn't mind taking her time, elevating the angle of her derrière that stuck up into the air, and raising her miniskirt in a provocative way, just in case Bruno happened to come back in and find her in this compromising position.

But he didn't come back, and her knees began to hurt, so she stood up. She returned the folders that, as she had noticed, contained the usual, familiar business documents, back to the corner of the desk from which she had displaced them. But when she checked out the scholarly book about Momaday's *House Made of Dawn* that she pulled out of the wastebasket, she was irritated. She knew he spent too much time reading stuff like this. Why? What did it have to do with the business of De Carlo & Wittgenstein? Or with anything else in his life? If it had been a sexy book, she wouldn't have minded as much. Or even one of Jack Peterson's bestsellers. They would have indicated he was interested in sex, or at least in the San Francisco notables he should cultivate in the line of business.

Then she looked at the papers stuck into the book. What the hell was this? Aliens? The Seti project? Obviously off the Internet. And what was this long email about? Hitler's twin? Good God! She skimmed through it. From the CIA in Washington, DC? Jean-Louis Lamour, this French artist was Adolf Hitler's brother? Has Bruno gone nuts? Is this some kind of practical joke? The pages looked authentic enough. But she obviously couldn't read them now. What if Bruno came back to the office? Did she dare take them with her, scan them or make photocopies and then put them back? What if he found out? No, she decided, that could ruin everything forever. She made a mental note of the correspondent's name—Olaf Knudtson, of the CIA's biotechnology and genetics division. She could check this out later. Now she would have to make a quick exit; she thought she heard Hermann's voice talking to Gaby outside Bruno's main door. Bruno's partner might enter any minute. She stuck the loose pages back into the book. Then she placed the book back under the folders and slipped out the door to the hallway.

14

FOUR DAYS BEFORE THE reception a call from Esperanza Dicarlomini woke up Bruno after midnight in his Russian Hill house in San Francisco.

"Hello," he said sleepily when he picked up the phone after the fourth ring, just after the recorded message on his answering machine began to claim he was not at home. He could hear his mother's voice responding to the answering machine message in Italian, telling it to speak Italian to her, that she couldn't understand its English. He tried to speak over the message and her voice to explain that she had to hold on and wait until the message and the beep had run their course. She went right on talking, however, and when the message was done and he asked her to repeat what she had just said, she reprimanded him for not listening. He countered that she had woken him up, and she accused him of being lazy. She was eighty-five now, and maybe he shouldn't expect her to remember that there was a nine-hour time difference between Monteriggioni in Tuscany and San Francisco, California. On the other hand, she'd always been difficult about everything.

Thinking that an elegant invitation to the artist's reception might be persuasive, Bruno had decided to make another attempt to get her to California, but now she announced she wasn't coming.

"Oh, Mama," he complained. "But you promised. I sent you the plane tickets—*first-class* tickets. And I've reserved you a beautiful suite at the Ritz-Carlton. It's all arranged."

"Did you say, the Ritz-Carlton?"

"Yes, Mama. It's a wonderful hotel. I know you'll love it."

Silence.

Bruno was annoyed. This was just like her, to throw a monkey wrench into his plans. How could he convince her he wasn't a fake and a failure, that he hadn't just squandered the money she'd given him over the years from his father's trust, if she wouldn't come and see for herself? He wanted her to know the truth before she died. He wanted her to see De Carlo & Wittgenstein's flourishing auction house in the Gerard Kerry buildings on Treasure Island, his hard-working employees, his stunning showcase home that had been featured in *The Chronicle*'s *Sunday Magazine*. He wanted her to attend the glittering reception of artists, writers, journalists, and society people he was hosting for the young French artist. He also wanted her there so he would have an excuse to ignore Crystal Beatty.

The night before the reception at De Carlo & Wittgenstein's galleries, Gloria Majestic dined in Jack Peterson's suite at The Pines along with five Reading Roundtable members, including one of the founders, Mme. Françoise Hayes. The superstar had flown up from Burbank early in her private jet, because she wanted more time with the elders who had impressed her when she taped her book program. As her producer had predicted, the show had been a huge success, watched by a larger viewing audience than usual, the excess composed, as it turned out, largely of seniors. It came as a shock to Ms. Majestic that there was a neglected audience out there, an overlooked market. But that fact was less interesting to the Gloria Majestic she was today than to the Gloria Majestic she had been a couple of decades ago. Then, she had embraced her celebrity status with enthusiasm and had projected that genuine gusto onto the screen. Now she realized much of it was a slick act, a performance at which she was a master. Internally, she had begun to feel dried up and bored with the repetitive nature of her phenomenal success.

Her visit to The Pines had stirred her interest in something else. What that something was exactly, she couldn't articulate. Yet she knew she had been keen on viewing the tapes when she got back to her studios, both the tape of the show and the extra footage her crew had filmed. She had viewed and reviewed it. Then she had put together the best book show ever. Why? Because the audience had been so very perceptive; their comments had been so critical and thought-provoking. They had been sincerely engaged with the material and had expressed their opinions with candor and grace. Beyond that, the extra film her crew had shot of The Pines's residents' daily lives and opinions had been intriguing, illuminating.

Now as she sat listening to Mrs. Mitzi Rochester tell about her interest in pharaonic Egypt, she realized there was something real here, something authentic, something important to know. Perhaps even something to do—something new. She had an entire list of questions and no camera crew this time to distract her. She was here for a different type of experience. She was here to listen.

"Mama!" Bruno exclaimed as his wiry little mother was pushed into the SFO arrival hall in a wheelchair. His offer to lodge her at the Ritz-Carlton had tipped the scales. Holding a bouquet of two dozen red roses, Bruno had waited over an hour at the railing that separated greeters from arriving passengers. He watched everyone that emerged from the automatic doors so as to be sure to see his mother right away. "Mama!"

He rushed up and bent down to embrace her, and as he tried to kiss her, she said, "Business class. You promised me first class, and they put me in business class!" she complained in Italian.

"But Mama, that can't be. I got you a first-class ticket. We'll go complain at the British Airways desk right now. They can't do that to you, Mama."

"No, it wasn't British Airways. That was first class. It was that Lufthansa flight—from Florence to London. That was business class. You couldn't lie down."

"Oh, Mama. I'm sorry. I thought I explained they didn't have any first-class seats on that flight. I would have got them if I could have. You know that, don't you Mama? And that first leg was only two hours. I thought you'd be OK in business class for two hours."

Bruno's mother only rolled her eyes and shrugged her shoulders in a resigned way that signaled, "What can you do?"

"But the flight from London to San Francisco—that was OK, wasn't it, Mama? There you were in first class, and you could lie down and sleep, couldn't you, Mama?"

"Well, I guess," she conceded.

"And the food was good, wasn't it, Mama?"

"They only had French and California wines, Bruno. No Chianti Classico."

Bruno didn't try to explain this to his mother. "But you could watch movies on your monitor and listen to music with your headset. Did you watch any movies, Mama?"

"No."

"Well, why not, Mama? You love movies, don't you?"

"I was asleep."

Bruno realized they were blocking traffic with their conversation and set the roses into her arms, so they could move on. He slipped a fifty-dollar bill into the hand of the wheelchair aid who smiled broadly and quickly stuck it down the front of her blouse. The aid began to whistle as she pushed the slight Italian octogenarian with her distinguished-looking son toward the international parking lot.

When they reached the dark green Jaguar on level four, Esperanza asked, "Is this your car, Bruno?"

"Yes, Mama. Well, it belongs to my company. It's mine to use, as president of my company."

Esperanza shifted her eyes from the front to the back of the car. She was wealthy, too, but she didn't show off like this. She didn't buy a bigger house; she didn't wear expensive clothes. Aside from her computer and office equipment that nobody ever saw, she didn't own expensive things. If she'd known how to drive, she would have bought a small, used Fiat. Not that she didn't appreciate fine things. But the things she spent money on were gourmet meals and wine and first-class train tickets to her daughter in Siena—things you consumed immediately, that gave you pleasure but then vanished, except for your memories, which were rich. After you'd had your pleasure, you couldn't flaunt it in front of your neighbors, who would be envious. Nobody wanted to hear about your travels or your good meals. She didn't even own a washer-dryer. She washed her clothes by hand and hung them out her kitchen window to dry, two floors above street level. Or she took them with her on her visits to Siena, where her daughter did them in her washer-dryer.

Bruno swung his mother's suitcase into the trunk. Then he took her cane and deposited it there, too. Good God, what would they think of this cheap, worn, cloth-covered suitcase at the Ritz-Carlton? And this impossible cane that looked like it had been whittled from a tree branch some dog had dragged back from the woods outside of Monteriggioni? Having forgotten he had already tipped the wheelchair attendant, he pressed another fifty-dollar bill into her left hand and was surprised to see her eyes widen as she put her right hand over her astonished mouth.

As they drove up Highway 101 past Candlestick Park, his mother answered Bruno's questions monosyllabically. Now he wished he'd sent Donald or Hermann to pick her up. He had had to reorganize his day to meet his mother's plane and was beginning to wonder whether he should have invited her at all.

In tight chartreuse-polka-dotted spandex shorts and an athletic top—polka dots were all the rage—Crystal pumped away furiously on her Flexgrind multivalent personal trainer machine with built-in internet access. Ear buds in both ears, she glanced at the digital readouts and upped the treadmill's speed. Then she switched the monitor back to the website she'd found about

Adolf Hitler. She studied the old pictures of Hitler, from his childhood through his adulthood: Hitler in *lederhosen* in Austria; Hitler in a suit smiling at Eva Braun and petting a German Shepherd at his alpine *Eagle's Nest*; Hitler in his Nazi uniform ranting at a large Nuremberg party rally.

Crystal was sweating, and she tossed her head back and forth so her long, blond hair whirled up off her neck before settling back down in disarray on her shoulders. Now she looked out of the gym's window in her penthouse toward the East Bay. A sliver of moon hung over Oakland. The port was full of freighters and huge container cranes that looked like mechanical dinosaurs. The Bay Bridge was festooned with lights.

A pretty sight.

When she looked down at Treasure Island, she could just see a part of the outline of the crazily shaped auction house of De Carlo & Wittgenstein. To her this structure looked like a tumble of children's building blocks that had been glued together in random fashion. Now, it made her think how jumbled and confusing life was, and about the weird signs and clues. She had secretly read more of the poorly hidden documents in Bruno's office and was stymied. A second Hitler? The Seti project? Foreign cultures? Bruno's loss of interest in sex? She got off the treadmill and onto her stationary bike and began to pedal furiously. What the hell did it all mean?

As promised, Donald called Hermann when he left Lombard Street, about eight minutes from Hermann's home. This gave Hermann time to turn off the computer, grab his coat, and get to the sidewalk. Hermann cringed when Donald made a U-turn in front of his house and rammed the BMW's right front wheel into the curb. Donald had miscalculated the car's turning radius once again, but Hermann didn't remind him how that put the wheels out of alignment. He didn't wait for Donald to open his door but opened it himself and climbed in.

"Where is he?" Hermann demanded. Donald was supposed to pick up Jean-Louis first, then Hermann, and after that, Bruno's mother at the Ritz-Carlton. But the car was empty.

"Who's he, boss Hermann?" Donald replied in a low voice, feigning innocence.

"Who's he? Who's *he*?" Hermann roared back at Donald. "I can this not believe," Hermann continued, reverting back to German word order. "You know exactly who I mean, Donald: Jean-Louis Lamour!" Hermann almost shouted this.

"He. Was. A. Little. Late," Donald replied slowly with an inscrutable smile.

"Late? What do you mean? What's the matter?"

"It's cool, Hermann. Nothin's the matter. It's jus' that his girlfriend, you know, the cute little Korean at the art school—Soonie—she takes longer than some, man. And Louis, you know, he's in no hurry. He be a patient cat. He knows how to please the ladies."

Hermann didn't feel cool or patient. He was responsible for getting the guest of honor and Bruno's mother to the reception on time. "Good God, Donald. Doesn't he know this is his big day? The whole event is for him. Lots of important people will be there. Couldn't you explain that to him—how important this is?"

Hermann sometimes thought it would be better if Donald called him Mr. Wittgenstein, then maybe Hermann wouldn't have that feeling Donald was more in charge than he was. Especially when things didn't function the way they should. But now, of course, it was much too late.

"Sure, I told him. He knows. It's OK."

"Well, when *will* he be ready?"

"Oh, it won't be too long now, I guess. But we may as well pick up Mr. De Carlo's mama first. I'm pretty sure he be ready by then."

Hermann should have made this suggestion, to show he was in charge. But now Donald had said it first, and it would be pointless to contradict him.

Hermann told the woman behind the Ritz-Carlton's reception desk he had come to pick up Mrs. Dicarlomini. The receptionist then gestured toward the petite old woman seated on the chair upholstered with scenes of the Bayeux tapestry. She was partially concealed behind the large fronds of a potted palm. For an instant, Hermann thought he could be looking at his grandmother back in East Germany, or maybe at Myrtle. He had expected a jolly and robust Italian mama. Bruno hadn't told Hermann how frail and wiry his tiny, gray-haired mother was. Hermann felt an immediate urge to protect this person who was so easy to overlook.

"Mrs. Dicarlomini?" Hermann said, as he approached her. Then he remembered to say, "*Buon giorno,* Signora Dicarlomini," as Bruno had instructed him. He suddenly felt much too big in front of her, unacceptably large, and he instinctively bent way down from his waist as he extended his right hand toward her. When he sensed he still hadn't managed to reduce his size sufficiently, he set one knee down on the settee next to her chair, so that he practically kneeled in front of her.

Esperanza Dicarolomini broke out into a broad smile and discovered some English in her. "I think . . . you Hermann?"

"Yes, ma'am. I'm Bruno's, your son's partner, and I've come to take you to the reception. I hope you are feeling fine today, ma'am." Hermann returned her smile and she kept holding onto his large hand.

"Yes, I know. Yes, I am happy. Why you call me ma'am . . . Mama?"

Hermann laughed when he realized she didn't know what "ma'am," meant. It reminded him of his own linguistic past. "It's like when you say 'sir' to a man. It shows respect," he explained.

"Respect?"

When Hermann realized she hadn't understood "respect," he gave up and said, "It's because . . . I like you."

"You like me? Yes, good. Yes. I like *you*! Yes!"

Esperanza laughed and beamed and let Hermann pull her to a standing position. Then she pointed to her cane and purse at the side of the stuffed chair. Hermann picked them up, then Esperanza took a tight grip on Hermann's right arm and let herself be led out of the hotel to the BMW where Donald held the back door open for her. She slid across the seat to make room for Hermann.

When they left the Ritz-Carlton and Donald headed not for Presidio Heights but the Fillmore, Hermann realized Jean-Louis was once again staying at Donald's. De Carlo & Wittgenstein had rented a beautiful furnished flat for the French artist on Clay Street within walking distance of the New Age Art school and not far from the Presidio. But in the month since Jean-Louis moved in, he rarely used it. Since Bruno's mother was with them in the car, Hermann didn't say anything to Donald this time. But he worried about the Hitler duplicate, since he thought Donald was a bad influence. He couldn't understand how anybody, even Hitler's brother, could stand spending time in Donald's bizarre, dark flat. Maybe identical twins were less sensitive and didn't notice things as well as nontwins. Or maybe there was something sort of Wagnerian in this character's genes that liked spooky, dark grottos. He couldn't stop shuddering internally when he thought about Donald's place, and he worried about the idea of a potential dictator running loose.

Hermann had broached the subject of the artist's unhealthy penchant for Donald's apartment with Bruno, but his partner didn't want to take any action. Bruno also told Hermann not to refer to him as Adolf. He might be Hitler's twin, but he was legally and for practical purposes Jean-Louis Lamour, a French citizen, with all the rights an individual enjoys in a democratic country—well, most of the rights if you ignored the CIA's justified surveillance and agenda for his life. He was a guest in the United States, with a valid visa and work permit. Hermann should try to think of him as such. The main point was Hermann shouldn't be prejudiced, even toward the twin brother of Hitler, because in America everyone was innocent until proven guilty. Besides, artists couldn't do their best work if their liberty was restricted, so they often cultivated unconventional habits. He reminded

Hermann their mission was to promote Jean-Louis as an artist and make him wealthy, satisfied, and complacent.

Since fleeing East Germany, Hermann had come to appreciate the concept of liberty. Still, he had problems with the idea of an innocent Hitler. If this was, indeed, another Hitler, then he, Hermann, had a responsibility to the CIA in its mission. He trusted the American government to do the right thing to contain a potential monster. Now that Hermann was an American, it was his patriotic duty to help. It would be one way of repaying the adopted country that had been so good to him.

Hermann was jarred out of his ruminations when Donald ran into the garbage can outside his apartment near Yoshi's, and a startled Esperanza grabbed Hermann's hand. As Hermann stroked her hand to soothe her, he made it clear to the chauffeur if he didn't produce Jean-Louis within twelve minutes, he Hermann, would come in and get him. Donald left his chauffeurs' cap and gloves in a compartment in the driver's door and shot into the building at a rate that suggested the black man's oft-repeated complaints about painful knees had been creative fiction.

In the car, Hermann entertained Bruno's mother as best he could and glanced frequently at his watch. After eleven and a half minutes passed, he tried to explain to Esperanza that he would have to go in himself but would be back shortly. He gave her Donald's pager and showed her how to press the orange button if she needed him. Then, as he turned to go, Donald, Soonie, Fisto and Jean-Louis bubbled brightly onto the apartment building's outside landing.

Good God, what a crew, Hermann thought. He glanced at Esperanza and noticed she gaped at them as they started down the wooden steps toward the street. In his snazzy blue uniform with the silver stripes, Donald looked more like a member of Sergeant Pepper's Lonely Hearts Club Band than his usual lookalike, Pope John XXIII. Soonie, Jean-Louis's Korean girlfriend with the waist-length glossy black hair, wore a tight, yellow-and-black-polka-dotted sweater and the shortest mini-skirt Hermann had ever seen. In her arms she carried not only a patent leather polka-dotted purse to match her sweater, but also a scruffy Fisto, who was licking her chin. Still at the top of the landing, Jean-Louis let the door behind him close on the coattails of his full-length, slick black trench coat and was jerked back awkwardly. He dropped a cigarette from his lips, and a little glass vial fell out of his hands onto the landing. He started to laugh hysterically.

Um Gotteswillen! Hermann thought. He must have been smoking pot again. And he couldn't believe how this character looked. His long scraggly hair was now disrupted by half a dozen or so tight miniature braids tied with bright yellow ribbons, while his beard seemed inches longer than the last time he'd seen him. He had on purple-rimmed, wrap-around sunglasses; his clothes were beatnik black except for his shoes (which didn't go with anything except Soonie's sweater), and extra thick-soled, rubbery, yellow-and-black-polka-dot basketball shoes. He looked ridiculous. *This can't be Adolf Hitler's double*, Hermann thought. Anybody with any of Hitler's genes simply couldn't look like that. But then he thought, maybe anything was possible, after all. Then he wondered, what had the French artist dropped on the landing?

Hermann, who was now out of the car, rushed up the stairs to help free a giggling Jean-Louis from the door. Fisto struggled out of Soonie's arms, ran up the stairs in pursuit of Hermann, and barked and nipped at Hermann's pant cuffs. Kicking at Fisto, Hermann struggled to release Jean-Louis's coat from the door. He also managed to make out the label on the bottle of men's perfume that the artist had dropped—*Fatal pour Hommes*. The glass vial hadn't broken, but the cap was loose, and some perfume had spilled.

His coat liberated, Jean-Louis picked up his favorite perfume, wiped the excess onto his hands and rubbed them through his hair. With a triumphant grin, he raised the bottle with a broad sweep of his right hand and waved it back and forth from his wrist, his elbow straight, presumably at Soonie, before he snatched up Fisto and bounced down the steps in his rubbery shoes. When Jean-Louis handed Fisto to Soonie as she got into the car next to Esperanza, Jean-Louis wiped the bottle dry on Fisto's fur.

15

THE MAIN GALLERY AT De Carlo & Wittgenstein's postmodern auction house was full of Jean-Louis Lamour's *boulist* paintings, both watercolors and oils on paper and canvas. They had been hung on the sidewalls of Building One, which Bruno had named "Casa Firenze," as well as on portable walls that had been set up throughout the center of the huge hall. These portable walls had been arranged not in the usual straight lines and right angles, to create rooms for viewing different periods of an artist's life or certain themes or motifs. Rather, these wall sections, curved themselves, had been put together in seemingly random, undulating or circular patterns, as if, from an overhead view, a handful of cooked spaghetti or Medusaesque snake tangles had been flung out onto the floor. This organization made it impossible for viewers to see the paintings in any particular order or even to be sure if they had seen them all. It had the effect of complementing the curves of Lamour's work.

This design had been Bruno's idea, since the owner and CEO of the auction house hadn't discovered any development, any evolution in the *oeuvre*, but rather a dogged insistence on repetition of the same motifs or forms. Bruno knew certain artists had become very successful through devotion to such monomanic activity, often late in life. Claude Monet's creation of that tree-lined pond with the water lilies in Giverny had arrested his development. From then on, he painted only that pond, those same water lilies and willow trees—in spring, summer, fall, and winter—in hundreds of variations. Peter Paul Rubens became almost as stuck on his fleshy female nudes; he seemed to love nothing more than pink cellulite. El Greco, on the other hand, insisted on painting gloomy, dark, unnaturally thin, and elongated figures, as if he suffered from an ocular malady. Similarly, when the fourth-rate artists of the 1950s, Walter and Margaret Keane, created their first set of large, dark-rimmed, sad eyes, it changed their lives. Thereafter, they kept replicating those same kitschy eyeballs in endless variations—on children, men and women, the young, the middle-aged, and the elderly. Pondering why both Monet and the Keanes didn't get bored with the same subjects day in, day out, Bruno conjectured that whereas Monet produced variations on beauty, which earned him the financial success and security he achieved late in life, the only thing that must have saved the Keanes from fatal boredom was their frequent trips to the bank. Wealth accumulation, in their case, staved off the insanity that would otherwise have surely set in.

When Bruno looked at Lamour's curved villages and landscapes, he saw something that could make Lamour as wealthy as the Keanes. In such a case, it would be preferable if viewers didn't actually see all of the work. And journalists and art critics would be able to make much of this unique presentation where the design of the exhibition space reinforced the art. They might throw in some insights about the audacious, revolutionary architecture in which the event took place.

Lamour's French works had been shipped to San Francisco by the large *Galerie Soleil* in Montpellier that had had good success in selling the work to tourists for the last two years. It had been there, after all, in the *Midi*, where the term *boulist* was born in a conversation between the well-known art historian and critic Bernard Delavigne and his friend Antoine Bourget, owner of the *Galerie Soleil*. After Delavigne had disparaged Lamour's paintings, saying they reminded him of round imitations of cubist landscapes and mocked them with the term *boulist*, the gallery owner had transformed this little joke into a successful marketing slogan. With it, he had convinced foreign tourists who visited his upscale gallery—especially Americans—this art was part of a new trend, a *debut-de-siècle* phenomenon you might call it, the first new twenty-first-century art movement, and the contemporary legacy of the avant-garde artists who had worked a century ago in the same general region—Picasso, Manolo, Gris, Dali, Masson, etc. He recommended visitors go to the Museum of Modern Art at Céret, close to the Spanish frontier, where some outstanding cubist works of Picasso and others were housed, so they could compare and contrast *boulisme* with *cubisme*. Soon thereafter, Americans were shipping Lamours back to Spokane and Des Moines, Céret was overrun with well-to-do yankees, and a local French stone mason amassed a fortune when he constructed a large underground parking lot in the middle of that town, which had clean, modern pay toilets.

As part of the exhibit, De Carlo & Wittgenstein incorporated a video documentary about Lamour's youth in southern France on large and small monitors and interactive media throughout the exhibit. The video was also accessible on the website, and information about Lamour was contained in the pamphlet that guests could refer to as they browsed the paintings. There were bars and mini bistros stocked with food and wine next to each multi-media station manned by tuxedoed waiters and waitresses. Everything was ready.

Near the gallery entrance, Bruno conversed in high spirits with Gaby Wittgenstein and some camera and security people wearing spiral-wired ear buds. At any moment, Hermann would arrive with Jean-Louis and Bruno's mother. Her presence would help him keep Crystal at bay. Just then he realized he hadn't seen the heiress and wondered, momentarily, where she was. Then the journalists would arrive, and the celebrities, Gloria Majestic and Jack Peterson. He wondered how the elderly genre writer had managed to persuade the superstar to attend. Whatever he had done, Bruno was pleased. It would be a dazzling affair. His mother would be impressed.

First to arrive were the local television crews and some newspaper reporters. Bruno provided them with insights about the exhibit and suggested they enter and get a preview ahead of the crowds. As guests began to arrive, they were immediately surrounded by waiters plying them with delectable *hors d'oeuvres* and French champagne before they wandered off into the tangled exhibit.

Bruno was watching from inside the glass entrance when a company BMW rolled up. He saw Donald get out and open the back door. The French artist tumbled out laughing, followed by Soonie and Fisto. The dog jumped up and down excitedly, almost as high as the bottom of Soonie's mini skirt. Hermann got out of the front passenger side looking worried, and he opened the door for Esperanza who offered him a wide grin and clasped his arm.

When Bruno rushed forward to greet his mother, he noticed how her grin morphed into a grimace. He wanted her to take his arm, but she didn't let go of Hermann. Only when Bruno told her Hermann had some important work to do did she relent. After Hermann excused himself, wondering what it was he should do, Bruno gesticulated expansively at the huge, festively decorated gallery and asked his mother what she thought.

Esperanza peered into the gallery for a moment. She looked across the cavernous space and up at the high, multi-angled ceiling with the retractable skylights arranged in stunningly crazy, geometrical patterns. She seemed to take it all in—the multimedia booths, the bars and waiters, the reconstructed Mediterranean gardens featuring grape vines, red poppies, thyme, lavender, and potted Cypress trees. Bruno thought he detected a trace of a smile when she looked at these plants. Then she looked at him and asked in Italian, "Why is your business called 'De Carlo & Wittgenstein?'"

"Well, Mama, you know my partner's name is Wittgenstein. You've just met him—Hermann Wittgenstein."

"I know that, Bruno. I mean, why is it 'De Carlo'?"

Bruno's heart sank. He realized his mother wanted to know why he'd shortened his name, their family name, from Dicarlomini to De Carlo. Was this all she could think of to say?

"Oh, Mama. I explained that before." Bruno had explained it a hundred times to his mother during his visits in Tuscany—how Dicarlomini was too long a name in California; people had trouble with it; he needed a good business name that sounded distinguished. Esperanza always countered that Dicarlomini *was* distinguished, it sounded good; it was spelled just like it sounded. Was he ashamed of his family name? His father's name?

It was a terrible argument to have with his mother. He knew where it led—to a shouting match and then to her tears and withdrawal. It was worse than the one about her refusal to get a washer-dryer or even the one about his getting married that went around in circles and upset both of them. It was the last thing he needed at this moment.

He started to tell her that he was forced to shorten it by the State of California, since together with "Wittgenstein," there would have been too many letters for registering their business. He began to regret this lie when he saw her eyelids begin to compress the way they did before she began to cry. His mother wasn't stupid. She could tell when he was trying to pull a fast one on her, and she was prepared to take her revenge by making a scene right there at the entrance of his major event.

Just then the limousine carrying Jack Peterson, Gloria Majestic, and three of Peterson's guests from The Pines arrived in the semicircular driveway in front of Casa Firenze. As the cameras flashed, Esperanza opened her eyes back up and directed them toward the approaching spectacle. Bruno then swept her into the introductions, and miraculously, Jack Peterson and Ms. Majestic took an immediate shine to her. When they sucked his mother into their little group that was buffeted with food, drink, and reporters' questions, Bruno found himself alone. He was free to greet the growing flood of guests streaming in.

An hour and a half into the reception, Bruno realized he still hadn't seen Crystal Beatty. This wasn't like her. Where was she? He was relatively unencumbered now, free enough to wander from group to group. He was pleased to note most guests were busier socializing with each other and commenting about the exhibit's design than in studying the works of Jean-Louis Lamour. He was also pleased to note many guests tried out their French on the colorful young artist with the purple shades and the polka dot basketball shoes and the Korean girlfriend in her matching sweater.

Jean-Louis Lamour held court in one of the artificial Mediterranean gardens so Fisto would have ready access to a cypress tree. A uniformed Donald stationed himself next to them. Hermann had thought Donald should stay with the cars in the garage, but Bruno had said Donald could come in as long as he kept his pager on him. In his own, inimitable English, Donald was half-translating, half-interpreting whatever Jean-Louis said to the curious guests when their French reached their limits.

"Yes, ma'am. Mistah Lamour here's from that *très petit* village, Colombières-sur-Orb that be in the Languedoc. That's near Provence. You been to Cannes, the Film Festival? Cool. Well, Louis's works been shown in Montpellier. That Montpellier's a university town . . . with a famous medical center. You maybe been there too?" Donald's southern French accent of these place names was good, people thought.

When somebody asked Donald to ask Louis what inspired him to create his boulist paintings, Donald already knew the answer, "*Pastis*, man! Yea, lordy, pastis. It's this drink they drinks in the *Midi*, with the kinda licorice taste. Yum!" Donald rolled his eyes, and everybody laughed. "No shit, Messieurs, Dames. It was the pastis. That's the secret."

Some guests asked how to say "polka dot" in French. Others tried to make jokes about the dog and about their experiences with doggie poop in Paris. Fisto yapped and nipped at people's cuffs and hems, snatched *hors d'oeuvres* out of Jean-Louis's hands, lapped up spilled champagne, and peed against a cypress tree pot. Jean-Louis rattled on in French to whomever approached about whatever subject they broached. About his childhood he said he was too young to remember much; he thought he had caught a case of amnesia.

Donald explained, "It was the pastis, man," rolled his eyes again, and everybody laughed.

Bruno observed his ward from a short distance, how well he got along with the public. Despite his minimal English, this young Frenchman managed to attract attention. In his odd way, he had obvious communicative skills that would benefit his *entrée* into the American art scene. Jean-Louis obviously didn't mind crowds. On the contrary, he seemed perfectly at home as the center of attention. The more people gathered around him, the more relaxed and charming he seemed to become. Occasionally, he would come to the end of a story, then fold his arms across his chest and smile, while Donald came up with an unforgettable translation. The enraptured circle of listeners clapped with delight and enthusiasm, which drew attention to them and provided a steady string of curious fans who wanted to meet the soon-to-be-famous French artist. Bruno was more confident than ever that Hitler's twin would do well with his help.

High above, undetected on a catwalk under one of the geometrical sky-lights, Crystal instructed one of the cameramen she had hired to zero in on Jean-Louis Lamour with his telescopic lens and to film him for the duration of the reception—discreetly. Then she headed for an elevator. In Bruno's private restroom she combed her hair and touched up her make-up. She rubbed generous drops of *Fatale pour Femmes* perfume around her neck and behind each earlobe and checked that the wireless microphone embed-ded in the nametag she intended to attach to Jean-Louis's lapel was func-tioning. He was already wearing a plain name tag, but she would insist the celebrated artist take it off and wear this special one that contained both the De Carlo & Wittgenstein embossed logo as well as a tiny Lamour reproduc-tion in the corner, not to mention the electronic bug. She would pin it to the artist's shirt at an opportune moment when Bruno, Hermann, and Gaby were not around, and later, after Lamour's voice had been recorded, find a pretense to remove it again. She intended to compare the artist's voice with Hitler's voice from old WWII film soundtracks and radio broadcasts she would listen to. She had to get to the bottom of what Bruno was up to. It was possible he was suffering some kind of mental disturbance and needed help. She tossed her hair back, practiced a smile, and headed for the gallery.

It took her about thirty minutes to work through the crowds. She had to chat patiently with those who greeted her; many knew she was a Beatty and that she worked at or with De Carlo & Wittgenstein. Many assumed wrongly, however, that she was a partner in the enterprise. No one would have believed she worked as its accountant. And, of course, she never told anyone her real motives for working there. When you were a Beatty, the world made its own assumptions about you and your life, and no matter what you said or did, the world remained constant in its inaccurate opin-ions. It was only one of the many annoying prices you paid for extreme wealth.

Eventually, she came in view of Jean-Louis and his entourage. They were surrounded by a large crowd of guests, and this peculiar-looking char-acter, Crystal thought, seemed to be having a wonderful time, talking rap-idly in high-pitched French, holding a champagne glass as a woman might hold a teacup, with his pinky sticking out. Donald was standing on a rock in the Mediterranean garden to make himself taller, and Jean-Louis swept his right hand up, bent at the elbow, and slapped it down on Donald's shoulder when he wanted his African-American friend to explain something to the crowd. Then he'd smile and sip champagne while Donald translated. Everything Donald said drew laughter or applause from the crowd, and then Donald and Jean-Louis would high-five each other. At this, a straggly little black dog barked and jumped up and down and Jean-Louis would slap one of his thighs. Crystal wondered how that mutt got in. Dogs weren't allowed on the gallery floors. The scene looked to her like a form of street entertainment. Certainly, this Jean-Louis, whom she hadn't yet met, didn't look like Adolf Hitler. For one thing, he slouched, and there was so much hair all over his face, he looked more like that dog than anything else. Was that *his* dog?

She moved in closer to make her official approach. Only a few people separated her from Jean-Louis, and now she suddenly noticed something else about him, something indefinably subtle, a kind of aura that radiated from him, a certain something that was . . . appealing. She stepped past the last invitees separating her from the artist and felt a definite pull of his presence. It seemed to her, also, that before she stepped into his sight, he had noticed her, too. He had stopped talking in mid-stream, looked around—right through the crowd—as if alerted or alarmed, and tipped up his nose as if he'd scented smoke and was looking for the fire. She noticed Donald looked at him to see if something was wrong. But after that, she became oblivious to her surroundings. The crowds seemed to vanish as she took the final steps into his circle of influence and approached the young man who smiled at her and leaned forward to kiss her on each cheek, and then returned to the first cheek but bypassed it to place his lips softly on her ear, where he seemed to breathe in and out while his nose lingered above her ear. The hairy head that brushed her face seemed to her as smooth and soft as mink, and she felt a strange tingling behind her ears as he slowly pulled his head back to gaze at her face as if moonstruck. And she, in turn, felt flushed all over. Her heart was pounding. She forgot to exchange Jean-Louis's nametag.

16

LATE IN THE EVENING of the reception a taxi driver first delivered an elderly Italian woman to the Ritz-Carlton. In the back seat she had argued with an elegantly dressed man, and when he attempted to kiss her on the cheek, she scurried off toward the hotel entrance where she smiled at the doorman and vanished inside.

Now the driver stopped his cab in front of 999 Greenwich, and the driver twisted his neck back toward the gentleman, who emitted the aura of a sophisticated Italian actor, and said, "Wow, is this your place, sir?" The passenger nodded and the driver said, "Some pad!"

"Thanks," said Bruno. "What do I owe you?"

"Sixteen dollars and thirty cents, sir."

Bruno got out of the car and handed the driver a hundred-dollar bill. "Keep the change."

"Wow, boy!" said the driver. "Thanks a million, sir! Hey, let me give you my card, sir. If you ever need a cab . . ."

But the gentlemen had already buzzed open the pedestrian security gate with a remote control. The gate shut and the man vanished inside the ultra-modern structure, a home that suited his classy appearance.

Inside his expansive marble entrance, Bruno walked to the elevator and took it to the second floor. He had remodeled the house two years after Myrtle's death. The best architects had transformed it from a recognizable San Francisco Victorian into a postmodern marvel of simplicity and style. The interior was cool and lean, understated, full of stark, sometimes fanciful Italian furniture and odd modern sculptures; the walls were covered with an eclectic collection of paintings. A romantic Fragonard picnic in the countryside hung next to a humorous Paul Klee stick figure, and that next to one of Picasso's hideous female heads. It was an outstanding collection, but Bruno knew that the mix was hard to take, especially for Crystal. He'd made the mistake years ago of inviting both her and her parents to his housewarming party. Her parents alone would have been fine, but once Crystal had been there, she somehow had a way of reappearing and spending nights in his bed. And once she'd spent a few nights in his bed, she felt she had the right to criticize the way he'd hung his paintings. One morning, he found her downstairs wearing nothing but one of his shirts, a coffee cup in hand, staring at a wall where she'd switched the position of several paintings. After that he had the security company out to recode his house and his remote, so that she couldn't enter on her own. He kept making up excuses why he didn't have her remote updated to the new code until she quit asking. He returned the paintings to their original places in order to annoy her all over again whenever he weakened and, against his better judgment, let her spend the night.

Now he stepped off the lift on the second floor and entered the one room, a den, that he had left in its original state—in the style of Myrtle Halstead. There he kept his collection of her music tapes as well as the silver candlesticks, her books, and a few trinkets she wanted him to have. He pulled out a tape of Schumann's piano quartet, opus 47, and spooled it forward to the sad and lyrical *Andante Cantabile* in the old-fashioned tape deck—an anachronism in this age of home theaters. Out of respect, he didn't want to digitize her tapes. As the music played, he walked over to the window and peered at the city lights. He thought of the old woman, his cultural mentor, who had done so much to inspire his interest in literature. He knew his involvement in art and antiques was about business and profits, and consequently less genuine. He used the visual arts to become rich. He knew a great deal about art, and the paintings on his downstairs walls were there to impress wealthy friends and clients. He didn't really love or even like the heads of Picasso's women, for example, or even the simpering, romantic Fragonard. These were simply things money made possible and which increased his portfolio. But he did love to read. He loved to go to the theater. He lost himself in the universe of literature, with its purposeful characters, their passions, their catastrophes and triumphs. And he could lose himself to the sounds of great prose or poetry, to beautiful language. It had not always been the case, but it had become so due to Myrtle. Now it was a high pleasure, a skill he had cultivated, a gift he had earned. It couldn't just fall in your lap, like wealth could. It was two gifts, really, because great literature was accessible to him in English as well as in his native Italian. He preferred English nowadays, since Italian reminded him of his mother.

Bruno turned away from the city as the music bathed his ears. He went to the antique cherrywood credenza and looked at the framed photos of his mother and of Myrtle. The latter would have understood him; *she* would have been proud of him. Too bad *she* couldn't have attended the Lamour reception. She would have reveled in the scene, and they could have talked about it for hours over lunch the next day. He would have felt good about himself. He passed from the photo of the young, robed Myrtle as a tragic actress in Euripides's *Medea* at UC Berkeley's Greek Theater to one of his mother leaning out of her kitchen window in Monteriggioni above the laundry she hung out to flap in the breeze.

How could a wealthy woman be so gauche, even if she lived in an Italian village? Why did she insist on washing her clothes by hand and then complain about how hard she worked? Why did she have to display her underwear in public? *She* still sent *him* money. To prove he didn't need it, *he* now sent *her* more money than she'd ever need. It was an absurd recycling potlatch, but neither was willing to end the vicious cycle. In her situation, a new washer-dryer was a mere pittance, a negligible drop in the bucket. Good God, she could have her clothes, including her underwear *dry cleaned* every day and never notice the cost. He knew she sent him that photo to remind him of his village background. Unlike Myrtle, *she* was very much alive. He flew her in for the exhibit so she could be proud of him. And he wanted to do her a favor, to show her a nice time. But all she did was complain, pick on him about little things, the same old things. Not that she didn't seem to be enjoying herself. She seemed to get along with everybody else—Hermann, for example, and the strangers she met at the exhibit. And people seemed to like her, even though she really couldn't speak English. Even the Ritz-Carlton staff apparently liked her, despite her disreputable luggage. She just didn't seem to have the time of day for him. Why couldn't she be more like Myrtle?

The *Andante Cantabile* came to an end. Bruno didn't want to hear the rest. It was late. He was tired. As he turned off the stereo, he noticed the red light of his answering machine flashing in his office in the next room. He walked in to check it. A message from Crystal from that morning, before the reception, to tell him she absolutely had to see him in his office at 10:30 tomorrow. Her voice sounded high-pitched and strained.

"Damn it, Bruno, what's going on with this French guy?" she said. "Who the fuck *is* he? Is there something wrong with *you*? I've got to talk to you. Now! This is a pressing matter, you know? Call me, damn it!"

Her voice morphed from angry to inquisitive to frustrated and back to angry. This was obviously not just a new ploy to weasel her way into his home and bedroom. She must have gotten wind of something. If so, why had she avoided him at the reception? And why had he seen her cuddling his dog and smiling next to Lamour for the photographers? *Maledizione!* This could be serious. Bruno pressed the erase button so hard he split his fingernail. He should have had that taxi driver stop for cigarettes. He thumbed through the pile of mail his butler had left on his desk and picked up the morning's *Chronicle* that lay next to the mail. He took the paper to his bedroom and flipped through a few pages before falling into a fitful sleep. Tomorrow he would have some explaining to do.

The photo that appeared in the following morning's *Chronicle* pictured Esperanza, Gloria Majestic, Jack Peterson, Donald Washington, and Jean-Louis Lamour holding champagne flutes, and Crystal Beatty cradling Fisto in her arms. All were smiling radiantly at the stunning reception for the new *debut-de-siècle boulist* artist from southern France. A long article reported that the exhibit's unique, nonchronological design was the perfect complement to this new wave of timeless art, the curved aspect of which suggested the cyclical, nonlinear nature of seasons and time, thereby rejecting and confounding Western notions of linear development. Lamour's work evoked an inclusive blend of nature with a landscape of everyday objects in reaction to the dehumanizing effects of technology. All of this was realized by a French and thus Western artist, and, presented in the postmodernist Gerard Kerry structure, the haphazard geometrical angles of which complemented its opposite in the art—namely circular forms—and thus reconciled conflicts. The *Los Angeles Times'* article, entitled "Amazing Maze of an Exhibit," called the show a stroke of genius.

A week later, *The Daily Cal* on the Berkeley campus published a review submitted by a university student who worked part-time for De Carlo & Wittgenstein and who had helped hang Lamour's paintings on the serpentine walls. The student writer noted the banal paintings, which were blatantly deficient in craftsmanship, had an obsessively repetitive quality, that the curved nature of the objects in every landscape, for example, the supposed *debut-de-siècle* counterpart of the Cubists, was an absurdly transparent marketing notion designed to conceal a thoroughly mediocre talent and boring exhibit. Compared to the Cubists, these latter-day works could only be seen as a degraded, degenerate form thereof, if there was any relationship at all. Not wanting to lose his job at De Carlo & Wittgenstein, the student signed his article with a pseudonym. The precaution was hardly necessary, since no one with any influence in the real world read *The Daily Cal.*

17

THE MORNING FOLLOWING THE reception, Crystal called Gaby at 10:00 A.M. to tell her she was sick and wouldn't be coming to work and to please cancel her 10:30 A.M. appointment with Mr. De Carlo. Gaby found it strange, since Crystal always called Mr. De Carlo "Bruno" and not "Mr. De Carlo." Furthermore, she always wanted to talk directly with Mr. De Carlo and never wanted to leave messages. When he wasn't around, she always wanted to know where he was, what he was doing, and when he'd get back. This time Ms. Beatty showed no interest in his whereabouts.

After Crystal set the phone down on the orange crate that served as Donald's night table, she reached across the bed to stroke Jean-Louis's straggly long hair. He was still smiling and sound asleep. Her call hadn't disturbed him in the slightest. It was cold in the apartment. She didn't know how to turn on the heat; and even if she did, she had no reason to get out of bed now. Donald, who had spent the night in a sleeping bag in his living room, would already be gone to work. She didn't hear the whimpering of the Korean girl, Soonie, who had locked herself in the bathroom. She snuggled down under the covers and cuddled close to Jean-Louis; he grunted and grasped her hand to his chest when she put her arm around him. He began to snore. She closed her eyes and thought about the events of the last twenty-four hours.

God! Nothing like this had ever happened to her. She had recently turned forty-eight. She was filthy rich, desirable. Never married, but she'd had lovers, some good ones. Bruno should realize that. And she was a good lover, too. Bruno, of course, didn't appreciate *how* good. She'd read all the how-to sex books—the classics like the Kinsey Report, Masters and Johnson, the definitive *Sex Atlas*, and those recent best-sellers, *Celestial Sexuality,* and *Spiritual Sex*. But Bruno had no understanding of the spiritual, medieval, and mystical aspects of sex. He just laughed at imminent, radiant sexuality, sexuality that transcended the human sphere. What did he know? Maybe he had no talent for transcendent sex. But this Frenchman. . . She stroked Jean-Louis's back. Maybe this was what those books were all about.

Earlier that same morning at 7:59 A.M., CIA agent Latrone Sanders pulled his unmarked government Toyota Camry up to the curb, where his colleague, who had finished the night shift, had just pulled away. It was a good spot, just across the street from Donald Washington's apartment. His contact had informed him that a woman with long blond hair, who resembled the rich bitch, Crystal Beatty, had entered the apartment at 1:30 A.M. along with Mr. Washington, the Korean girl, Soonie, and the French artist, and that no one had come out since then. Why Jean-Louis Lamour insisted on sleeping at his black friend's place in the Fillmore was beyond Latrone's comprehension. And if the blond was indeed Crystal Beatty, well, that was incomprehensible, too. But it was his job to monitor the artist from 8:00 A.M. until 5 P.M. this Thursday and make note of any unusual activity.

Up until now he had speculated that Hitler's twin was gay and had a relationship with De Carlo & Wittgenstein's chauffeur. But, good grief, the chauffeur was an eccentric, aging codger, and Jean-Louis was only twenty-one. On the other hand, Latrone had noticed at the reception how the Frenchman held a glass with an extended pinky, which seemed pretty gay to his mind. But then again, the CIA had given him some training in cultural differences, so he knew that French people don't normally give you a house tour when you're invited to their homes, and that chrysanthemums were appropriate funeral flowers in France. He remembered how you were supposed to twirl and sniff the wine in your glass before you took a first sip, but he couldn't remember what if anything was said about what to do with your pinky. So maybe it was just a French thing. Or maybe an aberration due to the fact he had been frozen as a baby. Then again, he knew the artist had this cool-looking, slim Korean girlfriend whom he'd somehow nailed his first week in San Francisco. Now he knew the chauffeur had driven not only Jean-Louis and this girlfriend back to his sorry pad, but also, maybe, the billionaire heiress, Crystal Beatty.

The more Latrone thought about it, the more confused he became. After it became clear Jean-Louis rarely stayed in his beautiful flat near the

Presidio, De Carlo & Wittgenstein provided the artist with a huge, trendy warehouse loft near AT&T Park that contained both living quarters and a spacious studio. At least Jean-Louis went there to paint. Immediately, he started inviting his students from the New Age Art Institute to the loft, and they would all get tipsy on pastis and then start slapping those ridiculous, colorful round balls on huge canvases. People paid lots of money for them, even though Latrone knew many of them were done by his students rather than by Jean-Louis. To Latrone they all looked more or less the same.

Latrone sighed and stopped trying to figure things out. He had enough experience with the CIA to know sometimes you didn't understand things until a case was closed. And sometimes you never did. But you still got paid. He retrieved a *Playboy* from under the driver's floor mat, began to leaf through it, and let his mind wander.

Later that morning, when agent Sanders glanced up from his absorption in a *Playboy* centerfold that depicted a slim, sleek, Asian female with silky jet-black hair that cascaded around her breasts and fell all the way down to her low-cut silver bikini bottom, he saw the door to Donald Washington's apartment open and Monsieur Lamour's Korean girlfriend, Soonie, stumble out and start down the stairs toward the street. She looked unkempt, her black hair was flying about, and tears streamed down her face. Articles of clothing hung over her shoulders, and she carried two brown paper grocery bags full of who knows what. At the next-to-the-bottom step, she tripped, and everything went flying. She yelped and landed in a sprawl on the sidewalk. Sobbing, she twisted her body to clutch her right ankle as if in pain and tried laboriously to pull herself back up onto the bottom step. Apparently, no one in Donald's apartment noticed any of this. The front door had slammed shut, and the shades were drawn; in fact, the entire street still seemed asleep. Latrone, who had never forgotten his mother's injuries back in the Loma Prieta earthquake, and who hated to see women suffer, took a quick second glance at the centerfold, dropped the magazine to the floor of the car, jumped out, and ran to assist the Asian woman with the tears welling from her eyes. As he crossed the street, he had two thoughts—whether rendering assistance could get him in trouble at work, and what the tearful Asian woman would look like in a silver bikini.

18

"WHAT'S THIS?" BRUNO ASKED himself when he picked up his thick paperback copy of *The Brothers Karamazov*, and a paper fell out of it onto the floor of his office.

Four months since the reception, Bruno was pleased the mission was going so well. Crystal, probably aided by that pheromone perfume, seemed to have fallen under the spell of Jean-Louis and had forgotten about any suspicions she might have had. Lamour's *boulist* paintings were commanding ever-higher prices, and he was prolific beyond everyone's most optimistic expectations. He was a star instructor at the New Age school and a media darling who welcomed journalists and photographers to his loft or school, day and night. He always had time for interviews, usually translated in idiosyncratic and entertaining fashion by Donald, who in the meantime was relatively fluent in the southern French *patois* of Languedoc. Jean-Louis's English remained broken, but his admirers found his accent charming. They tried to brush up on their French so they could better appreciate his long-winded, scrambled, and cryptic commentaries. The more attention he received, the more pastis the artist drank, and the more he smiled. In Washington DC, Olaf Knudtson couldn't have been more appreciative of Bruno's brilliant work. To top it off, Bruno was pleased Crystal had stopped using his private restroom. Donald confirmed she had been spending a lot of time with Jean-Louis. When he thought about it, Bruno realized Crystal had been absent several afternoons without calling in, and she had taken a few days off without giving a reason. It wasn't like her.

Bruno bent down and picked up the fallen paper to find a copy of the anonymous critique of Jean-Louis's artwork that had been published in *The Daily Cal* following the gala opening. Bruno recalled the review but wasn't concerned about it at the time since *The Daily Cal* had no influence in the art world. But how did the article get into his book, which had been underneath a stack of business documents on the swivel stand attached to his cutting-edge recliner? And why? It wasn't anything Gaby would do. She was straightforward, beyond suspicion. She didn't have a manipulative bone in her body. Hermann was also out of the question. The janitor barely spoke English. Crystal hadn't been in his office for a long time. If she had an amorous relationship with Jean-Louis, she wouldn't have a motive. He wracked his brains for other possibilities. Finally, Hermann's administrative assistant occurred to him. He had access to both Hermann's and Bruno's offices. Bruno called Gaby. "Gaby, could you please email me the employment application and dossier on Hermann's assistant, what's his name . . . Hernando, no, Fernando?"

In less than a minute, Bruno's computer's ping announced new mail. Bruno opened the documents on Fernando Seed. An odd name, he thought. Let's see: born in Salzburg; parents Dr. & Mrs. Philip Seed; enrolled at UC Berkeley; grades in the sciences below average, good grades in the humanities; working on a double major in Spanish and English when hired part-time by Hermann at De Carlo & Wittgenstein; wrote reviews of concerts and art exhibits for *The Daily Cal*. Wait a minute, thought Bruno. Fernando *Seed*? *Seed* is the name of the scientist who discovered the frozen baby in Austria and brought him back to life—*Dr. Philip Seed!* Bruno sprang up from his desk and opened one of his locking file cabinets. He pulled out some of the Lamour documents from Olaf Knudtson that he should have shredded a long time ago.

Yes, there it was on the fourth page in the background material on Philip Seed. It had been a while since he read it. He sat down at his desk to concentrate: after giving up the "glacier boy" to government authorities, Seed and his wife, Carmina, had returned with their toddler, Fernando, to Chula Vista, where Dr. Seed worked in a lab at UC San Diego. Mrs. Seed was killed in a car accident when Fernando was three years old. Philip Seed never remarried and raised his son on his own. The father tried to steer the boy toward science, but the young Seed showed no interest in it.

Bruno quickly double-checked Fernando's birthdate on the application. By God, it was the same as Hitler's twin's reanimation, or rebirth day!

Dio mio! So, this fellow was a sort of half-stepbrother to Jean-Louis for the first year of their lives. And he works for us. How disconcerting!

Bruno rose from his desk and paced. Then he eased himself down into his ergonomic chair. It was clear Fernando Seed was the only one who could have planted the article. Why? He reread it now with attention. The writer was very articulate, and he was right to attack the quality of Hitler's brother's artwork. After all, Hitler, the historical Hitler, had been a mediocre artist and had failed to gain admission to the Vienna Art Academy. It stood to reason his identical twin would share a similar degree of artistic talent, or lack thereof. But Bruno knew in this day and age, quality was irrelevant to an artist's success; marketing was everything. And success in the current American art scene, after all, was the government's concern and therefore Bruno's mission. If Hitler's brother became successful, he wouldn't have the time or inclination to develop any *other* talents. But why did Fernando Seed want Bruno to read this?

Four days later, Gaby placed a copy of the *Los Angeles Times Sunday Magazine* on the center of Bruno's desk. She opened it to the lead article, complete with color photos, about Jean-Louis Lamour's life and work since his arrival in San Francisco. It was entitled, "Jean-Louis Lamour—A French Imposter?"

When Bruno picked it up after he entered his office, he didn't bother to take it to his recliner. He read the headline standing up. Stunned, he finished the body of the article and sank into his chair. Someone who called himself Charles Magnus had written an absolutely brilliant and scathing analysis of Jean-Louis's work in an insightful, literate, and elegant style. The vocabulary was rich and the diction and article's cadence impeccable. Although it was a review, on another level the text itself was also a caustic piece of art. Its writing style resembled that of *The Daily Cal's* article. And it was full of photographs—of Jean-Louis teaching at the New Age Art Institute, and of Jean-Louis's loft full of large *boulist* canvases. There were more photos of Jean-Louis and Donald being interviewed, and even a photo of the one small Jean-Louis painting on the south wall of Hermann's office. Jean-Louis had made a present of it to Hermann, and Hermann couldn't refuse to hang it up. Only an insider could have taken that photo, thought Bruno, who wouldn't dream of hanging a *Lamour* in his office.

All the previous articles and reviews had been full of praise and thus benign. Hitler's brother was a media darling. But this Charles Magnus claimed a large number of paintings sold under the name Jean-Louis Lamour were not painted by him, but by his students, and their work was no better than that of their teacher, whom the article thoroughly demasked as a sham and charlatan—a cultural manipulation worthy of the greedy corporate art world. In the article, Jean-Louis was expertly chastised. Bruno was shocked by its message—not that he disagreed—and dazzled by its style. Through reading the classics, Bruno recognized good writing: this and the author of the *Daily Cal* article were undoubtedly one and the same. But this was in the *LA Times*! What would happen if this article garnered too much attention, got syndicated and started a media buzz?

Bruno didn't have long to wait. Charles Magnus created a firestorm. The following Sunday *LA Times* was full of letters to the editor with emotional reactions—both pro and con—to Magnus's claims. Talk radio and CNN news picked up on it. Larry King invited Magnus to his show two weeks hence. Olaf Knudtson called Bruno with the information that Charles Magnus was a pen name for Fernando Seed, his employee, Hermann's assistant—which Bruno already knew. How was he going to arrest this potential disaster and prevent it from metastasizing?

19

"HERMANN, I'VE GOT A special assignment for you," Bruno announced the next morning after he called him to his office.

"What's that?"

"It requires you to use some of your former skills. I hope you won't mind."

"Well, I haven't done any electrical work in a while, but I probably still could." Hermann wondered why his boss didn't just get their maintenance department to take care of whatever the problem was. Then it occurred to him it might be a problem in Bruno's house, not at the company, and maybe Bruno wanted him to fix it just for old times' sake. "I've still got my tools at home. So, what can I do for you?"

"It's not really for me, Hermann. It's for our mission—for America."

Hermann sat up straight in his chair. America had enabled him and his family to attain a good standard of living, a very good life, actually, an upper-class life. Few East Germans had been as lucky as he. Of course, now those East Germans were a lot better off in a reunited Germany, but most of them hadn't been able to come to San Francisco, to meet great people like Bruno and Myrtle, who had helped him. His kids didn't know how lucky they were; they could barely remember East Germany. That griped him, because they were grown up now and not interested in German history. If they had been, they would have had a better appreciation for all their advantages. Hermann didn't really understand his children, but then a lot of Americans thought that was normal. But that was beside the point. Now he and his boss had undertaken a dangerous mission, well maybe it wasn't all that dangerous, but at least it was an *important* mission for the American government, to prevent Hitler's twin from turning into another Hitler. If America needed Hermann's skill as an electrician, he was ready to work for America, for free.

"Well, yes, sir. Just tell me where and when, and I'll be there in my overalls with my tools."

"Actually, Hermann, this job requires something of your old East German skills."

"Well, OK, but Gaby's really better at translating German into English than I am. Her English is better than mine. She also knows of a professional translation service in the city."

"No, Hermann. I don't need translations. What I mean is, I need you to use your skills as a former police spy. I need you to break into Fernando Seed's apartment in Berkeley and download everything in his computer for me."

Stunned, Hermann sat back in his chair. Mr. Seed? His assistant? Bruno—and America—needed his old *Stasi* skills?

Hermann couldn't sleep. He didn't want to keep Gaby awake by tossing and turning, so he crept out of bed as quietly as he could, went downstairs to the kitchen of his spacious Marina District home, and pulled a Beck's beer out of the refrigerator. If you drank enough of it, beer was a soporific, and it calmed the stomach. He walked to the picture window that looked out toward Sausalito, but couldn't make out any lights across the bay through all the fog, let alone at the Yacht Club or on the boats docked in its marina.

After Myrtle died and Hermann learned about her generosity to him in her will, he had sworn to himself he would never spy on anyone again. Especially not on his boss and partner, Bruno, who had also been so good to him. He felt so guilty for having suspected Bruno of harboring evil designs on Ms. Halstead that he resolved to renounce spying forever, as penance for his guilt. Besides, he had learned all kinds of new business skills in the meantime. And maybe he wouldn't even remember everything he needed to break into Mr. Seed's apartment, figure out his secret computer codes, and leave no fingerprints or other traces of his entry.

As he thought about the process, a thrilling little shiver rolled up Hermann's spine, and his heartbeat accelerated. He recalled the adrenaline rush his old work sometimes provided—the only good thing you could say for it—but then he felt ashamed about the positive twinge, however slight, in this memory. He knew enough history in the meantime to realize his East German *Stasi* skills had affinities with the Nazis' Third Reich. The German

Democratic Republic was a misnomer for the country in which he grew up—which was the opposite of democratic. Both those systems shared similar mentalities and styles; they were both totalitarian.

Hermann looked at the clock—3:40 A.M.—and looked out the window at the fog again. Of course, he couldn't tell Gaby he had agreed to a dangerous, illegal assignment. She would forbid it if she knew he had to break into someone's apartment. Only he and Bruno knew Jean-Louis was Hitler's twin brother. Oh, and, of course, Donald knew it. But Donald knew everything, and it made no difference. Donald never judged anyone for any reason. And he was discreet. Hermann couldn't understand Donald—certainly not why he lived the way he did now that he could afford a nice, clean apartment. Donald was like someone from another world, like a peculiar angel in human disguise, or like someone who had had another life and could remember it and everything he had learned in it, so that he knew twice as much as everybody else in this life. He was the most tolerant person he had ever met. Too tolerant, probably.

Hermann went back to the kitchen and took another beer from the fridge. What if he got caught in the act of breaking into Seed's apartment? If he were arrested? But he would be acting on higher authority. The legal implications weren't clear to Hermann, but he guessed Bruno would work them out with the CIA if anything went wrong. Of course, Bruno would take care of his family if he, Hermann, had to spend time in jail, and jail in America wouldn't be half as bad as all those wasted years in East Germany. And since it was Bruno who was asking him to take up spying again, maybe he wouldn't have to feel guilty about going back on his promise to himself.

Hermann thought and thought while he drank his second Beck's. He weighed this and that angle and drank a third beer. Then he thought some more. He took another look out the window at the fog, which had only thickened. Then he fell asleep on the living room couch with one last question in his mind: *What would Myrtle Halstead think?*

20

It had been really easy, a breeze, as Hermann told Bruno four days later. Fernando lived in the downstairs flat of an old two-story, shingled, south side Berkeley house that must have been rented to Cal students for decades. The entrance on the downstairs east side of the house was almost overgrown with ivy, and the door had no deadbolt. Hermann knew Fernando was at work in San Francisco that afternoon.

"Getting in was a piece of pastry," he explained excitedly to Bruno. "I was shocked how messy it was inside and dusty. We know Mr. Seed is very clean and well-dressed when he comes to work here, but in his apartment were his clothes all over everywhere. And there were stacks of books and papers sometimes three or four feet high all over the floor, and much dust on many things. All walls had bookshelves that were full, and many too full so that books were hanging out halfway sometimes, and some had fallen onto the floor. And there were magazines, lots of books and magazines about writing, like *Writer's Digest* and *Publisher's Weekly*, and journals with stories in them. Also, lots and lots of newspapers. Also, lots of stories and manuscripts by him, with his name, "Fernando Seed," and some by "C. Magnus" or "Charlie Magnus" or "Chuck Magnus." I don't know why he uses different first names and this false last name, but maybe he thinks someone will publish his manuscripts if they are written by someone with an important-sounding name like Magnus."

Hermann was anxious to present his boss—he couldn't stop thinking of Bruno as his boss even though they were partners—with all this information he had obtained on Fernando Seed. He hoped he had done something helpful for America.

"Excellent," said Bruno, smiling. "Now, were you able to obtain the contents of his computer?"

"Yes, of course! I used nonpowdered vinyl gloves so I wouldn't leave fingerprints and I downloaded his hard disk onto my laptop and I've already sent it to your computer. Just look under *Magnuseed*. I gave the file half of both of his names, so you could remember it. I hope this will help America. If this country needs anything else from me, just let me know," Hermann exclaimed.

"Good work!" Bruno smiled in approval. "With any luck, that should be all we need."

Bruno dismissed Hermann, then he asked Gaby to bring him a double cappuccino with skim milk. He adjusted the swivel stand on his marvel of a chair to accommodate his laptop and opened the new file labeled *Magnuseed*. It was 1:25 P.M. He didn't notice when Gaby left the office at 5:30. He didn't notice when the sun set over the Golden Gate and dusk turned to darkness and the lights of downtown San Francisco came on. Later in the evening when he became aware of a hunger pang and looked at his watch, Bruno was surprised it was after 8:00 P.M. He got out of his chair, went to the restroom, and called *Il Fornaio* to deliver him their veal scallopini, an insalata mixta, a half bottle of Monsanto Chianto Classico, and some tiramisu. Close to midnight he felt a little dizzy from all the reading and ordered a cab to drive him home.

The next day Bruno asked Hermann to find out what he could about Fernando Seed's father, Dr. Philip Seed's, current life. Hermann should ask Olaf Knudtson at the CIA if he needed help. Then Bruno went back to reading the *Magnuseed* file in his laptop.

Two days later, certain things had come into focus in Bruno's mind. In a lesser talent, the fact Fernando used the pen name of *Magnus*, which meant "great" in Latin, would have seemed a sophomoric gimmick, but Bruno had read in his laptop unpublished stories and novel manuscripts of such depth, eloquence, wisdom, and artistic beauty, he was convinced this young Seed was a rare literary genius. So why was he working for De Carlo & Wittgenstein? And why did he bother to debunk the visual art of Jean-Louis? Bruno now had incontrovertible evidence he had written the anonymous critique for *The Daily Cal*. He found a draft in the files Hermann had copied, and Seed had obviously stuck the copy into his volume of *The Brothers Karamazov*. Bruno feared the furor caused by his *LA Times* review could do irreparable damage to his French protégé's artistic trajectory and thus the US government's mission of containing the potentially dangerous Hitler twin. If this brilliant young Seed learned too much about Jean-Louis, his investigations might come too close to the truth. Whatever his motives, he had to be stopped.

Two days later, after Hermann sat Fernando down for a man-to-man talk, Hermann had new information for Bruno. Seed was a poor student. He had had to slow his progress toward his degree at Cal to earn money—hence, his employment at De Carlo & Wittgenstein. Fernando admitted he had tried to make some money while in school with his writing but failed. He was twenty-one years old, and his old father had stopped supporting him when he turned eighteen. His mother, who had been much younger than his father, died when he was three—Bruno already knew that—and his elderly father was a retired scientist who lived alone in Calistoga in a mobile home park.

On a Tuesday afternoon, Bruno sent an email to Fernando Seed, stating he wanted to see him in his office on Thursday morning. On Wednesday, Seed told Hermann he had developed chills and nausea; he was probably coming down with the Bhutan flu that was going around, and he would have to go home and stay in bed a few days. He asked Hermann to tell Mr. De Carlo about his illness and that he hoped his Thursday appointment could be postponed. He left work early. On Thursday, Hermann called his assistant's cell phone—he didn't seem to have a landline—to see how he was feeling, but he got no answer. There was no answer on Friday when Hermann called again. When there was no answer the following Monday and no response to Hermann's emails and text messages, Bruno instructed Hermann to go to Seed's apartment in Berkeley, and if necessary, employ his *Stasi* skills to see what the matter was.

"*Mein Gott*, I didn't have even to break into to Mr. Magnus's apartment," Hermann reported after returning from his Monday expedition to Berkeley. "When I got there, the door was wide open and a woman wearing an apron was shaking the dust out of a bathmat at the side of the house. You wouldn't believe it. There was really a lot of dust! And from a bathmat. I couldn't believe that. And before I could think what to say, she said, 'I guess you're here to fix the toilet.'

"I was in my overalls, so she must have thought I was a plumber and not an electrician or a spy or a very well-off businessman, like I am. So, I just nodded, and she said, 'I'll show you,' and I followed her into the apartment, and I couldn't believe my eyes. Almost all of his things were gone. I mean, most of the books and the clothes that were all over the place before. Gone. But the furniture was still there. The woman said she wanted to fix it up before renting it out again, and the last tenant obviously hadn't ever cleaned it up, the pig, and he'd left in a big hurry. I guessed she must be the owner, or maybe the manager. I asked did he break his lease—I'm glad I thought to think of that question—and she said, 'He just paid month to month, and the last month was almost up, anyway.'

"I looked at the toilet, and even though I'm a trained electrician, I know enough about toilets to see it needed a shorter chain, so I said if there is a paper clip around here in this apartment somewhere, maybe I can fix it without charging you for a part—if there is a paper clip. She shrugged, so I suggested maybe I could find one somewhere. She shrugged again, so I thought she meant she didn't mind if I looked for a paper clip, so I thought it was OK if I looked in the living room first. I tried to make a little conversation and I said to her this was a pretty nice place and I knew someone who might like to live in it. Did she rent it furnished? 'Yea, all this furniture comes with the place.'

"I looked around the bookshelves where there was still a bunch of books and asked if they were part of the furniture. She said, 'No, the last tenant left them.' And, guess what, I didn't even need to ask, because she said to me, 'Do you want them? You can have them.' I said, 'Yes. I want them. I know someone who likes a lot of books.'

"She started mopping the kitchen floor, and I grabbed up some of the books and put them on the entrance porch. I also saw a stack of old papers and letters in a folder between some books, so I put that whole stack at the front door, because I thought she wouldn't mind if I took the papers, too. After I had all that looked interesting, I said, 'Hey, I found a paper clip.' She said, 'Good for you,' and went on cleaning the linoleum floor in the kitchen.

"I shortened the chain in the toilet with the paper clip and flushed it a couple of times. There was a crack in the old rubber ball, but I didn't tell her that. Instead, I said I thought it would do it for a while—the paper clip on the chain in the toilet. She said, 'Thanks. What do I owe you?'

"I said, 'Nothing, I've got another job close to here, and the paper clip doesn't cost a thing, and these books are as good as bucks.' You see, I made a little joke with her, and she stopped her mopping and said, 'Great, then we've got a deal,' and she smiled at me.

"Then I took the books and papers and went back to my car. I looked back to see she wasn't looking at me before I got into my BMW. She might have gotten suspicious if she'd noticed my car, because then she would have thought I'm not a real plumber. And I wondered what she would have thought if the real plumber showed up after I left. But then, I thought maybe she'll get suspicious and not let him in."

Hermann was almost breathless when he finished his story. He placed a large cardboard box of books and papers on Bruno's table.

21

CRYSTAL DIDN'T USUALLY READ newspapers. She had often told Bruno, with a coy smile, reading wasn't her favorite pastime. She had been a good accountant for De Carlo & Wittgenstein, in fact a smart and meticulous one, Bruno had to admit. She didn't mind reading and calculating numbers. Her mathematical talent might have been an inborn and in any case a useful trait in a wealthy heiress.

Today she was hopping mad. Bruno had never seen her like this—stomping, literally stomping back and forth in front of his desk. Her blond hair shook at every step, and her pleated mini skirt swished with every turn. She astonished him by whacking what seemed to be a rolled-up newspaper or magazine on his desk as she sputtered and swore at him.

"How could you? How could he? That dirty little weasel fink! Bruno, how could you allow this?" She whacked his desk again. "Do you know what this means to Jean-Louis? What if he finds out?" Whack! "Where is the cowardly snot head? Huh? Where is he, the dirty bastard?" Whack, whack, *whack!*

"Crystal, *ma petite*," Bruno cajoled as he rose from his chair and reached an arm out to try to calm her down. She was rather pretty in her anger, and he felt a fleeting erotic twinge—until she whacked his outstretched arm with the magazine so hard he cried, "Ow! What are you doing!"

"Don't you *ma petite* me, you, you, you . . . I don't know what you are! Tell me what the hell is with this?" She brandished the magazine threateningly toward him like a conductor directing the first emphatic beats of Beethoven's *Fifth Symphony*. He feared she would hit him on the head on the second downbeat and stepped back out of her reach.

"Sorry. But what are you talking about?"

"You know what I'm talking about!" she hissed.

"No, I don't. Couldn't you just tell me?"

"Why should I, you dirty rat?" Her vocabulary wasn't much more imaginative than Hermann's when she was excited.

"Because you obviously have an issue with something. How can I address it if I don't know what it is? Here, do you want to show me that, that paper or magazine? Is that what's bothering you?"

Crystal's mien suddenly went from fury to sorrow; she quit stomping and began to whimper. Before she could say anything, she began to cry. Uncontrollably. Soon mascara was streaming down her cheeks. She threw the magazine vehemently onto Bruno's desk. It was the *LA Times Magazine* that contained Charles Magnus's attack on Jean-Louis.

"Oh babe," Bruno started to say in an attempt to soothe her.

"Don't you *babe* me," she choked out the words between sobs.

"But this is old news. The furor has died down. Charles Magnus has disappeared into the woodwork." In actuality, Hermann had, just a few days ago, received a cryptic email from Fernando Seed in Barcelona. "You really don't need to worry about this." He tried to placate her in a soothing tone of voice.

"Oh yes, I do! Shit, shit, *shit*! You don't know anything!" Crystal cranked up the decibels with her reply.

Bruno pulled the ivory silk Lagerfeld handkerchief out of his navy silk Tournaboni suit, and stretched it toward her carefully, alert to any sudden motions on her part, in case he needed to avoid another body blow. Crystal raised bloodshot eyes toward him, yanked the handkerchief out of his hand, wiped an ample amount of black mascara onto one half of it, and blew her nose loudly into the other half. She paused and looked down at her feet.

"Jean-Louis saw it," she said in a softer, calmer voice, "and he made Donald translate it into Languedoc French for him last night." She spoke in fits and starts.

"You're telling me he found out about the article? About what's in the article?"

"Yes, damn you! What do you think I'm trying to tell you?" Crystal shouted, frustrated with Bruno's slowness. Then she tried to compose herself. "I entered the loft after Donald had already begun to translate for Jean-Louis. Six of Jean-Louis's students were working on projects at the south end of the room. Jean-Louis was on a roll. I can tell when he's inspired. He was working on this wonderful painting—ten by twelve feet—and it had the greatest round spheres of Victorian houses, like on Bush Street, in really old-fashioned psychedelic paisley patterns—what a great idea!—and he and Donald were drinking pastis, and Edith Piaf was singing *chansons* on the iPod. It was so beautiful." Crystal couldn't suppress another sob. She blew her nose forcefully into Bruno's handkerchief again and when she went to fold it over cried, "Oh shit. Now my nose is fucking bleeding! Fuck!"

"Here, sit down and tip your head forward, and hold your nostrils together," Bruno suggested and offered her his desk chair.

Crystal didn't resist and plopped down into it. Bruno adjusted it to an upright position and she leaned forward. With his handkerchief in her left hand and her right thumb and forefinger over her nose, she continued.

"Anyway, I think Donald skipped the worst parts in his translation; he made it sound better than it was. But Jean-Louis isn't used to being criticized. He's very sensitive!"

Crystal sounded like a congested child with a nasal twang. Bruno could barely understand her. She released her nostrils and blew some more blood into his handkerchief, but managed to leave a red spot on the tip of her nose.

"Yes, yes, of course he is," replied Bruno. He refrained from telling her she looked like the red-nosed reindeer.

"Well, yes," continued Crystal. "He's not stupid, you know!" Crystal shouted when she thought she detected a hint of condescension in Bruno's voice.

"Did I ever say he was stupid?" he retorted.

She squinted and seemed to launch daggers from her eyes as she stopped talking.

"What happened next?" Bruno asked.

"Why should I tell you, you . . . *moor*!" This time she found a word for him, but she didn't see Bruno smile when he realized she meant *boor*.

"Because, I want to help. Please tell me what happened." Bruno said this in a tone that contained all the diplomacy, courtesy, and respect he could muster, considering the black streaks on her cheeks and the blood congealing on the tip of her nose.

"Well," Crystal hesitated for a moment. "Well, I can't really describe it." She paused and looked down again before she continued, this time in a low voice resonant with gravitas.

"Jean-Louis got the message, I mean, he understood the criticism in the stupid article, and he sort of froze at his easel. I mean, I had never seen him stop painting in the middle of a work before; he always finishes any painting he starts during the day before going to bed at night, no matter how late it is. He's really disciplined, you know. It's kind of a rule with him. Like his rule that you have to make love at least once a day, before the clock strikes midnight.

"I tried to grab the article away from Donald," she continued, "because I could tell it was really confusing Jean-Louis, and I thought I ought to read whatever it was before Donald continued. But Jean-Louis ordered me, in such a cold voice—one I had never heard before—to let Donald finish—so I was scared to interfere."

Crystal sniffled and blew her nose again. She glanced up briefly at Bruno.

"And he didn't even look at me when he told me to sit down while Donald finished. Jean-Louis just sat there on his stool with his paintbrush in his hand. And he didn't look at Donald either when he said, 'Finish the article, Donald,' in this really cold, clipped voice. I think even Donald got a little scared."

Crystal paused, as if searching for the right words. She continued in a very soft voice, full of profundity.

"Then something really strange happened. A window suddenly blew open by the fireplace, and a cold breeze blew in and sort of swirled around in the loft. It startled us. I mean everyone except Jean-Louis. Fisto—he'd been curled up by the wood-burning stove—well, Fisto woke up and ran over to Jean-Louis and started yapping and jumping at his legs. Pretty soon, he was barking and howling and running circles around Jean-Louis, in a frenzy! We couldn't get the dog to calm down, and we couldn't get Jean-Louis to move or to talk to us. He had always picked up Fisto before, whenever Fisto came to him. Always. It wasn't like him. Poor Fisto was going crazy. We poured some more pastis in the glass that he always has on the table next to his easel and coaxed him to take a drink, I mean Jean-Louis, of course, not Fisto, but he just kept staring at one spot on his canvas, as if he was catatonic."

Crystal paused, sighed, and wiped her cheeks with the handkerchief, which smeared her mascara in broader streaks across her face.

"I'd never seen him like that. It was so awful."

Now a tear rolled down Crystal's left cheek clearing a narrow path through a mascara stain. Bruno stared at her, not daring to disturb her story.

"Well, Donald got us all to his place, and I got in bed with Jean-Louis, as usual. But, damn it, he didn't talk to me all night long, and midnight came and went, and he didn't make love to me. We've made love every night since we've been together. It was a sacred rule with him. *Damn it*! He's the best lover in the history of the world. I know he's the love of my life. I knew it the moment I came close to him at the reception. He knew it, too. It was love at first sight, sheer magic. It happened just like that, like a lightning bolt—real love, physical and spiritual love. You wouldn't understand that. Now everything is ruined! *Ruined!* I'm going to be fifty in a couple of years, and then sixty, and the best years of my life will be over. I'll be a lonely, wealthy spinster, and that's all! *Fuck! Fuck it!* Life's not fair!"

"Oh Crystal, baby, let's just slow down and think about it. Things don't just change overnight like that. I'm sure he'll snap out of it. How was he this morning? Did he talk to you?"

"Well, yes. He spoke to me again, thank goodness. But his voice sounded different, and he said he thought he would change his profession; he thought he was tired of painting. He thought he would try something else. He said he was going to take a walk so he could think things over. I said I would walk with him. He said no. When we got up Donald had already left for work. Jean-Louis said he wanted to be alone, and he told me to go home, or to go to work, as if he didn't care what I did!"

Crystal began to whimper again. Now she allowed Bruno to rub her forearm tenderly.

"Damn it, Bruno. I'm afraid. He seemed so different. Like he *had* changed overnight. Like I didn't know him. If he only hadn't found that article and made Donald translate it for him. What am I going to do?"

Bruno couldn't answer Crystal's question.

What are *we going to do?* And then he thought, *What would Myrtle do?*

Jean-Louis had an atrocious headache. He knew he hadn't had enough pastis the night before at the loft. That wasn't all. He was stunned by the article Donald had translated for him. There was someone out there who disliked his paintings, his grand circular designs; someone who disagreed with his aesthetics, who was trying to thwart his progress, who was a threat, who was his archenemy. Whoever it was had the audacity to say it out loud, to publicize it openly, to oppose his intentions. This was new!

Fully conscious now, he flung himself around in bed and kicked off the covers. He had sent his girlfriend away, and Donald had gone to work. Alone, rage swelled up in him. He made a fist and hit the pillow next to his own pillow. It felt good to punch something, so he pounded it several times before flinging it across the living room, startling Fisto who started to yap. The dog's yapping made Jean-Louis's headache worse, so he pulled himself up, dragged himself to the kitchen where he heated some milk for the dog and himself, and swallowed a couple of aspirins. Once his dog was quiet, he moved slowly into the bathroom and looked into the full-length mirror that hung on the inside of the door.

After he wiped some spots off the mirror, he regarded his reflection. His dark hair, parted in the middle, was straggly, straight, and below-shoulder length. Sometimes he tied it in a ponytail with a rubber band. A couple of times, just for fun, when Soonie was his girlfriend, she would divide it into five thin ponytails around which she tied five different colored bows and then braid the ponytails. They would switch sunglasses and articles of clothing, get high, and go out in public in order to *épater la bourgeoisie* (shock the middle classes). He had taught Soonie the phrase; she had a cute way of saying it. It was hard to shock San Franciscans, since the city's denizens were used to gay parades and eccentric individualists. But Jean-Louis and Soonie would giggle when tourists from, say, Kansas City, stared at them. He smiled at the thought but noticed he could barely see his expression change through all the hair on his face.

His thick, dark moustache stretched from one cheek to the other and connected seamlessly with his beard, which had attained a length of about six inches. He liked to let the moustache grow as long as possible—until it covered his upper lip and got in the way of eating. Then he reminded himself of Fisto; people often said dogs and masters look more and more alike the longer they lived together. He realized he hadn't really seen his entire face since puberty, when he let his moustache grow out back in Colombières-sur-Orb. In France he had always had a hairy face, but the long beard was part of his *look* the last few years. Today he felt confused. The more he looked into the mirror, the less his face revealed to him—because of the hair. He tried frowning and then smiling and saw it didn't make much difference. Maybe if he could see his own facial expressions again, he thought, they could tell him how he really felt, give him clues as to how he *should* feel in this new situation, and therefore what he should *do*. He turned on his heel toward the wash basin, where he reached for his toothbrush and accidentally knocked some bottles off the counter onto the tiled floor—the only floor in Donald's apartment that wasn't carpeted. He was too absorbed in thought to register the broken glass.

Ten minutes later, Jean-Louis left Donald's apartment and wasn't seen or heard from for four days.

On the second day, while Crystal was weeping in Bruno's bathroom at De Carlo & Wittgenstein, Hermann and Donald were combing through Donald's apartment for clues to Jean-Louis's disappearance. Hermann pieced together the shattered fragments of two perfume bottles and their labels he found on the bathroom floor—*Fatal pour Hommes* and *Fatale pour Femmes*. He almost gagged at the cloying aroma that rose like steam from that puddle. He wondered why, *um Gotteswillen*, Donald hadn't bothered to clean up the mess the day before, but then he was glad he didn't, because it might constitute valuable evidence. He opened the medicine cabinet and noticed several more unopened bottles of each perfume. He saved the labels off the broken bottles, some of the glass shards, and some drops of perfume in sealed baggies and stuck them in Donald's freezer; then he mopped the floor and sprayed the area with Lysol from Donald's kitchen sink.

By the third day, Olaf Knudtson had been awake in Washington, DC for forty-four hours, and his acid reflux was erupting uncontrollably during his frantic phone calls all over the country.

Late afternoon on the fourth day, a clean-shaven, spikey, short-haired, light blond Hitler twin walked back into Donald's apartment to find Donald trying to comfort a weepy, red-eyed Crystal, who was stroking Fisto in her lap, as well as Hermann, who was wringing his hands, and Bruno, who was standing in the corner of the living room talking on his flip phone. Over in Corte Madera the French artist had treated himself to a clean shave and a hair styling that left him with gel-spiked blond hair and eyebrows. He had wondered why the hair artist had grown less and less talkative the more hair he removed. He even caught the guy leaning out the door of his shop and looking in his direction after Jean-Louis left and walked down the street. In fact, it seemed like a lot of people had taken second looks at him or pointed surreptitiously during the ferry crossing from Larkspur. But he was, after all, a Bay Area celebrity, and they probably recognized him in spite of his new look.

Now he said *bonjour* nonchalantly and saw how Crystal, Donald, Hermann, and Bruno dropped their jaws in unison. Fisto stood up in Crystal's lap and started growling and trembling. He jumped off the couch and howled piteously. Jean-Louis said gently, "*Tais toi, Fisto. C'est bon, tout va bien. C'est moi.*" But Fisto shook and snarled and snapped at the Frenchman's outstretched hand. Then the terrified canine backed up under Donald's record player chair, where he whimpered and cowered in the shadows.

Bruno quickly ordered Hermann to take Crystal home, because he had to talk to Jean-Louis privately. He was afraid she would have noticed the young Frenchman's resemblance to Hitler and wanted her out of there as quickly as possible. When they were gone, he had a few private words with Donald outside on the landing; then he left, too.

At home that evening, Bruno prepared himself a pesto pasta he had once made for Myrtle in her Pines apartment. He finished with a dessert she had particularly praised—raspberries soaked in marsala and lemon juice and spooned into a depression in a ripe half papaya. He liked to cook for himself from time to time; it was a meditative activity that helped him think, and this evening he needed to calm himself in order to sort out the startling new developments. He would confer in depth with Olaf Knudtson tomorrow. If they put their heads together, they would come up with a workable plan before things spun out of control. Because he knew he could count on master alchemist Donald, who possessed a magic apothecary, Bruno was less worried about the short-term than about Jean-Louis's long-term career as an artist. And now that she had seen Lamour's face, Crystal, too, was a worry. She was more intelligent and observant than he liked to admit, and if she had suspicions before, she had surely noticed the Hitler resemblance now. He hadn't told Crystal about the glass fragments from the broken perfume bottles Hermann had discovered on Donald's bathroom floor, and that Hermann had cleaned and sanitized the tiles. He thought it best that the lovers take a breather, at least for a while, and that withdrawal from the powerful perfumed potions was required. He might have to tell Crystal the truth about Lamour's identity and the CIA mission, and he would need her help to assure a positive outcome—but he hoped to put it off. He thought she would need time to absorb the new information and to come down from her extended erotic high—not too long, however, to get her thinking about him, Bruno, again. It would be difficult. It would require some human engineering. But how best to manage all of this?

After eating, he paced for a long time as contradictory thoughts competed in his brain. Finally, he forced himself to sit down and willed himself to concentrate on something else. He filled a cognac snifter full of Otard and selected some classical music on his iPod. He picked up the worn copy of his favorite novel, *Les Misérables*. He often read with soft music in the background since it didn't disturb his concentration. In fact, classical music usually enhanced the enjoyment of his reading.

He opened the book to reread the pivotal scene of the Champmathieu affair in Part 1 where Jean Valjean shows up at the trial of the poor bastard who is about to be condemned to years of prison for a petty theft that he, Valjean, had committed. Now a successful and benevolent mayor and benefactor of a small French town, Jean Valjean, is, of course, mightily torn between his desire for freedom and his conscience that doesn't want an innocent man to suffer.

As Bruno read the climax of this monumental moral struggle in the French novel, he became aware that the third movement of Brahms's *Third Symphony* was playing in the background. Now the music penetrated his consciousness with a singular clarity; it seemed to underscore the passage he read.

By God, it was Myrtle's favorite symphony, and her favorite movement! He read on.

It was uncanny and seemed to portend some special meaning. What could it be? Bruno read to the chapter's end, almost holding his breath. The Brahms movement came to an end at the same moment he finished the chapter. Despite the inevitability of dire consequences for Jean Valjean, the hero told the truth. And Bruno resolved to tell Crystal the truth.

22

By LATE THE FOLLOWING morning, Donald had obtained a very expensive artificial hairpiece, moustache, and beard and attached them to Jean-Louis's head. This hadn't been easy at first. Hitler's twin didn't want to cooperate. He wanted to give the clean-shaven look a try, because he might want to change his profession. Donald would hear nothing of it. He poured something special into the *chocolat chaud* he always fixed for Jean-Louis whenever they ate breakfast together at Donald's digs, and within a very short time, Jean-Louis was not only compliant but charmed by the new look, which was not dissimilar to his old look.

At the same time in his office on Treasure Island, Bruno tried to calm Crystal. Why hadn't he told her before that Jean-Louis was Hitler's double, his clone, his twin or whatever? Bruno was an evil person! He had let her sleep with him over and over again . . . and let her fall in love with him! With Hitler! Didn't Bruno have any respect for her? Did he hate her? She wanted to kill Bruno!

"Crystal, why do you say that? What makes you think Jean-Louis is Hitler?" Bruno countered, weakly.

Crystal didn't tell Bruno that after Hermann drove her home, she took a taxi back to Donald's and spent the night in bed with Jean-Louis—one more time—even though she had seen he was a dead ringer for Hitler. She felt so sorry for him. She didn't tell him he looked like Hitler, because maybe *he* hadn't noticed. At least, he hadn't said anything. She knew he hadn't had much education in rural France, so maybe he didn't know anything about Hitler or what he looked like. Seventy-nine percent of American high school seniors didn't know who Adolf Hitler was, either. Anyway, the thrill was gone. For the first time he wasn't turned on by her. He wasn't frozen, like after Donald translated that awful review, it wasn't that he didn't talk to her, but he didn't make the slightest move in the night to touch her. And she didn't feel like touching him, either. She could tell when it was over with a man. And it was all Bruno's fault!

"Well, duh!" she spat. "The minute he walked back into Donald's apartment with that spiked blond hair and his face all smooth, I knew, damn it! All that garbage you were reading about the Seti project, and alien cultures and that crap about Jean-Louis from the CIA. I hadn't believed it when I saw that stuff on your desk."

"You read documents on my desk?"

"Well, yes, fuck you! Why did you print out all that shit if it was supposed to be top secret? Anybody could have seen it. Gaby could have seen it!"

"What do you mean? I *hid* it! You were *snooping*! Gaby would never snoop, but *you* did!"

"Well, *you* were a careless slob, *asshole*! And careless with a *secret* CIA mission, for heavens' sake! And besides, how the fuck did *Donald* know? Why did you tell *him* and not *me*? I mean, he's only a chauffeur, so why does *he* rate?"

Bruno had not told Donald. But both he and Hermann knew Donald simply knew everything; they couldn't explain it. That was just the way it was. And there was no way to explain that to Crystal.

"I thought maybe you had some loose marbles at first," she continued when Bruno didn't answer, "but then I forgot about all the crazy stuff, that Seti, alien, frozen baby shit, especially after Jean-Louis and I fell in love—*at first sight*. But after Jean-Louis returned all clean-shaven, it was obvious. I knew it had to be true. He *was* Hitler, damn it all! So, I called this Knudtson guy in DC . . ."

"You called Olaf Knudtson?"

"Well, hello, of course I called! Early this morning."

"And Knudtson told you about Jean-Louis's identity? He confirmed it?"

"Yes, but I didn't need *him* to tell me. Anybody could see it. And now, on top of everything, Knudtson and the CIA are *vetting* me! *Me*, of all people! Isn't it enough that I'm a Beatty? That I'm a wealthy heiress? *Everybody* knows that. Doesn't that count for *anything* nowadays? Knudtson is flying in special agents tomorrow to interrogate me. *Me*! Who are *they* to interrogate *me*?"

Crystal didn't know whether it was worse that *she* was being inter-rogated or that she would be *interrogated*. But either way, it was an affront.

"But babe . . ."

"Don't you babe me!" she yelled and then began to whimper. "And why the fuck aren't they interrogating *Donald*? Life is not fair!"

"Crystal, look at it this way, it's an honor to be interesting to the CIA. You've become privy to a state secret of enormous importance. How many people would they trust with such a secret?"

"Some honor! They don't have a choice. They *have* to trust me, whether they vet me or not, since I already know!"

"But think of it, you'll get a high-level security clearance. How many people do you think have that kind of status?"

"Status, schmatus. What the hell good is status compared to lost love? And the humiliation of having fallen for another Hitler? No self-respecting woman would want to be another Eva Braun! Let me tell you something—that *sucks big time*! You let me fall in love with Hitler. You let me sleep with him over and over again."

"I didn't make you sleep with him."

"Oh, shut up, you jerk!" Tears welled from her eyes.

"And he's not really Hitler, not Adolf Hitler, anyway. That Hitler's been dead for over half a century."

"So, I've been sleeping with some fucking frozen corpse that somehow sprang to life again? How creepy is that? How am I supposed to feel about that? Do you ever think about *my* feelings, Bruno?"

Bruno tried more arguments on Crystal—that she wasn't sleeping with a reanimated corpse, because DNA wasn't dead in the same way flesh could die, and she would be part of an amazing assignment, an undertaking, a mission, and she had a duty now, and she would have a part in accomplishing something more important than probably any other heiress in history had accomplished. But Crystal wasn't buying Bruno's arguments. Her emotions were a Medusa head of writhing poisonous vipers. And her nose had begun to bleed.

Crystal let herself down into Bruno's ergonomic chair and reclined it all the way back. She turned on her side with her back toward Bruno and put her hands over her face. She wept in despair. Didn't he have any respect for her? Who did he think she was? Did he hate her?

Bruno stood next to her, moved by a genuine pang of pity. It wasn't really his fault, but a bizarre chain-linking of unlikely circumstances that had brought them to this point. He took a packet of Kleenex from an inside jacket pocket and carefully slipped it into one of her hands. He wanted to bend down and place a comforting arm around her shoulder, but he feared she might take a roundhouse swing at him.

23

A WEEK LATER, THE mirror in Bruno's private restroom at De Carlo & Wittgenstein was again smudged with Crystal's mascara and makeup base. Crystal was spending her fourth day in Bruno's office, reading the CIA reports on Hitler's twin, a.k.a., Jean-Louis Lamour, her ex-lover, and some background on Adolf Hitler's rise to power, his role in WWII, and in the Holocaust. She had passed her vetting brilliantly and was now privy to all the relevant and sensitive information in the strange case. Occasionally she sighed audibly or blew her nose, but she didn't break out in tears, much to Bruno's relief.

While she was busy with her studies, Bruno read through an entire stack of publishers' rejection letters Hermann had confiscated from Fernando Seed's old Berkeley flat. He also read some email attachments from Olaf Knudtson that revealed what Bruno already knew. Seed's father, a retired biologist with a peculiar personality, was widowed when Fernando was young, and he currently led the life of a withdrawn hermit in the Napa Valley north of San Francisco. Other than that, recent information on Dr. Seed was sparse. Before leaving work in the late afternoon, Bruno made a call to Philip Seed in Calistoga and arranged to drive up there the following day for a luncheon meeting; he wanted to talk to him about his son, Fernando, and his career possibilities. He was pleased the old man agreed to the visit. He wanted Hermann and Crystal to come along to help pick up clues.

It was a gorgeous October morning. Hermann drove a company BMW convertible. He put the top down once they reached the Silverado Trail on the east side of the Napa Valley. The wind whipped Crystal's long hair in glorious golden plumes and billows until she tamed it with a scarf. The hillside vineyards displayed a splendid spectrum of autumn shades; an occasional grape-harvesting vehicle slowed them down, and a cyclist who swerved out of the bike lane almost side-swiped the Beamer, but Hermann was able to outmaneuver and avoid him. When the threesome reached Philip Seed's mobile home adult community, the guard at the Vintage Citizens Manors' gate looked wide-eyed at the well-dressed visitors in the expensive convertible with the De C&W personalized license plates who wanted to visit the strange old recluse, Dr. Seed.

The party of three couldn't find a doorbell at Seed's entrance, so Hermann knocked on the metal screen door and tapped the window with his keys. After a long wait, an elderly man in ill-fitting, scruffy clothes opened the door and peered at them through the screen before asking, "Who the heck are you?"

"Good morning, Dr. Seed," Bruno spoke up. "I'm Bruno De Carlo, and this is my partner, Hermann Wittgenstein, and this is Crystal Beatty. We're here for our 10:30 A.M. appointment."

"An appointment? What appointment? What do you mean, appointment?" he snipped, looking down at his slippers and shaking his head with its sparse gray hair.

"Well, yes, we agreed to an appointment at 10:30 A.M. today."

"Today? What day is it?"

"It's Wednesday—the sixteenth. Remember, I called you yesterday, from San Francisco."

"No, it's not Wednesday. It can't be Wednesday," Dr. Seed replied, shaking his head quite decidedly. He made no move to open the screen door, so Hermann did so without asking permission. Dr. Seed continued to look at his slippers while dandruff drifted down from his head and accumulated on the shoulders of an old navy blue sweater that appeared too large for his slight frame. About five feet eight inches, Dr. Seed was thin and poorly shaven. Wiry white hairs sprouted from his eyebrows, nose, and ears.

"I can show you my calendar," said Hermann, and started to go for the Blackberry on his belt clip, "and you will see it is Wednesday."

But Bruno quickly pushed Hermann's arm down and said, "Ah, Dr. Seed, perhaps we have erred on our date. I'm so sorry for the misunderstanding and for disturbing you unexpectedly. Please accept our apologies for this intrusion on your privacy."

Seed's eyes moved up now from his feet and met Bruno's ingratiating smile. Bruno continued, "We certainly don't want to bother you at an inopportune time. I can only imagine how busy a world-renowned scientist of your caliber must be, and we wouldn't want to impose on any of your valuable time."

Seed's confused expression began to vanish and morph into positive interest.

"Well, we all make mistakes," he conceded after a pause. "I guess I could take a break." Then he asked, "What's your name again?"

Bruno repeated the introductions and told Dr. Seed his son, Fernando, had been working for their company, and he was such a promising young man that they wanted to promote his career. They thought his father might be able to share some insights about how best to help him.

Dr. Seed seemed puzzled. "My son? What did you say his name was?" Ferdinand?" He scratched behind his left ear, releasing another small puff of dandruff. He looked down at his worn leather slippers and the one blue and one brown sock that stuck out of them. The sock that came through the front opening of the left slipper had a hole that exposed a large toe with a yellow, ragged, overgrown toenail. Philip Seed seemed to search his mind for what to say.

Bruno hinted, "Would you mind if we came in for a minute, and perhaps we could talk about your son, *Fernando,* and his career?"

"Well, I don't know. You say Fernando is my son?"

"Yes, indeed, and he has great intelligence and formidable talents, in our opinion. He's the son of a scientist, after all." Bruno said this with a charming smile and wink.

"Well, I guess that would be all right. I guess I could take a break."

The shades were drawn inside Seed's mobile home, but enough light came through the windows to reveal a disorderly living room and a television tuned at high volume to a shopping channel. Old scientific journals were stacked on top of the set, threatening to fall off. The walls were covered with old photographs—snow-covered mountains, pine trees, mountain goats perched on sheer rock cliffs, Dr. Seed wearing a lab coat bent over a Bunsen burner, and the doctor with what might have been family members smiling at a birthday cake with candles. Stacks of newspapers were piled up in corners of the living room in such good order that they appeared unread. A satin lampshade sported a large scorch mark on a vanilla-colored pole lamp, and an old table lamp lacked a shade altogether, although a fluorescent bulb was twisted into its socket. Dr. Seed made no move to offer his visitors seats, and the visitors couldn't think of anything complimentary to say about his living quarters. For an awkward moment, the visitors sought for a way to generate conversation. Finally, Hermann, who gestured at one of the photos on the wall, said, "Oh, Dr. Seed, I think maybe this is a picture of your son, perhaps."

"My son?" Dr. Seed seemed confused. The visitors didn't know whether he couldn't recall that he had a son or that he had displayed a photo of his son.

"Yes," said Hermann. "Here, in this photo, is this a photo of you with your son, Fernando? I am sure he is our employee in San Francisco, the same one." Hermann gestured toward the old man and the photo with two outstretched arms.

Dr. Seed looked down at his feet. Bruno took him under the arm and gently turned him in the direction of the photo at which Hermann pointed.

"Perhaps you could tell us about the picture, Dr. Seed. How old was Fernando in the picture? Where was it taken?" asked Bruno.

Dr. Seed allowed Bruno to guide him close to the photo. Hermann pointed at Fernando. Philip squinted at it for a long while and finally said softly, as if to himself, "My son." Now it sounded less like a question than an affirmation.

"Here," said Hermann, "I will show you a more recent picture in my BlackBerry of your son, with me, at our company."

Hermann tapped on his BlackBerry. When he handed the device to Dr. Seed, the scientist's placid composure began to change. His face grew red, his forehead developed deep furrows, his brows seemed to compress, and he began to breathe heavily, almost pant. Suddenly, he raised Hermann's BlackBerry above his head and shook it so violently Hermann was afraid he would smash it on the floor.

"Damn him!" Dr. Seed exclaimed. "Damn him to a pit of serpents writhing in flames and brimstone, the ungrateful wretch! That miserable idiot of an unworthy offspring, that sorry excuse for a son!"

The photo seemed to have sparked at least one clear memory in the old scientist's mind. Hermann, Bruno, and Crystal watched him in alarm as Hermann seized the phone in one hand and with the other held the old man's arm and half forced and half helped him to sink into a chair with a worn cushion on it, fearing he might collapse from excitement.

"Now, now, Dr. Seed, we didn't mean to upset you."

"Upset me?" he retorted. "The only thing in my life that ever upset me was fatuous Fernando and his futile literary ambitions. The boy had an IQ of one hundred ninety-three. He could have been a brilliant scientist—an astrophysicist, a geneticist, or a biologist, like me. We might have collaborated, become an unparalleled father-son team that would have astonished and awed the world. But no, he goes off to Berzerkeley and after his first year tells me he wants to be a writer, a *creative* writer, the idiot, and that he was a staff reporter for the students' moronic paper, *The Daily Bullshit*. He asked me, 'Aren't you proud of me, Pops?' Ha! Proud that he wanted to write when he was wasting his brain and talents? When he'd end up a starving bohemian in a dilapidated, unheated apartment?"

"Oh, you mean *The Daily Cal*?" Hermann tried to correct him.

"Call it what you will, it's full of sophomoric dribble," exclaimed an excited Dr. Seed.

"And he joined some silly Hispanic Latino Club and contributed to their newsletter. He's fluent in Spanish; his mother was Mexican, you know."

Hermann almost confirmed they already knew that, but Bruno was able to step on Hermann's shoe to warn him not to. He didn't want the old man's loquacity to wane, now that he was on an verbal roll.

"What a crying waste of a brilliant brain! Alas, alas," Seed continued. "The best made plans of mice and men do often go astray! I should disown him, the puerile, pathetic, misguided moron. He was Nobel Prize-caliber, but now he'll just waste his life."

The three visitors watched in amazement as the old man's emotions suddenly collapsed in on themselves as he dropped his head into his hands supported on his knees and covered his face. Was he crying?

Crystal, in the meantime, had found the remote control and muted the sound on the TV shopping channel. Seed had not noticed. Now they waited to see if he would recover. Dr. Seed finally raised his head and shook it slowly in a gesture of resignation.

With glazed eyes Dr. Seed rose to his feet and shuffled toward the wall with the photos. The visitors observed him expectantly as he focused on a glossy black-and-white photo of an alpine cow with a bell around its neck examining a pretty clump of Edelweiß flowers.

"That's in the mountains, I think," Dr. Seed pronounced.

"That is interesting," said Bruno. "Which mountains are they?"

"Oh, let's see, I think it was . . . well, I'm not sure. I seem to have forgotten the name. But that's not important. It was very cold some of the time. Yes. I remember the cold. It was cold, indeed."

"Does Fernando like the mountains?"

"Fernando?"

"Yes, your son."

"I have a son?"

"Yes, your son, Fernando Seed. You just told us about him."

"I did? Who are you again?" Seed's memory must have been overtaxed by the allergic topic of his son.

Bruno introduced them all again and told him about De Carlo & Wittgenstein.

"And where did you say you were from?"

"San Francisco," Bruno replied.

"Ah, San Francisco," mused the doctor. "Is that in the mountains?"

Bruno gave up trying to question Dr. Seed and devised a new plan.

"Dr. Seed," he said, "we are very honored that you agreed to have lunch with us. You know it's time we go on over to the restaurant."

Crystal and Hermann both looked at their boss, who gave them knowing looks.

"Crystal, could you check with the restaurant to see if everything is ready for the three of us, please?" Bruno continued, before turning to the doctor again. "Unfortunately, my partner, Hermann, won't be joining us at the restaurant. It was kind of you to offer him to stay here while he makes his calls; he expects they will keep him tied up until early afternoon, when we will bring you back. But Ms. Beatty and I will be delighted to host you at the restaurant."

"Restaurant? Are we going to a restaurant?"

"Yes, remember when I called for this appointment, I said we wanted to invite you for lunch?"

"Oh, did you say that? I don't remember that."

"Oh yes, you said you enjoyed eating out."

"Well, I guess I do, but I don't like squid. I won't eat any squid. You know, squid just disagrees with me," replied Dr. Seed.

"I promise you won't have to eat squid, Dr. Seed—only things you like. And remember Hermann will be working here while we are at the restaurant."

"Did you say Hermann was my son?" inquired Dr. Seed.

Bruno suggested to Dr. Seed he put on some shoes in preparation for the lunch, and while Dr. Seed disappeared into his bedroom, he told Crystal to contact a good, local restaurant and make a reservation. He told Hermann to look busy when Seed came through again and to gather all the relevant information from Seed's dwelling he could while they were gone. Bruno would call him when they finished lunch and were on the way back. Then Bruno went quickly to the BMW, got a briefcase out of its trunk and brought it inside for Hermann.

24

DURING THE WEEK AFTER their visit to Philip Seed in Calistoga, Bruno went through the materials Hermann pilfered from the senile scientist's mobile home. Now he and Latrone Sanders were finishing up a conference call with Olaf Knudtson regarding Fernando Seed.

"One more thing, Mr. Knudtson," said Bruno, looking out the window of his office toward Alcatraz and Sausalito. "Do you have any theories about Fernando Seed's pseudonym, *Magnus*?"

Olaf Knudtson was happy to answer this one, because he hoped Bruno, who was so well versed in literature, hadn't thought of it.

"Well, I think the young Seed chose a pen name that would sound illustrious. And if you remember your Latin, *magnus* means 'great.'"

"Yes, yes, I knew that," Bruno replied, feeling a bit irritated, "but what about 'Charlie' and 'Charles?'"

Now Knudtson could shine, although it was one of his junior staff who had pointed out the connection. "Charles is the English version of Karl, and *Karolus Magnus* the Latin for 'Charlemagne.'"

Damn! I hadn't thought of that! Bruno thought, feeling slightly outdone. The cultural competition annoyed Bruno, but he had no counter. It was only later he recalled what Myrtle had taught him—about Charlemagne's reign as a model for the Holy Roman Empire that came later, and about Charlemagne's *scriptorium*—which probably factored into young Seed's choice of a pen name.

Knudtson continued now, sounding a bit more modest, "I'm no expert, but I agree young Seed's attack on our subject's art was well-written. You'll be amused to know Philip Seed sometimes held little audio speakers to his wife's belly during her pregnancy and played recordings of music and audio books—and who knows? maybe lines of Shakespeare or Hemingway to the fetus—believing that hearing these things would make it smarter. And it's medically true that from about the second trimester, fetuses can hear music in their mother's womb when the mother plays an instrument; they can even hear loud music further away in a room or in a concert hall. Maybe Carmina Seed's fetus picked up some of the rhythms or cadences of English prenatally. We'll never know what Carmina thought about this. Some weird husband that Dr. Seed must have been. He probably drove her nuts."

Bruno sighed. "And he can't help us anymore, either. The poor devil obviously suffers a kind of selective dementia. The only thing he remembers clearly is his anger toward his disappointing son. From his perspective his attempts at prenatal education obviously backfired. He should have played recordings of math or chemistry formulas for the fetus," he laughed.

"That's a good one, Mr. De Carlo." Knudtson enjoyed a laugh too. "Yes, it's sad about the old man. Maybe if he'd devoted himself to stem cell research, he would have found a cure for his own dementia. But now, of course, our first order of business is to contain any threats against our subject."

"Certainly," agreed Bruno. "I'm afraid our young Charlemagne's literary prowess is as enormous as is his resentment and disdain for Jean-Louis Lamour's success. He's also contemptuous of both the publishing and the art *businesses,* of their *crass commercialism.* So, we will a need two-pronged containment plan, one that includes Fernando, too."

"Yes, absolutely," agreed Olaf. Then, remembering his agent, Latrone Sanders, hadn't said anything, he said, "Mr. Sanders, you're apprised of the situation. Do you have anything to add?"

Latrone, who had listened attentively during the call, felt that the cultural exchange was over his head.

"No, sir," he said. He just hoped that in his assignment in the new plan, he wouldn't have to fly anywhere. Soonie hated to fly, too. They had that in common.

25

It was 10:20 p.m. in Spain and a dark night. Air Iberia from SFO was scheduled to land at Madrid-Barajas at 10:25 p.m. High winds buffeted the plane, and rain was streaming down the window in economy row thirty-eight where Latrone Sanders sat, gripping Soonie's two hands in both of his. He didn't know whether it was his or her cold sweat that made their palms and all twenty of their fingers clammy.

With tightly curled, short, silver-blond hair, blue contact lenses, and grannie glasses, Soonie had an entirely new look so that Jean-Louis wouldn't recognize her if he saw her deplane. Of course, he wouldn't see her during the flight, because Hitler's twin brother sat in front in business class. Besides, Jean-Louis was busy reading and rereading the papers that criticized—no, condemned—his artistic achievements, articles that, despite everyone's best efforts, he had obtained from one of those art school students. Hitler's twin was therefore unaware of the dire aeronautical straits in which they were entangled but to which Latrone Sanders, CIA agent, was acutely attuned. Latrone had installed a bug in Donald's phone, and the agent had listened to all of Jean-Louis's frantic calls to the airlines when he tried to book a flight to Europe. The only thing Lamour could get was a flight to Madrid, and Sanders had had to scramble to get reservations on the same flight, since he was to trail him. Other agents would also get involved once they landed in Europe. He told no one he was taking his Korean girlfriend along.

At 37,000 feet Latrone worried, *Why aren't we descending?* The plane had been pummeled by fierce Atlantic headwinds and side winds, not to mention frightening updrafts and downdrafts. The white Airbus with the red and gold stripes across the fuselage had climbed and descended in numerous futile attempts during the last five or so hours, to attain a comfortable altitude where it wouldn't be knocked about so cruelly. This airplane, Latrone reasoned, would be low on fuel due to those headwinds, the turbulence, and the precipitous climbs and descents. The ocean was immense and treacherous, especially in the fall. The pilot had only spoken Spanish to the passengers, and that only once, shortly after takeoff from San Francisco. Why didn't he tell them when they would be landing? Why didn't he address them in English? He looked at his watch and thought, *the plane should have started its descent long ago.*

Ten minutes earlier the monitors and audio programs in economy had suddenly gone dead. When he asked a flight attendant what was wrong, she just smiled and said *No hay problemas. No es grave, señor,* and Latrone thought that *grave* sounded like "grave," which sounded bad to him. She didn't even try to explain the problem in English; she just vanished. There was probably something wrong with the plane's electronics, probably with the entire navigation system. The pilot was probably lost and was embarrassed to admit it.

Suddenly the plane took a sharp, precipitous dive. Latrone gasped, and at the same time felt his body grow lighter, almost weightless.

Jesus!

Soonie gripped his hands tighter and asked, "What is happening?"

Air Iberia then banked sharply and sickeningly to the right. Latrone tried to be brave.

"I'm not sure. I guess we're beginning our descent to Madrid." He wanted Soonie to think he had the steely nerves of a secret agent.

Suddenly the monitors and audio came back on. A flight attendant announced in Spanish that passengers could view the landing on their screens if they wished. Latrone couldn't understand the announcement and buzzed again for a flight attendant. No one came. The fasten seat belts light came on simultaneously with another announcement from the cockpit. This time the instructions for passengers to return to their seats, close their tray tables and put their seatbacks into the upright position were sounded in Spanish *and* in English, but the latter was barely intelligible because of a thick Spanish accent. The voice sounded quivery to Latrone. Was it the captain or the purser? No way to tell.

Sanders peered out his window hoping to see the lights of a town or city, but everything was black. Rain streamed wildly across the window—horizontally.

He peered at the monitor, which displayed similar blackness and rain pounding straight into it. There must be a camera mounted somewhere on the plane that captured take-offs and landings. What was the point of terrifying the passengers by showing them these last moments of dark blankness before they crashed into oblivion? If he survived this flight, Latrone Sanders would demand a desk job at the CIA, or give up his government career to seek less gut-wrenching work. The plane had been descending for much too long. If it had cruised at 30,000 to 40,000 feet like the pilot claimed, it would have to be at sea level or below by now. Latrone's window was now a river of water and so was the monitor. Soonie was babbling swiftly to herself in Korean; maybe she was praying. Latrone's thoughts shifted to his poor mother, how alone she would be if . . .

He squinted at the monitor again. Then he squinted again, harder. Now he thought he saw a tiny pinprick of light through all the water. He blinked a few times and squeezed his eyes closed for a moment. When he opened them, he peered again at the monitor. Sure enough, there was a barely perceptible pin prick of light through all the rain. Could it be an island off the coast of Spain? Or maybe just a freighter at sea that the plane had spotted. Could an airliner land on an aircraft carrier in an emergency? He remembered reading that a passenger jet, maybe Air France, had once run off the far end of Papeete's runway, which was obviously too short, where it was stopped by a coral reef. Then he thought, *Madrid isn't at the coast, it's inland.*

"Look, Soonie, there's light on the monitor. Maybe it's the airport."

"Oh, oh, oh, oh, ok, ok, ok," whispered Soonie.

Latrone still couldn't see anything out the window. From this side view he wouldn't be able to see the city the way the camera with the frontal view could. He looked around the plane at the other passengers in the economy section. Some were sleeping; some read newspapers. The man across the aisle had stretched a long leg into the aisle and was yawning. Latrone tried to muster up enough courage to yawn.

Now he could see two faint lines of parallel lights through the pounding rain on the monitor. The airbus was attempting to land in a terrible storm. It rocked to the right and then to the left of those parallel landing lights. Latrone knew that side winds during landings were particularly perilous. They could lift a wing and knock a fast-moving jet off track and twirl it right off the runway, especially a slick runway. *Why, a plane could probably hydroplane,* Latrone thought for the first time in his life. If a car could hydroplane on a slick freeway, then this plane could also skid right off the end of the Madrid-Barajas runway after a normal touchdown, especially if its tire treads were low.

It looked to Latrone as if Air Iberia was going to strike the runway at a forty-five-degree angle, if it even made it onto the runway.

Oh, my God!

He gripped Soonie around her head and pulled it close to his just as the monitor went blank.

When Air Iberia opened its doors and the first and business class passengers debarked, Latrone made sure he and Soonie were among the first economy passengers to exit the plane in order to trail Jean-Louis into the luggage and customs areas. Two CIA colleagues would be at the greeting area outside of customs, one to trail the suspect if Sanders were separated from him and the other to drive Sanders, and now Soonie, too, whom he would introduce as a relative, in a separate car and to communicate with the first agent. All went smoothly. Soon M. Lamour was checked into room 312 in the Marriott in central Madrid, and a Mr. and Mrs. Sanders were a few doors down the hall in 325. European agents surveyed the hotel that night.

26

It was Bert Wittgenstein who called his mother, Gaby, about the article in the Madrid newspaper, *El País*. Bert had learned Spanish in high school and kept up his third language by reading Spanish newspapers on his iPad. When Bert noticed the article about Jean-Louis Lamour, he knew his parents would be interested. Now Gaby told Hermann, and Hermann told Bruno and gave him the article he printed off the Internet. Hermann thought Bruno, since he was a native Italian, would be able to make sense of the Spanish.

The article about the French *boulist* painter in San Francisco was brilliant and derogatory and written by a Charlie Magnus. The agency had tracked him to Spain, and now Jean-Louis had fled to the same country. Fernando hoped he could make a living as a writer in Spain, which seemed a safe distance away, and Jean-Louis felt threatened in his aspirations as a painter and wanted time and distance to sort things out.

Bruno felt ambivalent about this news. If young Seed attacked Hitler's brother's paintings in Europe as well as in America, well, negative publicity was also a form of buzz that could stimulate interest in the artist. Controversy, after all, could add to an artist's repute. But it was equally possible it could have a deleterious effect on his career and shorten it. An artistic rage could easily become a short-winded fad, and a popular painter could sink back into obscurity following his fifteen minutes of fame. This was a possible outcome if the brilliant Seed were left to his devices—and, considering

Seed's writing talent, much too risky. Bruno had rarely been as impressed with anyone's writing skill, aside from the great classic authors, of course.

Troubled by his thoughts, Bruno rose from his desk, walked down the corridor past his private bathroom and entered the stairwell no one used. He walked up two flights of metal stairs to the roof garden, which was empty, and strolled to the roof's edge and looked west toward the Golden Gate Bridge. The afternoon was sunny and windy, cloudless and clear. Whitecaps speckled the bay along with the colorful sails of boats that skimmed through choppy swells. His thoughts turned inevitably to Myrtle Halstead. Maybe Bruno didn't know how to get on the good side of his mother, but he now had a plan for Fernando Seed that would also constitute an oblique way to repay Myrtle. Bruno descended the stairs and reentered his office. He told Gaby to set up a conference call with Jack Peterson and Gloria Majestic.

27

WHEN THE CHAMBERMAID ENTERED the Madrid Marriott's room 312 at
10:15 A.M. central European time, she woke up a young man, who had had
a bad night after a transcontinental flight. He told her in French and English
to go away and come back later. She wasn't sure of what he said, but she retreated and hung the *No Molestar* sign on the outside door handle, to warn
the maid on the next shift to be careful about entering. She wondered about
the casually dressed foreigner wearing ear buds who seemed to be loitering
down the hall.

When Jean-Louis checked out of the Marriott early that afternoon, he
had to pay for an extra day. The hotel concierge arranged for a one-way train
ticket to Toledo and reservations for a week in the *parador*. Seated in first
class on the train, Jean-Louis found himself as upset as he had ever been and
ordered the steward to bring him a pastis. He was not accustomed to the
prickly feeling of unease that had plagued him ever since the initial shock of
the article in the *LA Times*. Donald had translated the English subtleties and
innuendos for him into a French vernacular he could understand.

He had always been a relaxed person. His French parents in Colombières-sur-Orb had appreciated that, and his memory of his early childhood didn't extend back any earlier—although he was puzzled by recurrent
dreams of snow and high mountains. The only traumatic event in his life
had been the death of his *copain*, his buddy, Pascal. Then he had drowned
his grief in pastis and had come through that period when he discovered

painting and threw himself into it. At first, he felt compelled to paint, as if to satisfy an addiction, but in time he found he simply enjoyed creating one circle after the other, in endless variations. Lucky circumstances had made him famous in California, where everybody loved his work and he was celebrated—with only one exception now. This writer, this Charles Magnus, had claimed he was a mediocre, second-rate talent. How could that be since he was so immensely popular with so many people—wealthy, prominent people as well as poor students who hung on every word he uttered, people who wanted to wine and dine him, to be close to the aura he emitted? What was wrong with this Magnus? Who was *he* to question the rightness, the genuineness of his art, his important message of *boulism*?

He needed to get far away from San Francisco, to clear his head, to ponder this utterly new and unexpected development, this unsettling turn of events. Air Iberia had helped in that. Could there be something to Magnus's criticism? With his flawed English, he couldn't judge the quality of the critic's writing, but he had forced Donald to give him an honest assessment of Magnus's talent, and Donald had admitted the guy could write—like a celestial poet. Jean-Louis trusted Donald's judgment about everything. He knew Donald had uncanny powers, even if he wasn't the best driver in the world. If there was some truth to Magnus's criticism, he needed to get to the bottom of it. But first he needed to get away from the familiar influences. And he needed time. Despite his confusion and exhaustion, he also felt he might be on a journey of self-discovery. He pulled the devastating article out of his shirt pocket and tried once again to make sense of it. When the steward came down the aisle of his first-class car, he ordered a pastis.

Although he tried to nap at the Parador de Toledo, Señor Lamour only twisted and flopped from one side to the other of the king-sized bed with the heavy dark bedposts. Was it jetlag? He had experienced jetlag after his arrival in San Francisco. No. It was Seed's attack on his work, his art, that kept him awake. Maybe if there had been a woman in his bed. Or even Fisto. He might as well give up on sleep. At least he had slept a few hours in Madrid.

It was dinnertime, so he dressed and descended the cold tile stairway to the *parador*'s bar and ordered a pastis, which he sipped slowly while staring at a soccer game, for which the volume had been muted on the television that was suspended above a long shelf of bottles behind the bar. After a while he absentmindedly slid off the bar stool and carried his almost empty aperitif glass through the open French doors that led to a broad red tile patio alongside the hotel. Across the river the old city perched on a hill, its *alcazar* and cathedral outstanding in the skyline in the darkish blue of dusk.

Gray clouds hung over the city; a few sparse evening lights twinkled to life, and Toledo presented itself as a dark, rather ominous ball of an entity, or rather, with the river that seemed to form a parameter, as a unit that could be seen as a ball unto itself, or . . .

Jean-Louis stopped himself. Perhaps it was stupid to look at a city this way. To look at everything as if it were a ball or circle. What was the point of it? Confused, he sipped the last drops of his milky, anise-flavored drink, turned on his heel, and went inside to find the restaurant.

The menu only made him feel worse. It would have been alright in French, but the English translation of the Spanish menu confused him, and he didn't know what to order: "eggs with brains; air-dried deer; garlic soap with eggs floating; typical yolks; shrimp cocktail in apple juice; stuffed pig trotters; typical porridge with pork; fried ice cream in tulip shaped; fried dream with grapes pudding." He never should have left San Francisco without Donald. Donald would have known what to do.

Jean-Louis downed the eggs with brains, wondering whether extra brains might help him think. He followed the entrée with the fried ice cream in tulip shaped and another glass of pastis. By the time he finished dining, it was dark, and the city of Toledo was sprinkled with myriad points of light. The cathedral spire and the *alcazar* towers that were bathed by spotlights seemed to draw Jean-Louis in their direction as beacons of hope. He was tipsy, but he wasn't sleepy, so he walked down the hillside, across the bridge to the main town, and up into the narrow streets and alleys, where a festival was in progress. Street musicians were scattered in large and small plazas, and crowds of people milled about—entire families with children, lovers holding hands or with arms wrapped around each other hugging or kissing in the shadows of buildings. Colorful banners spanned the streets at rooftop level. Loaded down with two and sometimes three teenagers, high-pitched, unmuffled motorbikes darted around recklessly with an insouciant disregard for everyone's safety. The noisy confusion was overwhelming. Jean-Louis walked around aimlessly until he found the cathedral and entered in the hopes of escaping the commotion.

Here and there people sat in pews and prayed; a few tourists gazed up at the stained glass that was illuminated dimly by the outside floodlights. Jean-Louis had never entered a cathedral before and felt immediately overcome by the cavernous space, by the polished black-and-white-checkered floor, the soaring columns, and the unending throngs of baroque cupids and priests and robed figures and angels and suns and birds and flat round turds of gold and stars of gold with radiating gold shafts and semi-nudes and angel wings and organ pipes and musical instruments and scepters and scrolls and tablets and unidentified objects floating toward heaven, and horses and dogs and swords and miters that peopled the baroque ceilings and made him dizzy when he craned his neck back, his jaw hanging, and stared at the ceiling until he began to feel faint. Or was it the fourth glass of pastis he was feeling?

He crouched on the floor and lowered his head so he wouldn't pass out, and when he felt a bit better crawled over to a pew and sat in it with his head bowed and his eyes closed. After a while he was able to look around and spied what he realized were dusky wooden confessionals lined up along one side of the main body of the church. Perhaps he could talk to someone there, someone with a sympathetic ear, someone who was a wise counselor. He dragged himself over to the first one and found it locked. He knocked on the second one, which was also empty and locked. He pounded on the third and the fourth without receiving a response. The priests must all be out to dinner.

Passing by the scaffolding and construction canvases that covered the Capilla de la Descensión, Jean-Louis continued to wander semi dazed until he came upon a bank of small electric lights under thick plexiglass and a group of Spaniards. A fat little Spanish boy, perhaps ten years old, in a white starched uniform with gold fringed epaulettes on his shoulders, white patent leather shoes, and a large gold cross hanging from a thick gold chain around his thick neck, tried to activate the box. His family—a father, mother, grandmother all in black, and a smaller brother, all dressed formally—stood by watching the boy in the white suit expectantly. Proud as a peacock, he held out his hand to his father, who dropped a coin into the chubby palm. The boy dropped the coin into a slot at the end of the sturdy plastic box that contained four rows of ascending light bulbs with eight in each row representing candles. None of them lit up as a result of the coin drop. Jean-Louis could see the Spaniards hadn't followed directions, which were posted in four languages—Spanish, German, English, and French— that instructed worshippers to drop in not one Euro, but three Euros if they wanted to illuminate any electric candles. When nothing happened, the father looked angry, the mother gasped and covered her mouth with her hand, and the grandmother looked up at a window. When the second coin the father gave to his dandy of a son also failed to illuminate anything, the little brother, who had been holding the father's hand, broke away and began to kick and yell at the box. He pounded it with his fists, unaware he was violating sacred decorum. When the mother seemed to stagger and the grandmother grew pale and vacant-eyed, Jean-Louis, who had seen the alternate slot for a credit card, stepped forward and inserted his Wells Fargo Visa card into the slot and punched a few buttons, with the result that not only the box with thirty-two electric bulbs lit up like a Keno board, but piped organ music began to play the opening *Kyrie Eleison* of Bach's *B Minor Mass* throughout the cathedral. At this the mother began to cry and said, "*Gracias, muchas gracias, Señor*," but her younger son began to attack Jean-Louis as if he were the electric box, kicking his legs and stomping on his feet with an agitated intensity. The boy managed to bite the artist below his knee and unleash a nasty blow to his crotch before his parents were able to subdue and carry him squealing out of the sanctuary. Jean-Louis shuffled over to the nearest pew and lay down on the bench clutching his groin and gritting his teeth. He closed his eyes tightly, trying to hold back tears, and waited for the pain to subside. When he opened them again, the first thing he saw was a statue of the Virgin Mary with fresh flower leis piled up around her neck that loomed directly above him attached to a thick, soaring stone column. She held a baby Jesus in her left arm like a football and clutched her right breast, as if it hurt, in her right hand. She seemed to stare right down at Jean-Louis Lamour as if to say, "*Ce n'est pas grave, mon ami.*"

Maybe it was the gothic cathedral, maybe it was the assault on his groin, or maybe it was the pastis, but when Jean-Louis finally stood upright, he virtually staggered outside the church, tripped at the top of the stairs and skipped crazily down two or three steps at a time toward the open plaza that was teeming with people. He tried desperately to catch himself from falling into the cobblestone street by lunging forward in awkward long strides . . .

Witnesses to the accident reported to the police, who were quick to arrive at the scene, that at first they thought the foreigner might have been drunk, but then they concluded unanimously that the Virgin had given him wings and instilled in him the intention to save the poor little boy. For in the same instant Jean-Louis was plummeting into the street, one of those whiny, raspy, shrill insects of a motorbike came screaming around the corner and would surely have killed the precious little ten-year-old boy in the white uniform with the gold-fringed shoulder epaulettes had not the brave stranger literally flown into the street and collided with, or rather embraced, the child, who had momentarily escaped the grasp of his father's hand and had darted directly into the speeding vehicle's path. With no regard for his own safety, the stranger had, in a magnificent display of athletic skill, managed to shield the boy with his body and take the full brunt of the motorbike hit, risking his life and sacrificing a number of his bones as well as his nose in the miraculous rescue. One could understand if the poor foreigner babbled incoherently in French and English after receiving such a shock and while bleeding profusely. And the large crowd that had formed and the Toledo police had to be excused if in their animation they attributed the accident victim's pastis breath to the gasoline and motor scooter oil that had spilled all over his clothes. The motorbike's driver had flown over the handlebars and landed in a fountain, drenched but unscathed. Jean-Louis, recalling the fatal accident that had killed his friend, Pascal, and seeing the uniform of the ten-year old Spaniard in his arms, observed not a drop of blood or oil on the immaculate white suit—nothing, in short, that would have given him a clue as to what he should do next—before he lost consciousness.

28

"Bruno," he said, answering the call he was expecting.

"Good morning, Mr. De Carlo. Gaby here. I've got Mr. Peterson and Ms. Majestic in Burbank on the line for your conference call."

"Thanks, Gaby, and good morning to both of you, Ms. Majestic and Mr. Peterson."

Ms. Majestic uttered a hello and Jack boomed, "And a very good morning it is here in beautiful Baghdad by the Bay. Wouldn't you agree, Mr. De Carlo? Isn't it time we persuaded Ms. Gloria to move her operations to San Francisco, ha ha?"

"A splendid idea, but that would be up to Ms. Majestic, of course."

"How nice of you to suggest that, Mr. Peterson," Ms. Majestic remarked, to be polite.

"Well, I want to thank you both for your time." Bruno now took charge. "As you know from my emails, this has to do with the literary career of a De Carlo & Wittgenstein employee, Fernando Seed."

"Yes, yes, he's quite something," Ms. Majestic said. "Very impressive."

"I'm glad you agree, Gloria. I hope you've had time to read the documents we sent you—his articles for *The Daily Cal*, his short stories, the unpublished stage plays and the unfinished novel manuscript?" Bruno had excluded Seed's attacks on Jean-Louis Lamour on purpose and hoped she wasn't aware of them. The remarkable texts she was privy to were among the papers Hermann had confiscated from Seed's abandoned Berkeley apartment. Seed possibly had copies on a computer he had taken with him, but to be safe, Bruno was careful to preserve them.

"Absolutely, I couldn't put them down. I was bowled over. You know, I've hosted a very popular book talk show, and I've read more literature in the last fifteen years than most lit professors, and I've met some terrific writers, but this Seed is in a category by himself—if I have any basis on which to judge."

"I'm very glad you agree," Bruno said. "I certainly respect your opinion."

"Well," chimed in Jack, "I didn't exactly always get whatever it was he was getting at about the book business and publishing and everything, you know, what exactly his gripe was. I mean, anyone is free to publish anything in America, and it's not that hard. I mean, when I think back to the good old Reading Roundtable with Myrtle Halstead, well, that was all the inspiration I needed. So, I'm not sure I get what's bugging this young fellow."

Bruno and Gloria Majestic both cringed at Jack Peterson's input. They knew Peterson produced formulaic novels and thrived by catering to the lowest levels of literary taste. They knew there was a difference between popularity and quality, but they both wanted Jack's help. Ms. Majestic was planning, aside from her ongoing book talk show, a new project focused on older San Franciscans, and Jack's network of contacts was extensive.

Bruno had a two-pronged interest in Jack's help. He needed to quash Fernando's campaign against the second-rate artwork of Hitler's twin, and he intended to do so by getting the young man successfully published and promoted. Until Seed had a successful career, he was a loose cannon. But there was more. Bruno also wanted to leave a lasting legacy, to be part of something larger than himself, larger than his business, larger than even his work for the CIA. Adolf Hitler had wreaked disaster on the world during the early twentieth century, but now he was gone, and the world had moved on. That's the way it was with political movements, even cataclysms. But the works of Shakespeare, Cervantes, and Hugo were still alive and always would be, he believed. Hitler's brother, even if he were to become infamous and cause trouble, would eventually die and forty years later school children wouldn't know who he was. Good literature, on the other hand, transcended time. It offered insights, beauty, hope, humanity, wisdom—things that were eternally valuable to posterity. Bruno wanted to have a part in promoting a Nobel Prize-caliber writer. It wouldn't mean much to his mother, but it would have meant the world to Myrtle. It would be a legacy in which he could take pride.

Bruno explained his plans to Gloria and Jack. De Carlo & Wittgenstein would get Mr. Seed back from Europe, and Gloria and Jack would help catapult the promising young writer to well-deserved recognition and wealth.

It was several hours later when, snoozing in his ergonomic chair, confident there were solutions to all problems, Bruno was awakened by an urgent telephone call from Olaf Knudtson. Jean-Louis Lamour had been badly injured in a bizarre accident in Spain, outside the Toledo cathedral. The first medical reports indicated he was stabilized, but with severe injuries to his face, right arm, and hand. The full extent of the injuries was not yet known. Knudtson was already worried Lamour's painting days might be over.

By God, this is serious, thought Bruno, jolted into full consciousness by the news. Just when he felt confident about his plan for handling the latter-day Charlemagne, a new problem had arisen. Bruno paced in his office, wondering what Myrtle would have advised. Then he called Donald in for a debriefing and consultation. As Donald was about to exit Bruno's office an hour later, the chauffeur said, "That's the best plan, Mr. De Carlo. You just call Ms. Majestic right away. Don't wait. She's gonna help. Because she can."

"Yes, hello again, Gloria," Bruno said, once the superstar was on the line. "I'm sorry to bother you a second time today, but I hope you can give me a few more minutes. An urgent matter has just come up."

"Well, yes, I've got a break before a taping begins. What's up?"

"You remember our young French *boulist* artist, Jean-Louis Lamour—you were at the opening reception last spring?"

"Oh, him! Ha, ha! Remember him? Lordy, yes! That character with the unforgettable hair and the shaggy dog, his green glasses, and his ridiculous paintings. What a kick, Bruno. You sure pulled one off! Loved it. What a coup. So, what's up?" She sighed and tried to catch her breath after laughing so hard.

Bruno was taken aback. Aside from Fernando Seed's negative reviews, no one else, certainly no one in San Francisco society, had openly laughed at Lamour's art. "So, I can see you're not a fan of our Frenchman."

"Well, you aren't either, are you, Bruno? Come on. I mean, you can promote him, but you don't have to admire that puerile stuff he paints, do you—seriously?" It came out more like an affirmation than a question. "I mean, *boulism* as opposed to *cubism*—that's a good one! Who came up with *that*?" When De Carlo didn't answer she thought she might have overstepped a line and tried to backtrack. "Of course, something can be said for his use of colors, I mean the variety of colors. Is Monsieur Lamour a relative of yours, by any chance? I really don't mean to offend you, because the reception and the exhibit's staging were quite brilliant."

"No, he's more of a . . . actually, I'm more of a guardian, well a sponsor, because he had a rather sad upbringing, because he was . . . well, orphaned at birth and had a rather deprived childhood. I'm just trying to help him make something of the talents he has. It's a long story."

Bruno's tone suggested she wouldn't be interested in the long and boring story. And he worried Donald might have been wrong about Gloria Majestic's willingness to help. But he was relieved by what she said next.

"Look, I can relate to that. And there's no harm in a mediocre talent becoming rich and famous in America," she conceded. "I've transformed a number of bad writers into wealthy best-selling authors because I felt sorry for them. I'm not naming names, sweetheart. Anyway, I'm sure the process is the same in your art world."

"Well, yes, it is, Gloria. But I happen to believe even people of small or mediocre talent have a right to live and create and thrive. And successful people have an obligation to help those who cross our paths needing assistance, whether we think them great or not. We can't help everybody, after all."

Bruno knew he was fudging on his philosophy of quality for the Burbank superstar. After all, he had already compromised himself for the sake of a greater good—something much more important than the truth about his personal opinions of Hitler's twin's artwork.

After dealing with Jack Peterson and with the much more impressive women of the Reading Roundtable, Gloria Majestic had vowed, in order to regain a sense of her own integrity, she would express her real opinions about the writers she promoted to her colleagues in the business—to the insiders, that is—even when her promotional publicity sometimes deceived the public. She considered De Carlo a colleague and thought he wouldn't be shocked.

"Look," she said, "between you and me, let's agree this character is not a great artist. But," and she paused a moment before continuing, "if his future is important to you, I'm willing to help. I've got a big business and we can find something for him, if that's what you want. I noticed he could work a crowd and charm them. He seems to have the gift of gab. We're going to develop a series of new commercials for my book talk program for next season, and you know how Americans love a French accent."

Bruno hardly needed to explain about Lamour's accident and injured hand. That didn't matter to Ms. Majestic. She had to go to her taping. It was all settled.

29

"DAMMIT, SANDERS, I'D FIRE you right now if I had anyone closer to the case in Spain," Olaf Knudtson barked from his DC office. "What the fuck have you been doing? How could you let this happen? Do you need *us* to tell you where he is, for Chrissake? You're our man in the field! Get your sorry ass down to that hospital, *now!*"

Latrone put down the hotel phone in the Madrid Marriott. It must have been unplugged by the previous hotel guest or something, because it was a hotel employee who had pounded loudly on the door and then entered their room with the news of an emergency call from Washington DC. That staff member brought in a new phone, plugged it in, tested it, and removed the old phone. It was on the new phone that he talked to Knudtson.

Latrone and Soonie had overslept—*way* overslept. It was almost midnight in Madrid and 6:00 P.M. in Washington, DC. After their jetlagged arrival, Latrone had forgotten to plug in his cellphone on which he had set the alarm, and the battery must have gone dead during the night. And he had neglected to ask the hotel for a wakeup call. It was an unacceptable slip-up—he knew it. Knudston had told him his European backup had followed Lamour to Toledo, where the artist was in a hospital as a result of an accident. And the backup agents were pissed.

Latrone called the concierge. He could get him and his companion on a train to Toledo at 7:05 A.M. the next morning.

At 5:30 A.M. the following day Latrone and Soonie turned on the TV as they packed to leave. Although neither spoke Spanish, they could still glean from the news that there had been a traffic accident accompanied by a feat of heroism in Toledo involving a French or, by some reports, an American hero. His identity had not yet been determined—but Latrone and Soonie knew who he was.

Before boarding the train, they bought a copy of *El País* at a newspaper kiosk. Bold headlines reported that a brave French-American had saved the life of the Duke de la Mancha's young son in Toledo the night before.

A couple of hours later, once the taxi driver had deposited Latrone and Soonie at the Hospital Virgen de la Salud de Toledo and they had ascended to the fourth floor, they could barely squeeze into Jean-Louis's hospital room 1918, overflowing as it was with aromatic bouquets and flower wreaths from the grateful folk of Toledo, who had witnessed the accident—*miracle,* actually—during the Festival of the Virgin. Dorothea, one of Jean-Louis's nurses who knew some English, explained to the foreign visitors that the heroic actions of her patient, who was obviously the Virgin's emissary from San Francisco—or was it France? He sometimes said things in French—had saved the precious life of the son of the wildly popular Spanish rock star, the Duke de la Mancha, a.k.a. Carlos Allejandro de Saavedra Marquez, who was a descendant of Padre Junipero Serra's extended family. Only the Virgin would have had the supernatural power to send someone directly from Alta, California—which, according to the Spanish, was discovered in the eighteenth century by their expatriate priest, Serra—to rescue the poor little boy on the day of his confirmation. The simultaneity of events was too astonishing to exclude divine intervention.

The surgical masks that both Latrone and Soonie donned to hide their visages from Lamour proved superfluous, as Jean-Louis's entire head, excluding openings for his mouth and nostrils, was bound in bandages like a mummy. As a precaution, the nurse explained, because of their proximity to his serious nose injury—his eyes were also covered. Unfortunately, his right thumb had been crushed and might have to be amputated. His left leg was in a cast and in traction, as well as his right arm; a drip emptied into his left arm. A heart monitor seemed to indicate normal function as far as the visitors could judge. The nurse said the surgeons intended to wait a couple weeks before operating on his nose. Having assumed the motionless patient was asleep, the nurse and visitors were now surprised to hear him utter in a weak voice, "*Donnez moi un pastis, s'il-vous-plaît.*"

None of them understood what he was saying.

Four days later following an operation on his thumb, the hero of Toledo lapsed in and out of consciousness in the recovery room at the hospital. The mummy bandages were gone from his head, but his nose was covered with dressings, and he was black and blue—purple, really—around both eyes. A masked nurse in a light blue uniform hovered over him and said, "*Buenos días, Señor*," when he fluttered his eyelids at her.

Buenos días?

"Comment?" he whispered, and immediately abandoned any attempt at further communication when he perceived an uncomfortable pressure of something, he didn't know what, weighing on his upper lip. He dozed off into a dreamless sleep. An hour later the tension of a blood pressure cuff tightening on his upper left arm roused him again. This time he opened his eyes to see a nurse in a green uniform wearing a headscarf with red polka dots hovering over him.

"Good evening, Mr. Lamour. I am Dulcinea," she said in fluent English.

"Good . . . *merde*! *Ça fait mal*! That gives me pain, *mon nez*!"

"I'm sorry," she smiled at her patient, not understanding his French.

"*Merde* . . . nose, my nose!" He wanted to touch his face, but his right arm was still suspended in traction and his left arm was on a drip, and when he tried to move either of them they hurt.

"Yes, yes, I'm sure it's painful. Just a minute and I'll add some medicine that will take away the pain."

"Wait *un* moment. *Ou*, where am I?"

"In the Virgin of Health. Do you remember your accident? You've broken your nose, and some other things."

"The Virgin? *Mon nez*? *Montrez le moi*, show me it, please!"

"But it is not pretty, Mr. Lamour. Are you sure you want to see it? It is covered by a bandage."

"*Oui*, yes, show *moi*."

The nurse fetched a mirror and held it in front of Jean-Louis's face so he could peer at his disheveled hair, scratched forehead, his swollen purple-circled eyes like that of a defeated boxer, and the ridiculous white bulbous bandage over his nose. "*Mon dieu! Quelle horreur!*" he exclaimed. "*Donnez-moi un* pastis, please."

The nurse didn't understand his request, but she added some painkiller to his drip, knowing it would be a few more hours before he would be leaving the intensive care unit, and she could take it easy if he were asleep.

Imagining his nurse was adding pastis to the cocktail in his drip, Jean-Louis lapsed into a semiconscious torment of confused thoughts and swirling impressions—about a long flight next to a boy in a white military uniform; Fisto biting the boy's pant leg and lapping up eggs with brains;

spherical paintings of Toledo nailed into Donald's walls in San Francisco; an enormous credit card overdraft set on fire by candles in a cathedral; a snow sled racing a high-pitched motorbike from which a confetti of newspaper articles were flung into a crowd of mocking onlookers; and other variegated bits and pieces of mental and visual flotsam and jetsam that failed to make sense. Convinced Crystal Beatty's blond hair whipped his face and clogged his nostrils, he woke up with a muffled snort five hours later, harboring black thoughts from his dark night of the soul.

For the first time since the accident, Jean-Louis made a sober effort to sort things out. He tried to retrace events—how he had tripped down the stairs outside the cathedral into the path of a motorbike; before that, the ca- thedral and the family and the electric lights and his credit card. Before that, there was the weird food at the *parador*. Before that the train ride and the long flight to Madrid. Before that there was San Francisco and his success as a *boulist* artist. But there was also that fellow who had attacked his work in that article. *That* was what got him to this pathetic situation. Who *was* that guy? What did he want? He had to be stopped, whatever it took.

Jean-Louis launched mental daggers at Charles Magnus—yes, he remembered his name now—but it only made him feel worse. When he thought of doing him harm, he thought of eggs with brains and his bad dream. Then he thought he, after all, was a famous artist, while this writer was a nobody, and he might turn the tables and attack Charles Magnus pub- licly. Then he imagined Fisto being bitten by a little boy, and it made him want to cry. When he tried to think of other scenarios, they were confused. He had no place to turn. He missed Fisto. Why wasn't Donald here? He found a red button and pushed it. A nurse came running. He asked her for a pastis. She gave him some more sedative and he slept, but he continued to suffer atrocious dreams.

When Jean-Louis woke again in a single room, he was relieved at first that his nightmares had only been dreams. But then he was depressed to notice the enormous bouquets and wreaths of flowers that reminded him of Pascal's funeral. Was he going to die here? Why didn't they unwrap his nose? Only the tips of his four fingers stuck out of the cast on his right arm. And they were black and blue, more black, really. Where was his thumb? Had his artist's hand been damaged? There was that big bandage over his nose. Was he terribly disfigured? Maybe it would be better to die. Two days later he finally persuaded a nurse to bring him a pastis and was able to drink it though a straw, which didn't bother his bandaged nose very much at all.

The morning after the pastis, Jean-Louis Lamour woke up feeling much better. Though still in casts, his broken arm and leg were out of trac- tion and he was able to sit up in a wheelchair. That afternoon his doctors would allow him to receive official visitors—the mayor of Toledo and the famous Spanish rock star the Duke de La Mancha. In the meantime, one of the nurses gave him copies of the newspaper articles about his accident— Spanish newspapers out of Madrid and Toledo, *Le Monde* and *Le Figaro* from France, and the *International Herald Tribune*, all of which had headlines or lead articles about the miracle of Toledo and photos of him, yes, of *him*, Jean-Louis Lamour, the prominent, sensational *boulist* artist from San Francisco.

He stared at the photos and the headlines of *Le Monde, Le Figaro, El País,* and the *Tribune* in that order, and then he switched the order and looked at the photos again in the opposite order. There he was, with Donald and Soonie and Fisto at De Carlo & Wittgenstein's exhibit, and there he was in his studio and at the New Age Art Institute being filmed by young videographers who were submitting their documentary to the Sundance Film Festival, and there he was at the New Age school being photographed for next semester's course catalogue. Those weren't the only photos in the papers. There were also photos of a nighttime accident scene outside an ancient cathedral, and a crowd surrounding a body lying in the cobblestone street, and a mangled motorbike, and a small boy in an inexplicably immaculate white suit with fringed shoulder epaulettes, and a skinny young man dripping wet, and a gurney with a body being shoved into an ambulance, and a police motorcycle cavalcade roaring ahead of an ambulance, and of an ambulance delivering a patient to the *Virgen de la Salud de Toledo's* emergency entrance while police motorcycle lights flashed. That's where the accident photos ended and were followed by an equal number of photos of Spain's beloved hip-hop-metal-salsa-rap star, the phenomenal Duke de la Mancha, of the long given-name.

When it occurred to Jean-Louis he should also read the articles, he began first with the French reports. He realized during his months in San Francisco his French had suffered, while at the same time his English hadn't improved much either. But he got the gist of the reporting: he was a national hero in Spain. He had selflessly, without regard to the peril to his life, jumped into a situation where angels would fear to tread, and saved an innocent youngster from certain destruction. Such an act of unparalleled courage and altruism hadn't been witnessed or even heard of in the environs of Toledo, or for that matter, all of Spain, since the lunatic heroism of the fictional Don Quixote who had embarked upon his gallant but misguided adventures four centuries earlier. This Lamour artist, however, was *real*; he was *the real thing*, the *Ding an sich*, as the *Frankfurter Allgemeine* suggested in a moving editorial, which Jean-Louis never saw and wouldn't have been able to read. Such heroism was rampant in American Westerns, and perhaps the bold and naive influence of the American West at the edge of the Pacific in San Francisco had had the salubrious effect on this creative artist of compelling him to this triumphant moral achievement. Such was the speculation of one of the French writers. *Mon Dieu*, thought Jean-Louis, and didn't know what to make of it, but the praise made him feel good. Much better than before.

Late that afternoon, after the mayor of Toledo and Carlos Allejandro de Saavedra Marquez were ushered out of Jean-Louis's room by his nurses, because their patient needed to rest, Jean-Louis felt better still. Very carefully and slowly, so as not to disturb the drip's needle, he lifted the medallion, which was attached to a gold chain that the mayor had placed around his neck, off his chest and tried to decipher it. Despite the bulbous bandage on his nose he could see that in relief it depicted a snake and an eagle and a lightning bolt positioned on what appeared to be a mushy bed of eggs with brains out of which an olive tree grew, all of which were surrounded at the medallion's edge by Latin sayings: *Verba movent, exempla trahunt* (words move people, examples compel them) and *Virtutis fortuna comes* (good luck is the companion of courage). But Jean-Louis's head soon dropped onto his chest from exhaustion, and he fell asleep in his wheelchair with happy thoughts of the promised public celebration of his grand deeds scheduled for the next week in the *Virgen de la Salud de Toledo's* garden courtyard.

30

WHILE THE INJURED LAMOUR was safely in the hospital, Latrone Sanders and his girlfriend tracked down Fernando Seed to a dingy attic room in Barcelona's Gothic quarter. It was an easy assignment for Latrone once they determined Fernando didn't leave his cramped room until about 11:00 A.M. every morning to spend the next several hours with his laptop drinking espresso a block off Las Ramblas in the Las Pulgas Tapas bar. Always attired so as to create a new look, Soonie sat at a different table every day in the same bar. She hid her face behind a newspaper in order to observe Fernando discreetly. By arrangement, she called Latrone's cell phone whenever Fernando left the bar. Inside Fernando's room in the Gothic quarter, Latrone then had time to replace any of Fernando's documents he had been photographing or scanning, exit his apartment, lock his door (which he had opened using elementary CIA break-in skills), descend back to street level, and meet up with Soonie in front of the *La Boqueria* marketplace on Las Ramblas—before Fernando might return to his room.

Latrone's foragings unearthed the young man's correspondence with his father in Calistoga in which they argued over his literary ambitions, the father discouraging him from this unpromising pursuit, and the son bemoaning the lamentable state of the literary arts in contemporary America. Latrone noticed the father, who never addressed anything else in his letters, seemed to have suffered a compartmentalized version of dementia about most things, but not about his son's substandard life. Perhaps Philip's singleminded fixation on his son's failings had brought on the dementia. Also significant, thought Sanders, were new articles that Fernando had submitted for publication to *El País* and the *International Tribune's* Sunday cultural sections with strident claims the popular *boulist* artist, Jean-Louis Lamour of San Francisco fame, was an artistic fraud, a mediocre thinker devoid of vision, prominent only because of the worst catering by clever American corporate interests to the lowest common denominator of the uncultured American masses. Fernando claimed the artist had fallen under the spell of big money and had been seduced by De Carlo & Wittgenstein's influence in the art world. The prestigious galleries and auction house had, for unknown reasons, evidently sacrificed their standards when it came to contemporary art, to the money Moloch. Fernando knew Europeans enjoyed feeling culturally superior to Americans, especially when their economies weren't as strong as their North American rivals, and he confidently expected to be published and paid by their papers, ever since his first critical article had appeared and evoked some notice. He was hopeful he could become a successful freelancer in Europe and eventually an employed journalist with enough time to pursue his true passion—writing novels.

Several days after the news broke of Lamour's heroism during the Festival of the Virgin, Soonie was hiding behind an old copy of *La Stampa*. When she sat down and opened the paper to shield her face, she failed to notice the old date and the front-page article with the photo and the name of Hitler's twin splashed across the headlines. At this moment five tables away, Fernando stood up and headed for the restroom. As he was about to pass by her the bold Italian headlines caught his eye: "*Jean-Louis Lamour, Artista, Eroe de Toledo!*" He stopped abruptly, bent down and did a double take at the headlines. He realized they were in Italian, and he realized *eroe* was the same as the Spanish *héroe* without the "h," and that the accent was a negligible quantity. *What were the Europeans doing now to lionize mediocrity?* he wondered, stunned, *especially after they had the benefit of my article.*

Buried in his work, Fernando rarely read newspapers and he didn't own a television. He hadn't yet heard the news of Lamour's heroism.

During her last discrete peek around the coffee house, Soonie had noticed Fernando Seed's laptop was abandoned at his table. Now she realized Fernando himself was hovering over her, and it became uncomfortable to pretend she didn't notice. He broke the impasse.

"*Perdóneme, señorita,*" he said.

"*No hablo Español, señor,*" Soonie replied, very softly. That much Spanish she knew.

"English?" Fernando tried the universal language.

"Yes, I speak English," Soonie replied almost inaudibly, continuing to cover her face with the newspaper.

"Oh, good," said Fernando. "I'm sorry to trouble you, but I just noticed an item in the newspaper you are reading, and if you happen to be finished with the front page, I would very much appreciate it if I could borrow it from you for a few minutes. I'll return it momentarily."

"OK," said Soonie and attempted to extricate the first page, which constituted the backside of her shield, without lowering the rest of it to reveal her face, a maneuver she performed reasonably well. She thrust it in Fernando's direction, who took it back to his table with a "*Muchas gracias*, thank you very much, *madame*."

Soonie sank low into her chair, and, after a few minutes had passed, peeked around the side of the remaining paper in her hands to see Fernando poring over the front page intently, tweaking his nose nervously, raising his eyebrows, shaking his head, and finally whistling a long, shrill note, half whistle and half sigh. This attracted the attention of other bar patrons who looked over at the intense young man—probably a struggling foreign student to judge by his scruffy clothes—before returning to their own business. Suddenly, the young man folded up the newspaper, stuck it in his back pocket, placed some coins on his table, folded up his laptop, tucked it under an arm, sprang up, and dashed out. Soonie dug her phone out of her purse and called Latrone to warn him that Fernando had left the tapas bar.

31

STANDING ERECT IN FRONT of Bruno's desk, Donald Washington looked expectantly at the CEO of De Carlo & Wittgenstein. Holding his cap with his white-gloved hands, he looked uncommonly snazzy in his chauffeur's uniform. Hermann stood several paces away, looking skeptically at Donald, as the chauffeur spoke to Bruno.

"OK, boss," he began, "you're in charge, Mr. De Carlo. I don't mind at all goin' to Spain. Why, I never been there, and I think it be a mighty fine country—with dark-haired ladies with red hibiscus flowers behind the ears, and twirling skirts and lace shawls and dark red lipstick and sunshine and beaches and deserts and gazpacho. Yes, sir, Mr. De Carlo, I do love that Spanish gazpacho, especially with a corn tortilla when it's hot, and I don't mind at all goin' to Spain in the line of my work. Now I'd be happy to rent a car for the company to bring Monsieur Jean-Louis back from Toledo, back to the airport, if that's what you wants, Mr. De Carlo, boss. And I'll take Fisto. You know, Mr. De Carlo, that's Jean-Louis's little pup. Before I depart I'll take Fisto to the canine salon and get him bathed and gussied up so he be looking fine and smelling good for the journey."

"No, Donald. I don't want you to take Fisto along," Bruno replied.

"But Mr. De Carlo, since Jean-Louis's been in the hospital in Spain way far away from everything and everybody, Fisto missed his master real bad. He stopped doing his jump rope trick and his bug-eye roll over and snarl trick, and everything, like if the life just putted out of him like the air out of a balloon. And I'm sure Jean-Louis misses his little dog. I'll bet it would cheer him up one whole lot."

"I'm sure it would, but your mission is to get Mr. Lamour back here, to San Francisco. So, you can tell him Fisto misses him terribly and can't wait until he comes home. Hermann and Gaby can care for the dog while you're gone, can't you Hermann?"

"Sure boss, I mean Bruno," said Hermann. "Gaby likes animals."

"Well, and Mr. Boss De Carlo," Donald spoke up, "Jean-Louis needs to come back, 'cause his students at the New Age school, well, they just lost. I mean, they just kinda wandering around and don't know what to do. They done stopped painting and they jus' sit around pretty glum and depressed. Like without Jean-Louis, nothing happens."

"Yes, that's not good. I understand how students need their teachers, and miss them when they're gone," Bruno said wistfully. He threw a quick glance at Hermann, then looked at Donald again and said, "One more thing, Donald, I want you to take this note from Gloria Majestic to him. He might remember her from the big reception. She would like to talk to him when he gets back."

A week later, Donald sat next to Jean-Louis in the first of five rows of seats on an outdoor tribune erected for the occasion in the hospital's large courtyard. Reporters, photographers, and television cameramen buzzed around below and above this stage to film and broadcast the celebration to honor the extraordinary Hero of Toledo. Curious and enthusiastic crowds of Toledans, and Spaniards from neighboring villages, and even from Madrid, had come to see the hero and to take advantage of the free sangria, tapas, paella, and the music provided by the grateful Duke de la Mancha and his band. Spectators streamed into the courtyard to the sounds of the Duke's novel and idiosyncratic blend of hip-hop-metal-salsa-rap music while the Duke's chubby ten-year-old son, who wore the same snow-white uniform in which his life had been saved, strutted back and forth across the stage like an albino peacock, raising one arm and then the other and waving to no one in particular in the growing crowd. Bright red and yellow flags of Spain, along with French, American, and California flags were draped in vertical banners from the courtyard's rooftops, and multicolored pennants hung from cords that crisscrossed the space in an "X" above the crowd and flapped gently in the afternoon breeze. Satellite trucks jammed the parking lot behind the hospital, where a large screen and loudspeakers enabled the overflow crowd to watch the proceedings.

At 3:20 P.M.—the ceremony was supposed to begin at 3:00—the Duke de la Mancha's percussionist gave a drum roll and struck his cymbals repeatedly to signal the Mayor of Toledo was about to speak. The mayor stepped up to the podium, tapped the microphone, cleared his throat, and embarked on a long speech in Spanish, which neither Jean-Louis nor Donald understood. Whenever the mayor crossed his hands over his chest and then clasped them together and pointed them at Jean-Louis and bowed his head toward the hero, the crowd applauded its approval. And the noise grew louder whenever Jean-Louis attempted to smile or wave, encumbered as he was by his nose bandages and arm cast. When the mayor finished, the Duke, the grateful father whose son had been saved by the stupendously courageous act of the French artist from San Francisco, gave a really long dissertation in Spanish about the miraculous event. It didn't matter that Jean-Louis and Donald didn't understand it, because they saw the tears that came to the Duke's eyes and the drops that rolled down his cheeks, and they heard the cheers of the crowd. They saw the handkerchiefs that grown men and women employed unabashedly to blow their noses and wipe their faces, and how they lifted their toddlers and infants toward the sky or clutched their older children close to them, or both, as if grateful Jean-Louis had saved them, too. The Duke had pulled his all-white son to his side while he spoke, and when he finished, he bent down and kissed and embraced the boy. Seeing this, the crowd gulped down the lumps in their throats and choked on their tears. Some applauded wildly, some kneeled, some muttered *ave Marias*, while the boy, the unscathed one, stood proudly next to his father staring placidly at the adoring assembly. He slowly raised his right hand as if to bless them, feeling it was all about him.

Under a stone archway in the courtyard, about twenty meters from the speakers' platform, a disheveled looking foreign student stood gape-mouthed at the proceedings. He was dressed too warmly for the mild autumn day, with a long, thread-bare army-green knitted shawl around his neck that was unraveling at the ends, a navy blue knit cap pulled over his ears and dark glasses. A couple weeks' worth of dark stubble sprouted from his face, and his worn brown leather jacket might as well have come from a thrift shop. Spectators around him later told police he cursed and shook his head frequently, and sometimes, during the speeches, hit the side of his head with both fists in a gesture suggestive of astonished disbelief, and that they had been suspicious of the bulging burlap bag the strange *señor* carried over his shoulder. They testified he became quite agitated when Jean-Louis came to the podium accompanied by his black friend, and that the young man kept dipping his hand into the burlap bag and taking it out again in an indecisive manner.

The hero's approach to the podium was preceded by a moving new song that the Duke de la Mancha had composed especially for this occasion and for the man who had saved his son—a song that combined musical elements of "We are the Children," "Amazing Grace," and Pachelbel's "Canon" woven through it in his unique and indefinable hip-hop-metal-salsa-rap mode. An adorable children's choir, all dressed in dazzling white, sang what were surely lovely Spanish lyrics, which the hero and his African-American friend failed to understand. Yet they had to have been beautiful, judging by the buckets of tears shed by the throng.

As this musical offering gradually faded away, the mayor of Toledo signaled for the hero to step forward. Propped on the arm of his faithful friend in the sharp blue uniform, Hitler's twin rose carefully from his wheelchair and walked slowly toward the podium and directly into a sunbeam, which appeared as if on a heavenly cue, from behind the billowy white clouds that had previously obscured his radiance. Seeing how, as if on purpose, the sun transformed and illuminated both men, the spectators, who had been reduced to a sea of quivering, blubbering souls, more moved, as many among them believed, than by anything they had ever witnessed, grew silent—all of them—hushed as if by a heavenly magic wand.

Fernando, observing the spectacle from underneath the stone arch, couldn't believe the misplaced adulation displayed by these sadly deceived Spaniards. Digging into his burlap bag with his right hand, he turned around and around mumbling over and over to himself words like, "Fraud! Deception! Incredible! Trickster! Mediocrity!" and the like, looking more wild-eyed by the minute. People around him wondered if he hadn't drunk too much free sangria.

When Donald and Hitler's brother reached the podium together, and Jean-Louis grasped the side with his good hand and rested his other arm in the cast on top of it, the crowd's deafening silence was now broken by someone's slow clap, and then another and another until everyone began to clap and many stamped their feet so the sound of applause crescendoed into a booming thunder that echoed through the courtyard and resounded beyond it. Anyone outside of the hospital grounds might have thought there was a *corrida* going on inside, except the roar and clamor were almost continuous and accompanied by shouts and wails of emotion.

Jean-Louis told his buddy to speak first. Now, Donald Washington— the dignified, elderly, dark-skinned Californian—when this small, exotic, and enigmatic figure in the magnificent navy-blue uniform finally raised both his arms to the sky and smiled his beatific Pope John XXIII smile, the crowd finally settled down to listen.

"Woowee, howdy!" Donald said into the microphone. "That be some welcome you people of Spain give my friend and buddy, Jean-Louis, and me. Yessiree! So, we be grateful to you people and the big boss of Toledo and everybody for comin' out today. So, *muchas gracias, amigos!*"

Holding a microphone at a discreet distance from the podium, the official translator translated Donald's greetings into Spanish: "Ladies and Gentlemen, Mr. Lamour and I wish to thank you for your kind and gracious welcome today."

But no one in the crowd heard the translation, because the crowd resumed its previous roar at the same volume and intensity as soon as Donald paused. They didn't care what the translator said, or for that matter, what Donald said. They were just happy that the black man had spoken and smiled at them.

Under the arch, Fernando Seed turned around and around as if chasing an invisible tail. He studied intently the spectators surrounding him, searching in vain for one that might have a wrinkle on his or her forehead, a skeptical look on his or her countenance, even the hint of a doubtful mien—in vain. Even the children, who couldn't have understood the event's significance, seemed entranced, enchanted by the fraudulent magician on the stage.

The din of the throng increased to new levels now that Señor Washington stepped aside, allowing Jean-Louis a chance at the microphone. The hero opened his mouth and said, "*Hola! Buenos días, amigos.*"

These few words were met with a roar of applause that swelled up suddenly and washed over Jean-Louis like a wave of pleasure so that he had to laugh with sheer delight and forget about his injuries. He had to wait a long time before he could continue, and in the meantime he relished the feel-good atmosphere and large turnout. He and Donald exchanged thumbs-ups at each other, and the people imitated the gesture and shouted, "*Olé!*"

Jean-Louis didn't mind waiting in the warmth of the sunbeam. He realized he felt better than he had for a long time. He took a sip of pastis, which the sponsors, knowing it was his favorite drink, had generously provided to him in order to relax him in case he was nervous. But Jean-Louis felt as comfortable before this medium-sized mass of humanity as he had with the public at his big reception in San Francisco, and as he had rapping with his adoring art students at the New Age Art Institute—perhaps even more so. He wasn't nervous at all. On the contrary, he felt at home, in his element, as if he were born to do this. As the sun glinted off the gilded medallion around his neck, he raised his glass to toast the crowd, and the audience raised their paper cups of sangria, their baby bottles full of milk, and some of their babies if their arms were free, and toasted him back with alacrity, shouting, "*Olé! Salud amigo* Jean-Louis!" and similar words of affection.

Moved by their enthusiasm, Jean-Louis embarked on a spontaneous speech of thanks in English and French to the crowd—for turning out, to the Mayor of Toledo for creating this wonderful event, to the Virgen de Salud hospital, to his nurses, Dulcinea and Dorothea, and the doctors, whom he insisted on calling forward to receive the recognition they deserved, to the great country of Spain, to his friend Donald who had come so far to be with him during this pinnacle hour of his life, to anyone he had forgotten to mention, and to the Duke de la Mancha. The only individual he forgot to recognize was the unscathed one, the all-white one, the miraculous one, the little chubby one whose buttons stretched the cloth of his jacket across his belly in an unbecoming fashion and who had sat down with his legs dangling over the front edge of the stage, swinging them back and forth in an unbroken attempt to attract attention.

As Jean-Louis spoke, and before the translator could put his words into Spanish, the crowd, which had understood a few of them—Toledo, Virgen de Salud, Spain, and Duke de la Mancha—broke out repeatedly into paroxysms of weeping and thunderous applause, as well as waving handkerchiefs and the miniature flags of Spain and California that had been handed out with the sangria. And Jean-Louis became consciously aware for the first time of something about the power of his voice. He noticed how the crowd reacted to it—to its rhythms, cadences, and the rising and lowering of its pitch. It didn't matter to them what language he used, because they couldn't have understood what he was saying, or that he spoke with a French accent. Whatever it was, his very voice alone evoked reactions; it evoked their emotions, more emotions, he realized, than his paintings had aroused in their viewers.

Jean-Louis beamed at the adoration with a radiance commensurate with the bright sunshine of Spain. He looked down beatifically at his worshippers and thought, *This is great*, and *Hey, it's not about that prissy little brat in the white uniform, it's all about me! Cool! Formidable!*

Finally, when Jean-Louis perceived that the crowd's intensity did not abate and they were in danger of suffering a collective nervous collapse from their hysteria, he raised his left hand high, because his right hand in the cast was too stiff, as if to give them a benediction, and lowered it to signal them to calm down. He had them under his control, for they grew silent immediately, the way an orchestra reacts to its conductor, and awaited his next command.

But then the unexpected happened. Something so altogether extraordinary no one could have predicted it, but something Latrone Sanders should have prevented. A barrage of luscious ripe Spanish tomatoes hurled by an angry young foreigner stationed next to an arch at the side of the courtyard assailed the grand hero, Jean-Louis Lamour, and his friend, Donald Washington, surprising them and soiling their clothes. One of those fruits struck M. Lamour on his bandaged nose and splattered over his face.

Headlines in *El País*, *Le Monde*, and the *International Tribune* reported the next day that two policemen were injured trying the save the alleged tomato thrower, an American named Fernando Seed, from the outraged crowd, and that Fernando was recovering from his injuries in a wing of the Virgen de Salud hospital, under police guard. One English-speaking witness to the incident who had been under the same arch, told reporters the suspect had appeared to be insane, that he babbled unintelligibly and cried out insults as he launched the missiles from the burlap bag, such as: "Insufferable mediocrity!," "Deplorable abomination!," "Malevolent charlatan!," and "Fatuous imbecile!" Police reinforcements had been called in to subdue the rioting crowd, a number of whom had fainted. Most of the injuries had been minor, and three days later the magnanimous hero, Jean-Louis Lamour, not knowing who the perpetrator was, once again displayed his moral grandeur by declining to press charges against the tomato-thrower.

32

THREE WEEKS AFTER HIS nose surgery—performed the day after the celebration by a team of the finest plastic surgeons from Madrid, who volunteered their services—Jean-Louis was sitting in a lounge chair on his private balcony overlooking the courtyard where his celebration took place, sipping a pastis. Donald sat next to him drinking a bottle of Spanish beer. The sun was setting.

"Hey buddy, *mon ami, passe moi le miroir*, please," Jean-Louis said.

"OK, man. They gave you a beautiful nose, *très beau*! Here, *voilà*."

Donald handed him the mirror for the umpteenth time. He understood why Jean-Louis wanted to look at himself, over and over again. The new nose was gorgeous—aquiline, long, straight like Nikola Tesla's, with a slightly upturned, nicely pointed tip, rather like Czar Nicholas II. It was as beautiful as you could imagine, as beautiful as any man in Western civilization had yet sported. It had the perfect physiognomic proportions—from between the eyes to the bottom—the Golden Ratio of 1:1.6. The surgeons did themselves proud. Their work had healed so quickly the bandages came off in six days. The nose skin, part of which had been harvested from Jean-Louis's left thigh, and the skin around his eyes that was initially black and blue, were already turning a healthy pink. The new nose changed Jean-Louis's appearance, and he liked it so much he thought he might dispense with a moustache and beard going forward in favor of a little goatee and sideburns. He would cultivate a brand-new look. The only flaw about the new nose that would remain, probably for the rest of his life, were scars—they would fade somewhat in time, according to his doctors—down the front of the nose, where two equally long parallel lines marked the bridge of the nose and were intersected by a "V." These scars appeared to form a symbol, reminiscent of a cattle brand, that might be interpreted as a capital "M." The scar's effect was felicitous. Jean-Louis showed Donald the similar scar on his left thigh, where the surgeons had extracted the skin-graft. Donald said the nose scar made him look distinguished, transfigured, almost wise.

After Donald left Jean-Louis and returned to his room at the *parador*, Hitler's brother gazed a while longer at his new visage, thinking about all that had transpired since that nasty article appeared in the San Francisco paper that threw his life off course. He still didn't know what it meant, or where it might lead.

Deep in contemplative thought he soon dozed off for a while, but as dusk turned to darkness, he woke to the sounds of guitar music—beautiful music, the antithesis of the Duke's odd-ball, chaotic, pulsing music. Jean-Louis had never heard classical guitar music before—Rodrigo, de Falla, Boccherini, Bach—and now pieces by these composers were performed by a woman seated in the courtyard. Jean-Louis noticed other patients, those fortunate to have rooms overlooking the courtyard, came to their balconies, most in their bathrobes, some pulling portable IVs attached to their arms, drawn like bears to honey by the mellow sounds. *Mon Dieu!* thought Jean-Louis, *This is heavenly. I've never heard anything like it.*

Now the patients, Jean-Louis included, leaned against their balustrades and strained to see the unknown guitarist, the woman who transported their souls to a better place, who quelled their fears of their illnesses and injuries, even if just for an hour, who soothed their senses with beauty, with sounds so subtle and exquisite, as if celestial.

By God, there are heavenly things here on earth I never knew about, he thought as tears began welling up.

Despite all the tears the crowd had spilled for him, he hadn't shed a tear at his own hero's celebration. Now he felt sheepish thinking about it. Guilty, actually. After all, he hadn't tried to save the little white-suited brat. It hadn't been his intention when he tripped down the cathedral steps. But he hadn't told anybody that truth; he hadn't told the Duke or the Mayor, or his nurses, or doctors, or anybody who had showered him with credit and praised his heroism. Of course he had been injured and had undergone surgery, and after the surgery he couldn't really talk without it hurting like hell, and he was unconscious and sedated and confused a lot, and by the time he could remember what really happened, it seemed too late and too difficult to explain, and after all, everybody, all these Spaniards had been so happy about the miracle, and who was he to undermine their faith?

Jean-Louis's thoughts tumbled around his brain like wet cement in a cement truck drum while the music worked on his conscience and heart. The small woman who sat on the edge of the central fountain and held her guitar so gracefully, nodded modestly at the applause of her patient-audience that stood appreciatively on their balconies. Why did she do this? Jean-Louis wondered. She looked poor. Did the hospital hire her? He would tell Donald to give her a generous tip tomorrow, if he could find her.

Jean-Louis's thoughts troubled him deep into that night. He tossed and turned and eventually crawled out of bed and put on his bathrobe. Artists came to mind—Picasso, El Greco, and Dali—painters he had learned about since he'd been at the New Age Art Institute. He had been amazed to see they could produce anything they wanted. They were real *virtuosi*, skilled craftsmen, with genuine talents, who could *think* and create new ideas and execute them—brilliantly—while all he could do was paint circles and circular objects, over and over again. Leaning on a cane, he shuffled back and forth in his room in a distressed sweat. Maybe he was one big fraud, like this Charles Magnus claimed in his article. What was he doing with his life? He finished a bottle of pastis, climbed slowly back into bed and toward morning finally fell into a fitful sleep and had a dream. In it the wonderful guitar player sat on the edge of a fountain across from him and fixed his gaze. Her expression was intense and serious, yet kind. She told him that she played out of love. She played for the patients, not for herself, and that Jean-Louis should do something good, something out of love—for others.

The next day the guitar player was gone, and no one could tell him anything about her.

33

TEN DAYS LATER THEY were all on the same flight, Avianca 876, from Madrid to San Francisco. Sequestered in splendid isolation in the dome of the 747, Donald and Jean-Louis drank champagne and ate caviar and crab cakes. Latrone and Soonie sat in the back of the economy section, where Latrone was well aware the tail of the long airplane swayed back and forth and rocked up and down more than in its mid-section. He was keeping an eye on Fernando, who sat further forward in economy in the middle seat in a row of five, with an ill-tempered, squirmy three-year-old girl directly to his left and an enormous, sweaty, fat man on his right. Before take-off the young Fernando already knew he would be physically uncomfortable for the next twelve hours. Not only the cramped quarters but also his injuries, some of which were still painful despite his treatment in the Toledo hospital, made that a certainty.

Every once in a while Fernando held his head in his hands and mumbled something under his breath, asking himself why the imbecile had declined to press charges against him after he bombarded him with tomatoes in Toledo. Several hours into the flight, when he had to disturb the baby and the mother to his left to let him out to go to the restroom, the man on his right noticed the scribbles on the notepad on his empty seat: sketches of what looked like bubbles or clumps of grapes and the words, "Why?" underlined three times, and "incomprehensible," "insufferable mediocrity," "must be stopped," "end of civilization." The passenger worried the young man was disturbed and resolved to call a flight attendant at any signs of suspicious behavior.

Donald and Jean-Louis arrived at SFO refreshed after the good food and lengthy naps on the pleasant flight. Hermann met them in a company Mercedes and drove them to Donald's pad in the Fillmore. Agent Sanders and Soonie arrived, exhausted from the turbulence and tasteless pasta at the back of the aircraft, and went to visit Latrone's mother before buying hamburgers at Jack in the Box and going to Latrone's apartment in the Mission to sleep. By the time Fernando exited customs, the others had left the airport. Latrone's CIA relief agent would trail Fernando, and Latrone was convinced Hitler's brother would be fine overnight with Donald. He emailed this to Olaf Knudtson and Bruno De Carlo. He knew Fernando had an appointment at his old employer, De Carlo & Wittgenstein, two days hence, but he had little money and no place to go.

Fernando found out he could take a bus to Napa in two hours and a shuttle to Calistoga that left Napa every thirty minutes. He also knew his father wouldn't remember anything about him except his disappointment in his choice of profession.

34

"Who the hell are you?" Philip Seed yelled at the scruffy young man sleeping on the couch in his mobile home in Calistoga. "What are you doing here?"

Fernando awoke from a jet-lagged semi-slumber, groaned, rubbed his eyes and said, "Hey, Pops, it's me, Fernando, your son. Remember?"

It was two days after his Avianca flight had arrived at SFO, and the young Fernando felt terrible. He hadn't had a decent sleep in days. As always, his demented father was angry at him. He, Fernando, had been arrested for criminal behavior in Europe and had ruined his chances with his former employer. His aging father had squandered his money in bad investments and was living in near poverty. How would he be able to support his dad, let alone himself? On top of it, that French artist-charlatan might change his mind and still press charges against him, and De Carlo & Wittgenstein might sue him for slandering their protégé. They were powerful. Maybe they could sue him for breaking his contract, abandoning his job, and leaving the country. Maybe his father was right, and he should have studied science at Cal. He could have had a PhD by now and a job in a pharmaceutical company with an income that would support them both.

"My son? I've got a son?" the old man scratched his head.

"Yeah, Dad. You've got a no-good son, who's not a scientist. One who wants to be a writer, remember?" said Fernando raising his torso to face his father and supporting himself on an elbow.

"Oh, good God! That son! Yes, I remember you now. You're the one who lacks common sense, who rejects my good advice. You're the one pursuing those hare-brained goals that lead nowhere. Where did I go wrong?"

He scratched the back of his head and sent a shower of dandruff adrift in the sunlight that streamed through a crack in the curtains.

When the phone rang, Philip picked it up. "Yes, yes . . . Well, all right, I guess . . . Fernando? I don't know a Fernando . . . There's no Fernando here . . . Who are you? . . . De Carlo and what? . . . Do I know you?"

Fernando stood up and gestured to his father to give him the phone. Philip spoke into the handset, "Well, there's somebody here who wants to talk to you, whoever you are," and handed the phone to his son.

Gaby reminded Fernando that he and his father would be picked up at 10 A.M. by a chauffeur and driven to San Francisco for the meeting. Could they be ready by that time? Fernando assured her they would.

With a heavy heart, Fernando poked at some Cheerios and milk while his father ate gustily. Then he showered and dressed and tried to get his father to change into some decent clothes, but when the driver arrived in a dark green Jaguar, his father refused to come along if he couldn't wear his old sweater and his comfortable slippers.

On the drive south through the beautiful Napa Valley Fernando thought if he had studied chemistry, he could have become an oenologist, worked in a winery, and earned a good income that way. He had burned his European literary bridges behind him by the tomato-throwing incident and police arrest. No respectable European journal or publisher would touch him now. And here he was in trouble with powerful art brokers. But what the hell did they want with his father? Did they know he was incompetent? He had no answers and no options but to face the music.

Seated in Bruno's beautiful office, Gloria Majestic expressed her wish to use the powder room before the others arrived.

"Of course," said Bruno and led her to his private restroom in the hallway behind his office. He hadn't noticed that a few days ago Crystal had abandoned a half-empty vial of *Fatale pour Femmes* behind the box of tissues next to the basin.

After Ms. Majestic washed and dried her hands, refreshed her lipstick and pulled the first tissue out of the box, the yank, as often happens with the first difficult tissue, pulled the entire box forward revealing the elegant hidden vial. Ms. Majestic was familiar with many fine perfumes, but not this one. Intrigued by its deep amber color, she held it up to the light. She knew what "femmes" meant and wondered whether Mr. De Carlo used this perfume because he was gay. She opened the stopper and took a whiff, and then a second whiff. By God, it smelled divine. De Carlo would never miss it if she dabbed a tiny little drop behind each ear. Then she called her hotel on her cell phone and ordered five vials of it sent to her room.

That same morning when Jean-Louis woke up at Donald's pad in the Fillmore, he felt good. He had enjoyed two good nights' sleep since their long flight. He was with his best buddy in the world, and it struck him that San Francisco felt like home. Spain and all that had happened there seemed a strange dream, except for that beautiful guitar music and the new realization that he possessed a remarkable voice, a voice that could inspire, a voice that moved people to wild applause. The Duke de la Mancha's music had disappeared from his memory, but that classical guitar music stuck with him—its timbre, sweet tones, and subtle rhythms. He even remembered some of the melodies and harmonies. It made him happy when they ran through his brain, which was often.

To top it off, Hitler's twin was really happy with his new nose. People gave him admiring, even envious looks; they couldn't seem to take their eyes off his gorgeous nose with the distinguished-looking scar. And even though yesterday an orthopedic specialist at UCSF hospital told him his right thumb would never be serviceable, Donald had told him better things awaited him, career-wise. And Donald was never wrong. Jean-Louis had almost forgotten about the malicious review of his art that a guy named Magnus had written about him. He had decided to put that behind him and to look forward to a positive new phase in his life. He dabbed a bit of *Fatale Pour Hommes* that he found in Donald's medicine cabinet behind each ear. Even though it was almost Christmas, when the buddies left the Fillmore for Treasure Island, it felt like springtime.

Gaby announced Jack's arrival to Bruno on the intercom, and soon he, accompanied by his personal assistant, Linda, entered the room.

"Well, a hearty good morning to you, Mr. De Carlo," Peterson boomed as he shook Bruno's hand and squeezed it to demonstrate his virility.

Bruno winced and answered, "Same to you. Good to see you, Mr. Peterson."

Gloria stood three steps behind Bruno ready to greet her writer acquaintance from The Pines, who had reached the venerable age of ninety-five, along with such undeserved literary fame.

"And to you as well, my dear Miss Majestic," said Peterson, and instead of shaking her hand, he brought it to his lips and kissed the back of it. "It's a lovely day in the city, don't you agree, Gloria, my friend, and high time you should transplant yourself here, don't you think? Ha, ha."

"I'm happy to see you're well, Mr. Peterson," replied Ms. Majestic.

"Thank you. Yes indeedy, I'm fit as a fiddle. By the way, this is Linda, everybody, the best assistant in the world," Peterson declared to everyone, just as Hermann entered, "and don't you try to take her away from me, Ms. Majestic or Mr. De Carlo, now that you've seen her!"

Just as Hermann and Jack exchanged greetings, Crystal opened the back door from Bruno's hallway, and in stepping into the office, nearly tripped in her four-inch spiked heels. She caught herself and simultaneously whipped her long blond hair around in a flashy flourish she hoped Bruno would notice. His attention, however, was directed at the main office double doors, which Peterson and his best assistant in the world had failed to close, where he caught a glimpse of Donald's blue uniform and Hitler's twin, who had been abroad for over a month. With the kindest words of sympathy for his injuries and lofty words of praise for his heroism, Bruno welcomed the injured artist back to San Francisco in the warmest way, and Gaby arrived with a tray of tall glasses for everyone, a pitcher of ice water, and two bottles of pastis.

While Gaby poured some of the alcohol into the glasses, diluted it with water and ice, and distributed it to the guests, Bruno said he wanted to make a toast to their prodigal son, so to speak, who had returned to California, which he hoped would become his permanent home, and to a new phase in an already illustrious career. Two of the glasses were not yet claimed, and before Bruno could continue, the last of the guests, Philip and Fernando Seed, appeared at Bruno's office door. Hermann ushered them in.

"Where are we?" asked Philip. "Who are these people?" He directed his questions to no one in particular, standing there in his old slippers in the elegant surroundings.

"Good morning, Dr. Seed," said Bruno. "I am Bruno De Carlo. This is my partner, Hermann Wittgenstein, this is Ms. Gloria Majestic from Burbank, this is Mr. Jack Peterson." Bruno by-passed Jean-Louis, who, with Donald, had wandered over to the large window that faced the bay, and he offered Dr. Seed a comfortable chair and handed him a glass of pastis, which he downed in a single gulp.

Looking at the assemblage, Fernando began to suffer a bit of vertigo and a weakness in his knees. Olaf Knudtson and Latrone Sanders, who were watching the meeting remotely on their computers—via video cameras hidden in Bruno's office—saw the color had drained from the young Fernando's face. Knudtson instructed Hermann, who was wearing an ear bud in his left ear, to have Fernando lie down so he wouldn't faint.

When Jean-Louis, who had been enjoying the sight of sailboats on the bay, turned around, he didn't recognize either the unshaven young man in the shabby clothes or the old man in the shabbier clothes. But Jean-Louis knew what it meant to feel faint and sick, and he knew what it looked like, and he knew how much it meant to a sufferer to hear some soothing sounds, and he knew, moreover, that when he spoke it didn't matter what he said because he could soothe and comfort and inspire joy, even in strangers. So he hastened to comfort the ashen-faced young man stretched on his back on the beige leather couch and began to tell him how sorry he was that he wasn't feeling well, and to offer him the rest of his pastis and to put his hand on his forehead and to assure him everything would be all right. Fernando, at that touch, however, averted his eyes from the trickster with the beautiful nose and lost consciousness.

As Jean-Louis knelt next to the couch ministering to the young Fernando, Gloria, remembering her first-aid training from long ago, came forward, and told him they should lift his feet up onto the arm of the couch so gravity would help his blood run back into his head. She could see he had fainted and was not in danger; he would come to in a short time. So, she lifted Fernando's left leg and Jean-Louis lifted his right leg, and in doing so they brushed arms, and Ms. Majestic and M. Lamour both noticed the electricity that passed invisibly between them—more than a quivery *frisson*. More like a distinctly pleasurable shock. At the same time they stole glances at each other, they registered something extraordinary, a *je ne sais quoi* as sweet as a fragrant rose and as tempting as the morning aromas of a bakery.

The rest of the meeting was lost on Hitler's twin, who only had eyes for Gloria Majestic. Bewitched by the beauty of her luscious, caramel-chocolate skin, he could barely follow as she, somewhat breathlessly now, explained how she needed a spokesperson, someone with an outstanding voice, who was not shy with crowds or in front of the media. If he was willing, Mr. Lamour would bring to this new position—doing voiceovers and commercials for her next authors' television series—the perfect basket of skills, including innate rhetorical talent and proven oratorical competence. The job would involve frequent travel to Burbank, and if he needed an assistant, Mr. De Carlo had already suggested Donald Washington.

Jean-Louis couldn't quite trust his ears and looked to Donald to translate for him. Donald, of course, had read his mind and in the English his French buddy best understood he explained, "Jean-Louis, *mon ami*, you got to look at it like this. If you don't paint no more, all those balls, *les boules*, you painted up till now, well, they all get more and more valuable, like every day. The price for your stuff goes up every day, *chaque jour*, because there won't be no more of it coming. So, they become *très, très cher*. And besides, everybody, *tout le monde*, knows how and why you can't paint no more, 'cause your hand be crushed, and you're a big hero in Spain, so they'll want to buy up all of your paintings they can get, and the price just keeps going up and up and up! So, no worries, dude. You gotta take this job!"

As the truth sank in, and Jean-Louis realized he wouldn't have to paint again to make a living, and he beamed across his beautiful nose at Ms. Majestic, he slapped his thighs in exultation.

Bruno was grateful to Donald for his excellent job of persuasion, and smiling, clapped Donald's shoulder. "Now that that's settled," he continued, "the other order of business today involves our young writer friend, Fernando, and Jack Peterson, the latter of whom, along with Gloria, has agreed to devote a generous amount of his energy to promoting the work of this brilliant new literary talent."

The young Fernando, upon hearing his name as through an echo chamber, came to his senses expecting the worst. But, on the contrary, he heard Jack declare to all present that as he had no offspring of his own, he would be proud to mentor the promising young Fernando whom Ms. Majestic was convinced was writing the great American novel—and he would do this willingly without any compensation, in honor of his own literary mentor, Myrtle Halstead. Afraid he was dreaming, Fernando pinched his thigh and peeked into the room, the elegant office of De Carlo & Wittgenstein's CEO. No one noticed he was awake and listening to the discussion.

"Mr. Wittgenstein," Ms. Majestic now addressed Herman, "you did an invaluable service to your adopted country and its culture, when you discovered the unpublished novel manuscript in the Berkeley apartment of Mr. Seed, who employed that clever pseudonym of Charles Magnus. *The Magpie Conundrum* will shine next to the classics of Melville, Twain, Faulkner, Steinbeck, and Hemingway in the American literary pantheon."

Jack couldn't restrain himself from interrupting, "Aren't you forgetting something from that pantheon? Ha, ha?"

"Oh, well, yes, there's the incomparable *Resurrection in Venice*, which was Mr. Peterson's very first and rather unforgettable novel," she conceded. "And with the assurance of Mr. Peterson's advocacy and help, and with a beginning print run of 200,000 in my *Majesticwerke* publishing house, not to mention appearances on my book talk show, why, an enormous success is guaranteed for Mr. Seed's novel."

"Dr. Seed," Gloria continued as she walked over to Philip Seed who, with an empty glass in his hand, was sitting quietly in his chair off to the side. She took hold of his right hand and said, "I want to congratulate you on the crucial work you have done for us. I'm afraid you'll never know what an enormous contribution you have made to world peace and culture and for producing an amazing literary genius in your son, Fernando."

"Did you say I have a son? Fernando?"

"Dad," Fernando now called from his couch, "Dad, I'm your son, Fernando. Remember? The son who's not a scientist."

"Oh yes, you! You good for nothing. Just look at him, Miss. While all of you people are discussing important business, that no-good, lazy son-of-a gun is sleeping on the couch! By God, I worked hard when I was young. I spent long hours in a laboratory. And I hiked high mountains to keep in shape. And I worked in foreign countries. And I made some important discoveries. And . . ." Now Dr. Seed scratched his head releasing a snowfall of dandruff that made Bruno worry he might remember something from the distant past that shouldn't be revealed.

"Yes, yes, Dr. Seed," Bruno hastened to insert. "You are a truly distinguished scientist who made incomparable discoveries and contributions to science, and for those reasons everyone present would like to raise his or her glass to you in a toast of admiration and appreciation for your outstanding accomplishments."

Gaby got the hint and filled up Philip Seed's glass again with pastis and ice water, and before everyone had raised their glasses, Dr. Seed emptied his.

In the meantime, Jean-Louis, who hung onto Gloria Majestic's every word, dropped his jaw and glowered at Fernando when he realized he had aided his enemy. Donald was quick to notice the change in his friend's demeanor and placed his hand on Jean-Louis's forearm. "It's cool, *mon ami*," he assured him quietly. "Don't worry, bro. Bruno the boss man, he's taking care of that writer dude. Jus' forget him. He don't matter no more. Just enjoy your good fortune with Miss Majestic."

Reminded of his new love, Hitler's twin yanked his head back in her direction, and his heart swelled with joy. Donald's words were like a magic wand that removed all fear and animosity he might have harbored toward the unkind young writer. *The brave new world of California is big enough for both of us,* he concluded, *to develop our potentials and pursue happiness in our own ways.*

Ms. Majestic went now to the couch where Fernando raised himself up slowly on his elbows. Color had returned to his face, and with it his wits, and he said, "While I slumbered here, I fear it were but visions that appeared."

She took his hand. "No, not visions, my dear Fernando, but people who wish you well, people who want to set your spirits and your talent free to soar."

Bruno joined them, knelt next to Fernando and said *sotto voce*, "Just one bit of advice. Stop attacking Jean-Louis; he's finished as a painter. And I know how you feel about your father. In a few weeks we'll have lunch and I'll tell you about my Italian mother." Then Bruno placed his hand on the young man's shoulder and said, "Hermann will take you shopping for clothes after lunch and loan you a car so you can drive your father back to Calistoga."

Now Bruno stood up. He took Gloria's hand and led her over to her new collaborator, Jean-Louis, who looked at her through adoring eyes down his gorgeous, scar-branded nose. She returned his amorous gaze. Crystal, who noticed their attraction, thought they must both be on pheromones.

Bruno nodded at Gaby who emptied the second bottle of pastis into the glasses. After the final toast in which he also wished everyone a Merry Christmas, Bruno went around shaking hands. Good cheer reigned. Hugs made the rounds. Philip Seed got up and joined in the hugs. Fernando hugged his father who pushed him back, but only slightly. Crystal held onto Bruno snugly, who smiled at her and didn't resist, and Jean-Louis and Gloria embraced tenderly, as if they had missed each other for a long time and had just been reunited. Someone from outside looking into the office would have seen everyone smiling. When Bruno even hugged Jack, Mr. Peterson winked at Linda and said, "This is a man hug," and with a hearty laugh and a toothy smile on his face, he toppled over backwards and crashed down onto the marble floor.

Later that evening Fernando drove his father back up the west side of the Napa Valley toward Calistoga in a BMW that belonged to De Carlo & Wittgenstein. While thoughts of the day's events swirled in Fernando's brain, his father slumbered in the passenger seat, snoring gently and mumbling a few words in his sleep—"snow," "Schreckens glacier," and "frozen baby." At least that was what Fernando thought he heard. A bit south of Calistoga, Fernando could see geothermal steam rising from various spas in unearthly clouds, partially obscuring the lights of the town. As Fernando made a right turn off of Highway 128 onto Lincoln Avenue, Philip Seed woke up with a start. He looked out the window and seemed to take an interest in one of the rising sulfurous clouds. Then he turned his head, and, looking intently at his son, addressed him.

"Fernando," he said, "I found a frozen baby in an Austrian glacier on the day you were born. He's a French artist named Lamour, and he's a twin of Adolf Hitler." Philip Seed now squinted intently as if trying to recall something more, but then he looked away from his son and down at his lap and dropped his chin on his chest as he fell asleep again.

Fernando smiled and realized his father must have had a crazy dream. But by the time they reached the Vintage Citizens Manor mobile home community and he parked the car, Fernando felt a twinge of disquiet. Still seated in the BMW he woke up his father and said, "Pops, I want to ask you something. Think hard now: What did you just tell me about a frozen baby, a glacier, an artist named Lamour, and about Adolf Hitler?"

Philip took a look at the stranger next to him who posed these questions and said, "Who are you? Where are we?"

35

On January 3, 2009 Bruno, Hermann, and Crystal drove across the Bay Bridge toward Alameda in Bruno's classic red Thunderbird convertible with the top down. It was a clear, mild day for early January, and Bruno, who was in a good mood, was at the wheel. Seated next to him, Crystal didn't bother with a scarf, and the wild flashing of her blond hair in the wind caught the attention of nearby motorists, who wondered for a moment if something wasn't on fire in that convertible. Bruno took a couple of surreptitious side glances at Crystal. Before she donned her sunglasses, he had noticed for the first time the budding crows' feet next to her left eye. They gave her a new aura of intelligence and maturity. She had suffered, after all, and had grown. When she tamed her wild hair, he realized, she was handsome and distinguished. And, in spite of everything, she still loved him.

In a sharp dark blue uniform, white gloves, and chauffeur's cap, Donald followed a few vehicles behind them at the wheel of a company SUV that carried Dr. Philip Seed and his son, as well as Gloria and Jean-Louis, the two of whom held hands in the back seat and occasionally whispered sweet nothings into each other's ears.

The Elysian Society boat left the dock late in the morning with everyone on board. Across the estuary, Latrone Sanders instructed the captain of a small boat hired by the CIA to follow at a discreet distance. As his boat pulled out, agent Sanders checked for the fourth time the buckles, emergency whistles, and flashlights on his and Soonie's life jackets, as well as the boat's fire extinguisher and the condition of the inflatable zodiacs. Despite the dramamine he had taken thirty minutes earlier, he began to feel seasick as they motored out into the hazardous waters of San Francisco Bay, known for its treacherous tides and currents, accidents, and shipwrecks. If it weren't for the fact his mother was so proud of his work, he would begin to look for a different job the very next week.

As they motored past Angel Island, Bruno gathered the Elysian passengers together. He had to retrieve Gloria and Jean-Louis, who had spent most of the time nuzzling each other at the aft of the boat. He said a few words of thanks and farewell to Jack Peterson and announced some surprising news: the previous day Peterson's estate lawyer had informed Bruno that Mr. Peterson was willing his telescope and his suite at The Pines to the first new talented writer Gloria promoted on her book show, and that happened to be, of course, no other than their own Fernando Seed. Peterson's estate would pay all expenses for the new occupant at The Pines, because Peterson knew a good writer would gain inspiration for novels as successful as his own from the unique location of his suite and the particular view it afforded of the city. Fernando smiled in amazement and declared his gratitude, but his preference would be to house his father in that suite, if possible. Bruno said that could be arranged, and Fernando hugged his father who asked him, "Who are you?" and "What do you think you're doing?"

Fernando then confessed to the passengers that he had done his best work in his Berkeley apartment, and he wished to move back to the university town for his inspiration. He would, of course, visit his father frequently at The Pines and make good use of the telescope. Bruno nodded and smiled his assent at Fernando, and as a large swell picked up the boat and tilted it gently to one side, Crystal pretended she couldn't help but lean against Bruno and pressed one of her breasts against his side. And Bruno welcomed it, placing his arm gently around her waist.

When the boat was a good distance beyond the Golden Gate Bridge, the Elysian Society representative, holding a box wrapped in brown paper and tied with string, stepped into the circle of passengers and announced, "It's time to commit Mr. Peterson to his resting place, according to his wishes."

Bruno set the box down, cut the string, unwrapped the paper, and opened the box. He pulled out a plastic bag and walked to a back corner of the boat. The others followed and watched as he poured Jack Peterson's ashes into the Pacific Ocean. Everyone could see the ashes were swallowed up in a small vortex or whirlpool that seemed to form for no reason—a watery gyre that consumed Jack's remains in one unceremonious gulp. None of Peterson's ashes were caught by the breeze, nothing blew up or back at them, nothing sailed through the air. They all just sank and disappeared. The sight of the round water vortex startled Jean-Louis and brought back memories of Pascal's round blood drops on his thigh and all his subsequent *boulist* art. But one glance at his new love and at Donald reassured him all of that was of the past. It was history, as the Americans say, and it was behind him as surely and quickly as the ash-swallowing gyre had vanished and blended with the waves.

When Hermann looked up several minutes later, he recognized a rocky promontory near China Beach, and knew the boat was near the spot where Myrtle Halstead's ashes were poured two decades ago. He went up to the bridge to ask the captain to make a couple of slow circles in the vicinity and was surprised to find Donald at the helm and the captain several feet behind him, smiling at the neophyte's obvious sailing talent. When Hermann made his request of the captain and the captain nodded toward the uniformed black man, Donald, perfectly at home in his new role, gave Hermann a broad smile and snapped a salute off of his cap. Hermann couldn't help but shake his head and smile to himself as he descended to the deck.

Hermann now called Bruno to the port side of the vessel and reminded his partner that this was where Ms. Halstead's ashes had been released into the water, and he handed Bruno six of the dozen red roses he had brought on board to honor her memory. Then Hermann tossed a rose over the side, and Bruno, who had wrapped an old pale-green cashmere scarf with two gold stripes around his neck, followed suit, and they alternated dropping roses onto the water one by one until all twelve flowers formed a rough circle bobbing on the waves.

Leaning on the railing watching the roses as the boat idled, both men fell into silent contemplation, absorbed by their thoughts and memories. Neither spoke. Hermann dabbed at his cheeks with a linen handkerchief. The others kept a respectful distance. A minute or two passed, when suddenly, from the center of the dispersing circle of roses, a dolphin sprang high out of the water into the air close to the boat. The animal spun its glistening body in a beautiful, athletic twist and salute, which sent a shower of seawater—a fine, dazzling spray of droplets tinted gold against the sun—raining down upon the passengers. Everyone gasped with surprise and delight, and Jean-Louis slapped his thighs. Bruno and Hermann were the only ones to notice the water streaming across the dolphin's sleek body seemed to form for an instant a transitory symbol that resembled an "M." And they would have sworn the creature smiled at them as if to say, "Well done," before it plunged back into the Pacific Ocean and disappeared, swimming west.